SHADOWS OF GLORY

Owen Parry
[Ralph Peters]

STACKPOLE
BOOKS

Books by Ralph Peters

Nonfiction

Lines of Fire
Endless War
Looking for Trouble
Wars of Blood and Faith
New Glory
Never Quit the Fight
Beyond Baghdad
Beyond Terror
Fighting for the Future

Fiction

Cain at Gettysburg
The Officer's Club
The War After Armageddon
Traitor
The Devil's Garden
Twilight of Heroes
The Perfect Soldier
Flames of Heaven
The War in 2020
Red Army
Bravo Romeo

Writing as Owen Parry

Faded Coat of Blue
Call Each River Jordan
Honor's Kingdom
Bold Sons of Erin
Rebels of Babylon
Our Simple Gifts
Strike the Harp

Published by
STACKPOLE BOOKS
5067 Ritter Road
Mechanicsburg, PA 17055
www.stackpolebooks.com

Printed in the United States

10 9 8 7 6 5 4 3 2 1

Cover photo courtesy of the Library of Congress, reproduction number LC-DIG-cwpb-03920

Cover design by Tessa Sweigert

Library of Congress Cataloging-in-Publication Data
Parry, Owen.
Shadows of glory / Owen Parry.
p. cm.
ISBN-13: 978-0-8117-1134-0 (pbk.)
ISBN-10: 0-8117-1134-X (pbk.)
1. Jones, Abel (Fictitious character)—Fiction. 2. United States—History—Civil War, 1861–1865—Fiction. 3. Welsh—United States—Fiction. I. Title.
PS3566.E7559S53 2012
813'.52—dc23

2012003815

To Maisie,

Who endured many a battlefield

GLENDOWER:

I can call spirits from the vasty deep.

HOTSPUR:

Why, so can I, or so can any man;
But will they come when you do call for them?

—Shakespeare, *Henry IV, Part I*

ONE

I SAW HER FIRST AT THE BURYING, BEHIND THE WICKED crowd. With the mob of them cursing and shaking their fists in the snow, twas her I saw. Still as if frozen she was, and only her eyes betrayed the fire devouring her. Aglow like embers in a winter hearth, those eyes would burn us all, and haunt me when she was gone.

Fanned by the wind, a lock of hair flamed from her shawl, scorching across her forehead. I would tell you that her hair was red as blood, to give you the vividness of her, but such would be untruthful. I know the look of blood, see. Her own would spot the snow before my eyes. Her hair was a darker thing than blood, though not so dark as her story.

I should have felt the queerness there at once, from the way the rest of the Irish kept off her. Careful they were with the lovely, though otherwise a bad pack. The men slurred and jostled. Drunk under noon, some of them were, and ragged. Bleezed with spite, their women put me in mind of white-faced crows, hard and deprived. Even the little ones come hating to the holy doors that day. For the Irish fear an informer more than the devil, and death excites them always. I worried that the coffin would not pass the gauntlet they made outside the poor boards of their church. As the representative of our Federal authority, I should have made order my business. And I meant to. Then the look of Nellie Kildare drew me from my duty, and I leaned—one fateful moment—on my cane.

But I must not go too quickly. There was blame in this death, and a bitter portion of it was mine. Had I not lain abed with General McClellan's own typhoid upon me, I might have come north a month the sooner, as Mr. Nicolay and Mr. Seward first intended. Our agent might have lived. Better it would have been for the widow and the little one, not to speak of the poor, blundering fellow himself.

They had tormented him before they killed him. I saw the marks of their work when I come fresh from the train that morning, fair running from the station, with ice on the streets of the town, and my leg bad in the cold, and the weakness still upon me from the fever. The coroner's assistant held the coffin open for my arrival, then disappeared. The Irish priest kept the widow away from the box. Kind doing that was. I ran into the church all snow-pestered and unready for the shock of it. How long I stared at the dead man I cannot tell you now. Long enough, though, to singe my eyes. Twas small of me to gobble so much time, for the widow was keening away in a locked room. But such matters bind us, and we forget consideration. My hands curled into fists beside the corpse, and not only to fight the cold there in that church. There is cruelty, I thought. Savagery. I had not seen so grim a sight since India and the inferno of the Mutiny.

I am a poor beast, as all men are, and would not question the Good Lord's grand design. Still, I wonder at that which He allows.

When I finally stepped away, two paddies nailed the box shut. Muttering and careless, they made it clear enough that they wanted no part of the business. But the priest fell hard upon them and soon they were jumping about and jabbering their sorries. Their voices took me back. I knew those accents from my old red regiment, the gurgling of that unextinguished tongue, harsh as lye-water in the mouth. Each fellow smelled of whisky.

The priest brought in the widow then, holding her up on her feet with one big arm. His other black sleeve held her babe. The little thing was bawling as if it knew all.

Beneath a statue of the sort the Irish idolize, the woman found her strength. She plunged forward, young and worn in her tattered dress, black shawl flying about her. Flinging herself upon the raw pine, she nearly upset the bier. Splinters soon bloodied her hands for the beating she gave the boards. Her wailing echoed in the empty church, raising a swell of laughter beyond the doors.

"The hoor's upon 'im now," a woman cried, triumphant. Her voice pierced the walls. "Oh, bring ye out the traitor's hoor. We'll give 'er what she's a-coming."

To calm the widow, the priest forced her babe into her arms. The woman's raw hands bled on the infant's face and wrappings. They prayed then, in the different way they do, all Latin and sorrow. The priest had eyebrows that met in a black knot and his shoulders were those of a navvy. Not young, not old, there was a worn solidness to him. He might have done for an elder soldier, had he not been a soldier of his faith. His name was McCorkle and he was no more born to America than I was.

I prayed my own prayers. Off to the side, and quiet like. I will not be small and think the Good Lord tends only to us chapel folk. For all the pagan coloration, there is a faith in your Irish Catholic that must call down pity from above. They do the best they can with what they know, and I would not damn them out of hand. But then I have found good among the Hindoo and the Musselman.

I prayed first for the dead man, then for his shattered family. Careful I was not to face their painted statues, but looked to the windows and Heaven beyond. Next, I gave my thanks. First for my Mary Myfanwy and our little John, and then for the passing of the old year. I believe I was as glad to see the back end of 1861 as was Mr. Lincoln himself.

I will not forget that awful year. First the coming of the war and the separation from my family, then the savaging of our Northern pride and the ruination of my leg at Bull Run. After that I fell into the Fowler matter—the needless, bitter death of that young man—and next come the typhoid that would have been the end of me in an army pest house had my friend Dr. Tyrone not taken affairs in hand. He was gone to the western armies now, called to Cairo, Illinois, and I missed him and waited on a letter. I prayed for Mick Tyrone. Not just in that cold church, but nightly. He was one of those stubborn, educated Irishmen who will not ask God's favor for themselves. And I wished a blessing on dear Mrs. Schutzengel, my Washington landlady, all girth and goodness, and then on that no-good Molloy, who doubtless would have been eyeing the communion silver had he been by my side. Finally, I prayed for the mob grumping and growling beyond the shut doors of the church, for such was my duty as a Christian.

The priest lifted the woman and child away from the coffin. He started in to barking, all sour, "Come ye now. Come here, ye."

I thought he was admonishing the Lord.

Twas the pallbearers he was addressing. Bent things they were. The two who had labored with hammer and nail scuttled forward again, followed by a pair of their butties. Each wore the dirt of a lifetime polished into his face, and they had not a full set of teeth between them. I could not understand a word they said. But they did not want to shoulder the load. That was clear from the way they glanced toward the noise beyond the doors.

They hoped in vain for rescue, for the priest, Father McCorkle, was a very Caesar with them.

"Out now, and into the wagon," he said against the widow's sobs. "And none o' your capering nonsense."

The priest arranged the procession with himself in the lead and the widow trailing closely, with her infant swaddled against her. By rights, the bereaved should have followed the coffin, but the priest knew his doings. He was no slave to ritual, I will say that for Father McCorkle. So the box bobbed behind the mourning wife and the little one as we started down the nave, with the pallbearers cowering at the thought of the mob.

I brought up the rear at a respectful distance, wondering if I could not have raised myself from my convalescence sooner.

Had this poor fellow died because I lolled out a sick man's leave, reveling in Christmas by my own hearth while he did our nation's duty? I was not yet recovered to my full strength, but strong enough I would have been to come by rail. I should have sensed the urgency. But Mr. Nicolay himself told me to gather my health first, and didn't I grasp the excuse of it like a bad child? How easy it is to fall from our duties. And the results are as bitter as Peter's denials. I had only reached New York City when the coded telegram from Mr. Seward overtook me, instructing me to make all possible haste.

I well recall that foggy night in Washington when Mr. Nicolay, who was Mr. Lincoln's confidential secretary, recruited me with the warning, "They killed the last man we sent up there." And now "they" had killed another on the back roads of New York. Yet, we knew not who "they" were, but for a rumored Irishness. Mr. Seward, the fierce blaze of brains who had become our secretary of state, feared insurrection. New York was his state and he knew the war was not popular with all the souls left to the Union, least of all with the Irish lately come among us.

Mr. Lincoln himself had taken an interest in the matter, for much had begun to fray. As if the Confederates were not enough, rumor had the English on the edge of war with us, for their sympathies lay with Richmond. Canada, domain of eskimaux and the mighty bear, sheltered our enemies. To top it, some young fool of a naval officer of ours had boarded one of the Queen's ships to seize a pair of Rebels. My adopted country needed every honest man to stand to. And selfish Abel Jones had let better men down, enjoying his fever.

The priest threw open the doors. The stove inside the church had gone unlit and the nave stood dreary chill. Still, I was unprepared for the blast of wind and snow that swept in. Twas cold as death's own hand.

A gray world waited beyond those doors. The snow rushed against a near, gray sky. The gray-wrapped mob wore gray faces. They had tramped the earth to a gray muck. It was a prosperous little town this Penn Yan. You saw that even on a skip from the railway station. But you would not have sensed it from this worst of buryings.

I expected a great howling to greet the opened doors, like the delight of Mr. Gibbon's Romans at their spectacles. Instead, the crowd fell silent. The mob parted before the priest, just wide enough for an unhindered passage, and our little procession descended into the slush. The pallbearers went slowly, careful of the ice on the steps and fearful of their neighbors. They crouched beneath their load like beaten dwarves. I followed apart and last, for I wanted the local Irish to see me proper. I had hit upon a strategy in the church, if I may dignify a moment's inspiration with such a mighty term, and wanted every man to mark my presence. But let that bide.

One voice—twas a woman's, for they are ever the boldest—cried, "Look at the traitor's slut, would ye? Look at the informer's hoor and 'er bastard. Bury 'em with 'im, says I . . ."

That set them going again. Loud as the sounds of battle. The gauntlet tightened around us. More than a hundred of them there were. A bandaged fist shook in my face, and then I realized it was not bound in bandages, but in rags to keep off the cold. None of them dared touch us yet. But our safety was fragile.

Twas only the power of the priest that held them back. I saw that. He was their own even when he stood against them.

But I could feel the devil's hand descending.

There is wicked, see. At that moment of danger, did I think of the poor widow and the infant in her arms? Oh, no, not Abel Jones. I thought of the fine new uniform I wore under my greatcoat, the grand blue frock with the oak leaves and the handsome striped trousers my Mary Myfanwy had presented me for my Christmas, an incitement for me to finish my cure and rise from the bed. So proud she was. When I told her it was too grand a cut for the likes of me, she reared right up and said that John Wesley himself wore silver buckles on his shoes, and silk, too, and a bit of braid was becoming to an officer newly risen to his majority. Ever proud of her I was, and heathen proud of my new soldier suit—though I had meant to leave such doings behind. I knew how she had saved and sewn to outfit me. So, too, we fall from duty. Selfish man that I was, I thought not of the unfortunates before me, but of the risk to my precious new uniform.

That, too, would be torn in time.

I bullied myself round to my task again and straightened my back. I am not one of these tall fellows, but I do show strong in the chest and shoulders. I kept my cane tight to my bad leg to brace my stride. A major of United States Volunteers shall not be daunted by a pack of hooligan Irish.

"Give way, you," I ordered one great lout.

"Why, ye little Welsh cod," he answered hard. But give way he did.

The priest led on in silence. A buckboard wagon waited in the street in a canyon of snow, the horses smoking. A shabby carriage lined up just behind.

I thought we were safe. Twas then I saw her, that woman who would reach into our souls. Well to the rear she stood, beyond the want of the wind-scraped faces—narrow as lies—and the pair of worried police fellows, their slouch hats wreathed with snow. It was as if she had called my name. As if a cry of "Abel Jones!" slashed through the mob. When I turned, I found those eyes upon me. Under that flame of hair.

Look you. There is a quality in some folk, though not in many, that commands us to see more fully than is our custom in the to and fro. They grant us a peek at the richness of life, and tantalize us with possibilities. The girl, God bless and forgive her, might have been the only one of the hundred of us who was fully alive on that day of death.

And so alive she was! Framed in the dour propriety of her garments—they were not rags—her skin had the whiteness of porcelain. The snow on her shawl showed filthy by compare. She was white as clean milk, as good paper. But for the burning spots on her cheeks. Her features were clear and definite, with a handsome angularity that scorned common beauty. Slender and tall, she stood encased in dignity. The sight of her stopped me cold.

And a snowball smacked the back of my head.

My hat tumbled, and with it the mob's hesitation fell away. They surged around us, stinking of sweat and whisky and home-made salves. Now I am an old bayonet, may the Good Lord forgive the follies of my youth, and my cane soon cleared a space about me. But I was not the object of their wrath. Twas the coffin they were after, and the widow.

The wooden box went down, pursued by screams. The priest set about him with his fists, cursing like a heedless sergeant, and none dared strike him back. He pulled the woman and child against himself and they disappeared as the crowd surged in again, with the snow twisting and screwing to confuse us all.

"Oh, feed the turncoat bastard to the dogs," a voice shouted. "Burying's too good."

"Judas!" a harridan shrieked. *"Judas!"*

I heard a wrenching and breaking, and wordless howls of rage.

Then the world changed. The crowd's pitch dropped of a sudden. Their motion slowed, then froze. One voice hushed another as a hard sobriety fell upon them. Slowly, one by one, they began to move again. Backing off, shunning their purpose. I heard gasps, and slivers of devout language from the women. The aura of children caught out settled over the crowd.

They had gotten their way, for all the good it did them. The box lay broken open in the muck, and the corpse had spilled onto its back. They all got a gander at the devil's handiwork then. I do not think they saw his cast-off suit, or even the broken skew of the fingers. No, they all saw what I had seen at first look, and no matter the rumors they might have heard, the brute doings shocked the hardest of them.

The top of the man's head—scalp and flesh—had been burned away, the skull charred and the eyes cooked out. Only the bottom of his face remained human, streaked here and there with pitch roasted into the skin. He had died with a grimace of agony. The coroner had taken the rope off him, of course, but the neck was still pinched small and scarred deep where the noose had gripped. The thought of death by hanging has always held a special dread for me, but I hoped for this man's sake the hanging had come before the other business.

"Whiteboys . . ." someone whispered behind me.

The priest had not been quick enough. Before he could shut his hands over the widow's eyes, she saw what they had made of her husband.

Her scream will never leave me.

The priest clutched her and the babe against him. For just a moment, he shut his own eyes, as if gathering strength. Then he gave it to the lot of them.

"Damned ye'll be for this. Damned all. *Damned.*"

Even the hard men made crosses on their chests and lowered their eyes. The women began to blubber, then to wail, and the children cowered behind skirts.

There is foolish, you will say, when I tell you what I did. I looked for the pale young woman with the flame of hair down her forehead. The girl who stood apart.

She was gone.

Her spell broke with her absence, and I turned to duty. The pallbearers had scuttled off to their holes, so I summoned a voice from drill fields past and ordered a few of the Irish lads to help me gather the body back into the coffin.

They were not so much unwilling as afraid. They are a superstitious people, the Irish. I could not get a one of them to move.

The police fellows come up then. They had been but two against the mob and knew better than to go into it. And one of them looked Irish himself. But now they sensed that the danger had passed. We got the body back into its place, though not before I saw enough to haunt me. The corpse still smelled of burned pitch and, queerly, of spent powder. We set the lid on the box again.

Commanding a raisin of a woman to hold the infant, the priest let the widow collapse in the snow and weep while he helped us lug the coffin to the buckboard. He had a workman's hands.

Twas I who come back first to help the widow to her feet. With the guilt in me. Her wet eyes were as dead as her husband's body, and she smelled of milk and misery.

We headed for the boneyard, with the police fellows riding behind. The crowd dispersed into the falling snow. The priest would not look at me, or at any man.

I did what I could for the widow. But four years passed before the government could be persuaded to grant her a pension for her husband's services. By then the child was dead. That, too, was bitter to me. But it does not bear on the tale I have to tell, so let that bide.

"HELL OF A FELLOW, SEWARD. *He's* the one should have been president," Sheriff Underwood told me. He laid aside the bill of fare with the strong hand of a farmer—he had risen from the fields—and gave a tug to one of his mighty ears. "Don't order the pork. It's kept over from New Year's. Lamb's fresh killed, though."

He waved to a waiter. The serving fellow was as fancied up as the price of a meal was high. The Benham House was a topper of a hotel, with a piano going in the saloon bar and no spit on the floors. Plush chairs and dark wood set the tone in the dining room. Now there were fine hotels enough in Washington, and I had not come north for my pleasure, but glad I was of the warmth and the softness of my seat. The cemetery had been a cold, bleak spot of earth and my ride on the buckboard merciless.

"Tommy . . . I'll have that lamb I heard bleating out back," the sheriff said. The long tails of his mustache willowed as he spoke. "And you tell 'em I want it cooked good and dead."

"Yes, sir. And the major?" The waiter looked down at me. Twas no surprise he could read a rank. The hotel lobby had been speckled with military men, competing recruiters all, bursting with promises and bounties. Well quartered in Penn

Yan's finest establishment, they seemed to have no regard for the terrible expense and deserved to be brought up on charges. There are always those who will find luxury at the back of a war.

"I will take the stew, if you please," I told him. There was an awkwardness to my mouth, for I was still thawing.

"One lamb plate, and a bowl of stew. Thank you, gentlemen."

"Stew?" Sheriff Underwood said as the waiter retreated. The afternoon had mellowed to amber in the dining room, and the tables had lonelied. Many of the guests who had congratulated my host upon his new position were gone already. *"Stew* won't keep a fellow going. You've got to eat for the weather. Red meat, man. Red *meat!* That's the thing. Feed yourself up."

The sheriff had a prosperous physique. You would have taken him for a politician, rather than a law man.

"I like a good stew," I said. For such men will not hear of economies. "It is healthful and warming on such a day. Sheriff Underwood, may I—"

"Call me John. And I'll call you Abel. If I'm able . . ." He laughed and gave one of his remarkable ears another scratch.

"John . . . " I tried the sound of it. First names do not come so quickly to me, see. I must become a better American that way. I looked at the sheriff, who was an imposing fellow in his very prime. Big, that one. He wore a bright neckcloth, well knotted and trailing, a bottle-green jacket and waistcoat of plaid. All looked of good quality, though a bit roguish by chapel standards. I would have given him the advantage of the fist over a criminal, though not of the chase, for his person did give evidence of a fondness for the table.

Before I could put my question, the sheriff rose to shake hands with yet another well-wisher—for he had been sheriff only since New Year's Day. A brief conversation ensued between the two of them, so I will take this time to tell you of those ears.

Now, we are not to speak unkindly of another fellow's peculiarities of person. Nor would I appear basely excitable. But the man had the ears of an elephant. Bristling with hair like a boar.

They did not protrude bumpkinlike, but lay flat and fair shielded the side of his head with their length. Twas as if someone had hung red cutlets on the man, such great devices they were. He looked to have ten years advantage of me in the wisdom of age, which placed him square in his forties, and thus time had accustomed him to his awesome companions. But I had a ferocious time keeping my eyes from them. Powerful ears they were, and appropriate, see. For a man of the law must hear things others cannot.

Sitting again, and pleased with the world's respect, the sheriff told me, "Have to get you up to the farm. Show Washington what a New York welcome means. You can keep all that Secesh hospitality. Won't be served by no slaves up here. Just the wife and the house-girl." Smacking the prosperity of his physique with the flat of his hand, he laughed. "Wife's a devil of a cook. And sometimes she's just a devil. Don't I know it? Won't go near the jail, let alone hear tell of moving into it. Won't leave that farm even to visit the place. Would be a comedown, of course. Though the county built a nice enough set-up." His big fingers combed the bristles sprouting from an ear. "Turned it over to my deputy and his wife. Free livings. And aren't they glad of it? But that one can't cook to save her life, that Sarah Meeks. Couldn't very well invite you back there and feed you spittle and grease. So here we are." He gestured at our handsome surroundings. "Hotel don't put on a bad spread. Though it can't compare with good home cooking."

Now I am fond of my victuals, though I will not have extravagance, but it always seems to me a distraction to conduct business over food. The business is only half attended to, and a fine meal but half appreciated. It is how the better sort will have things done, y.et I would as soon have met him at his jail and spared the cost.

"Sheriff Underwood?"

"'John.' Got to call me 'John,' Abel."

"Well . . . John . . . I would like to know the details of the finding of our man's body. I must have the facts, see."

The sheriff frumped his chin, pulled an ear, and nodded. "Well, we aren't going to hold anything back from Bill Seward's personal agent. No, sir. That's fact number one right there. You'll have my personal support." But he sighed. "Don't you think we should save the grisly side of things for a glass in the club room?"

"I have taken the Pledge, sir."

A spark of light, perhaps of laughter, lit his eyes. But he mastered his demeanor. "Well, then . . . I guess there's no purpose in waiting, after all. Is there?" He deviled his ear again. "Look here, Abel. I want to get this business straightened out as badly as you do. Worse, I expect. I'm the sheriff, for crying in a bucket. Can't have folks running around like the old Iroquois, scalping and burning and hanging Federal men. Now can I?"

He slumped back, as though the cares of office had already overtaken him. "Bill Remer, now. Used to be sheriff. Gone off to Albany and bigger things. Worst doings he had to face up to was that serving girl drowned her little one in the outhouse last summer. Then that first fellow of yours got himself killed back in November. But Bill Remer knew how to bide his time. Don't I know it? Just packed up and handed it all on to me. He's off to the legislature, and it's all on my head now. And here I've got Bill Seward sending his own special agent up to reckon with me, in case I can't tell a bull from a milk cow. What kind of sheriff is that going to make me look like in front of my voters?"

I almost told him that I was Mr. Lincoln's agent, not Mr. Seward's, but that would have been a needless display of pride. And, frankly, Mr. Seward seemed to have more play with the man.

"I have not been sent to chastise or bother," I declared. "I am prepared to work together, see, and would steal no man's credit."

He shook his head slowly. "If only old Thurlow wasn't off gallivanting in Europe . . ." Then he braced himself up. Stroking back hair and ear with a big hand, he said, "All right, Jones. I mean, Abel. Here's what I know. And I regret to say it isn't all that damned much . . ."

A farmer had found our fellow hanging from a tree beside the high road east of the lake. Our man, Reilly, had been recruited from among the local Irish by my predecessor—before his own death—and had not been a felicitous choice. Young Reilly had the curse of the drink upon him and talked grandly in his cups. His boasting of secret entrustments brought him low. His widow said they took him in the night, the masked and silent men who did the deed. She had gone to the priest, not the sheriff, and by the time Father McCorkle went to the authorities with his lean report, Gerald Reilly's head had been crowned with hot pitch, sprinkled with gunpowder, then set alight. They left him hanging in the winter winds.

"But . . ." I said, " . . . surely they hanged him first? Before this burning business?"

Sheriff Underwood looked at me with calculating eyes. Gray they were, like the weather. He petted the ends of his mustache where they hung below his chin. Then he reached for an ear. But this time he stopped himself and lowered his hand again.

"I couldn't say that. And, frankly, I didn't think to ask Alanson. That's the coroner. Alanson Potter. Related through the wife, by the way. Farm's the old Potter place. Grand old family, the Potters. They—" He caught himself drifting and shook his head. "Should have asked, I'll admit. But I didn't. Anyway, Potter's set off to the war himself. Go myself, if I was a younger man. Right thing to do. Essential, if a fellow expects to have a political career afterward. Of course, a sheriff does his part, too. Anyway, Potter's assistant might know something. We can ask him. Strikes me, though, that it probably went the other way around. With the burning business first. Somebody wanted to lay out a lesson. About the price a fellow has to pay for turning on his kind."

"But that's a torment like—"

"Like something out of a damned book of martyrs." The sheriff wrestled himself into a more comfortable position in his chair. "Don't I know it? Hardly the sort of thing the voters are going to tolerate in a law-abiding, progressive place like Yates County."

"At the church this morning—"

He snorted. A last patron, leaving, gave him a look.

"Know what had that crowd all riled?" the sheriff asked.

"Reilly had become known as an informer," I said. "He was prepared to compromise this matter of an Irish insurrection and—"

"No such thing!" Underwood said. He slapped down a big hand and the table settings jumped. "No such thing, friend. Insurrection, my backside. Couldn't get those micks out of the saloons long enough to stagger down for a hand-out of free hams. Know what had 'em riled? Somebody spread the word that Gerry Reilly's job was to put together a list of all able-bodied Irishmen in the county. So they could be rounded up for military service. And they're terrified of it. Don't I know it? Frightened as all get out that Old Abe's going to force them into a blue coat and put a gun in their paws and make 'em fight to free the Negro. That's what had 'em going this morning, Abel."

I sat back. For I had believed I had seen the stirrings of rebellion. When all I had seen was fear.

"But these . . . rumors of insurrection?"

The sheriff held up a hand to silence me. An instant later, the waiter appeared at my shoulder. My stew shone thick, and smelled handsomely of beef and pepper.

"You just wait right there, Tommy," the sheriff told the waiter after the lamb had been laid before him. My host then took up knife and fork and cut deeply into his meat. Twas done to a cinder, and a shame that, for the chop might have made a fine piece of eating. "Now that's what I like to see," the sheriff said happily. "A fellow who listens to what he's told." He nodded his dismissal to the waiter.

When the man had gone, Underwood leaned toward me. He had spent much of his life out of doors and the history of it was written on his skin. He brought his face so close I could read the veins in his eyes, and the trails of his neckcloth flirted with the gravy on his plate. I could not fathom this gesture of secrecy, for we were now the only diners left in the room. I had been long at the burying and our meal had been much delayed.

"Well, I've looked into it," the sheriff said. "All this Irish insurrection business. Don't know how the hell the rumor got started in the first place. Not a thing Bill Remer could find, or that I can find. Nor any of the men—deputies, constables or police. Not that the local police are worth much. They're taking on Irish fellows themselves. But goings-on? I'd hear about it, if anything was happening out in the hills. Farmers know me. I'm one of 'em, for crying in a bucket. They aren't going to hold anything back for the sake of the Irish—or anybody else. They don't want trouble coming around to spoil things. War's trouble enough, with so many of the boys gone. Ploughing and planting's going to go hard this year. And the drummers now. They hear things, if there's anything to hear. And they know to pass it on when they do. Likewise, your parsons and such. Even the mechanics and teamsters. The canal people. They all know enough to pass any word of trouble along to the sheriff, whether he's a new sheriff or old."

Elbow on the table, he made a great fist. Twas a sign of confidence, not anger. "I *know* what goes on in this county, Abel. And I haven't heard one squeak about an insurrection that hasn't come directly from Washington." He took time out for a chew and a swallow. "I'll take you down to the Irish boozers later. Down the way on lower Main. Then we'll go over to Jackson Street. Used to be all free Negroes back there. Now the Irish are crowding 'em out, and it's a change for the worse. Let you have yourself a look. And you can tell me if those sorry lumps of rags look ready to break out in armed revolt. Hell, they're just worrying about getting their next bowl of porridge—or their next drink—and staying out of the county jail." Speech done, he applied himself to his plate with masculine vigor.

I had been content to listen and eat my stew, for I would have it hot and healthful. Oh, I love to thrust a spoon into the hot, brown joy of a stew and to raise up the treasures the cook has concealed in its depths. But twas my turn to speak.

"Who, then, killed Reilly?"

The sheriff dropped his fork on the plate. It made a great clanking and spatter. "Criminals. Murderers." He grunted. "Don't you worry. I'll find 'em. You can be sure of that."

We both went at our eating for a bit, and lovely my stew was, though pricey and not to the standards of Mrs. Schutzengel, to say nothing of my Mary Myfanwy, or the wife of Hughes the Trains, or other famous cooks of my experience. Although I am told it is considered improper by some, I took a swipe of bread to the gravy leavings in my bowl, for waste is a sin. The sheriff did not seem to mind my habits, and I must tell you the fellow had failings of his own. All in all, I found these New York country folk a practical sort, and much to my liking. But let that bide.

"Have you ever," I asked, in my warmth and satisfaction, "heard anything of 'whiteboys'?"

I could see by his face he had not. He raised a lamb bone to his mouth, but paused long enough to say, "Never heard of such a thing."

Neither had I. Perhaps, I thought, I had misheard the voice in the mob. I let it go. For now I had a delicate subject to raise. But I would have an answer, for the truth of it is that I was cross. It had seemed to me a great oversight that only two timid police fellows had been present at the church that morning. And now that I realized Underwood had possessed reasons to fear trouble—based upon those rumors of draft lists and the hatred thus engendered—I was disturbed that he had not stood before the church himself, with the full weight of badge and law.

"I was surprised, John," I said, "that only two law officers were at St. Michael's this morning. There was a fuss."

He wiped his mouth, then his fingers, with his table linen. Rather than showing anger or resentment at my observation, he gave me a little smile of the sort gentlemen exchange in private.

"And you're sitting there wondering . . . if I know so damned much about what's going on . . . why the hell wasn't I out there with the militia called up and standing in ranks?" He nodded at the thought, amused, and squeezed the vast lobe of an ear.

"Abel, my friend . . . did you and Bill Seward have a sit-down before he sent you up here? You two have a good talk?" He held out a leather case. "Cigar?"

"I do not take tobacco, sir."

He nodded. As if he had expected as much. "Mind if I have a smoke?"

Twas his business. I gave my head a little shake and said:

"Mr. Seward did honor me with an interview."

"He tell you anything about Yates County?" The sheriff applied a match to his filthy roll of weeds. Soon he was issuing smoke like the Lower Depths, filling the room with a noxious, wicked, unChristian stink. Twas vulgar and foul, and doubtless pleasing to Satan. But we must not judge the vices of others too severely, and I will say no more of it.

"We concentrated upon the matter of insurrection," I said.

"Oh, insurrection, my backside. I don't think Bill Seward knows a damned thing about insurrection. At least not up here in Yates County. Maybe down South there. And I'll tell you honestly—I'm not going to pretend I have all that close an acquaintance with our distinguished secretary of state. But I've met him a few times, one political fellow to another, little fish to a bigger one. I know old Thurlow Weed a sight better. He's the money man, he's got the reins. But I do know this much, Abel. Bill Seward knows how every county in this state operates. Every last one. Best governor we ever had, and a politician to talk the drawers off a vestal virgin. He could have told you that Yates is a fine county. Most folks up here walk straight ahead and work hard." His eyes shifted behind a veil of smoke. "But there's this other thing. I'd explain it to you . . . if I could explain it to myself."

He looked past me now, and took a fortifying draught of his tobacco. "These hills . . . they're kind of a place people run to. Oh, I don't mean criminals. No, sir. We keep a rein on that. But other sorts. Most of 'em just religious folks who didn't get along back home and don't want bothering. But some of 'em are full-moon crazy on a sunny afternoon." He stroked his ear gently, coaxing out thoughts. I feared the nub of cigar between his fingers would set his hair alight. "There's just something up there in those hills that don't make sense to the rest of us. Maybe it's that magnetism folks are always going on about. But we draw all kinds. Prophets—or so they call themselves. Queer sects and the like. Why, we even had two spiritualist conventions right here in Penn Yan! Don't that make you wonder?" He touched the ends of his mustache with thumb and forefinger. As if connecting the current in a scientific experiment. "Sometimes . . . I wonder if there isn't just some kind of madness up there above the lake. Something in the water or the wind. Ever hear of the Publick Universal Friend?"

"I have not."

"You will. Before you leave. She started it all. Old Jemima Wilkinson. Going to build the New Jerusalem in the wilderness. That was on to seventy years ago. Now we've got everything from shouting Methodists to these Elsasser Lutherans up my way in Potter—good folks, mind you, but they don't speak a word of English. I'm not sure they even know they're living in the nineteenth century. Hard to give a stump speech to folks who don't speak English, don't I know it?" For just a moment, he fell into the pit of electoral memories.

After clearing his throat of a cough, he called the glow back to the tip of his cigar. "Point is, things are changing. Progress, Abel. Has folks confused, cranky. Don't know what to make of all the newfangled goings-on. Can't reconcile themselves to the old ways going. So they start dreaming of some Garden of Eden that never was—at least not up this way. Desperate for something to turn to. And this war now. It draws things out in people. Not all of 'em good things. Most folks are for it, more or less. Yates is a solid Republican county, and Whig before that. But not all folks see things right. Not by a long ways. And people up here always had strong opinions, right or wrong. Your Presbyterians over in Branchport, for instance. Presby*te*rians, mind you. Tighter with a penny than most men are with a twenty dollar gold piece. Few years back they went taking up collections to send Sharps rifles out to John Brown and those fellows in Kansas. And send 'em they did. 'Free men, free soil, and free the slaves.' Underground railway stations all over the county, both sides of the lake. But down county, toward Dundee, now that's a whole different story. Pennsylvania folk settled down that way. My own people were Rhode Islanders, so they were right-thinking. But those Pennsy fellows, they'd catch 'em a nigger running through and ship the poor bugger right back south for the reward money. Trussed like a hog." He paused to give me the fullness of the image while he enjoyed the last of his smoke.

"So," he resumed, "we've got wild-haired abolitionists, other folks who don't want anything to do with freeing any slaves, caterwauling Bible-whackers, mystic fellows and mesmerists, and now these Irish on top of everything." He gave me an intense look. "You realize more than one in ten residents of this town is Irish nowadays? And near every one of 'em turned up within the last fifteen years."

Yes. The Famine. My friend, Dr. Tyrone, had stories to tell. The blight on its praties had sent the Irish nation wandering. My regiment in India had teemed with the children of Erin.

The sheriff pushed his plate away, as if the sight of it suddenly offended him. "Now why am I telling you all this? What do you think? Well, first, you tell me something, Abel. How long have you been in this country yourself? And I mean no offense."

"I am four years an American."

"No offense intended now. The Welsh work hard, don't I know it, and they're always welcome. But what I want to get across is just this: The country—*our* country—runs on elections. No kings or queens, no dukes of this or that. Votes and voters, that's what we're all about. One man's right to choose, and another man's right to get himself elected. Now you just look at the scrambled-up mess of folks we have here in Yates County. And tell me a sheriff—or anybody else who stands for public office—doesn't have to think about how he plants his boots."

"And you believe Mr. Seward should have told me these things?"

"Hell, no. Not all of 'em, anyway. Don't expect he's got time for that. With this Mason and Slidell business and what not. But he should have told you about our Irish."

"What about the Irish? Specifically."

The waiter came to clear away our plates. The sheriff held back his words until we sat alone again.

"Well, think about it. More than one potential voter in ten here in Penn Yan's an Irishman. That's a lot of votes. And, of course, they're contrary, your Irish. Democrats to a man. And plenty of people—I'm speaking of the people who count now—they figure we can just ignore the boggies. But *I* say we have to think of the future. We have to do what's right for this country. And this country's changing. Why, we even have Italians on the county rolls. No, I say we can bring the Irish over to Mr. Lincoln. If we give 'em a fair shake. And turn the screws just enough, when we have to. But there's no need to antagonize 'em by sending the law down to their church. If you see what I mean." He sat back again. "The Irish just like to make a noise. Then it blows over. What harm was done this morning?"

I thought of the widow and child, and the coffin broken open.

"You'll see," Sheriff Underwood went on. "The Irish are all talk and temper. But there's no substance to 'em. They couldn't organize an insurrection to save their souls—and, anyway, what do they have to rebel against? They have it good. All that business about dark-of-the-night plots—that's nothing but spooks and haunts somebody in Albany dreamed up to put a scare into Bill Seward."

He lowered his voice and leaned toward me again. "But I will tell you this. We have two Federal men dead now. Or one Federal man, plus a half-breed, you might say. And, frankly, I lay it to nothing but outsider meddling. Leave the Irish alone, and they'll make no trouble that matters. They'll just beat the daylights out of one another, or take a strap to their wives and children. But poke a stick at 'em, and you'll find yourself in a nest of rattlesnakes."

Gray eyes hard upon me, he said, "Now you tell me something. How the hell do you expect to run a secret operation when the first thing you do when you get off the train is march over to Father McCorkle's den of thieves and let the whole world know what you're after?"

"I don't intend to run a secret operation," I said. "I want the killers to know who I am."

He looked at me in wonder. As if he could not decide whether any man could be the fool I seemed.

"Well . . ." he said, " . . . if you didn't come up to my county to run a secret operation and look for some fairy-story insurrection, what *did* you come for, Abel?"

"For the killers," I told him. "For when we have them, we'll have the truth of the rest of it."

He snorted and scratched a great ear. "Oh, and I suppose you expect the killers to just walk up to you and give themselves away?"

"Yes," I told him, "there is the trick of it. I know the Irish, see." The fellow had finished his cigar, so I saw no fault in giving him a stir. "And now I would like to see where they hanged poor Reilly."

TWO

I HAD MISJUDGED THE SHERIFF. SET AGAINST THE extravagance of the hotel, I feared the fellow had become a devotee of fine living and but a political creature—for I will tell you, though it shock, that the moral ingredients of political men are not always what they should be. But Underwood proved solid. He was as tough as the hills and glens that spawned him, and he proved it soon enough.

But I must not go too quickly.

The sheriff ordered a sleigh from the livery stable behind the hotel, and didn't they jump to it? Waiting on the rig, we stood in the horse spew and trodden snow of an alley. The passage brisked with boys on commercial errands and men shortening the distance to their destinations. Every one of them tipped his hat respectfully to the sheriff, casting a curious glance at me. Underwood greeted each citizen by name.

Now I must tell you a thing: I do not love the horse. It is a beast infernal as the juggernaut, and my discomfort with the four-legged leviathan was compounded by the memory of the great fire in those Washington stables that climaxed the Fowler affair. Twas a nightmare, nothing less. I see and hear the burning creatures still. Their agony will haunt me to the grave. Oh, I would not slight the work done by the horse—I understand we could not do without him—and the Good Lord did see fit to breathe life into the beast, after all. But how I dread the aspect of the creature! I would sooner box a Bengal tiger than sit upon the back of such a brute. And yet such worries must not be revealed, lest others think us weak. It is a sadness of our human kind that we will sooner mock another's fears than like his virtues.

I propped up manly on my cane, trying to ignore the slattering of hooves in the icy yard. I wished the sleigh well ready, and not only to confine said horse safely in harness. Twas blade cold in that alley, for all the steam of the droppings. The snow had stopped, but a freeze glassed the air. Greatcoat or no, I wanted myself under the travelling blanket.

"Fine town," Sheriff Underwood cried out, his breath a gush of steam. "Growing by leaps and bounds. Industry's the thing, Abel. Mills going up all along the outlet canal, and six trains through a day, two of 'em freights. It's a boom, that's what it is. *Good* afternoon, Donald, 'afternoon, George. Missus feeling better? And agriculture growing to beat the band. Orchards, timber. Sheepers up Italy Hill. Just got to keep folks patient and sensible, and no tomfoolery. 'Lo there, Jimmy. You tell your pa I said hello. So when they found your . . . predecessor . . . face down in the lake, and then that Reilly . . ."

He stood unbothered in that chapping cold, wearing naught but a light cape, hands bare of gloves and ears scarlet. Twas all I could do to keep from hopping about, for the winter come right up through my boots, despite the good greasing I had given them. But Underwood was a walrus at his polar revels.

"*Fine* town," he recited, louder than required for the ears of Abel Jones, "*fine* county. Plenty of future up here. *Plenty*. Future to spare, bushel and a peck of it." He turned his head of a sudden. "Bucky, what's keeping that damned sleigh?"

At that, a sleek, black cutter left the barn, led on by a Negro. Rigged for two horses it was, not the customary one.

I was not pleased. A cutter is an open rig. And I saw no blankets. Only a shovel tucked beneath the cushion fall, as if for arctic snows.

"About time," the sheriff said, catching the reins. "Let's go, Abel," he told me, "if you want to get there before dark."

I clambered up beside him, wary of the beast harnessed to my side of the cutter. The sheriff took up more than half the seat, but I am not excessive in size, so it mattered not. He snapped the whip in the air, and I half expected chips of ice to fall from the heavens. The horses pulled away as though they longed to run.

"Bucky knows better than to set me a weak team," the sheriff said. "And he knows I won't have bells." He steered the sleigh into a street ripe with business, then quickly turned us into an even more vivid thoroughfare.

"Main Street," he said.

A farmer's wagon crowded in between the snow banks, forcing us a-tilt to keep from worse. The sheriff let a curse I cannot set to paper, for profanity numbs the good as surely as cold numbs the flesh.

"Over there now," he said, settled again, with the horses stepping as if they, too, were proud of their environs, "you'll want to remember that shop there. Hamlin and Sons. Fellow trying to make a go of one of your 'temperance' stores. Won't sell alcohol nor tobacco. I predict bankruptcy."

We slid by handsome fronts with painted names: RAPLEE'S BANK; the FRANKLIN HOUSE HOTEL, of which I had heard critical report; GEORGE R. CORNWELL, BOOKSELLER AND STATIONER; ROBERTS AND CO., FANCY DRY GOODS. The snow-lined street harbored apothecaries, photographers and harness-dealers, dispatchers and brokers and readers in the law, barbers, a watchmaker and, up a flight of stairs, a school of music. The windows of an emporium of gaieties had been soaped with announcements of price reductions to greet the new year, and pink-cheeked women rushed in with their baskets. A little world of its own, this Penn Yan was.

Then we come to Egypt.

Saloons and glooming whisky bins clustered by the bridge. Deviltry and shame, a curse upon the land. Forlorn figures hunched inside the doorwells.

The sheriff pointed his whip. "Those shabs there? Mick boozers. Stick your head in any one of 'em and you'll see familiar faces, that's a fact. Dirty as the glass they pour your poison in. I guarantee you half the crowd that was out howling at St. Mike's this morning are in there now. Glorying over their grand heroics and singing tearful laments about heroes and traitors and dying colleens. With their women home watering the last of the porridge and their brats dying like it's a cholera year."

A no-good in a hat with a chopped brim and a burlap scarf gave us the "go on, you" eyes. Fair daring the sheriff to stop. Underwood ignored the bravado, for he, too, understood the pride of broken men.

"On the other hand," he said, "you might not want to step in there just now. They do hold a grudge, your Irish." He laughed, get-upping the reins.

We skittered over a bridge dressed with ice and the sheriff insisted I look around. "Branch canal. Connects the lakes. You can go right up to the Erie Canal, all the way to Rochester, Buffalo—even New York City, way of the Hudson. Right from this spot. Miracle of modern engineering." He tugged an ear. "Oh, our canal may not be the biggest in the state. But we've got twelve dams and locks, with a three-hundred-foot fall. Every last lock built of solid stone. Puts the other canals to shame, if you're talking quality."

The white bed of the canal lay frozen over. A throng of boys skated, and joy they had of the day, although we might have wished them at their lessons.

"You wait," the sheriff told me. "Come March, she'll be going again. Soon as the ice breaks. 'Transporting our fair harvest to the sea,' as Staf Cleveland likes to say. Or to Albany, anyway."

"Deep, is it?" I asked, feigning an interest.

"Naw. Four foot most of the way. Got to deepen it. Hoping to. Everything has to be bigger and bigger nowadays. Bigger boats, heavier loads. Only way to make a venture pay is to think big. 'Course, it's going to take money. And Albany seems inclined to back the railroads nowadays. Then there's this war, top of everything else. Maybe you could put a word in Bill Seward's ear for us?"

He glanced at me, then did not press the matter. The horses trailed steam from their nostrils. Two gleeful boys ran after us.

"But your locks now," the sheriff continued. "That's a different story. They're deep enough. Gush like Niagara Falls when they're running. Power your mills, the way they set 'em in. That's where you get your drownings. In the locks. Fool kids. Terrible accidents. Have to take you out and show you the mills, though. Dozens of 'em. All the way down to Dresden. Grist and flour. Plaster. Flax. Two spoke factories and a wool carding manufactory. Industries of tomorrow. Oh, the future's going to be something up here, Abel."

"I do hear the railroads are hard on the canals," I offered. I had a personal interest there. "In Pennsylvania, where my wife and I—"

"Railroad's a fine thing, too! Nothing against 'em. All for 'em. We've got business enough for both up here in Yates."

We slid past the proofs of prosperity, from lesser houses set near the mills to fine gabled dwellings that climbed a slope. Turning right, we followed a main-travelled road.

"Lake's just over there," Underwood told me, pointing the whip across my chest. "Can't see it now with the weather. But you could throw a stone and hit it. If there's a lake more beautiful than Keuka on this continent, you'll have to show it to me."

I saw only gray, and a fall-off in the quality of the houses again, then open lots, and the lonesome look of gardens left till spring.

The road forked and we veered left up a hill. The sheriff touched the lead horse with the whip, just enough to keep him to his pace, and the sleigh rose into a crystaled fog. Black and shut, a farmhouse flanked the road. Twas a dark place of a sudden.

And cold. Now, I am not indulgent in my comforts, though I welcome a warm bed and ready meals. Nor am I unfamiliar with the winter, for the hills of Wales that bred me do not coddle. Yet this was cold to freeze forgotten parts. No Indus heat or sun of Punjab here. It was a very Russia of a place, if what I hear of Russia is half true. I sought to keep my shivering to myself, and sank into my greatcoat. For the truth is the typhoid had left me weakened.

I envied the sheriff's red hands, happy on the reins. My world felt hopeless drear.

There was melancholy, and I succumbed to it. Longing for wife and child and warmth I was, and wishing away my charge as a shirker will. What man would seem heroic, or virtuous, if we knew his private thoughts?

Sudden as a child's fear, a black form loomed before us. We had heard no sound. Yet there he was. Gathered like a ghost from shrouds of fog.

A horseman, coming on at a canter.

Perhaps I was too given to my dreaming, but the surprise of him made my heart jump. He pranced up beside us, great cape snapping out. His horse, if I may judge, was not so fine as his clothing wished itself. I saw a bearded smear of face set deep, shadowed by a broad hat of the sort artistics wear. His eyes were icy as the day itself.

Yet he was mortal, and seemed no menace, after all.

"A bracing afternoon, Sheriff," the rider called out.

I have an ear, see. It comes out of the Welshman's love of song. I can place a man by the music of his talk. And I picked out the rider as one of those Irishmen who strain to speak like an English gentleman. Worst of both worlds, you might say, if you were in a hard mood. He summed a lifetime's longing in four words.

The sheriff muttered half a greeting, and the lead horse gave his tail a be-gone flick. The rider faded toward the town and the hooves of our team crunched in steady rhythm. The horseman might as well have been a ghost.

"Fellow just went past?" Underwood said abruptly. "Calls himself 'the Great Kildare.'" He grunted. "'Great Bamboozler' would be more like it. Professor of a dozen kinds of nonsense. So he claims. 'Science of Mesmerism, Egyptology, and Spiritualist Phenomena.' Figure that out."

He applied the whip to keep the team from slackening and scratched a crimson ear. Frost had formed on his mustache ends. "Took a rent on the Kyle place. Down toward the Steuben County line. Might as well be on the moon, it's so far to the back of nowhere. Worthless soil. All high and barren. But who knows what a fellow like that has in his head? Not here to plant corn, don't I know it? So we keep an eye on him. Though there's no warrant out on him in New York State. Bill Remer did tell me that much." He shifted and possessed a bit more of the seat. "I warned you about those damned-fool types that drift up here. All spooks and hobgoblins. And damn me if honest folk don't take 'em serious. Must be something in the air."

The only thing I felt in the air was cold.

And then grace struck. The road crested, and the fog and cloud fell behind us at the turn of a wheel. Twas as if we had pierced a wall.

There was beauty.

Now I have seen the Kush of the Hindoo, in all its brazen magnificence, and am no stranger to the ravishing Khyber. Not least have I seen the sweet valleys of Wales in the spring. But this . . . this was glory!

The horses welcomed the relief at the end of their climb, and we rushed between broad fields chaste with snow. A red sun fell. Stripped trees shone ruddy, glowing. The snow crimsoned between the shadows cast by black pines, and bracken lit gold.

Yet this was but a meager preparation.

Waves of ridges stretched westward, as far as Heaven, arrayed in lilac snow and dusky rose. The crests scorched scarlet, as if with winter burning. Words are too weak for such beauty! We might as well attempt to write of love.

As I watched, the sky formed into ribbons. Lavender bordered the purple of wine, and watery orange met lemon. Who could count the endless shades of red? I would tell you Heaven blazed like a heathen market in that hour, but all comparison is false. For the great bazaars are harsh, and hot, and sharp with calculation, but the Lord composes gently in His grandeur, and His generosity is endless. He fires the lily, and softens the flame.

In between the highlands, valleys dropped. Deep. Blue and purple declined to moody gray. Those gorges seemed all mystery to me. Oh, how I felt the yearning of that landscape!

Far below the high road that we followed, a crooked lake shone smooth with mending snow. Yet there, toward the center, yet unfrozen, a steely wet warned. Houses, tiny against majesty, smoked in the hollows. On a bluff, a lone horse stood, rimmed by the bloody sun.

I full forgot our purpose and the cold.

Now you will laugh and say, "This Abel Jones is a queer one, given to romantical blubbering like some poet fellow." And I will grant my fondness for the beautiful, and let you think it makes me less a man, if so you are determined. But when the Good Lord sends us such a prospect, you will not find ingratitude in me.

Oh, wonder of ravens atop a fence, feathers oiled against the flaming snow. Broken stalks stood gilded in the bracken, tangled as our lives. In a farmhouse window by the road, the first lamp of the day shone.

"There is beauty," I said, helplessly.

"What say?"

I blushed, for I had never meant to speak.

"A fine view, that," I told the sheriff. "You spoke well of your county. There is true."

He made a sound deep in his throat. "Got to get you out to see the mills, man. Industry's the thing."

So we rode, with the afternoon dying around us. We traveled some miles, though a shivering man cannot measure finely. Now I am hardy, as a rule, and a good healer. I showed the ones who said I'd lose my leg. But even the glory of all nature could not sustain me. I will not give excuses like a child, but the typhoid had blown me good, and I was not yet my old self. Cold it was, yet sweat come to my skin.

The landscape changed, although I could not say clearly when or where. Gone lonely, almost desolate, there was a wrongness about it now. Despite the blanket of snow, I sensed the poorness of the soil. The trees not cut for timber had a stunted look, and cattail fringes marked the moors and barrens. Twas the sort of place where the last-come farmer must work twice as hard for half the harvest. But beautiful still, I give the country that, though it lay a world removed from the prosperous town behind us.

"Should've told Bucky how long we'd be out," the sheriff said. "Could've mounted us a pair of lanterns. Won't be much moon."

"Is it far, then?" I asked. The muscles of my face were fair frozen, yet my back was slimed with sweat.

He shook his head. Melt sprayed from his eyebrows and his ears, and the trails of his mustache crackled. "Just shy of the tavern crossroads. Hop, skip and a jump."

The sleigh rushed through the spreading dark. Night swelled out of the ravines and copses, creeping up from the deep-set lake.

Without warning, the sheriff yanked back on the reins. As if we had come unexpectedly to the edge of a precipice.

We skated to a stop.

The lead horse saw whatever the sheriff had seen. He reared and fought the air. The mare beside him neighed and danced. I saw only empty road before us, and a sketch of blasted trees.

"Damn me to black blazes," the sheriff said, if you will forgive my frank report.

He jicked the reins, sending the horses forward again. Slowly. We hissed and scraped along ruts packed to ice. The sheriff stopped the team a length short of a great tree.

I saw it then.

Hanging by a rope from a black limb.

We both got down, my legs stiff as my cane.

There was little wind to feel, yet the figure swayed.

Too small to be a man.

Surely not a child?

Or . . . the poor widow?

I heard a queer rustling as we neared the figure.

Twas no man, but an effigy. A corn dolly of the kind the poor crafted for their children in the old country. Only this was bigger than any toy. And dressed in rags.

The sheriff struck a match.

The doll was garbed in blue, in a mockery of a uniform, with acorns fixed to the shoulders where an officer's rank would be. The top half of its head had been blackened with tar.

A signboard hung across its chest.

The match went out, and the sheriff struck another, holding it as high as he could. We struggled to read. Neither of us whispering a word.

LOOK HEER AND NO YUR FATE

The second match died and the sheriff made a clucking sound. He struck another light and turned to speak.

Twas then the shot rang out.

THE PANICKED HORSES NEARLY knocked me down. My cane went rolling. But the sheriff moved with startling speed. He grabbed the lead horse by the bit. When it failed to calm, he punched it on the side of the head. Then he hurled the slackened reins at me. I caught them as if tossed a lighted bomb.

The sheriff grabbed the whip from its socket and leapt off through the snow, heading for the grove that held the gunman.

"Hold the damned horses," he shouted back over his shoulder. "I'm going to cut that bastard to the marrow. Shoot at me, will he . . ."

Now, I've been shot at with a better aim. No marksman that one, for no bullet hissed near by. Perhaps it was only a warning. But the monstrous pair of horses meant me ill, and no doubt there. I felt it. I did. I stood with a death grip on those reins, looking to my balance on the ice of the road, for without my cane I was as tethered to the team as they to me. Twas awful. I would have chased a band of assassins with naught but my knuckles, rather than mind those beasts.

I turned my face away from the brutes. So I would not have to see their hellish eyes. Still, I felt their breath morbid upon my ear. A gruesome snout come nudging at my back. A great Sindhi cobra would have held less terrors for me. Better a pack of Pushtoons with their jezails, or dacoits with their daggers, than the horror of a horse.

One of the monsters licked me.

But I forget my tale.

The sheriff jumped through the snow like a very deer. Perhaps it is a trick New York folk learn to get them to the privy in the winter. Spry as a lad in his courtship days, the big man raced toward the trees from which the muzzle had flashed. With no attempt to conceal himself. Bold as a drunken grenadier. Waving the whip and cursing to shame the devil.

"You bugger," he cried. "You dirty, sneaking bastard."

Such were by far the softest of his words.

I feared a closer shot would strike him down. But none came. He disappeared into the wood, a black shape melting into greater blackness, and I heard him thrash about. Five minutes more and he re-emerged farther down the treeline, a dark bulk motive on a field of snow.

Twas night.

He come back sweating and steaming, going at his ears as if to tear them off in his rage. "Won't be the end of *this* business," he barked. Oh, there was anger in the man. "Don't you think it will. I'll track that fellow to Canada, if I have to. All the way to Californy. Shoot at the damned sheriff . . ."

"I do not think, sir, that he was shooting at you."

We both glanced at the doll hung from the tree.

"Aw, call me John, would you? For cripes sake. You're stiff as a corpse, you know that, Abel? And you're here with me. Somebody takes a shot at you, they're as good as shooting at me." In a last burst of anger, he trudged to where the effigy dangled, gave a barely successful leap—he was too solid a man to leave the earth for long—and yanked it by the leg. The dolly broke in twain and the bottom hushed to the ground, while the torso, sign and blackened head hung swaying.

"Oh, for crying in a bucket," he said, and kicked the fallen half of the doll.

"My cane," I said, pointing with my free hand. "Use my cane."

He took it up and knocked the dolly down. But for the head and neck caught by the noose. He tried and tried again, but could not reach the last of it.

Though not a quitting man, he finally stopped. He picked up the little signboard and tossed it in the sleigh, but left the rest of the figure.

"Well, you've seen the spot now," he said. "And seen it good. Reilly was hanging from the same damned limb." He patted at the lead horse and took the reins, offering me my cane. "Let's get on back to town. You're shaking like a man with the trots. Not used to the cold, I take it?"

I would not tell him of my bout with typhoid. For complaint makes us small.

We rode a while in silence, with the snowfields pale in the darkness. From a knoll, we saw lights in the distance, the town teasing us. A long, cold way remained.

The sheriff breathed hard long after his exercise, for such a body has great need of air. He puffed clouds. With an abiding fury upon him. Men of height and stature are not accustomed to challenge, though such is the lifelong lot of my slighter kind. Besides, he was a mighty man in his trim world, where all was subordinate. I knew the sort. The army makes them colonels, and they won't tolerate disorder or surprise.

I thought he had grown sullen. Then he laughed.

"Abel, my friend . . . you might be right about knowing the Irish. I'm not in a position to judge that. But it's sure starting to look like the Irish know you."

WHAT IS MORE WELCOMING than the glow of lighted windows, and the smell of woodsmoke, on a winter's night? The clouds were gone and starlight paled the streets. I longed for warmth, and the town seemed as welcome to me as home. Yet, behind its shutters and curtains, not all wished me well.

The villains knew I had come, whoever they were, and our match had begun. Now you will say, "What is this business of 'whoever'? Irish and guilty and done!" But the Fowler case had taught me to judge slowly. I would wait, and we would learn more of each other, like good enemies. The rascals would find I would not be discouraged by a doll or unskilled musketry. And I would find out what I could of them.

Still, I was glad I had packed the pistol given me by the boys in my old company to soothe our parting. It waited in my luggage. Now do not think me anxious to wield arms. I am a changed man from the hard days of my youth, when I thought a sergeant like unto a king, and I will not handle such tools but for necessity. Let us have amity, I say. But, sadly, not all men will have it so. So the thought of my Colt was a comfort.

Faint on the breathless air, I heard the sound of a harmonium playing "Annie Laurie." A maiden's voice joined in. Oh, music is a gift, and melody a blessing! Yet they are curses, too. For who can hear such sounds without recalling hearth and home? The ballad conjured my Mary Myfanwy and the nudging boy beside her, and soft hymns in the parlor of an evening. Her fair hands played the keys as brightly as she played upon my heart. How music gives us pain, yet we want more.

The sheriff snapped my revery.

"Set you down at the Benham House?"

Rich thoughts fled. After a moment, I told him, "That will be fine, sir."

"'John.' You've got to call me John, Abel."

"That will be fine, then, John. For there is as good as anywhere."

He swerved to miss a man drunk on a weeknight. Fair tumbling out of a whisky shab. "Irish, I'll lay you five gold dollars. You . . . are staying at the Benham House?"

I was not. For I would not have such grand accommodations at government expense, any more than I would at my own.

"I've arranged to board with your Methodist pastor."

He seemed stunned for a moment, then gave a mighty laugh. It rang in the frozen canyon of the street. "Well, you'll see precious little meat on *that* table, I promise you. Which one of 'em?"

"Which one?"

"Of the preachers? Which of our Methodist shepherds is going to put you up?"

I had not known the town held more than one.

"The Reverend Mr. Morris."

He made a sound twixt groaning and delight.

"I had not realized," I continued, "that there were two Methodist congregations. Now a fine town it is, your Penn Yan, but hardly of a size to—"

He snorted. "'Course, it's not. Your local Methodists went to feuding back in the forties. Scratching like cats. Half of 'em were pew-jumping abolitionists. 'Free the Negro,' and all that. Rest wanted to take things slower, not mix religion with politics. So they split. Breakaways built a new meeting-house and parson's hole just up from the courthouse. That's where you'll be heading, if you've set your mind to starve with Rev' Morris."

"So the Reverend Mr. Morris . . . is of the abolitionist persuasion?" Though not of fanatical bent, I wished the Negro free, and would not have a chapel shut its eyes to bondage.

"Oh, he's an abolitionist, all right. And everything else under the sun." Underwood laughed again. "You're like to have a lively old time. Though the housekeeper's ornery. And sparing with wood for the stoves, so I hear. Oh, you'll have yourself a time." He chuckled, unable to master himself completely. "You'll have yourself a time, all right."

His mocking tone—and such it clearly was—disappointed me. A man of the cloth is owed unqualified respect, and the sheriff sounded little better than a heathen. I began to suspect he was an Episcopalian.

Well, modern Penn Yan may have been, but it did not have a gasworks. The streets were lit by kerosene lamps set on poles. They cast a paler, harsher light than gas. Twas not late, but the town looked tucked in. The snow lay heavy on the roofs. Almost with the heaviness of death.

We slid along Main Street. Beyond the shops, the houses of the gentry shone thriftless. Money enables. The finest of the homes had columned fronts, like the handsome courthouse farther along.

Just past the court, the sheriff drew back on the reins. We halted with a skid before a row of lighted windows.

"Looks like some sort of to-do at Rev' Morris's tonight," the sheriff told me. "Maybe they're having a welcoming party for you. God only knows . . ."

The man had degenerated into shameless mirth.

"Got your luggage and all?" he asked as I stepped down. He pulled his ear hard, as if to hurt and keep himself from laughing. Yet he could not control himself.

"My bag was forwarded from the station, thank you."

He held out a big, red hand.

I could not but take it. If he was estranged from true religion, he had been brave and willing.

"Abel," he said, fair engulfing my hand, "I'm not sure whether trouble brought you to Yates County, or if you just brought more trouble to Yates. But I didn't like the looks of that nonsense back on the High Road."

"Indeed."

"Well, we'll get to the bottom of it." He seemed to mean it well. But even then he could not strap in his laughter. He let go of my hand and said, "You be sure to tell me how you like Rev' Morris's hospitality. And I'll make sure the Benham House has a room for you, if you need one. Don't you worry."

"A man of the cloth may live humbly, yet nobly," I assured him. "I will be content."

He grinned. His mustache spread, dripping beads of water and ice. "Well, we'll just see. 'Night now." He clicked his tongue at the horses to spare the whip and they stepped on.

A path had been cleared through the snow and I followed it up to the porch. The parsonage looked prim, but not falsely modest. Your Methodist works hard, and the results are to be seen in such provision.

A bell hung by the door. I rang it. Longing for warmth.

A conversation broke and footsteps come toward me. The door swung open and a clerical man stood before me where the light bordered the darkness. Lean and gray he was, with his hair combed up to a point and fixed with macassar.

"The Reverend Mr. Morris?" I asked.

He smiled as if in ecstasy. "The same, the same! And you're Brother Jones? Major Jones? You're Abel Jones? Of course you are, of course you are! She said you'd come in time." He fished a pocket watch from the billows of his waistcoat. "Right on the hour! See that? Right on the hour!"

The Reverend Mr. Morris seemed prone to enthusiasm.

"Come in, Brother Jones, come in!" he cried, clapping me on the shoulder in welcome. "You're just in time for our seance!"

THREE

NOW, THAT WAS NOT IN THE ORDER OF THINGS.

The fashion for the seance was not unknown to me, you understand. Popular they were back in Pottsville, too. I even knew of one good chapel woman who had thus indulged, longing to contact her lost daughter. Of course, my wife and I never succumbed to such irregularities. We read of such, and heard things, but no more. Deviltry the business was, and worse.

The seance was the stuff of charlatans and impostors, its audience a harvest of old maids, widows, enthusiasts and improvident youth. The hard-learned answers were not good enough for them, and they sat around their rapping tables, summoning spooks. It churned me to ponder such seductions practiced upon the weak of mind and forlorn. I had no doubt that money changed hands.

I dismissed the public's appetite for spirit contact as nonsense and would not be enticed by the demonstrations advertised. For I had seen the fakirs of the East and knew the clever tricks such fellows play. Our "spiritualists," all rappings, claps and ghosties, were only shadows to that Hindoo dark. Still, the common mind wants gulling. It is the stuff of magic shows and politics. But seances were not what we expect within a pastor's home.

I determined to have no part of the wickedness. I would as soon have sat me down to cards. And drink, too.

That is how I felt. I will admit my temper was not of the best, for the strain of the day had left me peevish. When Mr. Morris showed me to my room, to spare me five minutes for my personals, I flared at the prospect of such folly lurking in a man of God's abode.

I held my tongue, though. For hasty speech brings long regrets.

My room was clean, I will say that. Methodism does not spare the broom. My Mary Myfanwy holds to a useful rule: The hand that ends the scrubbing of a floor before the last verse of a hymn is sung—and a hymn of Charles Wesley's, mind you—has not performed the duty of a housekeep.

"Hurry, now. Hurry back down, Brother Jones," the pastor had cried, eyes all aglow. Like our small John's lit up on Christmas morn, bedazzled by the German tree. "They're waiting for you. They're waiting, waiting. She said you'd come! She foretold it! They're waiting in the parlor."

My bag stood beside the bed, properly delivered. I put dry stockings on my feet, then sat. I would not be insulting to my host. But seances were infamous, and wrong. Theaters of the devil they were. As if the common theater did not hold sin enough. Resolved to tell the fellow that I had a great need of rest—which was truthful, see—I went back down the stairs. I wanted supper, but would forego it if I might thereby avoid the spirit nonsense.

Oh, Sheriff Underwood's warnings had a different ring now that I knew the doings that went on. I wondered if the Benham House had rooms that might not be as pricey as the rest, perhaps the sort tucked up beneath the eaves. With longing, I recalled my handsome stew.

Well, down I creaked, glad anyway of shelter for this night. For I was too worn and weary to depart again. Tomorrow would do. My hands and face remained cold as the tomb, my limbs were slow, and I felt light of head.

The Reverend Mr. Morris stood waiting for me in the downstairs hall. Even the way his hair stuck up in a point annoyed me now. It seemed too gay and greased for his position, although his dress was dark and proper.

"Here he is!" he cried. "He's ready, he's ready! Here's Brother Jones!"

I heard a rush of whispers from the parlor.

The pastor seized my arm, as if to parade me down an aisle. I do not like such intimacy right off, but want a space around me until I know a fellow. Besides, I have my awkwardness of leg, and it is hard to keep step with another. I had to switch my cane to my left hand.

I had prepared a little speech that would allow me to retire politely—for rudeness is but a fist with no courage behind it. The words were on my lips as we went in.

Into that room that trapped me, heart and soul.

A red shawl wrapped the glass of the single lamp. The only other light come from the corner stove, its fire seething low behind the grate. The air felt as heavy as the parlor furniture. Hardly more than shadows, the other guests were seated at a table. Round it was, and large enough for six.

A vacant chair awaited me.

I saw too much too swiftly, despite the gloom, and must put it in order for you. As my eyes learned their way, I got a pair of shocks. Twas as if a boxing fellow had his one-two way with me.

Let me begin with the lesser astonishment.

Right there, between a pair of ladies in their prime, sat a great Negro fellow. Now do not misunderstand me. I have naught against the Negro. I wish him free and unsuffering, and hope he will again enjoy the pleasures of his African homeland. Nor do I think him less than other men in right, or soul, or even virtue. But surely you will understand my wonder that such a fellow, however finely dressed, had found a seat between two proper ladies.

And they were all holding hands!

Well, this was abolitionism sure.

That was the lesser matter. I saw it in a moment, for my eyes had no more time. Neither did I dwell upon the other man who sat there, although I recognized the horseman from the road. The one the sheriff called "the Great Kildare." His icy look meant nothing at the moment, for I had seen a sight that stopped my heart.

Twas the girl from the churchyard. The beauty whose beauty seemed wrong. She sat there in emerald velvet, red hair hanging free in waves of fire. The shadows adorned her, and her ivory complexion shone in the lamplight. Queer it was. Her features made no sense. All juts and angles, still they summed to beauty. But, above all, it was her eyes that called me. Brooding on such women, the Irish speak of spells, "come-hithers," put on boys and men.

Now, do not hear me wrongly. I do not hint at improprieties of deed or thought. For I was contented in my personal matters, and the blunders of my youth lay far behind me.

But she drew me! Those eyes burned. With the slow, deep fire of peat smoldering. There was no haste or drama in the girl. Or would you have me say "the woman"? For she seemed half of each. She gave no hint of pretense or imposture, but sat sedately. She might have been waiting for a coach.

And yet she ruled that room.

My mouth must have hung open like a boy's. I stood suspended. The tyrant Time had lost his grip.

She glanced up at me—only for a moment—and the spell abated. Perhaps she had decided to loosen her hold and let me go.

The party rose to its feet, as at a signal. One lank and bespectacled, the other merrily plump, the ladies fluffed their skirts free of their chairs. A great starched rustling they made as they fled the Negro's grip and ran to me. For his part, the black fellow straightened himself with a wonderful gravity of demeanor. Noble he seemed, all tall and grand. The bearded horseman kept himself apart.

But I must say a few words more about the Negro. Hued though he was, the good darkie had a polish lacked by many a paler man. He wore a wealth of hair, touched with gray and shaped like Pharaoh's in a lithograph. His dress was matchless neat and somber. Intelligence sat on him, as though he were no African at all, but dark-skinned by some accident of birth. Stern of visage, his eyes mixed wariness with boundless sorrow. Now you will think me odd, but I will tell you: I looked at him and thought, "There is a man!"

For her part, the red-haired girl sat in peace. As if the world were no concern of hers.

Excepting the horseman and the girl, the pastor's guests seemed easy and familiar. You sensed their acquaintance had been a long one. Without the least breath of impropriety, I will say there was great warmth between them all.

"May I present," Mr. Morris began, "my dear, esteemed friends . . . esteemed friends . . . Mrs. Stanton and Miss Anthony?"

And didn't those two thrust out their hands like they were men? Startled, I could but shake their mild appendages, though with a little bow to soften the presumption.

Mrs. Stanton was the one that did things first. Round and vivacious, she rushed at you. She grasped my hand as if it were the handle of a pump and gave it a hearty up and down.

"An honor, sir," she said, "to shake the hand of a champion of our noble Union. But you have suffered wounds?" She glanced down at my leg.

"A minor matter, mum," I said, embarrassed.

"Oh, Susan," she said to her friend, "I do admire men in their regimentals! Would that we could fight beside them!" Before I could withdraw, she grasped one of my buttons to inspect it more closely.

"Lizzie!"

"Oh, don't be a buzzard, Susan. This is the uniform of emancipation, and it is only proper that we admire it. Isn't that right, Mr. Douglass?"

Miss Anthony, the stricter of the two, offered a crisp, official sort of handshake. She looked right into you, that one, though one eye seemed awry behind her spectacles. Deep waters there, I thought.

"And surely you have heard," Mr. Morris said, pulling me free and facing me toward the Negro fellow, "surely you've heard of that great philosopher of freedom . . . philosopher and publisher . . . the journalist and orator . . . the great orator, Mr. Frederick Douglass?"

I could not say I had. I murmured, as we do in such circumstances.

The African stood a giant in compare to me—although size is not all that makes a man. Regal he was, though—and I am measuring my words. Laugh if you will, but had you been beside me, you would have thought him more the president than dear Mr. Lincoln. Dignity attended each of the fellow's gestures, and he took my hand with a solemnity nearly morbid. I know not if the Africans had kings, but if they did he come of such descent.

"I am honored, Major," he said, voice deep as the wisdom of Solomon. "*Hon*ored. We stand informed of your heroic deeds on the field of Bull Run." Up close, his eyes seemed lonely as the grave, and twice as deep. "You are welcome among us, sir. Ah, could we but accord a hero's due . . ."

I turned in alarm to Mr. Morris, who read the question on my lips.

"Oh," he told me, "no need to hide your light under a bushel, Brother Jones. No need to hide your light. The Reverend Mr. Abernathy took the liberty . . . liberty of writing of your exploits. He wrote of your exploits, sir, upon the field of battle . . ." He looked around at his guests. "Achilles stands among as . . . an Achilles!"

I do not resemble Achilles. Anyway, I have read my Homer and find all those Greeks a bad sort. Give me your Roman Cincinnatus, thank you. But I understood the fellow meant it kindly.

I will not tolerate exaggeration, though, much less error. I was no hero at Bull Run or elsewhere, but only did my duty, and that poorly. It is a wonder how these rumors start.

"You are mistaken, sir. I am no hero."

"Thus a hero speaks!" cried Mr. Douglass, raising an arm to hail me.

Kildare had crept up on us in the meantime.

"And here, Brother Jones," Mr. Morris said, "is our guest of honor . . . guest of honor. No. No, that's you, that's *you.*" He reddened. "The 'captain of our endeavor,' let us say. Yes, the captain! Of our endeavor, our exploration!" He beamed respect upon the swarthy fellow. "The learned Professor Kildare, Master of Spiritualism, Mesmerism and Egyptology . . . of Egyptology, sir! Think of it, think of it! And Doctor of Ancient Languages, as well! Of languages! Oh, how I wish I had a little Greek!"

The Great Kildare bowed with a tight smile. "At your service, sir."

"And yours, sir," I said. Although I fear I did not mean the words. I am no friend to strangeness and was not at his service. Nor did I wish the man at mine. Yet social life demands these small dissemblings. We have fallen far from Eden.

Kildare stepped aside. As if parting a curtain. To reveal that pale vision of a girl.

"My daughter and apprentice," he said, "a vessel of the high arts of the ancients, of secrets lost for countless millennia—until recovered by myself from Arabia's sands." He flourished his hand like a common tout. "I give you . . . Miss Nellie Kildare."

The girl looked up. Her stare made me feel uncovered. I mean that in no vulgar sense, see. But twas as if she saw more than we are meant to.

I should have turned around and run away.

"Miss Kildare," I said, with a graver bow.

The girl made no reply. She sat divorced from her surroundings.

"Sit down, sit down," the Reverend Mr. Morris said. "How late it's become, how late! Everybody, please. Sit, sit!"

I meant to plead weariness. The Good Lord knows it is the truth. And yet I let them lead me to that table.

"Mr. Morris," I began, struggling with myself, "I really cannot . . ."

"Don't be shy! Don't be hesitant!" Of a sudden, he stopped and gave me an asking look. "Surely . . . surely, this is not a new experience, Brother Jones?"

"I dare not . . ."

"But here's your place! Just here. The place of honor. Of honor, Brother Jones!"

That vacant chair sat waiting by the girl.

I fought my fate, if weakly.

"Look you," I told them all, "I'm lately risen from a sickbed." Twas more than I had intended to reveal. "And there is tiredness in me . . ."

The pastor looked ruptured. "But Brother Jones? Brother Jones! We've been waiting . . . waiting. We cannot proceed without six. It must be six!"

Now I have been a keeper of accounts, and have sufficient skill to count to six. And they had six without me. Mr. Morris himself there was, and the two ladies. With that regal son of Nubia attending. Then Kildare and his daughter. Six. And no mistake.

"But I'm the seventh," I protested.

Mr. Morris wrapped his arm around me, as if I might flee. Twas a boney business, that arm, and made me think of meals too closely parsed.

"Not at all! Not at all! Professor Kildare cannot participate in the circle. Can*not* participate. It's the rule, the rule!" He gripped me in his skeletal embrace, all staleness and pomade. "We need you, Brother Jones, or all is wasted, all wasted!"

Lord forgive me, I sat down with them.

The girl. I smelled her. She wore lavender.

And then she closed her fine hand over mine. Mrs. Stanton took me by the other. But that second grip was bare of sensation to me.

"I want her to ask the spirits when we'll get the vote," Miss Anthony said.

So transposed was I that her words did not register. Until later. But let that bide.

The Great Kildare dropped himself into a chair by the stove. As if to leave the rest of us to our sport. Mr. Morris opened with a prayer, and nothing queer in it. Then each person nominated a spirit they desired to contact. Mr. Morris named Swedenborg, then Miss Anthony said, "George Washington." Mr. Douglass hoped to reach his mother, though he seemed somehow reluctant, and Mrs. Stanton asked for a visitation by Queen Elizabeth. Though goaded, I named none.

"Let the spirits find me," I said in jest.

Nellie closed her eyes—forgive me if I call her "Nellie" now. I think of her that way, see. Smooth as cat or snake, Kildare rose up again and come to her from the shadows. He took a stance behind her chair, so close I could smell the horse sweat on his trousers.

Her father waved his hands over her face and hair, then down over her shoulders. Modestly, of course. He repeated the motion again and again, each time bringing his palms and fingers closer to her, until it seemed certain he must touch her. His hands glided with unearthly smoothness, disturbing not a lock of hair or fold of fabric. The ritual went on long enough to make me drowsy.

The field of action of Kildare's hands narrowed until his fingertips circled just before her eyes. Smooth and constant as a gentle sea. Rocking like the waves. Watching brought back my lightheadedness. I had to force myself to look away. And even then the rhythms followed me. Kildare seemed to have taken possession of the room. I closed my eyes—I know not for how long.

When I looked again, Kildare was gone. Around the table, all other eyes were closed. Now I am not one to spoil a bit of fun, if it be decent. But there was something in the matter I still could not like. I had grown awfully tired, though, and found myself resigned to sit and let things pass to the flicker of the lamp. I would have preferred to lie abed, to sink into dreams.

The whole weight of the day, of my long sickness, settled upon me.

I closed my eyes again, in case they looked. For none of us wants blame for disappointments. I felt something delicious now, almost a swoon. I seemed to be sinking, and watching myself as I sank.

Twas then I felt the cold. I thought Kildare had raised a window.

The cold flowed from the girl's hand.

Her grip strengthened, becoming as hard as a man's.

I had never felt a hand so chilled. I feared she was ill, or in a seizure. I thought I must cry out. And yet I only flowed along. As if we were all flowing together. But there was a restlessness, a struggle, somewhere under the calm.

Her soft voice stilled me.

"She comes . . ." the girl said, " . . . she . . . comes, the tawny one . . . fair as a princess . . ."

I popped my eyes open. Fearing some imposture by Kildare. But I saw nothing. Only earnest faces, dimly lit. And my eyes hated the least light. Darkness they wanted. Rest.

That cold hand.

" . . . she's with us now . . . she's been waiting . . . waiting so long . . ."

Her grip grew so strong it hurt me.

" . . . she brings a message . . . for the little man . . ."

Hand cold as a tomb. And the lush, falling darkness all around me.

The girl began to sing. Wordlessly. Softly. Beautifully. A whisper of a melody.

Twas a cradle song I knew. From old Lahore.

And so I learned fear. I do not like to think myself a coward. But I could not move. I could hardly breathe. I sensed danger, as a veteran soldier will at the edge of an ambush.

Then she crushed me.

The next voice that come out was not her own, but one I knew.

"Beloved . . . oh, Beloved of Allah . . . Beloved of Krishna and the White God pinched with nails . . ."

In battle, you will see a new recruit freeze upright. He wants to run, but waits there for his death. Standing till a bullet cuts him down. Twas thus I sat.

" . . . a thousand mercies on you, heart of my heart . . . our son is with me here . . . we await our lord . . . here, in the turning wheels of time . . . the time that is so long . . . endless . . . a river . . . a river of blessings on the new wife you have taken . . . she is the rose of your heart now . . . the consolation of my love and master . . . your second son is strong . . ."

No bullet or blade could have pierced me like that voice.

" . . . rejoice, oh Beloved . . . as I rejoice . . . for now I know our gods are the same . . . though yours be killed and eaten by his children . . . Oh, favored son of Allah and your Christ . . . love those who live, but clutch us in your memory . . . your first son is a spirit beautiful!"

"Ameera!" I shouted. I leapt to my feet, breaking the hold of that wintry hand, plunging upward through the darkness. I could not stop myself, nor did I try. A shame it is upon me, but I was set to clutch my lost love in my arms.

Nothing met my opened eyes.

I was a weak, disloyal, shattered man. I know we cannot love two such at once. It is not allowed, and cannot be right, and there's an end to it.

Yet, I loved her still. Though loving my dear wife no jot the less.

The girl who had caused my torment began to cough. And the cough worsened. She fell forward, twisting and contorting.

Kildare jumped up and tore the shawl from the lamp. In the shock of light, he flew to his daughter's side.

She coughed and gasped as though no air would fill her. Eyes huge, limbs shaking. She would have fallen from the chair, but Kildare caught her. He forced a handkerchief into her fingers, though she could barely hold it.

The others clustered round, but Kildare chased them back.

"She's caught between the worlds," he warned. "The spirits need room to leave us!"

She coughed up spots of blood, crimson on white linen. Twas then I realized what her pallor warned, and why those roses on her cheeks burned so.

Indeed, the girl was caught between two worlds, already halfway from ours to the other. She was dying of consumption.

I STOOD THERE, a helpless ass of a man. When the girl had partly settled, Kildare wrapped her in a cloak.

"Our horses!" he demanded.

Mr. Morris stood amazed. "But . . . the girl can't ride . . . can't ride . . . she . . ."

"She mustn't leave this house," Mrs. Stanton insisted. A fighter she was, that one. "She must be put to bed."

Mr. Morris looked at her doubtfully. "But the neighbors . . . neighbors . . ."

"I don't give a toot about your neighbors," Mrs. Stanton said. "Let 'em think what they want." She looked down at Kildare and his cringing daughter. "You'll kill that girl if you take her out on a night like this."

"Lizzie's right," Miss Anthony said. "Lizzie's always right about such things."

Mr. Douglass did not interfere. I expect he had seen worse.

Kildare swept his daughter into his arms and gave us all a look of scorn.

"The spirits will have her go," he fair shouted. "Do you think you can defy the spirits?" He turned his eyes and midnight beard to me. "*He* broke the circle . . . my daughter might have been lost in the darkness." I can't tell you the rage in him. "She *must* go home. I must consult my books."

He shoved past the pack of us, with the girl fainting in his arms. God forgive me, I did nothing to stop him. I had let myself be taken in by the hocus-pocus and stood stunned.

Kildare was strong enough to deal with daughter and door at once. That one had done more in his life than fuss over old books.

Then they were gone. Their horses must have been saddled in the back, in a shed or the like, for it was not long before we heard their hoofbeats. Two horses cracked the ice and crushed the snow.

I wanted to run after them. To save that girl from winter and her fate. But I lacked the force to move me from the spot.

All of their eyes were upon me. I had not even sensed it, so far gone I was.

"Why, Major Jones," Miss Anthony said at last, "you're weeping!"

THE REST OF THE EVENING was a thing of shreds. Perhaps I, too, was caught between worlds. Not betwixt us and some foul sham of ghosties, but between now and India.

I was not even by them when they died, see. The regiment had moved to an encampment to get us from the fevered city. The cholera took them, and they were burned to dust with all the others, long before I could return. I was a sergeant then, and had my duties. And young enough I was to misapprehend which duties are more important. They died with only the old woman to tend them, and why the cholera took them and spared the crone I will never understand. By the time the heat broke and we marched back, the rooms where we had loved were occupied by strangers, and all her ornaments had long been stolen. I did not have a shred of cloth to hold.

But let that bide.

What mattered was the stench here of conspiracy. How had these Kildares found out my history, and what was their wicked purpose? The only one on these shores who knew about my ghosts was Jimmy Molloy. And Irish and a talker though he was, I knew him to be back in Washington. And for all the foolish deeds the scoundrel had done in his life, I did not think he would betray me. Unless he was deep in his cups.

The voice . . . how did she get the voice?

The party broke up. Mrs. Stanton and Miss Anthony were making a circuit of visits, allowing Mrs. Stanton to say farewell to her friends around the counties. She was moving to New York City, where her husband had been given a fine post. The two ladies, who appeared to hold some extravagant beliefs between them, were staying the night with other acquaintances, since they could hardly share a pastor's rooms. And respectable hotels would not admit women traveling without escort.

Mr. Douglass, for his part, remained at Mr. Morris's. Twas the first time I slept under the same roof as a Negro, and odd it seemed to me then. But no harm come of it.

Mr. Douglass had traveled down from Rochester, where he had a newspaper office, to mediate a dispute over the right to labor. Penn Yan had long employed its Negroes to clear the snow from the streets. When the Irish began to arrive, the work was shared out. Now the Irish wanted the privilege exclusively for themselves, and there had been threats. Twas nothing like the business with the Mollies that I would face in years to come. But it put things out of order in Penn Yan, for the citizens were settled in their ways.

The Irish leaders had declined to talk to Mr. Douglass, if I may put it gently. His only interlocutor on the Hibernian side had been Father McCorkle.

"He cannot see beyond his own countrymen," Mr. Douglass told us, with that boundless sorrow ever in his eyes, "though he doesn't seem a bad fellow, for all that."

"McCorkle, McCorkle," Mr. Morris said, "leading his flock to damnation . . . to damnation and no less. No light in that faith, no light . . . all mumbo-jumbo, superstition . . . worse, worse . . . darkness of Rome . . . darkness . . ."

I took my weariness up to my room without a supper. For I still had to write my nightly letter to my Mary Myfanwy, although I feared the words would not come easy. And I wanted to hide myself away. For I was mortified by my outburst during their parlor game, and at how I had been taken in. I feared they might have misunderstood. And, to tell you true, I feared they might have understood too much. I did not want to appear a rogue or a fool before them.

I know pride is a sin, but who has none? I would be thought well of, and think there is no wretchedness in that. For concern with the opinion of others keeps us upright.

My unmentionables were drenched, as though I had gone wading and fell in. My sweat reeked of sickness. I started to change, but went too slowly. When Mr. Morris burst in the door, he caught me in the very guise of Adam.

He hardly seemed to see, though.

"Brother Jones, Brother Jones!" he cried. "I almost forgot . . . almost forgot! You had a letter by the evening train. 'Urgent,' it says, 'Urgent'!" He held the missive in a shaking hand, as if the envelope enclosed a bomb. Even his peak of hair shivered. "A high government affair, no doubt, no doubt . . ."

I feared he would linger to read it with me. But the fellow was selective in his foolishness. Perhaps we are all fools one way or another. Anyway, he left me alone with the letter.

It was no urgent matter of the state. But welcome it was to me. Twas a letter from my dear friend Dr. Tyrone. It had arrived in Washington as soon as I departed, and my good landlady, Mrs. Schutzengel, fearing importance in the missive, had gone to the trouble of expediting it to me.

I smiled for the first time in hours. Picturing the mighty vastness of Hilda Schutzengel as she impressed her will upon the postal authorities, wartime or not. Once set upon a course, the woman was not one to be blocked, and the letter had raced me to my destination.

Now there is good, a letter from a friend. When we are crushed by life and left alone, how warm such papers feel held in our hands. Twas as if Mick Tyrone had been the seer, not those Kildares. As if he had known his friend, the blundering Abel, had need of comfort.

Despair, too, is a sin. And, though tempted, I have never given in to it, excepting that time in India.

I thought of Mick Tyrone and wept again, this time for the goodness that is in mankind.

FOUR

Cairo, Illinois
December 31, 1861

My Dear Friend,

I was delighted to receive your communication of the 22nd instant, not least for the hearthside circumstance of composition described therein. Perhaps next Christmas, with the cruel necessity of war behind us, I shall find myself able to accept your gracious offer of hospitality. I long to make the acquaintance of Mrs. Jones, and to admire the son who so fulfills your happiness. May the coming year bring health and contentment to all!

But now, cherished friend, an earnest warning! As a man of medicine, I find your intended departure for the wilds of New York disturbing in the extreme. You must rest, man! Typhoid undermines the constitution with great violence, and the subject may imagine himself recovered before his health is properly regained. You will do no good through haste. Had I remained at your bedside, I would have enforced a regimen of complete rest well into the new year. I must tell you, frankly, what I concealed from you some weeks ago, during the crisis of your fever. Your case was the most severe example of typhoid I have examined that did not end in mortality.

You are a lucky man, Abel. If I shared your superstitions, I would say a "blessed" man. But enough humbuggery.

I applaud your transfer to your own hearthside for convalescence—these American hospitals do not approach the lowest European establishments, and our military hospitals would embarrass the plague. But you must calm yourself. You write of "duty." A medical man knows the meaning of that word as well as does a soldier. The first requirement of duty is fitness for the task before us. Have patience, lest you cause life-long impairment to your health.

Nor should you entertain the notion that you impress me with your nonsense about the "sturdiness of the Welsh." Firstly, my political philosophy does not allow me to share your belief in national characteristics—all men are brothers, Abel, and we must help them see it. Secondly, modern Science has defined the body as a machine of predictable and routine function, not unlike a mill or manufactory. The body's processes are all in common, until made eccentric by sickness, and its strengths and weaknesses are "democratic" when tabulated. Yes, some rare individuals may possess an innate robustness, but it is no matter of nationality, but, rather, of a peculiar heredity even now under investigation by Europe's most eminent doctors (I speak of the inheritance of physical advantage, not of the absurd charade of social rank through birth).

A few last riddles remain to Science, though we shall solve them in due course. Meanwhile, dear friend, do not succumb to some repugnant myth of national advantage over disease. You might as well believe in ghosts and witches!

For your own sake, man, rest!

Boundless thanks for your solicitude regarding my own slight misfortune. The wound was trivial, and free of subsequent infection. The bullet passed cleanly through the muscle and, though my shoulder retains an unaccustomed stiffness, I find I can saw through a femur as quickly as before. My dexterity in trying ligatures is not yet completely returned, but that will come.

I will admit a phase of alarm when I could not detect the formation of laudable pus during my healing period, but now conclude there was a subcutaneous manifestation of the substance which my body evacuated through healthy sweat. There is no other explanation. In short, I am well, and it is the height of absurdity for you to assume any blame in the matter. The fellows had to be stopped, and I am glad to have done my part in the face of such corruption. The risks you undertook were far greater.

Upon your return to Washington, please extend my compliments to Frau Schutzengel, our pie-baking evangelist of world revolution. I admire her, though I cannot share her enthusiasm for the Communist program. I have read her revered Mr. Marx and find him too heavy-spirited. He turns a strong phrase, but fails to allow for the temperament of our species. Communism is too thoroughly German for humanity at large—it will never expand beyond debating clubs and libraries. Marx is, however, not a bad journalist. I used to relish his dispatches in old Greeley's New York newspaper.

My greetings, also, to that acquaintance from your Indian service days, James Molloy. I believe you undervalue him. He is a perfect specimen of the individual of talent denied opportunity by an oppressive social hierarchy—and here I must lay down my pen and laugh. For I know you, Abel. Although our friendship has not yet been of long duration, I believe the bonds of mutual sympathy swiftly unveiled us one to the other. I see your eyebrows climbing up and your jaw twisting downward, as you tell yourself that my confidence in Molloy is but an example of one Irishman seeking to advance the other, no matter his flaws. I assure you, it is not so. Molloy has a gift. If, in the past, he has used it infamously upon occasion, let us hope that our fine, new country will enable him to rise above social obstacles—I believe this is the land where those "meek" of yours just might inherit the earth. And I will admit the fellow makes me laugh.

As to my present circumstances, I feel well rid of Washington intrigues and McClellan's indolence. Here, all is percolation. Although our military forays to date have been preliminary in condition, I believe major operations will soon commence. Once the mind becomes accustomed to the epidemic confusions of an army's endeavors, it begins to perceive the underlying thrust. It is not unlike diagnosis, in which the most obvious symptoms often mislead us. There are whispers of an advance up the Cumberland or Tennessee, into the enemy's heartland.

I must say that I like these Western men! At first, they seem rough—alternately drunken and taciturn—but they are honest fellows, and of good heart. When they say a thing, they will do it. I would not be surprised if they win this war while Little Mac dallies in the East like Marc Antony. Certainly, we, too, have our locust swarms of politicos in uniform, but there is no nonsense in General Grant's headquarters—and I have met a few fellows worth marking.

Firstly, I have made the acquaintance of a fellow surgeon for whom I have developed the greatest admiration. His name is John H. Brinton. As in "George Brinton McClellan." Initially, I thought him as pompous as his cousin. But that is only the Philadelphian sneer, as if they were all citizens of Athens gazing down at unlettered shepherds. He is a grand, hardworking fellow, and his accomplishments in organizing hospitals and setting up the rudiments of a field medical service have been splendid. General Grant admires him as much as I do. Brinton has made the going easier for all of us medicals.

Odd, too, that Brinton and I should only have met here, in this pestilential, rat-infested harbor—Cairo was chosen as headquarters solely for its command of the river junction (rivers are everything here, Abel, since the roads are nothing but quagmires). It appears that he and I missed intersecting time and again. Brinton studied in Vienna, at my old hospital, not a year after I fled to Budapest. We have numerous mutual friends and acquaintances, and he shares my curiosity about the theories of Dr. Semmelweis, whose personal demeanor has alienated so many—they say he is a madman, but I only found him a bother. Perhaps this war will bring us an opportunity to test his belief that a surgeon who washes his hands in chlorine solution between operations may reduce the rate of morbidity. I wish no wanton injuries upon our soldiers, but if make war we must, Science should profit.

Anyway, Brinton, who is near the top of the surgeon's roster (I'm near the bottom, of course), also served as president of the Medical Examining Board in Washington last year, departing just a week before my application was heard. But now we are met, and I find him an excellent fellow, of clear and scientific mind. I sense he was quite lonely upon his arrival here—a western river town is hardly Philadelphia—but he has made himself indispensable to the army and now, with my arrival, he can banter about the old days of his European studies and the like. A local apothecary of German origin even loans us the latest medical journals from Heidelberg and Berlin, where startling results have been obtained in the surgical theaters. Brinton is a sensitive man, for all his social position, and may be gotten to see the need for true equality in time.

Likely, you have not heard much of General Grant, unless you read of the engagement at Belmont in November (not Portia's Belmont, certainly). He is a brigadier, and my kind of soldier. I cannot predict his worth upon the battlefield, but I like him for his lack of pomp. He is, I am told, an old regular who served in the unjust war of conquest against Mexico, but failed in the peace. His detractors excoriate him as a bankrupt and a drunk, and I think he is watched by General Halleck's agents on the staff. Yet, I find him a quiet, good-humored man, of sound judgement and inexhaustible energies. His staff gets things done, and I have grown proud of my association with it. Grant is plain and short, and his russet hair goes unkempt. His uniform is proper, but Spartan and devoid of elaboration. He sits for hours over stacks of papers—that bane of war I never had expected—pipe in his mouth, calling occasionally for an adjutant. He reminds me, frankly, of a good surgeon—one who keeps the end in sight and will not be flustered by the radical measures necessary to a cure.

I have encountered a few other ranking officers of promise, although they are only in and out of headquarters, for Grant will not tolerate a lavish establishment. William T. Sherman, who visited, has the fire in his belly, and I would not want to get on his bad side. There is also one Lew Wallace, who writes. He has read his Gibbon and sees the tides at work in the affairs of men. But I fear he may think too much to make a good butcher. I do not like McClernand, who is proud.

You will note a large proportion of Scots among the highest officers, yet I have met no prejudice here against an Irishman such as myself. Well, these Scots are getting their own back on the English aristocrats transplanted to the South, I suppose. I will stand shoulder to shoulder with them, for if any war can be a good war, this is it.

Abel, you cannot imagine the plight of the Negro south of the Ohio! To read about slavery is one thing, and to see its tempered features in the streets of Washington yet another, but this is inhuman! The forlorn creatures run to us, following at the heels of our reconnaissance parties. We know not what to do with them all, and it is, of course, an issue of great sensitivity among the politicos. Grant and his staff wish the poor darkies away, since they become an impediment. But I, for one, am outraged by their suffering.

I must soon close, and apologize for my brevity. I have forgone the privileges of rank (a necessary evil in wartime) and volunteered for medical orderly duty this last eve of the year. It is my gift to those of stronger appetite bent upon celebrating the passing of the old and the coming of the new. There is much to do, for we have an outbreak of measles in the ranks. The men are tall and much to be regarded for their health upon arrival at the camps, but many are farm boys, who matured in isolation. They have not been exposed to those diseases that mark the passage from early childhood, and many die of illnesses an infant would cast off in a week. I study them as a man of Science, but feel their loss.

Tomorrow, Brinton has invited me to dinner to greet the new year, and I will go. He promises me "very good" wine, sent him by acquaintances back in his "civilized East." I know, my friend, you do not approve of any drink strong-brewed or fermented, but remember the pleasant story told of the Marriage at

Cana. If I cannot share the theology of the event, I applaud the sentiment. You know I am no drinking man, yet a glass of wine is a gentle consolation.

Well, I am tame, I assure you. At night, I fall asleep clutching a book. Have you read the Darwin I lent you?

Again, my dearest friend, your first duty is complete recovery. This war can do without you for a few more weeks. Study patience!

Kindly greet Mrs. Jones, and
kiss your little son for,
Yr Obt. Servt.
M. Tyrone
Surg. U.S.V.

Just such a man was my friend, Mick Tyrone. Blunt in his talk, but fine and eloquent with pen in hand. There is education for you.

I read the letter thrice. And then I knelt down in my nightshirt and prayed for all without stinting.

FIVE

I STOOD BESIDE THE PRIEST AS THEY RAISED THE BODY. The hooks they used to find her pierced her flesh and, as they drew her up, I imagined that those irons hurt her still. She rose between the blocks and shards of ice. Dripping deep water, her dress hung sodden down to her bare feet. She had left a second note in her shoes on the bank. Brogans they were, frozen hard. That last message said, "Give the shoes to Annie Slaney." She must have thought to write it in advance.

The first note, left in her shanty, said, "I am gone to the lock to see my Pat again. Pray care for my babes." The sheriff showed it to me. It was not spelled so well as I set it down now, but I will not mock her in her death.

I had gone, after a leaden sleep, to the priest's house that morning. I meant to query him about the affairs of his parishioners, but his housekeeper cackled, "Gone to the locks, 'e is, for the widder's drowned 'erself and they're drudging 'er up." I thought at first that she spoke of the widow of our agent, and I feared vicious murder. But it was not so. This was another widow, one Make Haggerty.

The men tried to be gentle, for they were Irish, too, and she was theirs. But their hands suffered from working in the ice and the water, and they were ill clad, and they wanted to make an end of it. An awkward business it was, reaching poles through broken ice to find her.

The girl come up reluctant. As if mortified by our attentions, and shamed. Hauled up between two floats of ice, she bobbed and sank again, trailing a blue hand. Then a second hook snagged her and the workmen lifted her free.

She was frail. As though she had not eaten in a year. You felt her ribs limn through her soaking woolens. Water poured from her.

And her eyes were open. I know not why, but I had thought the drowned all had closed eyes. Somewhere I read it is a peaceful death. But her eyes bulged in shock, framed by undone hair.

She was not free of the water half a minute before a queer thing happened. The moisture froze upon her skin. In the bright, cold air. A veil of ice covered her face and arms, her fingers and raw feet. The high sun hit her and she shone, a golden fairy dancing on their hooks. Frost gilded her rag of a dress. Ice formed in her streaming hair. She rose encased and gleaming.

They dropped her on the bank.

Her blood was thick with death and the cold, and it made little roses when they worked their hooks away. She lay there staring at Heaven, a magical thing. The priest went down into the gorge to close her eyes—he slipped and when he righted himself snow covered the backside of his cloak—but he could not make them shut.

He gave up and began to strip off his own garment to cover her, but the workmen dragged a tarpaulin from a shed by the locksman's hut. The folds were as stiff as her body. The navvies edged the priest away, careful as with an angry dog, and shrouded her in the canvas. Then they removed their hats in expectation of a prayer.

But pray the priest did not. He turned his back on them and started up the slope again, struggling to keep his footing. He wore a poor man's shoes.

The sheriff had stepped up beside me. "Told you those locks were dangerous," he said. "Now you see it."

"I would have thought them well frozen," I remarked. A smooth, white world surrounded the gorge, and I was mystified.

Such a one as her could not have cracked her way down through thick ice.

"They break up the ice on the locks," Underwood told me. "Keeps the force of it from ruining the machinery and warping the sluice gates. Can't drain 'em, cause you have to keep pressure up on both sides, or you'd get even worse. And the current still runs down deep. Enough to keep a couple of the mills going. Top freezes up again, and they bust it open again. All winter long. It's good wages for the Irish."

The priest looked huge and black as he hauled himself up, grasping at vines and sedge with reddened hands. It was a steep, wild place, with the canal forty feet down. Toward the town, the gorge was deeper still.

Below, the Irish drew straws for who would touch the corpse. Death moves them powerfully, and this one was unhallowed.

"She would have known," the sheriff went on, "that one. About the breaking up of the ice. Husband was a day-tender on the locks. Before he went and joined up. Decent fellow, no trouble with the law. McCorkle says she got word yesterday they buried him down in Virginia."

"I hear my name sounded," Father McCorkle called. As though he would thrash the two of us for taking the liberty.

"Just telling the major here," Underwood said, "how all this came about. Her soldier fellow getting himself killed."

The priest steamed from the work of the climb. "'Get himself killed' Pat Haggerty did not. The smallpox it was." He turned his black brows and blacker eyes on me. As if I were the spreader of that disease. "And there's the fine end to your bugling and drumming. Culling the best o' me boys with your rumors o' glory. Oh, there's a fine end to it, your lordship." He pulled the black cap from his head and feigned a bog-man's deference to my uniform. "Will I bow down to ye now, sir, and to your great guns and fine braids?"

"Father McCorkle," I said, "I'm sorry for this . . . misfortune. But there's no need—"

"Oh, is there none? Is there none, indeed?" He bore down upon me, and, if I may be honest, he looked more a brawler than a churchman. "An't it a worse mockery when the lot o' ye go making a war and turn to such poor, gullible lads as him to fight it for ye? Oh, off they went proud, to be sure. Marching like the boys o' Vinegar Hill. Pat Haggerty and Brian Brennan and the lot. To join up with the high likes o' Corcoran and Meagher, to prove the Irishman's worth! All 'green flag o' Erin' and moonshine. And not the ones we well could spare, no, but the best o' the boys run off, and husbands and steady workers among 'em." He bared yellow teeth. "Francie Kilgallen dead at your Bull Run . . ." He eyed the buttons on my greatcoat. " . . . when the rest o' ye went streaming off like hoors—"

I was shocked to hear such language from a priest, and fear my look betrayed it.

"—oh, like very hoors ye run. And Michael Duffy done o' the bloody flux, more glory to ye. And him with a family o' seven." His rage grew vast as the sky above us. "And what are the Irish to the lot o' ye, but white niggers and food for your guns? A feast for your black, murdering cannon." The fellow actually raised his fist at me. "You're bigger hoors than the Queen o' England!"

"Sir, you forget yourself," I said. "You have no cause to insult the Queen." My own fist tightened upon the ball of my cane. "And given her own recent loss . . ."

The Lord knows I do not love the English. But I will not have wanton insult heaped upon the good little Queen.

The priest spit on the snow. "That great hoor. The great hoor o' her. And what o' the Irish lost to buy her mounds o' jewels and satins? Starving by the million, with the grain pouring out to fatten the English purse. Driven here in the ships o' death by the little hoor, they were. And ye," he said to me, glaring, with maddened eyes, "ye are the worst o' the lot, ye runt taffies. Naught but slaves o' the English, ye are, and selling your tiny souls for English gold."

I saw then he knew nothing of the Welsh, and settled, and let him rant on. Now you will say, "You did not stand up for your kind, and proud you should be of the land of your birth." But the loss that day was his, not mine, and I saw in that instant the desperate sorrow of the man, and how he only wanted to hurt the world that hurt him and his kind. I was my uniform, not a man, to him.

"And *her*," the bull in the cassock cried, pointing down into the gorge. "Our lovely little Maire. Ye know well what ye've done to that one, don't ye? Oh, damned her is all. Even your black informer lies in consecrated ground. But not her, no. She'll sleep forever separate from her faith." And weren't there tears in the big fellow's eyes as he bellowed on? "Maire Haggerty was a soft one, she was. Not risen to the cruelties o' your world. Too soft and good for ye. And leaving two babes for to damn herself . . ."

The priest turned away. "Damn the lot o' ye," he barked. And he strode across the snow toward the town. Where the canal curved, a few chimneys smoked, marking hidden mills. The black plumes seemed to draw him.

We watched McCorkle go, John Underwood and I, until he was no more than a crow in the whiteness.

"I had hoped," I said wistfully, "to enlist his aid in my investigation."

Down below us, old-tongue voices rose. The navvies were hauling the dead girl up the slope.

"Wait until he calms down," the sheriff said, scratching one of his monumental ears. "He'll be sorry for taking on like that. That's just about the worst I've ever seen him." Then he clapped a hand upon my shoulder. "Come on, Abel. We'll leave it to the coroner's office now. Give you a ride back to town. Must've been some walk out here with that leg of yours."

We started for his cutter. But then he stopped again, looking out across the fields. Stubble quivered where the drifts had blown thin. The sheriff's eyes hunted for the priest.

"McCorkle's not really a bad sort," he said. "Just takes everything to heart, that's all. Irish are damned lucky to have him. He keeps 'em to the straight and narrow."

On the way back into town, with the horses kicking up a diamond dust of ice, Underwood glanced at me and said, "You walked all the way out here unarmed. Didn't you?"

I nodded. "Broad daylight it is. I saw no—"

"Have a pistol of your own?"

"I do. But—"

"Carry it."

I WANTED THAT SEWING MACHINE. Not for me, mind you. But for my Mary Myfanwy. It sat there in the window, the very engine she had wished for her Christmas, only to be disappointed by the one who loved her most. Twas a Singer & Co. No. 1 Standard Shuttle Machine, and wasn't it lovely? All black and trimmed with gold, as if for the royal household. A very panther of a device it looked, as though it would do a wonderful damage to a yard of cloth. And the bitter thing was that it stood reduced for sale. Twas a brute amount still, yet I would have bought it in a minute for my darling, had I held cash money enough that was not come from government funds.

Now you will say, "There is poor economy, for Abel Jones was a well-paid clerk before he put on his blue coat, and now he is got up high to a major's income. Where is the money of it, and why did he not treat his beloved proper?" Well, I will tell you. I did a curious thing before I come up to New York. I had been planning it over on my sickbed, and I discussed it with my Mary Myfanwy. She was not without misgivings, and downcast she looked to break the heart, but she knew the man of the house must make the great decisions.

In short, I bought railroad stocks.

Now you will say, "There is wickedness. For the buying of shares is but gambling and speculation, and why not sit you down to a round of American poker, oh, hypocrite?" But I did not think it wrong. I was buying tickets to the future of my new country, see. For my family.

Evans the Bags from the Miner's Bank tried to dissuade me. Now he is a well-meaning Welshman, though no relation to my wife's uncle, Mr. Evan Evans, also of Pottsville, or to my buttie Evans the Telegraph. Well, Evans the Bags said the safety of our little savings was best left to the vaults of his bank. But I would not be put off. For in the course of the Fowler affair, I had met one Mr. Cawber of Philadelphia. A rich man he was, and got up there by himself. I come to admire the devil, for he was no more born to privilege than I was. So I made inquiries as to the railroads Matt Cawber was backing, and there I put our savings. In the end, Evans the Bags bought shares for himself, as well. For a Welshman can tell a cow from a calf.

I was resolved that we would not end poor. For there is no country for the penniless, not even sweet America. One day my love would have the finest of sewing machines, and we would not contest the price, unless it were unreasonable. But the joy of that throbbing needle must wait a little.

Oh, yes, I was resolved! I would scrape every penny into our investment! But now, in hard January, the sight of the Singer in that shop window broke my heart. For I would deny my dear wife nothing.

I turned on my cane, careful of the ice, when a beggar boy gave me a tug. Pulling on the flap-over of my coat, all timid like. Then he stood away. Irish he was, by the nose of him, and I do not mean the snot but the puckered shape. Yet, he was American in his speech.

"A penny, gen'rul, please?"

Now thrifty we must be, if we are to buy railroad certificates or grand sewing machines, and begging is not to be encouraged, for it harms the moral constitution.

Yet, I fished out a coin for the little one, and more than a penny.

"Hypocrite again!" you will say. But I could think only of our little John, and of the fragility of all human protections. I have known the hurts of children in my time.

Off he ran howling in triumph, with me wondering whether I had given him too much for his own good.

I had no more time for the admiration of mechanical progress. For time is money, too. I had an afternoon journey before me, with the sleigh already ordered up and waiting.

First, I had a purchase to make.

I went along the lovely street, considerate of the ladies when we passed between the snow piles narrowing the boardwalk. Across the way, I saw Mr. Douglass take himself into a bookseller's. For my part, I went into Munger's, an apothecary shop advertising ALL MEDICINES AND SUNDRIES.

The place smelled of bitters. A bald-headed counter fellow grinned a great toother to see me approach.

This was a matter of some delicacy. Fortunately, we were alone.

"Look you," I said. "I have an acquaintance who is troubled in the lungs."

"A temporary affliction?" he asked, quelled in manner. "Or do we speak of . . ."

"Consumption," I got the word out. "I fear it is the consumption."

His smile bloomed again. "Well, we have just the thing! A miracle of modern medicine. The very latest elixir. You've come to the right place, my friend."

He scooted around from the back of the counter, bending forward in his hurry, and searched along a row of well-dressed shelves.

"Your friend may be thankful," he said, "that we live in modern times. Here it is. Right down here. 'Winchester's Hydrophosphates.' Guaranteed infallible, if the patient is susceptible to cure." He held the lettered bottle out to me. "It's the very latest in tonics, recommended by the best physicians of New York City and Boston."

"How much is it, then?" I asked.

He looked at me soberly. "Well . . . it comes in different sizes. Seven-ounce bottle for one dollar, or six bottles for five dollars. Then there's a sixteen-ounce bottle for two dollars."

Medicine is an expensive thing. But I was determined. Both for the goodness of the deed and to buy me an excuse to see her.

I did the mathematics. Now, I can be chary of expenditure, and I considered buying only a dollar bottle. But the larger bottle was the bargain, clear. And I would not be mean of purse with a dying girl.

"I will have the two-dollar bottle," I said. Before he moved for his cash box, I held him with my eyes. "A cure is guaranteed, is it?"

He laughed, but kindly. "Not from a single bottle, no, sir. But it's a start. Your friend can try it out. If he or she doesn't see a wonderful improvement . . . well, then we'll try something else. But hundreds of documented cases claim that a full course of Winchester's will rid the body not only of consumption, but of asthma, chronic bronchitis and . . . female complaints."

"But she will see results? She'll feel them?"

He nodded gravely, then smiled again. "As long as she's susceptible to cure. Nobody can do a thing for those who won't be cured."

That made eminent sense, and I paid him.

As I was going out, a grand fellow stopped me. Upright, with a mighty beard and a fine Sunday topper on his head, I would have thought him president of the bank.

"Major Abel Jones?"

"I am he, sir. But you have the advantage—"

"Stafford Cleveland," he said. "Editor and publisher, *Yates County Chronicle*." He extended his hand. And then I saw he was a scribbler sure, for ink blackened his fingernails and the creases in his knuckles. As we shook, he continued, "We're the paper on the right side of the issues up here. Lincoln party, you know." He handed me his card.

I could not imagine what interest a newspaper fellow would have in me.

"I have not yet had the pleasure, sir, of reviewing your newspaper. But I am a regular reader of the *Evening Star*, Washington's finest—"

"Major Jones, how about an interview? My readers want the Federal view on these murders and this conspiracy business. And I'd also like to do a story on Washington's view of the British threats of war and—"

"Excuse me, sir," I said, pushing along. For I realized I had been ambushcadoed.

The fellow followed me, near knocking down a woman with her packages.

"Where're you going? Major Jones? The people have a right to know!"

I stopped and gave him a look. Now I like a good newspaper, but where would we be if lowly government officials such as myself, who cannot see the great design above them, went blathering to the press? Oh, that would be a sorry time. You might as well let the village idiot preach the sermon and Frenchmen set your morals. No, silence is a virtue. Let the great men talk, for they know what is to be said and not.

"Sir," I told him, "I cannot talk to a newspaper man. And I must not talk to a newspaper man. And I *will* not talk to a newspaper man. For it is not my place to talk to a newspaper man."

"The people have a right to know, Major Jones. When there's a danger of insurrection . . . atrocious murder on the roads . . ."

I lifted the head of my cane and fair shook it at him. For his presumption startled me. What if all newspaper fellows were so? Demanding answers of every decent sort going about his business?

I will admit my reaction was too fierce, for Stafford Cleveland turned out a good fellow in the end, and he wrote a fair page. But that is hindsight. And I was not myself, given the troubles inside of me and out.

"The people have a right to know," I said. "But *I* have no right to tell them. Even if I had a thing to tell, which I do not. Perhaps you should talk to your own Sheriff Underwood, and not go nattering after a Federal officer at his duties."

He looked nonplussed. "But Underwood sent me to *you.*"

I saw the beauty of it then, for I am not always slow of mind. All at once, I understood how the game is played with these press fellows.

"You really need to talk to the coroner's assistant," I told him. "He's the fellow that knows, see."

I left him scribbling a note. Clutching the bottle of medicine, I hastened toward the livery stable. For I was late.

Nonetheless, I went a block out of my way to avoid the window with the Singer.

"I'M REG'LAR JOHN," my driver told me, standing ready by the sleigh. His Ethiopian visage gleamed against the winter paleness. "Call me that cause I does everything reg'lar. Yes, sir. Reg'lar to church, reg'lar to work here, and reg'lar home to dinner, long as work ain't got me held fast."

I thrust out my hand. "A pleasure to meet you, sir."

He looked at me oddly. After glancing around us, he briefly took my hand.

"You know your way then?" I asked him.

He gave me a ready smile. "Know my way? Reg'lar John been up and down this county summer and winter." He soothed a spark of restiveness in the lead horse—from which I kept my distance. "You just name me a rabbit by name, I take you right up aside his hole."

"You know the Kyle place then?"

Of a sudden, the fine fellow changed. Shrinking against the flank of the stallion.

"I knows it," he said, voice lowered.

The alteration in the man was pronounced. As though I had raised my cane to threaten him.

"You seem hesitant, sir. Something wrong, is it?"

He shied his eyes toward the grit and snow of the livery yard. "No, sir. Nothing wrong. We going anyplace you wants to go. It's only . . ." He lifted his eyes back to me, examining me more closely than before. " . . . well, there's an unkindness in folks down that way. Don't like the Negro. Or any other color of outside people. They figures if they does right and stays up there in the hills, we all ought to stay down here and let 'em alone."

Now, I have seen something of the world. I know the disdain of the African is not a phenomenon that stops at the boundaries of Dixie. And I had no wish to endanger the good man.

"Perhaps, sir, it would be better if I took another driver? If the residents dislike—"

He waved his head at a greater horror. "No, sir. *No,* sir. I'm the reg'lar driver. And I does everything reg'lar."

"But I would not have you endangered, see."

He shook his head again. His woolen cap had a tassel atop it. The little ball swung from side to side. "No danger now. I just minds my own business while you does your business. I just minds my own business and takes care of my sleigh and my team. Anyways, only other fellow could go is Bucky, and he's blacker than a bucket of coal. Can't drive worth a bean, neither."

"Well then," I said, for time was running, "shall we go? You have the blankets?"

"Plenty of blankets, sir. Just like you said. They all tucked in back, you see? You going to be plenty warm, don't you worry."

He climbed up on his perch behind the horses, did Reg'lar John. Although the cost was greater, I had specified a larger vehicle, so that I might sit on the bench behind, farther from the monstrous brutes who must pull us. Mind you—I paid the difference from my own pocket and did not beleaguer our national treasury.

When I was seated and settled, with the blankets snug about me, the driver raised the whip. Then he hesitated.

"Folks say the Kyle farm haunted now," he told me. "All kinds of haunt doings up there. With that magic fellow."

"You believe in spirits, sir?" It was a topic newly of interest to me.

He shook his head and the little tassel swung. "Don't matter what I believes. It's what *is* that matters. See now. In the Bible, Jesus . . . He raised up folks from the dead. Got up Himself, too.

So maybe some folks gets up ain't supposed to? Sneaky like? Though I'm not saying they will or they won't."

"Don't worry," I told the simple fellow, "we shall be safe." Although the truth was that I had my own fears in my heart. With the last sweat of my sickness down my back. And my pistol under my greatcoat.

We retraced the route the sheriff and I had taken the day before. I wondered if I had only been under a spell those lifelong hours ago, if those highland views would so affect me upon a second inspection. The splendor of the white-clad moors and glens, of that endless parade of ridges, had intoxicated me. But I had been fevered. And disappointment is the common reward of too much expectation. Much that we have seen is painted finer in the mind than in the fact.

I was not disappointed. We had not the glory of the setting sun, for it was high afternoon. But beauty has as many shapes as evil. Now, in the pure light, the trees seemed made of glass. Their iced limbs dazzled to hurt the eye. Weighted branches broke off, loud as shots, a skirmish in the groves. When big limbs fell, the horses shied, but my driver kept them under control handsomely. Where the road followed the ridgeline, you could see to China. Except for the teamster of a lumber sled, we did not pass another traveler.

Reg'lar John asked if he might sing, and I have never minded a pleasant melody. He had a warm, manly voice and, to his credit, the songs he chose were hymns and moral anthems. I joined him in a few, but did not assert the power of my lungs, for I did not want to shame the poor fellow. No one sings a hymn quite like a Welshman. And it was clear the horses were accustomed only to Reg'lar John's musicality, for they acted queer whenever I sang out.

We passed the tree where I had been hung in effigy. The cornshuck head still dangled by the rope, but the driver did not notice and I did not wish to alarm him. A bit farther along, we approached a settlement and Reg'lar John gave the horses a taste of the whip. We passed between a pair of taverns and turned toward the heart of the highland plateau. The driver did not sing as we shushed through the hamlet. Twas cold, and few bodies stirred. But a fellow leaving a privy and another splitting wood paused to look us over.

When we had gotten a piece beyond—following a slighter road with fewer sleigh tracks—Reg'lar John called back to me:

"Two taverns back there? One called 'Bull Run,' other 'Manassas.' Union-minded folks goes to Bull Run, but them that got no liking for President Lincoln and this here war, they goes to Manassas. Terrible fights when everybody gets to drinking. Nothing else to do up here in the winter. Not much in summer, neither."

"I would not have thought," I called out over the rush of the runners and the clop of hooves, "that there would be so many people opposed to abolition this far north."

Reg'lar John shrugged his shoulders, then leaned back toward me. The tassel of his cap dangled. "Some folks just contrary," he told me. "Even in the Bible, there's folks inclined towards hating other folks. Way I looks at it, poor white folks lucky to have the black man to go opposing. Otherwise, they'd have to go opposing themselves, for all the spite they got to use up." He teased the whip in the air, alerting the horses without lashing them. "There's just a meanness in this world," he told me. "Even Baby Jesus couldn't get it out of folks. So I just minds my ways and keeps reg'lar."

WE PASSED THROUGH COUNTRY POOR as the Pushtoon hills. The tidy farmhouses near the town had long since given way to shacks. Instead of barns, there were sheds of gray boards, their roofs buckled under the weight of ice and snow. If not for the occasional trail of chimney smoke smudging the sky, you would have thought the landscape abandoned. The sleigh rode roughly.

"Not far now, that Kyle place," Reg'lar John told me. He had given up singing entirely.

To pass the time, I asked if he knew Frederick Douglass, the Negro fellow who was my fellow lodger.

"Oh, yes, sir. Yes, now. Everybody knows Fred Douglass."

"And you think him a good man?"

"He's a powerful, speechifying man. Brave man, even when there's no call for it." He gee-upped the team.

"You admire him then?"

"Much as I admires any unhappy man."

"You think him unhappy, sir?"

"Well . . . I'm not saying yes or no. But he does put me in mind of that priest fellow them Irish folks got. All raging against what the Lord set down here, and bent on fixing it all by himself."

"But surely . . . you would not accept injustice? I'm told Mr. Douglass is a great advocate for your people. A shining example . . ."

He glanced back at me with a rag of a smile. "Folks are different. Big folks like Fred Douglass and that priest fellow goes straight for the bull. That's their way. But Reg'lar John going to work his way around that pasture, 'cause he don't got no business with any bull and don't want none."

"But . . . you said you go to church regularly, sir? As Christians, we must all stand up to injustice!"

"Kyle place just down there." He pointed his whip toward a brown house behind a gnarl of trees. "Sir, I hopes to be a good Christian and to die in the Grace of the Lord. But there ain't no hurry about the dying part. See, I figure if folks nailed up Jesus for speaking His mind, I better just go quiet and reg'lar about things. That just works out best."

HE KNEW I WOULD COME. For I had not been the first. Whatever else the Great Kildare was or was not, he was an experienced hunter of souls. And he knew the quarry would come for the bait he had set out.

He did not even make a game of it. He only looked me up and down as I stood atop the steps before his door. All of the previous night's anger had drained from his demeanor, leaving only a mocking smile behind his beard. He put things directly:

"You want to see my daughter, I expect?"

I did, indeed. No, "want" is too soft a word. I *had* to see her. For a night and a day, I had struggled against the thought of her and the message she had brought me from beyond. Throughout the long drive, I had jailed her at the very edge of my mind, in a place akin to a dream. But I had to see her. Had I glimpsed a thing forbidden, or only been a fool? I had to know.

I held the pathetic little bottle out toward him. He glanced at its jacket of brown paper, but swiftly raised his eyes to mine again. There was no kindness in those eyes, nor aught else that I could decipher.

"Medicine?" he asked, before I could explain. "Leave it, if you want."

"I *must* see her," I said. I stepped forward, as if to prevent him from shutting the door. Although he had not moved to do so.

"I know," he said. "But you can't."

I looked at him pleadingly. How do you force a man to grant you an interview with his daughter? I mustered up what little I knew of these types, these mesmerists and dark performers.

"I'll pay," I said. "To speak to her."

He nodded. Nothing I could do or say would surprise him. "Something can be arranged," he said in a dismissive tone. "But not now."

"Please, sir. I have . . . questions."

"Everyone has questions for Nellie. But let me save you further display, Major Jones. The reason you can't see her is that she isn't here."

"Where is she?" I demanded.

He smiled again. His lips did not part, but his beard bristled and spread, and the thin mouth curled.

The Great Kildare extended his arm toward the white horizon. "Out there," he told me. "Perhaps toward the lake. She communes with the spirits."

"I'll find her," I told him, desperate as a lover.

He kept his voice low and coldly polite. He did remind me of the Englishmen he aped. "I wish you luck. For all the good it will do you."

I took the shambles of my heart and my bad leg back toward the sleigh. In the yard of the place, two ugly men with trouble in their faces were giving hard looks to Reg'lar John. They had the Irishness upon them. My driver ignored the fellows, brushing the ice and slop from a horse's withers.

He was a good man, Reg'lar John, and he knew he had brought me down a bad road. But none of us knew it would lead to such a tragedy before the winter's end.

SIX

I FOUND HER. WE LOST NOT AN HOUR OF THE DYING day. For all those rambling miles of whiteness, the horses pulled us toward her as if she had called them. A black slenderness glimpsed across the snow, she stood where the earth fell away from the moors. Standing at the end of the world. There was no face to the figure, but I knew it was her.

The horses would have left the track and rushed across the highlands, but the driver stopped them. There were marshes, he said, between the road and the girl, and ponds concealed by snow. The sleigh would surely go under.

He reined back the beasts and managed their stamping, while I climbed down and worked my way toward her. A withering wind come up, dusting old snow across the heights, and I drew my coat in tighter. My hat would not hold to my head, so I used it to shield my eyes against the blow. Keeping her in sight, I plunged along, cane sinking into the drifts. I feared she might vanish if I looked away for an instant.

In a grove nearby, the branches clashed like swords. Warning me away. Garbed all in black she was, black in a white world, the only color a flag of red hair snapping out from her shawl. She faced the far ridges and the falling sun, and I felt her clinging to the last ghost of warmth.

"Luck," you will say. "He found her by luck." But it was fate. I will believe that until the day I die. And perhaps beyond.

My boots crunched and squeaked as I hobbled across the snow. Suddenly, my bad leg sank down in a drift, and I will tell you: The fears of a man disturbed as I was are the terrors of a child. My cane found no bottom as I struggled. But then I broke loose again, for we are made tenacious. Only a bad knit of bone in my leg did not like the cold that returned with my freedom. The weaker of our parts would sleep forever, and only will and duty keep us well.

"Miss Kildare!" I called, but the wind took my words. I feared surprising the girl, for she stood at the edge of the promontory and I knew not what waited below.

Toward the end of the field the snow had swept thin over stalks and stubble. I heard a whinny and saw a black horse in the trees, head down. Now I am a man who notices things. But horse I had not seen.

Only her.

Her.

I called again, but still she did not turn. I wondered if I might not be mistaken, rushing to disturb a farmer's widow.

The wind stretched out her hair, longing to carry her away.

I stopped ten feet behind her. In a world silent but for the keening of the sky.

"*Miss Kildare,*" I called.

She turned.

I had worried about the sick girl traipsing over the countryside in such weather. But now I understood.

Standing there, with the falling sun behind her, standing at the edge of the abyss of the lake, upright in that cold and matchless world, she belonged not to us but to Nature. She fitted it like the groves and bracken, like the lean fields and the sky. The rest of us were intruders on those high moors, but she had come home. For hers was no gossamer beauty, meant for parlors and lingerbeds, but a sum of wildness.

And beautiful she was. Not of a cast as common as our desires, but possessed of a beauty invulnerable to our smallness. Twas as if the wind were sculpting her before my eyes, defining her as I watched. That hair belonged as much to the sky as to her person. Her father had been right: Among us, the girl was caught between two worlds. But now she was where she belonged.

I had disturbed her. I felt as if I had touched her with coarse hands.

Yet she smiled. A meager smile to break the heart.

"I knew," she said. "I was waiting for you."

I stepped toward her, close enough to talk without raised voices. She seemed to have no fear or care of heights, but stood to dare the depths. The drop was not sheer, yet steep enough to kill, a long slide of ice. Far below, black trees pointed up from the lakeside. You would fall forever.

"Miss Kildare . . . I must talk to you."

A mask of hair covered her mouth. She swept it away.

"I cannot help you," she said.

All the miseries that I had held suspended since the night before, the devils I had fought down, the years of confined remembrance . . . of a love that scorched then died . . . all that swelled inside me.

I was not master of myself.

"Please," I said. "I must know the trick of it. How you learned those things."

She shook her head in a sorrow I could not grasp. "I'm sorry, sir." Her speech was good, but when she said "sir" it come out "sor" and Irish.

The wind scoured the fields, sparkling the air between us, stinging.

"Miss Kildare . . . I *beg* you. The things you told me . . . about the woman and child . . . the matters described . . . her voice . . ."

"I cannot help you that way," she said, voice gentle. Pitying me from a distance. "I would, sir, but cannot."

"Was it a fraud? Please, Miss Kildare. Did someone put you onto me? Now there is cruel. Was it a joke? *I must know.*" I looked at her through a veil of blown snow, adding, "I will not betray the secrets of your trade. I promise you."

She stared through me. With those peat-fire eyes. Behind the whips of hair, her forehead creased.

"Don't you understand?" she asked. "I thought you would be the one to understand . . ."

"Understand what, then?"

A crow rose from a thicket.

She closed her eyes and lowered her head. Her voice spoke from the depths of that storm of hair.

"That I don't *know*," she told me. "I don't *know* what I told you. In the trance . . . they come . . . the voices. But I can't remember! Don't *you* understand?"

"But surely, Miss Kildare . . ."

She parted a curtain of hair and the bones of her face re-emerged. In that moment, she looked mad.

"I see things . . . I see them now . . . spirits all around you . . . but so faint . . . I can't tell, can't make sense . . . how they follow you . . ." Twas her eyes pleaded now. "It's only the daytime things that I remember anymore . . ."

"You told me about a woman and a child. A woman . . . not my wife."

"I can't remember."

"Miss Kildare . . . I'll pay. If it's money, see."

That grieved her. "They all offer money."

"What do you want, then? For the love of God!"

"Peace," she said. "I want them to stop. I want them to leave me alone. I thought you'd be the one to understand. Spirits all around you . . . they told me you'd come."

She fell to her knees. At first, I thought she was in a faint and moved to catch her, fearing she would slip into the abyss. But she held herself straight-backed, mittens joined as if praying. Two tears fell, one from each eye. Their trails froze white.

"I just want them to *stop*," she said. "My . . . father . . . doesn't understand. That I can't control them. Why I can do one thing and not another." She raised wet eyes to me. "He was in a rage last night. He wanted me to summon Queen Elizabeth . . . to pretend . . . for the Stanton woman. He thinks I lie about the trances. He thinks the Stanton woman hides her wealth, but he's wrong . . ."

Carefully, I moved toward her. Anxious to bring her back to her feet. On the edge of that precipice. "Miss Kildare, you must rise. You'll catch your death."

She looked up and laughed.

"I'm not afraid," she said.

"What . . . do you see now?" I asked in a coddling voice, inching closer. I knew not what to make of her or her confidences. "What spirits, then? Look you. I need to know. To keep the devil off me. Something. Anything. Tell what you can, I *beg* you."

She lowered her eyes to the snow.

"They're like gauze . . . so soft. They move when I try to look at them. As if they're playing with me . . . teasing me. They're all around you . . . an army of them . . . protecting you . . ."

A queen accepting aid, she let me lift her. For a moment, we stood so close I smelled her sickness.

Her smile twisted. As if she read my thoughts. "You doubt me. You of all men." She put on a hard, common look. "Will stage tricks be enough, then? To convince you? Do you want to see the things they line up to pay money for? Is that what you want?"

"Miss Kildare . . ."

She closed her eyes. "Beneath your coat . . . you carry a revolver . . . given to you . . . by younger men . . . given to ask forgiveness . . . they left you to die . . . there were horses . . . have a care, the second chamber will not fire, for you set a bad cap to it. And in your pocket . . . by your heart . . . a letter from a friend who saved your life . . ."

She opened her eyes and gave me a forlorn look. "More, sir? Or is that enough?"

"But how . . ."

She shook her head. The hair free of her shawl lashed her white face. "I can't explain. I've always had the gift." The pair of tears left trails upon her skin. "I thought you understood."

"But you claim to communicate with the dead? In your trances?"

Her smile turned wistful and blown snow narrowed our eyes. "The spirits say there is no death . . . but I don't know. I don't know what happens in the trances. Perhaps the spirits lie. Like men. I've told you . . . I know only that which comes to me . . . when I'm like this. The things I see by day. The rest is darkness." She canted her head and her hair streamed. Pulling her away. "Men have souls of glass. Their thoughts are all the same. I see them so clearly. But you're a hard one. They flee, but you come on. Even your wanting is different. When they stand in front of me, they're running away inside. And the Irish . . . they all believe I'm a witch. They'd burn me. Or worse, if they could. But you'll never run away. You understand. You're not like them." Slowly, a rising scale, her distress grew. "They'd push me under the ice." She glanced to the side. "Or over this edge . . ."

"Your father protects you, of course."

That fragile smile again. "The priest protects me."

"But surely your father . . ."

"Counts the money . . . it's always the money with him."

The light was quitting us. Instead of a grand-hued sunset, as on the day before, this twilight was soft, weak. A gloaming of lilac and gray.

"Miss Kildare," I began in a businesslike voice, for I had done my mental accounts in that instant, "I know not what you're about. Though wish you well, I do. Yet, there is something queer here, and you might begin by telling me . . . why you appear to reveal so much to me, a stranger? A stratagem is it? For it seems you've told me much, yet you've told me nothing at all. And this last confidence, regarding your father . . ." An inspired question struck me. One that would test her "visions" well enough. "Miss Kildare—would you just tell me this, then: Is there to be an insurrection among your Irish? Against our Union?"

My dullness crushed her.

"There is no insurrection," she said blandly. "No rebellion."

"Anything else, then? Any untoward doings of which you know? Anything you see in your visions?"

She shook her head. Slowly. "I cannot tell you such things."

The last of the sun filled with color: Twas red as blood again.

"Cannot? Or will not?"

"Will not."

"But why? After you've—"

She reached out and laid a mittened hand on my forearm. It quelled me instantly. As if a force had poured into my body.

"Don't you see?" she asked, near pleading. "It changes nothing. What comes, will come. I can only watch. None of us can change it."

"Then why . . . talk to me at all?"

She stood back, haloed by the sunset. Heels on the edge of oblivion. There was strange. Twas she who looked baffled now.

"But you're the *one*," she said. "Don't you know? Haven't the spirits told you?" She looked near despair. Clapping her hands to the side of her head, as if her thoughts pained her, she cried, "Please, help me . . . they play tricks . . . they won't stop. I can't tell what you know and what you don't. Only that you're the one . . ."

"The 'one' what, Miss Kildare? What am I, then?"

She looked at me, her beauty on fire, amazed at my ignorance.

"The one who came to kill my father."

NOW WHAT DO YOU SAY to a mad thing like that? It shocked me. The very thought of such a thing. And that a daughter might say it so. I saw she was sadly touched, and not by mystic spirits.

She had jarred me with the parlor trick of describing my pistol and the letter in my blouse. But I had read enough of mesmerics in the newspapers to know that mountebanks had a knack for reading a fellow's eyes or getting their victim to suggest things with his expressions. I saw then that the seance of the night before had been a mere charade, its details but awaiting explanation. Naught but cruel mischief there. And I had been drawn in like a country lad by a recruiting sergeant. Weightier affairs wanted my attention, for I had a charge and a duty.

Yet, she drew me.

I sought to reason with her as the darkness gathered around us. But she was beyond the power of all but prayer, and only repeated that I was "the one." She said it in a voice that bore me no malice, but her words were all the madder for that. The air come colder over us, and I repeated my concern for her health. At that, she changed. Sudden as the tides of battle. She bid me *adoo* and fair leapt upon her horse. As if gone over to the spirits already.

I watched the beast carry her away, leaping drifts. She seemed a fearless horsewoman, but still I had no sense of her bravery. To me, she was only a lost girl, dying. Her cape and shawl streamed behind her, different shades of darkness. Then she disappeared into a swale. Twas a wild place, those high moors, and she as wild as any of it.

Reg'lar John awaited me along the farm track. "All reg'lar," as he said. Yet, he was relieved to see me.

"Ain't no good up here," he told me. "Nothing good never happens up this way."

The horses wanted to go, and we galloped along the ridge. Twas as if the beasts themselves were in haste to leave the place. They did not slacken until we had left behind the dueling taverns and the gibbet where the corn dolly's head still hung.

By the time the team had used up its spunk, we were back in the lowering of the ridge, where the farmhouses were larger and well tended, with proper barns. Yellow-lit windows cast their glow across the fields. Again, I saw the town in the distance.

Reg'lar John sang hymns as we descended. I felt the Colt hard against me and did not join in.

WHEN I COME INTO THE PARSONAGE, scraping the snow from my boots, the Reverend Mr. Morris and Mr. Douglass were already at table.

"We waited," Mr. Morris assured me, "waited as long as we could. Food getting cold, getting cold . . ."

"The major looks a bit chilled himself," Mr. Douglass said, rising from his chair to welcome me. As if I had become a valued friend. He really was a proper gentleman.

"Duty, duty," Mr. Morris said. "Brother Jones has his duties." He looked up from his plate, upon which a meager sadness of a meal lay sulking. "Are the killers discovered? Have you discovered the killers? Are we safe now?"

"The day," I answered, taking off my greatcoat, "went awry, see. But there is tomorrow."

"Dreadful about the Irish girl, dreadful," the pastor went on as he spooned up peas. "Weak creatures, so weak. Drawn to sin, the Hibernians . . ."

I sat me down, for the housekeeper had laid out a place for me, a paying lodger. "Sin," I said, tucking the napkin into my collar, "is in us all, is it not, sir? Did not the great Wesley—and I speak of John Wesley himself—did he not write in his *Christian Perfection* that no man can say 'I have no sin to be cleansed from'?"

"Surely, surely . . . Wesley, Wesley . . . but the Irish, Brother Jones . . . the Irish . . . magnitude . . . proclivities . . . proclivities, sir! And propensities!" His lacquered peak of hair shook at the ceiling.

I looked at Mr. Douglass, wondering what a Negro might make of such a judgement, for such a one must know what it is like to be convicted by his brother's fall. But the African only smiled a bit and applied himself to his plate.

"Mr. Douglass?" I said, wishing to change the subject. For I had Irish behind me and Irish before me, and would not have them with my supper, as well.

That solemn Nubian turned his eyes upon me.

"I have met one of your fellows this day," I continued. "A certain 'Reg'lar John.' He claims you are not unacquainted."

Mr. Douglass chewed, nodded and swallowed. "That would be John Brent." Suddenly, he grinned, with strong teeth. Now

Mr. Douglass was not a smiling man by nature, but mirth he saw in something I had said. "Tell me, Major Jones, how did this 'Reg'lar John' fellow strike you?"

"John Brent, our John Brent," Mr. Morris added in support.

I swallowed a mash of peas. "Why, a good enough fellow. Simple." I thought over the day. "Likes a good hymn," I said, with a glance at Mr. Morris.

Now there were any number of looks shooting about that table: Mr. Douglass at the pastor, the pastor at me then at Douglass, Douglass at me, and me looking at both of them in turn.

At last, Mr. Douglass laughed out loud, collecting a chuckle from Mr. Morris.

"Do you," Mr. Douglass asked when he had settled again, "hold acquaintance with many of the sons and daughters of Africa, sir?"

Well, I had lived some months in Washington, where the poor creatures were still enslaved under the law, if quietly. And freed men there were, too. But my contact with them had not been close.

"I have observed such, sir, but regret I cannot count them my intimates."

Douglass let a smaller laugh. "Well, regret it or not, I'll let you in on a little secret, Major Jones. The simpler a Negro appears, the more he conceals. It is . . . a hard-learned trait. Born of suffering." He smiled with unanticipated warmth.

"Suffering," Mr. Morris repeated, "terrible suffering . . . human bondage . . ."

"Now you take John Brent," Mr. Douglass went on. "Employed in a livery stable, yes. Although few people know that he is also half owner of the establishment. Some achievements are best enjoyed quietly, and a man must reckon his circumstances. But I will confide in you, as an agent of Mr. Lincoln's government: John Brent has been one of the great heroes of the underground railroad. Surely, Major Jones, you have heard of that desperate path to freedom?"

I nodded, for I had. My Mary Myfanwy had long been a great one for the emancipation of the Negro, and had tugged me to not a few lectures upon the subject back in Pottsville.

"Well, the underground railroad ran heavily along Keuka Lake here. Fortunately, we have ever less necessity of it now. But even in recent years, there was great danger," Douglass said. "Greater danger than you might credit. Slave-catchers, rewards, nightriders, the kidnapping of Negroes born free . . . none of it frightened John Brent. He would walk from here to Bath to lead our people to freedom. Why, he must know these hills better than any man alive. And a tireless man. Fearless. Yet careful, for bravado is the enemy of such enterprises. Still," that son of the equator concluded, "I understand he barely escaped the mob and a noose during the Dundee troubles, and remains unwelcome in some corners."

"Dundee, Dundee! Elder of the church, as well," Mr. Morris exclaimed. "An elder! You'll hear him in the choir this very night, at evening meeting! Evening meeting, Brother Jones!" His hair seemed to rise higher with his excitement.

Look you. I would have enjoyed an evening of prayer and community, for such is ever a comfort. But I had not yet done my full day's work. I had one last call to pay.

"I would come, sir," I told Mr. Morris, "and most rapturous. But government business intrudes, see."

"But where will you go, where will you go?" the pastor asked, in Christian disappointment. "It's night, night!"

"I believe the Catholic evening worship finishes soon?" I drew out my pocket watch to verify the time.

"Yes, yes. Gone to their drinking, gone to their drinking. Not like honest—"

"Well, then," I said, already done with my starve of a supper, "I will call upon Father McCorkle, for we parted upon a break that must be repaired."

"McCorkle? McCorkle? Surely, *he* could wait . . . evening meeting . . . congregation . . . meet the congregation . . . honored guest . . . honored . . ."

"I fear," Mr. Douglass interjected, with his deep eyes upon me, "that we are both disappointments to Mr. Morris. For though we share a commitment to abolition, I cannot share his . . . beliefs. I have moved onward."

Disappointment there. For such a grand fellow as he should have been a paragon of faith.

I am a plain man, and Mr. Douglass read my thoughts more clearly than the girl had done.

He smiled. Twas a request for understanding, that little twist of the lips. "I have no wish to offend . . ." He nodded to Mr. Morris. " . . . our gracious host." He turned his prophet's eyes back to me. "Or you, sir. Good men may have differences, yet work toward noble goals they hold in common. But I will not dissemble in the matter of religion."

I pitied the great fellow then, and not for his sable skin. For he was a handsome creature. But can you imagine the loneliness of men without faith? I thought, of course, of dear old Mick Tyrone. And now I recognized the sorrow that followed Mr. Douglass like an echo. They bent over books in their longing, and failed to lift up their eyes to the light. Now I like a good book, mind you, but would not trade my faith for all the libraries of London. Even if their science proved me wrong, I would believe. For there is no other lasting comfort, and kingdoms are nothing.

We all stood up to part. Mr. Douglass reached into his vest and drew out a card.

"I'm off to Rochester early in the morning," he told me. "So we may not have an opportunity to say farewell." He looked down at me, for he was a tall one. "I hope you have more good out of old McCorkle than I did, sir. No progress at all. Nothing to show for the time and effort. He's so pigheaded about his beloved Irish. And I've got a paper to publish." He offered me the calling card, then his strong hand. "If your duties ever bring you to Rochester, I would consider it an honor to be your host, sir. The world is short of heroes nowadays."

"I'm not—"

"No demurrals! No demurrals!" Mr. Morris insisted. "A hero, a hero!"

Douglass released my grasp. I had no inkling of the greatness of the man at that time, for I can be near of sight in some things. Nor did I have any notion of the disappointments that awaited him. But let that bide.

"I'll stop by the stable on my way to the train in the morning," he added, "and have a talk with 'Reg'lar John.' I'll tell him he can stop that good-darkie nonsense with you. He and I . . ." Here the great fellow's eyes clouded. "We both began our lives on the Eastern Shore of Maryland. Under circumstances foreign to human decency. We understand each other, John Brent and I." Then he snapped himself out of the past and repeated, "If you're ever in Rochester, Major Jones . . ."

"Time for chapel! Time for meeting!"

The truth was that I would have preferred to follow the Reverend Mr. Morris into the meeting hall, where my fellow Methodists were already gathering. For I had need of succor. And I will tell you: Selfish Abel had no wish to trudge off through the cold and dark. It is a weakness, how we love our comforts. But a Welshman is a dutiful fellow, most terrible in his determinations, and twas time to take matters in hand.

FATHER McCORKLE ANSWERED the door himself. The pleasure on his face was sublime.

"An't it the good Major Jones himself? Sure, and a blessing it is that ye've come to me door. For wasn't I thinking upon ye but now, and shaming meself for me doings and carryings-on? And here ye are, man. Made flesh, upon me word!"

Well, that was a change.

The fellow invited me in. Lean it was in his shiver of a house. Seizing my coat, he set me a chair by his own, close to the hearth. He poked up a blaze with a quivering hand and his shadow grew gigantic on the back wall. "And don't the winters seem longer with the years, boyo? But the years themselves grow shorter . . ." The firelight hunted over the crags of his face and the dark cliff of his brows. "Now Mayo's a hard place, ye know. But her winters are naught, held up to those of New York." He sighed. "When I was young I took meself to Rome, by the Grace of Our Lady, and wasn't that lovely and warm? Tis a joy in the memory."

We sat down. "Will ye have tea?" Then he gave me a wink. "Or there's not a bad poteen I can offer, for they bring it along to soothe me."

"I have taken the pledge, sir."

He raised his chin and lowered it again in approval. The firelight left half his face in shadow. The stern man of the burying and the titan of the morning were gone, leaving a worn old fellow behind.

"Oh, and a grand thing that is, the Temperance! I give poor Morris that, for all his follies. He does keep his flock off the bottle. Tis a curse on the Irish, the drink. But then so little they have . . . will it be tea, then?"

"I would join you, sir. If you're having a cup yourself, see."

He set a kettle over the flames, then parsed out leaves that had been used and dried. His furnishings were but sticks, dusty even in the dark. Twas a poor place set beside our Methodist comforts.

He drew his chair closer to mine. Until our knees all but touched.

"Oh, I'm a proud one," he said. "Tis my besetting sin. And so I delay. But there's no avoiding the act o' contrition. Sorry I am for my cursing o' ye. For the language. And for the sentiment, as well. Wrong it was, and wrong I was. Though disagree we will o'er Victoria Regina. No, ye just got in the way o' the storm and it blew on ye." He looked at me, but his eyes were lost in canyons of shadow. You saw but a gleam. "Am I to have forgiveness, then, Major Jones? What shall be penance enough?"

"Sir . . . we are all sinners . . . I'm hardly in a position . . ."

A slender log broke crisp and sparks rained upward, lighting a volume of Tacitus the priest had set aside.

He smiled and bent to turn the kettle on the irons. "Oh, ye Protestants. Couldn't I weep for ye, though? For ye do not understand the glories and gentlings o' forgiveness. It is a thing the True Faith has, if naught else . . . but are we mended then? Can ye overlook the madness that come upon me?"

It had been a great day for madness.

"It is behind us, sir."

"I thank ye for the kindness o' that! As I thank the Lord and his archangels." A veil of sorrow settled over his features. "The girl, it was. Our little Maire." He shook his head. Slowly. "The Lord has His wisdom, sure, and it is not upon the likes o' us to question it. But times there are when tis hard. For He calls the good wine to Him, and leaves the dregs behind." He searched my face, my eyes. "She was good, and wronged by this life."

"A tragedy," I said.

He mused on that. "Too small for a tragedy. But a sorrow . . ."

The kettle called. He lifted it barehanded from the irons and set it by while he dusted the tea leaves into a chipped pot. He poured the water slowly, with the steam rising about his hand. Twas as if all things in his life had to be measured. The carefulness of Mr. Morris's table was luxury to this.

"Sugar there's none," he said.

"There is good," I lied. "For I do not like sweetenings."

He raised one end of that line of brows. "And I thought the Welsh were great ones for their sugaring?"

"I have known such," I said. "But would have mine hot and clean."

"Hot it will be, then." He did not steep it long, but poured the pot empty, straining the beverage through cheesecloth to collect straying leaves. He handed me the better of his cups. The tea smelled sour, but the cup was lovely warm in my hands.

"Now ye'll be asking me," he said, seated again, "about all the bad doings amongst us. The lad bedeviled and hung, and your Federal man took up before him. And rumors o' rebellions and risings. Will ye not?"

I nodded.

"Tis to be expected," he said. "For ye have your duties, as I have mine. But there's sad little I can tell ye. Even was I to parley the secrets o' the confessional, which I am not like to do. But there's this much sure: Neither rebellion nor insurrection against the government. For what's to be gained by the likes o' that? No risings nor revolutions, Major Jones. But if it's unhappiness of which ye talk, you'll find a plenty. For the poor are always with us, and injustice. The hatred of Cain is upon the land."

The man looked even older now.

"But . . . if there's no plan of rebellion . . . if there's nothing," I said, "then why kill a Federal officer? And an employed agent?"

"A 'spy,' ye mean. For let us be plain. Oh, ye do not understand the Irish a jot, if ye fail to see the terrors an informer holds for them. Tis the bane of our nation's story, the informer." He leaned closer, lowering his teacup. "And what did ye hope to gain by such recruitments? Surely ye see that the silver of Judas only buys lies when the truth will not do? Tall tales he will tell ye, all smothered in a cream o' fine words. No, I will tell ye the truth of it—informers will be rooted out and done with. That is the way of it, and not even I could stop them. Though I will not excuse murder. No, there's no taming the wildness in them when they smell the stink o' the spy among them. Tis the way o' things, and a lesson taught by Britannia."

"And the Federal agent? Captain Michaels?"

"Sorry I am for the loss o' him. But there's nothing I can tell ye there. Mayhaps he crossed the wrong man, or the wrong line. They say he was a drinker himself, your Captain Michaels."

"Father McCorkle"—I called him "father," for that is how these people would be addressed, and meant it only as politeness—"surely you see that the government must pursue the matter. Look you. Two men dead. And killed ugly. The law will have its way."

He weighed an empty palm. "I cannot help ye. For I know nothing."

"But will you keep your ears open? Surely, you see the danger to your flock. I speak of prejudice, sir. America has been a ready refuge to the Irish, but murder will not be condoned and what will good citizens think—"

He closed a big hand over my knee. Twas my bad leg, but no matter.

"Speak ye o' America? And of a ready refuge? When men are paid starvation wages, and their women less than that? Do ye know, man, that I've so many cannot afford to marry that there's less being born than dying amongst us? They go talking o' Irish immorality, the fine ones. But let them look close and honest, and a sad crop o' spinsters they'll see, withering away. And young men all longings and rags. No, I'll never put the joys o' Temperance in their heads, though I shout meself blue in the face. For the lot o' them are naught but looking for a way to numb the pain till they're called." He sat back in his comfortless chair. "Maire Haggerty now. Who's to say she wouldn't have been better for the comfort o' drink than damning her immortal soul with her doings?"

"This country," I said, "is man's hope and pride. Now, in its hour of peril—"

He stood up. For he was past listening, though his mood fell short of anger. "Will ye come with me this half hour?" he asked. "For as ye lay claim to being a Christian man, there's a thing I would show ye."

"I am at your service, sir," I said. For I meant to indulge him. He was a compelling sort, and I wished to mend our relations. I recalled the drowned girl, frozen and shining, and the priest's rage above the canal. Twas all Heaven had been the object of his anger, and not small Abel Jones.

He tamped down the fire to ward off a conflagration, then pulled on the black cloak that served him for a winter overgarment.

"Come with me," he said, "and I'll show ye a thing."

We went along the darkened street, past little houses closed against the cold. He led me toward the canal. The houses became shanties, and the shanties grew smaller. Off to the left rose the black wall of a mill. In low barns, mules complained. Along the outlet, the barges were moored in ice. Kerosene lamps glowed behind the shutters and oiled-cloth windows of the cabins on the decks.

"The poor devils live on the boats year round," the priest told me, turning us right toward the lake itself. "For the canal's all a world o' its own, and a poor one for those that take their living from it. And the railroads go making it harder. For your locomotive needn't wait for spring and the thaw."

He near made me feel guilty about my investment. But progress is ever hard. I had seen that in the wretched streets of Merthyr, where I come into my young manhood.

"I had an encounter last night," I said, tapping along on my cane, "with a fellow who calls himself 'the Great Kildare.' He is of your country and faith, I believe?"

I felt the priest go darker than the darkness. "Perhaps o' me country, but not o' me faith, that one. Not with those doings o' his, and naught to it but eternal damnation. Tis Satan's business, and no less—and your Mr. Morris entertains the fellow! Wickedness and damnation!"

Now I had expected as much from him, for the Catholic faith is stern down deep, while ours is stern on the surface. But I did not expect the change that next come over his voice. For it softened.

"And yet I don't truly know the man," he said. "And there may be good stirred in with the evil. For the world is not so clear as you people would have it."

"Perhaps . . . there is good in the daughter?" I was testing him. For she had claimed the priest as her protector.

"I hardly know her but to see," he said. "Though I keep the worst of them off her. They'd kill her for a witch, if not for her beauty alone. She sets a fear in men, that Nellie. And worries them with wanting, besides." He sighed, and a fog of breath preceded his next step. "She'll be damned as sure as her father, if she doesn't turn back to the church before the cough takes her."

"She's very ill," I said. "She—"

But then I heard the music. It come jigging through the darkness. A dollar fiddle and a squeezebox, played to the pulse of a flat drum. Faint it was, but fevered. Growing louder with our steps. The path turned by a boathouse. Across a waste of snow, a barn bled light. Or perhaps it was a warehouse. For it was set by the water. Ramshackle, anyway, and overflowing with humankind. Those who could not get inside danced by a rubbish fire. Wild as the Pushtoon, they were, when that murderous savage capers to his war drums.

I expected the priest to put a halt to the business.

But I was wrong. He kept his silence, and the great dark shape of him hardly disturbed the revelers. A few cast wary looks upon our approach, but soon went back to their joys. Twas as if the priest had left his own dominion and entered another where his law did not prevail. We seemed but half visible.

Spirits, see.

A fighter-faced fellow leaned by the door, collecting the penny admission. He let the priest by unmolested, but had his cent of me. I did not like his eyes. Or the hammered look of his flesh, or the twist of his nose.

But in we went. A few of the young girls calmed their reeling at Father McCorkle's entry, lowering their skirts again to cover their petticoats. Even then, they swirled on, no more demure than the famed Spanish dancers of Gibraltar, whom I had seen when my India-bound ship put in—I was a foolish fellow then, and young.

But these girls flew! And not the girls alone, but the men, by whom the fairer sex was well outnumbered. Fellows danced with fellows, grinning silly. Couples past their best years trotted, too. There was but a small stove set in the corner of the vasty place, but the air was tropic hot and wet. The entertainment stank of sweat and whisky.

We stood at the back, the priest and I, amid the old men with their pipes. I watched the turning faces. Is anything more hopeful than a young girl at her dancing? With all her dreads suspended, and the moment a cloud of thoughtless beauty? Now there are those who would condemn such pastimes, and right they are that we must beware lasciviousness, for temptation is like any danger and finds us stronger on one day than another. Yet I would not forbid the dance, so long as things are done proper. For there is joy in the stepping, to be sure, and joy is a thing of sufficient rarity. I will even admit to tapping along with my cane, although I made no vulgar display.

Their faces careened before us, and soon the priest was forgot. The girls picked up their long skirts again, and, proof of the devil, I caught myself looking once. For I am not invulnerable to beauty, though a married man and content.

But their faces! If the priest had no dominion here, neither did misery, or poverty. For an hour these gay carousers reeled free of care. They whirled and laughed the darkness down, some aspects fair, others gray and toothless. Wart noses and cleft lips, or soft cheeks pinked by exertion, from handsome to haggard went the run of their features, from moony, pudding faces or chins as sharp as blades to the colleen splendor of young darlings. Some were clean, while others staunched the cold with layers of dirty woolens, but all had succumbed to the joy of the music, and the hoopla wildness, and the freedom of brief forgetting.

The priest said naught, but let me watch unbothered. And then, with the fiddler and squeezer and pounder gone off for a moment to fuel themselves up, a young man took the stage, led on by a baldheaded banty. Blind the boy was, but pretty as an angel, with a lick of hair falling over his forehead and the purity of his misfortune on his face. The young girls watched him, mired in regret, for such a one as he was not for marrying.

He sang. And I believe the night wind stopped to listen, and the stars come down closer to hear. He sang of a lost love, away in Killarney, her eyes soft as dew, and her lips like a rose. They were to be wedded, but winter come o'er her, and laid his love down 'neath a blanket of snow.

They all wept like children. And then he sang of lonesome Connemara.

They do have tenors, the Irish. I will give them that. But they will never have the power and unity of a Welsh chorus, for, though clannish, they cannot hold together in the clinch, but each will bully his own way. They are a folk for solos. I think it is the way the English beat them down the years, see. For one Englishman will set aside his differences and pull beside another until the dirty work is done, but the Irish would settle their differences first.

But let that bide. The blind boy moved me.

I drew out my handkerchief—for my Mary Myfanwy had accustomed me to the device, and I no longer believed it an affectation—and touched my own eyes.

Then I saw them. Watching me.

Across the big room, lolling about by a trestle where whisky was traded. Chewing little cigars.

Twas the two men I had seen in Kildare's yard. Night had not improved them.

I raised myself up on my toes to catch the priest's ear without a needless raising of my voice. He gave me a startled look, as if he had forgotten me completely.

"Those two. By the liquor seller. The big one and the lesser. Who might they be, then?"

He saw them at once. For they were not shy about their staring and did not stop.

"The O'Hara brothers," Father McCorkle told me. "Napper and Bull. A wise man would cross the street to keep shut o' them."

The fiddle called, and broken hairs flew from the bow. The fiddler stamped and sawed his little instrument, and the clapping began. Then the squeezebox joined in, and the round drum fixed the time. In moments, the company set to rollicking again, the sum of their joy beyond the mathematics of Mr. Newton. I lost sight of the brothers O'Hara in the confusion, and did not mind. For I will tell you true: The joy of that music reached me, although it was a raw thing and the makeshift dancehall no fit place for the respectable.

The priest bent down toward me, keeping his eyes on his people.

"This is what I wanted ye to see, Major. Look at them. A Christian man, are ye? Then look ye well. For there before ye are the people He came among." The priest's voice twined dreams and anger. "The Magdalene herself, I could point out to ye. And at least a pair o' thieves. Luke and John that take a poor living from the water. Mary and Martha, unmarried and waiting. And ye've had your Judas, haven't ye? And your innocents slaughtered? Oh, those are the ones He came down to. Not your fine bankers and senators. These are the ones who flocked to Him, who came to hear the Sermon on the Mount. Crawling, they were. Crawling on their bellies, when their weak limbs failed them. To hear the blessed music o' His words. Craving in their souls for one sight o' Him. The scorned and despised o' the world. *There* are your children o' Israel."

He turned his eyes to me then.

"Now tell me, Major Jones. Is this to be their promised land? Or did they trade one bondage for another?"

SEVEN

I MADE NO PROGRESS. A MONTH I STAYED, OR NEARLY. Twas time enough to make nodding acquaintance of the citizens who displayed themselves on Main Street, and to ride the county up and down in Reg'lar John Brent's sleigh. Sheriff Underwood was an honest man, ready to support me when I had need, yet I came to see that he wished no trouble upon his county and would not go looking for it uninvited. He did send a pair of constables to chop down the tree where Reilly then my effigy had hung. I got to know the place, and my sense of danger lessened with familiarity. I loved the land. Yet the winter was dreary, the days short, and the diet poor.

Although I found their range of interests a marvel and concern, I took comfort amid the Reverend Mr. Morris's congregation. For their faith was strong, despite the odd notions that crept in among them. And they liked their sacred music, as did I.

Now, I go at the singing of a hymn with a wonderful bellicosity, and blessed are the Welsh in their voices. My vocal expenditures astonished all. Good, humble folk, they could not even meet my eye when I sang out, but only smiled at each other in their delight.

A miracle it was, too, how the pulpit transfigured Mr. Morris. He shed his repetitions to reveal an orator all sharp and clear and true. He preached with a tongue of fire. That greased point of hair quivered, but his eyes steadied upon eternity. He opened the hand of salvation to all, and spoke of light where other men saw darkness. There was much love in the man, and it was revealed in his little chapel.

We are small and foolish creatures. I had all but dismissed Mr. Morris as a silly whack of a fellow before I heard him preach. Thus I learned for the hundredth time that our rash judgements will be rued.

Oh, I learned the back roads and the front pews, the passing faces and the names of farms, the shops and beggar boys. All this I did, but could not crack the Irish.

They have a way of talking grand and saying nothing, those Hibernians. Some look you in the eye but shut their souls. Others will not face you at all, but crab off muttering. I tried politeness and cajolery, appeals to patriotism for their new-gained land, and even threats. I visited their sick with Father McCorkle. I even tried to excite the charity of my fellow Wesleyans on their behalf, but truth be told they found it easier to love a distant slave than a day laborer down in a shanty. Armored in the rectitude of duty, I went into the whisky shabs to see what might be gleaned amid damnation. When that failed, I appealed to those who had climbed up a step—for some of the Irish had painted houses and clothes that asked no mending. But they feared the loss of the little they had gotten, and such were ever glad to see the back of me. The Irish remained as closed to me as the book with seven seals.

I tried to open back doors. At Hammondsport, at the bottom of the lake, I accepted the hospitality of a family of co-religionists while I nosed about, for the hotels were notorious. Now that was a sad little settlement, come near to ruin with the success of Penn Yan across the water. The population had no outlet canal nor railroad of their own, only a troublesome waterfront bunch and a demon scheme of growing grapes for wine. A shame it was, for I have never seen a prettier frame for a village—but, then, I have known many a place poor and beautiful at once. I believe that only prayer kept it from collapse, for the place was wonderful with Methodists.

Northward, in Geneva, I found high society and learning, but no plots. To the south, in Bath—a pretty place—commerce lifted all and even the Irish seemed contented. Elmira was a blue-clad town, with late-recruited soldiers in the streets and bunting on the saloons. Everywhere, I listened in vain for the whispers that would lead me to Irish plots or to the perpetrators of the murders.

The situation dragged my thoughts back to John Company and India. I do not speak of personal matters now. Twas the feeling of exclusion that was the same. We were as shut out from the world of the Irish as we had been from the schemes of the Hindoo or the Musselman. I found no least hint of rebellion, but well I remembered the Mutiny, and the signs we failed to see then, and the suddenness and slaughter that nearly finished us.

I sensed a darkness in the hills, though I could not find its source.

Look you. I would not pretend to Nellie Kildare's visions. Yet, there was trouble lurking just under the snows, and I knew it. My forebodings grew as January passed into February without event. For an old soldier knows that spring brings death, not life.

I knew not what to do, and felt a failure. But for a pair of queries, Washington trusted me, with confidence misplaced. Of course, the attentions of the great were elsewhere. Although Mason and Slidell, the Confederates our navy had seized from a British deck, had been handed back, the newspapers warned of London's surging truculence. The Rebels sought to parley Manchester's hunger for cotton into an alliance of war. Even the French were sniffing opportunity in Mexico like low mongrels. Meanwhile, we could not fight the war we had. Congress deviled Mr. Lincoln for results, with Mr. Seward damned in a new gazette each week. Twas a dark winter.

"He is not telling all," you will say. "For he was not quits with the spirit girl, that Nellie." But there is sad little to report. I went again to visit the Kyle place, where they abided. I took money along. For she had said her father had a hunger for it.

The Great Kildare allowed a *conversazione*, as he called it. We sat around a little table, the three of us this time, with the curtains drawn against the afternoon. But nothing come of it. The girl remained withdrawn in her father's presence, and the trance brought not the least hint of spookery. I felt she was resisting. In recompense to me, her father made her do tricks, like calling out a number upon which I concentrated. She brightened long enough to promise I would be happy, but I might have had that of a gypsy at a fair. At last, she fell to coughing. There was a new leanness to her, the sickness hewing her down, and her father quickly led her from the room.

Kildare returned for his money and explained that the spirits would not be moved that day. He pressed upon me a tract he had written on phrenology, along with a little pamphlet on "Swedenborg's Doctrine of Correspondences."

I left, with those O'Hara brothers watching from the barn door. As the sleigh pulled off, I heard Kildare's voice shouting at the girl.

When I went back again they were gone. Mr. Morris, whose admiration for Kildare had not faltered, explained that father and daughter had embarked upon a lyceum tour of a few weeks' duration. He showed me a handbill. The Kildares would go first to Elmira and Ithaca, then west as far as Erie and Buffalo, finishing with a "spiritualist gala" in Rochester. Young men and women would have their matrimonials predicted by the spirit world, and visions from beyond would startle all.

"He has to do that sort of thing," the pastor explained, "*has* to do it. Money for his research, money for his work."

At the end of January, we had a brilliant thaw. Patches of brown appeared in the fields, and there were birds in the air. If you went abroad at night, you heard the groaning of the ice on the waters. But all was false. With the start of February, winter bullied back. The wind screamed down, and the snows resumed in earnest.

One bitter day, when it was almost too cold for the horses to be out, John Brent drove me down to Himrod's Corners, where I wished to ask a few questions. In the course of our rides, I learned more from that man than from any other in the county. He had a handsome, even bookish speech when we were alone. If we neared other white people, though, he returned to the jolly dialect of the minstrel, for which he asked my indulgence. Twas the reverse of an Irishman, who will speak his best in your presence, then curse you in his brogue when you go off. But the Negro occupies a peculiar spot in our society, and I think it will take a generation before he is valued as equal to a white man.

Himrod's Corners was a barren, hardheaded place, a cluster of shacks excused by a meeting of roads. The sole tavern was low, its only patrons farmers going bad. I found no Irish. Still, my queries met silence or diversion, for these were closed-off folk from the glens. We soon began the ride home to Penn Yan.

The team trotted along a ridgeline and I watched a train cross the fallow land, peeling back the snow from the rails before it. Of a sudden, I saw that I had to leave. To return to Washington and make a report. And, perhaps, to recruit my own informer, though the matter lay heavy in my breast.

I will tell you: I was not unselfish in my plans. I would set my departure so that I might have a Saturday night at home, in Pennsylvania, along my way. For I had left a thing undone these last years that wanted doing.

I had tamed the spirits called up by Nellie Kildare, and saw the business clear for a fraud, if still an inexplicable one. The girl's sickness of body had unbalanced her mind, and her father, the mesmerist, had put things in her thoughts that he had learned on the quiet. How or why I knew not. But answers there would be in time to come, and no spooks or goblins would be found. Meanwhile, an earthly duty lay before me. Painful it would be. But that is the price of duty delayed.

I left Penn Yan in a snowfall.

THE RAILROAD MAKES US THOUGHTFUL. It brings us to one another with remarkable speed, and that is a welcome thing. But along the way it lifts us out of our familiar order. Old notions rise unbidden, and the journey—so eagerly begun—fills with a sense of loss. We feel uprooted, and we are. It is the times. For we live in an age of confusions, unlike the long and simple days of our grandfathers. Our world is a mighty locomotive, hurtling onward, regardless. And war worsens all. What man would not be glad of a little peace?

The train outraced the storm, and when I left the Tenth Avenue depot, all New York City was out in its finery along the avenues. There was bustle. Cheering sparked in the streets at the sight of blue uniforms—which I must say I found a grand and welcome surprise—and I was pressed to avoid the to-do spilling off the curb at each next public house. Fellows tried to fit great schooners of beer into my hand, congratulating me blindly, for too many are the men who associate patriotism with drink. I had to wave my cane to open my path.

With hours to spend before the Pennsylvania train, I walked across town to the district headquarters. Twas staffed by a plump, bewhiskered lot, all merry. They were drinking French champagne. In the middle of the afternoon.

"Haven't you heard?" a rotund colonel asked in response to my bewilderment. Waving his glass, he surveyed his fellow sybarites in uniform. "The fellow hasn't heard! Of all things!"

Fort Henry had fallen the day before. Our gunboats beat down its walls even as our army marched upon it. The fortress lay upon a Western river, such as those of which Mick Tyrone had written, and I prayed that my friend was safe. The officers said it was the start of a grand campaign and the beginning of a death blow to the Confederacy.

I found a sober clerk and sent a supplemental telegraphic to Mr. Nicolay, assuring him of my arrival in Washington on Monday. Then I wandered out the time until my train.

A bit too far I wandered. For not all was wealth and patriotic fervor in New York City. I come to slums that made me turn around. Irish, they were. And bitter. The inhabitants cursed me and my uniform by daylight, and on a wall I read a sloven script:

NO IRISH BLOD FOR THER BATTALS!
NO NIGUR KINGS!
FAIRE WAGES!

And a bummer spit on my boots. If insurrection broke out, it would be here. Not in the somnolence of Yates County.

Then there was a block of boys for sale, cheeky and got up fancy.

I fled.

I had to travel by way of Philadelphia, a city with harsh memories for me. From there, I found a space in a mail car going to Reading in the night, and, thanks to my uniform and rank, a bunk was granted me on a coaler returning to Pottsville with empty cars.

Twas dark as we clipped the last miles, but I could not sleep. I felt my newfound home rise up around me. The towns and farms of Little Germany slipped behind, and we curved into the water gap, where the Schuylkill washed the valley. Our own canal lay there, and the disordered settlements that had grown up at the landings. All sleeping now. We slowed but did not stop in Schuylkill Haven, home to well-fed Dutchmen, and chugged into Pottsville under a hint of light.

Twas a vigorous place, our Pottsville, built upon anthracite. The yards were quick with shouts when we come in. Our locked wheels squealed on the rails. Switchmen strained over levers. All smelled of ash, but the familiarity was sweet to me.

Despite the hard duty before me, I longed to see my love. For she was my joy. Twas not five weeks since last I had held her to me, yet it seemed a year. My young son drew me, too, but I will tell you truly, not like her.

I feared what was to come.

I had to speak to Hughes the Trains, to insure a place for a Sunday leaving. Meanwhile, I sent a boy along to warn my wife of my arrival. For enough surprises she would have, and to spare.

I TOLD HER ALL. We sent Young John to Mrs. Roberts, next house but one, and let that good woman think what she would. Then we sat in the parlor, for this was a serious matter, and I began straight out. No breakfast I allowed myself, nor pretension that all was well. She wanted but to hold me, my beloved, but I could deceive her no longer, and made her take a place on her proud cushions. I should have made a clean breast of it years back, before we married, when first I come back from India and found her in the garden. But men are weak, and I had been at my weakest then. Now I would be paid back with hard interest for my dishonesty and cowardice.

I told her of my dead love and the babe, and she learned at last why my letters had stopped for so long.

"I will not be false now," I told her downcast head. Her hair was pinned back sleek, her gray dress prim. "I loved Ameera. And the little one. Without benefit of clergy, we were. But a family none the less. For all the devils of India, I loved her. As I love you now and forever." Her head sank toward her knees and her small shoulders quivered. "As I love our little John."

I let her cry, and cry she did. Sobbing hard. She was a woman of great reserve in her parlor ways, but privately she kept no walls between us. She was better than I deserved, and I knew it and had taken the gift in silence. And never think that silence is no lie. It lulls the decent heart until it kills.

"I'm sorry," I said. "I'm so sorry, Mary. But you had to know the truth of it. Wrong it was of me to keep it from you. Wrong and cowardly."

"You . . . would not have left her, then?" my love begged. "Had she lived? You would not have . . . returned to marry me?"

The words come so heavy. But I would not lie to her now.

"I would not have left her. Or the child."

She wept from the depths of her, face in her hands. Tears ran down her wrists and into her sleeves.

I wished to be strong. But I could restrain myself no longer. I cast myself upon my knees before her.

"I'm so sorry. I've broken your heart . . ."

She cringed as if afraid that I would touch her, so I did not. Though I longed to gather her to me. I felt my fine life dissolving, and wondered if it would not have been better had I not risen from my fever bed.

"I've broken all your faith in me," I whispered, and I was weeping, too. "And brought you only disappointment . . ."

Suddenly, she straightened. Face fierce as the Black Mountains. She grasped my wrists with her little hands. Strong from the scrubbing, they were.

"Don't you understand?" she cried. "Oh, don't you?"

"I do," I assured her. "I'm so sorry, my love."

She shook her head. Denying that I could ever understand. Then, all unexpected, she flew from the chair and clutched me. Holding me hard.

"I'm such a wicked woman," she told me, sobbing. "It's me who's the wicked one, don't you see?" I felt the rise and fall of her breast against me. "I'd feared so much the worse of you, my darling."

TWAS NIGHT, AND OUR LITTLE JOHN SLEPT. We had already put certain things behind us, my sweetie and I. Too vivid in our love, we could not sleep.

"I don't know what to make of it all," I told her. For I valued her advice above that of all others. "Mr. Seward insists there's to be an insurrection. Yet I can find no clear sign of it. I feel myself a failure, see. And the business with the girl and her visions and sickness fair took my balance off." I sighed, turning to hold her the better. I loved the scent of her hair. "Well, I will go to Washington. And tell them what is and what is not. Then we will see."

"Then all agree there is no insurrection?" my love asked.

"Just so."

"Yet there is murder?"

"That, too."

"But Mr. Seward thinks there will be trouble?"

"He does."

"And so do you?"

"I do."

She got up on an elbow, hair cascading in the lamplight. "Then you are right," she said.

I gave her a look. For she must explain.

"There is simple," she went on. "There is murder, and trouble afoot, but no rebellion."

"And?"

"No 'and.' And you keep your mittens down, until we've done our talking."

I ceased my molestations.

"I do not see where you have gotten to," I admitted. For she was ever quicker.

"Look you, Abel. There is murder, and trouble, but no insurrection against the government. Well, that is it. No insurrection, no rebellion. But something else. You are looking for a goat because they sent you to look for a goat. And so you do not see the sheep."

"What sheep, then, my little shepherdess?"

She gave me a slap. "You will behave, Mr. Jones. Until we have gotten to the end of this. Or you'll get none of what you want, and plenty of what you don't."

She was ever a hard one, when she set her mind on a thing.

"And how many questions did you ask up in New York?" She tried a new approach to make me see.

"Questions, my little one? I asked a thousand. And every answer come back the same."

"That is because you did not ask a thousand questions, but one question a thousand times. Will you not see that there's no Irish rebellion there? Although there may be something else entirely, and Irishmen aplenty in the doings. Do you not see it, then? You will not have the right answer until you put the right question. Oh, I swear—"

"Mary!"

"Well, I do. Though only to you. And upon this one occasion. I tell you that I've never known a man so clever and foolish at once. You have the saddle ready before you've caught the horse."

"I would saddle no horse, girl."

"Look you," my love commanded. "If they will send you back, forget rebellions. Begin again. You've been working backward from what this Seward has decided. Without a true knowing. Instead of starting with the facts and going forward."

I saw it. I did. She was as right as I was slow of conception. It is my sense of duty, see. I would do what my superiors ask of me. Even when I should know better.

"Well, there is clever," I said.

"Clever there's none. You'll use the brains the Lord bestowed upon you. And come home safely."

When I looked at her lovely outline by the lamp, then thought of the mind that worked within my darling, I almost could agree with Mrs. Stanton and Miss Anthony as to Woman's possibilities. Although I know that is a foolish business, and trouble.

"Well, then," I said. "I have my orders. From General Jones herself. And but one question left to close the matter."

She looked at me all fierce, my little lioness. "What, then?"

"Would you turn down the lamp and come closer?"

"No. For we are not done."

"More, then?"

"More. The girl. This Nellie."

"Oh, Mary! There is naught between us. I never—"

She smiled at that and gave me a gandy look. "Oh, Abel, I know. I can see you're taken with her, but not in a way to trouble me. For I know that I will keep you, and fight I would, besides. But fight I will not have to, for you would fight yourself first."

"She's dying."

"We're all dying," my wife said. "That's what we do. She's only dying faster. Does it not seem queer to you, Abel, that we should all put in our claims for Heaven, but fear the going so?"

"The body fears what the soul would have. But there is strange. I do not think the girl fears dying. It's the living that frights her."

"Well, I meant not to be hard. That was not my meaning. Only that I think she knows more than she has told you, and I do not speak of spirits. You will need to talk to her again. And help her if you can, for that is Christian. But pity with a clear head. And that business with her father. There is a mystery. Perhaps he is like your rebellion."

"How, my little one?"

"Something other than he seems. I do not like the sound of him."

"Nor would you like his look. Different from the girl, he is. I wish that they were parted."

She rose still higher above me. "Do you? Do you wish that, Abel Jones? Without knowing the history of them, and what that girl needs when the doors are shut?"

"She's burning away," I said.

My love softened. "Oh, I know it. You've said. And though I have no fear, I will give you jealousy. When I hear you speak of her beauty. And know I will never be such."

I moved to hold her, full of words of praise and adoration. But she set her free hand to my chest and kept me back.

"Be careful," she said. "Only be careful, Abel. For I know how it is with these consumptives. When they're going, they crave the life of all around them. There is passion in them then, and heat. So much it is unholy. I know, for I have nursed them. And the girl's mad. Though not so mad as you think her."

"But, surely you don't believe in—"

"I believe," she said, looking down at her pillow, "in what I can hold. And in what the Gospels tell me. I'm a simple woman, Major Jones." She reached for the lamp. "And now I would hold my husband."

RISING FROM MY JULIET, I did not hear the lark of Mr. Shakespeare, but woke to early church bells up the hill. I took the nightpot outside, then washed in the cold under the pump, and lit the stove. I started to make the breakfast, then realized it was a kindness that would wound her. For she would want to break the eggs and spill the pancakes on the griddle for me. I only put the kettle on for coffee, that joy of good Americans.

My footsteps up the stairs woke little John, and he woke her. There was not enough time. A better man would have counted himself lucky to be home for even an hour, when vast armies were condemned to winter quarters and unbroken loneliness. But the torment of another does not lessen the hurt of our hangnail, and we are selfish creatures to the core.

I ate mightily, making up for a month at Mr. Morris's table.

We went to chapel as a family, but I had to leave before the final hymn. I heard them singing "O Thou who earnest from above," as I flew down the street with my bag. My eyes were so bothered I was nearly run over by one of Mr. Yuengling's brewery wagons, off to water some profane gathering up in the patches. That would have been a hard end for a Methodist.

EIGHT

"*OOOOCH,* MAJOR JONES! YOU ARE COMING AGAIN!" MRS. Schutzengel, my Washington landlady, waved her mixing spoon like a saber. Filling her doorway, she seemed a bulwark of all that is good and homely. "We beat them slave-keepers *gut und hart, nicht wahr?* Now pie I am making!"

Even as she said the word "pie," her rapture withered and her broad face sprouted worry. "*Ein Apfelkuchen ist schon gemacht,*" she continued, but the beauteous passion with which she customarily spoke of food deserted her. She looked me up and down, as if appraising a youth set under her charge who had ranged delinquent. "*Mein Gott,*" she declared, "he *ist* only the bones and all starfed! They have taken half of him away! Where *ist* you gone, Major Jones? And why *ist* you knocking and not coming in? *Sind Sie nicht hier zuhause?*"

Of a sudden, the woman puckered with tears.

"My dear Mrs. Schutzengel," I began, "there is good to see you again. I only thought that, since I'm no longer a boarder, I had best knock. I was hoping, see, that you might have an open room for a night or two, perhaps in the attic and—"

Now, I know that a bull is not a female creature, yet Mrs. Schutzengel was a bull of a woman. And that is nicely meant. It is her strength I would convey to you. And, yes, her presence of body evidenced a good table. Yet, delicate in her feelings she was. Tears fair poured from her, even as her great red face exploded with anger. She brandished the mixing spoon above her head again.

"Herrgott erbarme," she wailed, with her Communist eyes raised to Heaven, *"dass der gute Mann so wenig von der Schutzengel hält! Meint er, dass ich nur ein böser Kapitalist bin?"*

And then she began to scold. Still waving that spoon.

"Ooooch, now my heart *ist* all broken in *Stücken.* That you are thinking I am only after the money!" Oh, she wept. "*So geldgierig ist die Schutzengel nicht!* You will have a room in the attic? *Nein! Nein, bis zur Ewigkeit!* And what is wrong with the room you are already having? Is it not all *sauber und* waiting for you?"

"But . . . my good lady . . . I gave up my room when I went to New York . . ."

Didn't she give me the fierce then?

"You gived up your room. *Jawohl!* But your room is not giving up you! Even if them Rebels are coming, Hilda Schutzengel is guarding your room *wie ein alter Grenadier!*"

"But . . . I explained . . . that I cannot pay for two—"

She near slashed me dead with the mixing spoon. A hard end that would have been. Though not worse than mortality under a beer wagon.

"Pay? Who *ist* saying to pay? How else will Hilda Schutzengel fight for the Union *und die Freiheit?* For the freedom of the peoples, I give you the room when you are gone." Great choring muscles rippled beneath the cloth of her workadays. "*Ooooch,* if I am being a man, I make worse for them Rebels than Fort Henry! Over the head, I will hit them!"

A woman of passions she was. Of fire and mood. Again, she drooped into sorrow.

"But only the bones you are! *Nichts als Knochen!* Like the prisoner! Come inside. *Komm! Marsch, marsch!* Eat!"

The truth is that we would have liked to hug each other. But such things are not done in proper society. Even by Communists.

When my dear landlady shifted to allow me inside, I saw Annie Fitzgerald, the housemaid, standing behind her in the hallway. The stalk of a girl had been rendered invisible until then by the capacity of Mrs. Schutzengel's mortal coil. I had done Annie a small good turn once, but hardly expected to be remembered for it. Yet she cried to greet me, too. Now I would not have women weep for me, for I have never been the kind who takes joy in the suffering of the poor creatures—though some men do. But who does not like a nice welcome?

"Oh, Major Jones," Miss Fitzgerald said to me, "I dreamed you were gone into danger, and prayed to Our Lady til dawn."

Mrs. Schutzengel grunted. With a tad of jealousy in it. As if she had been trumped in her devotions.

"Major Jones must eat now," she admonished the girl. "And there *ist* plenty you are cleaning."

Humbled, Annie Fitzgerald curtsied and said, "Yes, Madame."

But Hilda Schutzengel truly did believe in the Brotherhood of Man, and her good woolen sense always conquered the high silk of her temper in the end. She softened and laid a mighty arm around the girl.

"*Doch,* first we are all having pie."

WITH MY BELT LOOSENED A NOTCH, I tapped along toward the President's House. The streets were mires. Even where cobbled, they had been muddied over by countless wagon wheels and the leavings of horses. Rain spit. Smoke and the smell of slaughtered cattle thickened the air. Twas past the visiting hour, so the fine carriages were put up, and nobody strolled for the joy of it. Only those without choices walked the streets, and the drabs kept to the doorways.

A regiment of pale recruits, not yet issued waterproofs, marched soddenly from one camp to another. They had the faces of long-punished children, and the sergeants failed to keep the step. Army supply wagons grumbled along behind delivery carts, the teamsters huddled low beneath broad hats and turned-up collars. The drivers lacked the spark to curse, which, though a blessing, tells you of the dreariness. Rats slicked about, unafraid. A miserable day it was, a winter Monday, bare as bones. It put me in mind of Britannia's damp, and of coughing children.

Yet, there was something in the town I liked. Perhaps it had only grown familiar. But I had spent a barren night in Philadelphia, delayed by trains diverted, and would not have traded the ferment of our capital for all the elegance of Rittenhouse Square. Although I might have wished for better sewerage.

The President's mansion was a shambles. The public hall was filled up dense as a barroom when oysters are set out free, and the look of the guests was no better. Shabbiness of dress vied with shoddy ostentation. Nor was every man sober. Now, I am told there is such a thing as a good cigar, but I smelled nothing of the kind that day. A cannonade does not leave smoke so thick. Twas a wonder the President's family could bear the stench.

The horde of men waited sullenly, for Mr. Lincoln would see all who waited upon him, but never soon enough to suit their vanity. Office-seekers and favor-beggars spoke loudly to one another, as if the volume justified their claims.

"Old Abe's forgot the likes of them put him in," a fellow with tobacco juice in his beard told his neighbor.

"Gone all high and awmighty," the next man agreed, "and thar's a fact."

Another visitor cut a souvenir from the draperies with his clasp knife.

As I went up to Mr. Nicolay's office, the supplicants lining the stairs complained about the military pushing good men out of the way and damned West Pointers—though I am far from such. I passed a bald man with the shakes and he called out, "Lookee there. It's a pegleg puss-in-boots." But when men speak to hurt, their own wounds show.

Mr. Nicolay himself answered my knock. He got me inside through the crush and complaints, then closed the door and locked it. The smoke seeped through.

The President's private secretary looked as though he had not slept in weeks. He bid me sit and took a chair himself.

"These people," Nicolay said, with just a trace of German heaviness, "I tell Mr. Lincoln they must go. But he lets them come. I tell him he must say they are to join the army, if they wish to serve the government. But he laughs and says that the best thing he can do for the army is to keep men like these out of it. What are we to do?"

Germans. Where the Englishman is only clever, the German is intelligent and earnest. And when he is not wanted, he keeps to his beer and cabbage. Loyal, too, your German, and he does not fear work. If only others made so little trouble.

"I fear," I told him, "I do not have a head for political matters."

He did not smile, for your German is a somber fellow at his workplace. But I sensed he was amused.

"The paradox of democracy, Major Jones. The bad man is born for politics, but governing requires the good man."

"Mr. Lincoln is a good man, it seems to me."

He sat up straight. Mustering all his Teutonic intensity.

"Mr. Lincoln is a *great* man. A very great man," he said. "They will see."

"Look you . . . I'm afraid my purpose has been frustrated in New York, Mr. Nicolay. I have done naught of value."

He half rose from his chair. "No, Jones, no. Your reports have been read, sir. You are a valued man."

"But I have found nothing."

"To the relief of all. Yet . . . your last telegraph message . . . implies doubts. You yourself continue to believe in insurrection, I think? Perhaps among the Irish? As Seward fears?"

I shook my head. "No, sir, I do not. Although Abel Jones has been wrong more than once in his life. I do not think the Irish are plotting rebellion. Nor will others rise against our government. Yet, there is something afoot. But there is strange. I cannot say what that something may be."

"You will continue to examine the matter?"

My shoulders shrugged before my voice could speak. "That's up to you, sir. And to the President and Mr. Seward. But I fear the expense to the government of my activities. When I come to you without result."

He did smile this time. Twas a rare expression on that man's face.

"Oh, we will bear the expense, I think." He chuckled. "General McClellan insists it takes a hundred thousand men to empty a slop pail. So I think one man is not too many for the peace of all New York."

"I wish I had more to tell," I said honestly. "But twas all in the cables and scribblings. I would not disappoint Mr. Lincoln, see."

Nicolay glummed at the mention of the President's name. Out in the hall, a round of laughter ended in coughs and phlegm.

"The President wanted to see you himself," he said. Downcast and sorrowing now, as if he had recalled a heavy burden. "But he's overcome. I can't even get him to sleep."

"The news from Fort Henry cheered him, I hope?"

His mouth twisted. "Oh. Yes. Fort Henry. The generals are already arguing about who should have the credit. The only thing they agree on is that none of the praise should go to any of the men in the field. To listen, you would think the war is fought in the headquarters alone." He sighed. "Well, that fellow Grant is marching on Fort Donelson. While the others talk. Perhaps we will not squander this chance entirely."

Now, you will think it disrespectful, but I will tell you: I never met a man I sooner would have employed as a clerk than John Nicolay, and that is high praise from one who has kept accounts. He had the soul of one who keeps good books.

The little German met my eyes again. "And . . . there's something else. The President's sons are ill. Perhaps you've heard the rumors? Well, they're true. Willie and Tad both. The doctors say it is a bilious fever. But I fear the typhoid. It is very bad, I think. And Mrs. Lincoln is not . . . always sensible. The President spends hours by their bedsides. It is hard to make him leave them. Even for the greatest matters. That is why he does not meet you."

"That is only sensible, sir. For his sons must come first."

Now you will say: "This Abel Jones does not understand the importance of great matters of state. Lincoln should have sacrificed his personal concerns, for he was President." But I will tell you: Even a war must wait for a sick son. It is a lesson I learned hard in India. And I had not even the excuse of battle.

"Seward wants to talk to you, though," Mr. Nicolay continued. "He said to send you over to his office this afternoon."

"Yes, sir."

"And Major Jones? Before you go?"

"Sir?"

"I had a message . . . from the clerk who manages the secret service fund. He . . . complains of irregularities. In your claims and account."

I do not think I ever leapt to my feet so fast.

"Irregularities? About money is it?"

"Now, now. It is a minor matter, I have no doubt."

"Irregularities?"

"Well, yes. He insists your claims are too low. You are not spending half of what the other agents do. He wondered if your receipts might not be incomplete . . . if you might not wish to revise them?"

"Revise them?"

"Well, he thinks you should be spending more."

"He . . . wants me to spend more? Of the government's money, then? He wishes me to make false claims? Waste and steal is it? I'd sooner—"

"I'm not sure I would say it in such a way, I think. But he fears it looks improper when your field expenses are so low and the other accounts are so much higher. A Congressional auditor looking into the secret service fund might wonder why those other claims are—"

"Well, let him wonder, see," I interrupted. For I was in a dudgeon. "I will not have waste and wanton expenditures! Oh, there is wicked, when men in service load themselves with luxuries, Mr. Nicolay. Our government is not a milk cow. So let this auditor wonder, and Abel Jones will tell him what is proper, if he comes asking."

Nicolay gave me his second smile of the day. This one showed teeth below his mustache.

"I see you are right, Major Jones," he said. "You have no head for political matters." He sighed. "Neither do I, I am afraid."

He moved to usher me out, for he had work in plenty. But I had to ask him, "Mr. Nicolay . . . think you that there are no good politicals, then? Besides Mr. Lincoln?"

He began to reply, then caught himself, as men must in Washington. And yet, he had spoken truly when he said that he, too, lacked a head for politics. After a pause, he answered me squarely, which is not the Washington manner.

"There's Seward," he said. "All thought he and the President would be enemies, since Seward was to have the nomination. They knew Seward's pride and expected jealousy. They would have enjoyed that, I think. But Seward is a bigger man than they believed. I think he has become the President's only friend in Washington, the only one to be trusted."

"But you, sir, are Mr. Lincoln's friend, and can be trusted."

A wistful look crossed his face as he laid his hand on the doorlatch. "I do not signify. I am a small man, meant for doing the little work. When God allows, I think I do it well. But Seward rises to greatness. He has kept us out of war with Britain. So far."

As if speaking to himself, Nicolay added, "I think of him as Saul become Paul."

"SONOFABITCH," MR. SEWARD BARKED.

Twas a hard greeting.

"Son-of-a-goddamned-bitch," he expanded. Chewing his cigar as if to eat it.

I knew my results had been poor, but I had been dutiful. I will admit disappointment at my reception by our Secretary of State.

"Son-of-a-goddamned-worthless-bitch," Mr. Seward continued, as if declining Latin. The paper in his hand quivered. In a room thick with smoke. All Cuba's tobacco might have burned there in a day.

"Sir," I said, "I have done my best, and if—"

"What the hell? Oh, Jones. Not you. Goddamn it. *Fred!*"

A moment later, a handsome fellow of perhaps thirty popped his head through the door.

"Yes, father?"

"Goddamned Canadians let two blockade runners into Halifax harbor again."

"Father, in the interests of accuracy," he said, with a glance at me, "I must remind you that Halifax is not part of the Canadas for diplomatic purposes, although it's administered by—"

Seward yanked the cigar from his mouth. It looked tormented. "Just get that bugger Lyons down here."

Fred Seward blushed royally. Or should we Americans say "blushed democratically"? Anyway, he slipped inside and closed the door behind him. His poise had deserted him.

"Lord Lyons is already here, Father. He's just outside."

Seward rammed the cigar back into his mouth then pulled it out again. "Well, let him wait, goddamn it. Can't have him thinking he has the run of the place. And get that goddamned picture of the Prince of Wales back out and put it on the mantel."

"Yes, Father. Would you like to review the latest correspondence from Ambassador Adams before you speak to the British ambassador?"

Seward grunted. I believe it passed for a yes. He was a small, bowlegged, bignosed, scrawny giant of a man. The sort who, despite his size, makes you think he could heave the world and have a hand to spare. A born scrapper, that one. Like the little pea-pod of a recruit who proves a demon in battle when the brawny waver. I do not excuse his lamentable excesses of language, of course, and would not report them were it not our duty to record the utterances of great men.

"Know Charlie Adams, Jones?"

I reviewed my acquaintances. "There was a Charles Adams in my regiment, sir. Died of too much gin in the Punjab."

"Not the same one. Hell. If Charles Francis Adams dies of any excess, it'll be an overdose of propriety. Damned fine ambassador to send to London, though. One of our own goddamned 'aristocrats.' Best kind to deal with old buggers like Palmerston. And that Russell. Buggers every one. Way they bring 'em up." He caught himself. "Not English, are you?"

"I am American, sir. Although born and bred in Wales."

"Don't have their proclivities, then. Good for you. Now tell me about this Fenian rebellion of ours. Cigar?"

"No, sir. Thank you, sir. There is no rebellion, sir."

"Sure of that?"

"I see no indication of such doings."

"You goddamned sure, though?"

"There is only so much certainty to be had in such matters, sir. But I see no insurrection against our Union."

He stood there before me, hardly taller than I was myself, with his neckcloth awry and ashes on his lapels. But his eyes, ladies and gentlemen! Fine writers tell of "piercing eyes." Well, Seward's went through you like roundshot. Looking back, I think he was too intelligent—certainly too well read, for he loved books—for the rough world of local politics through which he had risen. He had learned early to disguise his brains and learning, and now the rough disguise had become as comfortable as an old waistcoat.

"Well," he said, "my sources back home in Auburn *still* insist there's an Irish uprising in the works up there. Of course, the same thickheaded sonsabitches told me I'd be President." He gobbled smoke from his cigar. Augmenting the fog in his office, he continued, "All right, then, Jones. Tell me what *is* going on."

"I do not know, sir."

"But your dispatches, man. According to them, you think *some*thing's going on. Even if it's not an insurrection. Well, what is it, man?"

"I don't know, sir. But I will try to find out."

He began to pace. "Hell and damnation. Anybody giving you trouble up there? Getting in your way?"

"No, sir."

"They do, you let me know, goddamn it."

"Yes, sir."

"Well, what do you think, though? Man to man. One banty bird to another."

"Sir . . . I believe there is trouble coming . . . and it may well be Irish trouble. But I do not see insurrection. They are too few for a rising." The smoke was thick enough to hide in. "They know their weakness, see. And to what end would they do such a thing? There is no sense in it. The best of them are gone to the army, anyway."

He snorted. "First thing you learn in politics, Jones, is not to expect sense out of people. Just assume every last fellow's born crazy, but doesn't want anybody else to know. That's how this society works. Hell, *all* societies. Nothing but lunatics on their best behavior. Call it 'civilization.' Each last man and woman convinced they're the only one who's crazy and afraid to let it show. But give 'em an excuse and they'll be dancing naked as jaybirds in front of the county courthouse. And singing to beat the band."

That did not accord with my vision of mankind.

"Damn it, Jones. Keep on the matter. Would you? *Some*thing's wrong up there. We both agree on that. And this nation can't afford any more trouble now, internal or external. This Mason and Slidell business isn't quite as solidly behind us as the newspapers think. Damned British aristocrats *want* this country to fail. It's an example they don't like. An embarrassment. Afraid their own goddamned working classes are going to rise up and kick 'em in the pants. And their moneybags want Southern cotton for their mills. London bankers hate the damn blockade. Crown sent eight thousand more troops to Canada. Which doesn't strike yours truly, Billy Seward, as a friendly action. Goddamned 'Royal Artillery' and the like." He looked me up and down. "You served in Her Majesty's forces as I recall?"

"In John Company's ranks, sir. An East India regiment. But the Mutiny changed—"

"They any good? Can the Brits fight?"

"The men can fight, sir. And will fight. For the sheer delight of it. For they are not all good Christians. And the officers, begging your pardon, are too stupid to know when they have been beaten. It is a devil's combination, see, and they win even when they should lose."

He grunted. "Damnation. President's right, you know. He sees it. Don't underestimate that man. Did it myself. And how, I underestimated him. But he damned well knows his business. Fool the hell out of you, Lincoln. 'One war at a time,' he says. And he's right. Can't afford a war with Britain now." He dropped the ragged bits of his cigar into a brass bowl.

Twas good to hear him speak so. For I am loyal to our America, and no question there. But I do not long to fight another Welshman, nor any who had served beside me once. No, Abel Jones did not want a war with Britain and her armies and fleets.

"Anyway, Jones. Get to the bottom of things up there. Do whatever you have to. Money help?"

"I am adequately supplied, sir."

He grunted. "Well, don't be stingy with bribes. Especially with the Irish. And hire all the turncoats you want. Take some of these new green dollars. Federal-backed paper money. That'll make 'em think. You just box 'em in. Don't want any trouble up in New York, with Canada full of redcoats and bayonets just across the river and 'Merry Old England' spoiling for a fight. Can't have any appearance that New York's disloyal to the Union, either. John Bull needs to understand that we mean to hold together. Insurrection or whatever, you keep your thumb on it."

He briefly sorted through the chaos of his desk. Or perhaps it was only a private order others could not decipher, for he found what he was seeking soon enough.

He held out a sealed envelope.

"Here, Jones. Special orders. In an emergency, you're authorized to call up the militia on Federal authority. And to assume command of any U.S. troops or volunteers in the area. Rank immaterial." Those stabbing eyes cut through me yet again. "Don't hesitate. Least sign of trouble, crush the bastards. We need peace up there, and I'll pay in blood to get it."

"Sir . . . I . . ."

"Be *hard,* Jones. Don't look into their faces. Don't think of them as men. Just stop them. As if they were mad dogs. Make an example at the least sign of trouble. The Union's more important than any thousand of us."

I was just thinking that, were he not our Secretary of State, he would have made a splendid sergeant, when he turned back to the great business of his office.

"Goddamn it to hell. Now I've got to see that pompous bugger Lyons. 'Her majesty wishes to inform . . .' More excuses than an old whore caught filching. Succoring damned blockade runners and privateers . . ."

The door to the office opened. I feared it was Lord Lyons barging in, for Britannia is proud and impatient.

Twas Mr. Lincoln.

Stooping under the lintel, he was. All the great tallness of him.

Tears covered his face.

Now I am small and undistinguished, and I do not think Mr. Lincoln saw me at all that day. His ravaged eyes looked only at my host.

"Seward," he said, "my boy's gone."

IN THOSE DAYS, our Department of State was allotted a building hardly the size of a middling gentleman's country house. We were a nation that looked inward and not out, Westward and not East, though that would change. I left those cluttered offices and copy clerks for the lamplit world outside.

Rain spotted my coat.

I expressed no condolences to Mr. Lincoln, for we must know when we are not to speak. But it was not for lack of sympathy. Mr. Lincoln, see, looked a sad one on the sunniest of days, and think of the weight on him. Then this. I would say he was a very Job, but Job was no president faced with civil war. No, old Job faced the lesser trial. I slipped away, quiet like.

Twas clear that I must go back to New York in the morning, which left me with a list of things to do. I had meant to visit my friend Evans the Telegraph, and he would be wounded by my neglect, but time for such indulgence there was none. I would see Fine Jim, though, for but a moment. There was smallpox in the city, as well as the typhoid, and I feared to find him missing from his corner.

There he stood. An apprentice rooster, ragged and shivering by his pile of papers. When he saw me, Fine Jim fair lit like a rocket, running to meet me halfway across the street.

"Captain Jones!" he cried, smile wonderful. Then he corrected himself, "*Ma*jor Jones! Why, yer going fit as a racehorse! Ya all back then? Ya back to stay, sir? Ain't that leg looking good as new? Ain't it good as new?"

"Better," I told him.

"And yer back to stay?"

I shook my head and crushed the joy of his evening. And little enough joy the newsboy had. I recalled the misfortune he had suffered because of the overcoat I tried to provide him. He paid a high price for nothing, as the poor so often do. But let that bide.

"I only come by for my paper, see. A little visit it is. But I would know that you are well."

His smile returned. Oh, he was resilient. As children of privilege never will be.

"I'm tops, Major Jones. Just tops. Want yer paper, do ya?"

I looked at him. At the small, dirt-streaked face that found such joy in the moment. Twas a face born to sweat for great men who would never know his name, and to fight their wars and die for their speeches and pride. He stood shivering and wet through beside his stack of gazettes. A wrap of oiled canvas protected the merchandise, but not him. Perhaps Mick Tyrone and Mrs. Schutzengel are right about the injustice of the world and the need for changes in society, although I do not approve of uproar and attacks upon authority.

Fine Jim held out a copy of the *Evening Star.* He was little more than a matchstick shadow under the gaslight.

What do you see in a child's face? When life turns their way for just a matter of seconds? It may be the slightest transaction, a father's glance or the sale of a newspaper, yet they greet it with such delight. There is no gift so pure as a child's eyes. Now I speak of purity, not innocence. Too much is made of innocence, and we grow hard and unpardoning. Innocence perishes—too often through no fault of our own—yet purity may endure. I knew Fine Jim had seen things many a grown man has been spared. No, twas not innocence in his face, but a wonderful, gleaming purity. And faith. The faith that good will come, despite all. Is that not the soul of all religion?

"I must have not one, but three-and-thirty copies," I told him. For at three cents each, that made ninety-nine cents, and I might spare him the final penny without shaming him. "Here is the dollar." I held out the coin.

He looked at me, doing his own figuring. "But Major Jones," he said, "ya can't read but one."

"They are not for me," I lied. Yes, lied. "I have friends in New York who would each have their own copy when I return. I must not disappoint them, see."

He counted out the papers. I had reduced the stack by half. Perhaps he could escape the weather early.

Our business done, he could not meet my eyes. But only said, "We miss ya, Major Jones."

"You will see me again, boy," I told him. "For I am a bad penny, and will turn up. Keep well now."

I left him in his wet rags. Once, I looked back, and saw him watching me. Now I would not question the Gospels, for in them lies our salvation. But sorry I am of the warning that "the poor will always be with us." It isn't fair, see. And I would rather give a boy a chance than a dollar.

I WAITED UNTIL I HAD WALKED well out of sight, then laid down all of the papers but one. I tapped along as quickly as I could, for I had business to transact before the shops closed and more to do thereafter.

Slipped early from their duties, staff officers paired along the sidewalks, jovial and headed for Willard's Hotel or lesser establishments. Not a few would seek out Murder Bay, with its women of sorrow and liquor to blind. Provost riders clopped along, swollen lumps under India rubber capes, and clerks scurried across the mucky streets. A serving maid hastened on a late errand, basket clutched against her.

The shop was well lit and clean, as always. M. FEINBERG AND SONS. I needed a second major's get-up, see, for the lovely uniform made by my Mary Myfanwy was already wearing a bit and I would preserve it for ceremonies and Sundays. And Mr. Feinberg had treated me fairly in the past.

Now you will say, "That Abel Jones is so tight in the purse he buys Jew shoddy." But you will only make me angry. For I will tell you: When I clerked in the War Department, it was the great lot of uniforms from Brooks Brothers that we had to condemn, not the honest cloth of Moses Feinberg.

When I come in, the old fellow saw me at once. And didn't he drop the very business he was doing with a customer, throw his hands up in the air and rush toward me?

"A miracle!" he cried. "A miracle!"

Now I am glad of a welcome, but this seemed excessive.

He stopped before me, all beard and deep brown eyes, hands still upraised.

"A miracle!" he repeated. "Major Jones, your coming is a miracle!"

"I was looking for trousers and a frock coat, see."

But he had turned again, calling to his younger son behind the counter, "Levi, see to the customer, like a good boy. *Viel kaufen will er.* Where's your brother?" And then, to me again, "A miracle, a miracle!"

"Solly's in back, Pop. Like always. Where else is he going to be?"

The lad sounded as flinty and American as the old man sounded foreign.

"Come, Major Jones," the old man begged. "Come. Save my boy."

He led me to the room where they cut and sewed. Twas windowless, and heavy with the smells of flannel and digestion. The elder boy sat doing fine-work by a kerosene lamp. He was a handsome fellow, like the young men in those Bible prints, but lean as a diet of hardtack. Spectacles pinched his nose and he had the fingers of a lacemaker.

"Solly, you remember Major Jones? 'Not a penny more!' Remember?"

The young man put aside his work and laid his glasses on the cloth. He stood up respectfully. If there was a hundred pounds of him, I am Achilles, after all.

"'Evening, sir," he said, accent as purely American as his brother's. I noticed a volume of Walter Scott tucked behind the tailoring.

"Solly, Major Jones wants to talk to you. He wants to talk sense to you."

Well, this was news to me. But the old man explained:

"A terrible thing! Terrible! The army he joins. To go and fight for the *Schwartze.*" He pointed at his son. "Does he look like a soldier? I ask you. Tell him, Major Jones. Tell him what a fool he is. And ungrateful! Look at these hands, worked to the bone to put food on the table! He's breaking his mother's heart, and mine, too!"

I looked at the two of them. The father had naught but love and worry in his eyes, while the son burned with the determination of youth.

"I will talk to him, Mr. Feinberg," I said. Although I was not certain what I would say. For though the boy did not look like the material of a soldier, many is the man that would have said the same of me. And it was not my duty to discourage those who would serve our Union. But the weight of a father's love and loss had been impressed upon me that very afternoon. "Perhaps . . . you could leave us for a few minutes, sir?"

The old man went, muttering about miracles.

"Sit down, boy," I said.

He sat.

"Going for a soldier, is it?"

He nodded.

"It is a hard life. Blood and boredom. Only the fool finds joy in it. And not for long."

"You don't think I'd make a good soldier," he said, with gentle accusation in his voice. For he was alert to the world.

I waved my hand. "David may do as well as Goliath. Or better. I would only tell you that it is not all flags and trumpets. Or strolls with the ladies on Pennsylvania Avenue, with you in a fine uniform. There is death and misery, and the surgeon with his saw."

"I'm going to join up."

I nodded and fingered the head of my cane. "That is your affair, boy." I pointed at the novel that lay half-hidden. "I would only have you know that there is more of Cain and Abel in the business than there is of Mr. Scott and his stories. It goes hard, see. And there is always sickness, and the cold."

"I *have* to join," he said.

"And why is that, boy?"

He looked at me fiercely. "Because I'm a Jew."

I did not understand him.

"Because they all say we're cowards," he went on. "And thieves. 'Greedy Jews.' You know what they call us."

Yes, I knew.

He leaned toward me, a soul on fire. "If I don't go . . . when all the others are going . . . maybe they have a right to think that way. Why shouldn't I fight, too? Isn't this my country? Will it ever really be my country, if I don't join up like everybody else?" He looked at me in a transport of devotion to his vision. "By George, I'm going to show them, Major Jones. A Jew can fight as well as the next man. Better, too."

"Little is proved in war," I told him, though the words verged on a lie. For though we like it not, war is taken as a proof of too many things upon this earth.

Then he beat me completely.

"Don't you think this country's worth fighting for?" he asked.

Youth is cruel.

I took some time to answer. For the boy was right. Yet I feared for him. There was too much conviction in him, and too little fear. A certain fear preserves us, while conviction kills the saint.

"Yes," I said. "There is true. It is worth the fight, our Union. Still, not every man is carved for battle. Think on it, boy. Do nothing rash. Perhaps you should wait until you are a little older . . ."

The skinny little fellow jumped to his feet like a lion. "I'm twenty-one years old, and I'm going to join up." Then he looked at me with his father's lovely brown eyes. "It's our fight, too," he told me, softer-voiced. "If not here, where, Major Jones? If not now, when?"

"Only think on it," I said lamely.

Mr. Feinberg tried to give me too great a discount in gratitude, for he assumed I had succeeded.

I would not take any reduction.

"I do not know if the boy will listen," I said. "I do not even think he heard me."

The old man's face was sculpted by a lifetime's work, by joys and sorrows. Twas a good face, that.

"A man tries to do good," he said. "When a man tries, he should be rewarded."

"The price is fair," I said, "and I will pay it all."

The boy did not listen, of course. He joined up. I did what I could to ease his way. Working through Mrs. Schutzengel's acquaintances, I arranged for his transfer to a German-speaking regiment, for the Germans have less prejudice against the Jew than the rest of us. I hoped it would protect him, but he fell the next year at Chancellorsville. They told me he stood to his post while others ran, but that meant nothing to his father. The old man was inconsolable.

NINE

ANNIE FITZGERALD, THE HOUSEMAID, HAD MORE spunk than I knew. I thought the poor child a mouse, all drabness and devotions, running to mass whenever a moment come free. For there is a difference between worship and hiding, see. The Lord would have us pray, but live, as well. We must not run from life, but face it. We are enjoined to "fear not." And I thought Annie weak with fear of living.

How we misjudge.

Twas she who got me through to Jimmy Molloy.

But first, I must tell of the pot roast.

You will recall this was a Monday night. And beef was reserved for Sunday afternoons or payday Saturdays. Nonetheless, dear Mrs. Schutzengel covered the table with meat. You would have thought she'd coaxed a stray cow into her kitchen. Oh, lovely it was. Sliced thick and bathed in gravy, with carrots and potatoes, onions and turnips simmered in the gravy of it. It made me want to shout a hymn of praise, though I did not.

The steam itself was thick enough for spooning. The sauce gleamed. If beef could speak, that roast would have cried out, "Devour me!" No gray and withered cheapness on that platter, but fine brown slabs. Tender to a falling into bits.

Oh, glory!

The other boarders marveled at the splendor, and I think they were pleased to see me then. All but one. *Herr* Mager, a close-boweled compatriot of Mrs. Schutzengel's, could not like any matter concerning me. For he and I had fallen out over a matter of sausages some months before—twas but a misunderstanding on my part—and the German, for all his virtues, does not forget. Though I wonder if Mager was truly German, for he had the Frenchman's acid and his bile.

He scowled, but ate his share.

Well, let Mager bide. The chewing was glorious, and wasn't there pie and cake to help the beef home? Now I do not mind a sweet, and do not think the eating of such unmanly. Is there more robustness in whisky and the gutter than in a golden pie, thick with the apples of Eden? And your German can bake a cake, too. I used to think chocolate a queer thing. But one does grow accustomed to the way it paints up a fine, three-layered cake. And who does not admire the gentle springing back of a fine cake under the fork, and the delight of it in the mouth, and the last lick of frosting on the lips? I would say that a well-wrought cake makes children of us all, but my own youth was never as sweet as this. Yet, I must not favor the cake unfairly. That pie would not be slighted, with its apples soft as clotted cream in the mouth and a crackling crust to tame the wanton sugar. I had two pieces of each to show my appreciation. All washed down with coffee hot and black.

When the other fellows went outside to have a smoke and line up for the privy, I spoke to Annie, who was clearing plates. For she and Jimmy Molloy had made acquaintance during the Fowler case.

"Miss Fitzgerald?" I began.

She looked up from her gathering of the tinware.

"Would you . . . by any chance . . . know the present whereabouts of James Molloy?"

"Jimmy Molloy? Sure, and that one's never been hard to find, sir."

"You know where I might locate him then?"

She lowered her bouquet of utensils. "Oh, and will you look in on him, sir? Isn't that a kindness? For that one can always do with a bit of regulating."

I did not tell her that it was selfishness, not kindness, that drove me to seek out Jimmy Molloy, the regimental silver thief. Who should have been jailed in Delhi still. For all his wickedness, the man had talents, too. The Good Lord, in his mercy, is a spendthrift. And I had need of the fellow and his skills.

"I would look in on him, yes. If you can point me to him."

Mrs. Schutzengel came in, face huffed at Annie's slowness. When she saw I had engaged the girl, she calmed.

"Begging your pardon, sir, I can't do that," Annie said.

"So you *don't* know where he is?"

"Begging your pardon, I do, sir."

"Then . . . what is the difficulty, Miss Fitzgerald?"

"There's no describing the place," she said. "For it's over to Swampoodle. I'd have to be showing you meself, sir."

"Was denn?" Mrs. Schutzengel asked. *"Was ist mit dem Swampoodle?"* She had a curiosity, that woman. And all her heavy books could not appease it.

"I need to find Molloy," I told her. "You remember him, I believe."

"Molloy? *Der nette?* That sweet boy?"

Molloy was ever one for fooling the ladies. And the colonels. And even a sergeant, now and then.

"Yes, Molloy," I said. "Mrs. Schutzengel . . . if you wouldn't mind . . . if you'd do me the kindness . . . of allowing Miss Fitzgerald to guide me to Molloy's address?" Here I will tell you that I feared the worst, for Molloy was the sort who could fall while lying down. "That is, if Miss Fitzgerald has no objections? And if she judges there to be no danger, of course."

"Oh, none, sir. None at all." The girl seemed positively eager to be going. What poor housemaid will not escape her drudgery for an hour?

"But," Mrs. Schutzengel said, with heartrending disappointment on her face, "there is still cake for eating."

"Mrs. Schutzengel . . . my dear lady . . . I could not eat another bite."

"*Ooooch, ja,*" she sighed at the ingratitude of the world and its unfathomable lack of appetite. Then she looked at Annie. "*Geh mal mit, Kind.* Go with the major now. And clean your shoes before you come back in." Suddenly, she brightened. "Take the poor boy pie. And cake. I will make a package." She looked at me. "He has the great commitment to the world revolution, *der Junge.*"

Molloy had nothing of the kind, and I knew it. Twas all blarney. The only thing to which he was committed was roguery. And sloth, as well. Still, I said nothing. For I would not speak ill of a man whom I would shortly ask to risk his life.

I KNEW THE STREETS that led to Swampoodle. But no outsider knew the alleys within. The provost marshal's men went there only by daylight, and the Washington police did naught but collect the bodies floating in Tiber Creek. Irish, the place was, in the lowest sense. I'd taken a beating there once, in the course of the Fowler affair, and entered on my guard.

Before we plunged too deeply into that swamp of sorrow and poverty, I brought us to a halt.

"Miss Fitzgerald," I said, "I really cannot allow you to go any farther. For the place is a danger to all."

"Oh," she said blithely, "they'd not harm one of their own, sir."

"Really, Miss Fitzgerald, if you would only direct me from here, I'd—"

"Sure, and you'd never find the place, sir. Tucked away, it is. Where the landlord's own hounds would run circles."

"I cannot—"

"Come, sir. For I owe you more than ever I could pay. For you kindness."

"Twas nothing, Miss—"

On she went, carrying Mrs. Schutzengel's bag of treats for that unworthy Molloy, and what could I do but follow?

Soot and sorrow marked our way. Lost women who no longer had the looks or health for even Murder Bay haunted the darkness. Hard boys and drunkards patrolled their domain or huddled about dust fires. The gas lamps ran out and only the occasional torch of pitch and pine lit the muddy alleys.

Annie fit her arm through mine and pulled me close. As though we were . . . intimates.

"Miss Fitzgerald," I said, recoiling, "I will not take liberties . . ."

But she would not let me go. She had pulled her hood well over her brow, and her voice come from the darkness.

"Hush, sir. They must think I'm . . . one of those women. And that you're my gatherings of the evening."

"Miss Fitzgerald!"

"Please to hush, sir. For there is danger for you, if not for me. They're hard after them that goes about in Union blue these days, and they take officers for the worst. And a Welshie officer would be a terrible bait to them. It's the rumors of grafting them into the army, sir. They'll have none of it, the ones what are left." She pulled me closer still. So close I could feel the hungry childhood that trailed her through life. "You'll be fine, if you're quiet now and come along, sir. For the boys would not take the bread from the mouth of the lowest of women. We're not so cruel as your Protestants, begging your pardon, sir."

Such are the braveries we must remember when dark nights come upon us. The girl had known what she was doing from the start, and meant to protect me with the only armor she possessed: her honor.

We wound past shanties too poor for kerosene, lit by wicks afloat in bowls of fat, then trudged by hovels with no lights at all. Yet, you felt the life in them. Cradled babes cried out that life goes on. We were troubled by no more than a scattering of curses and surprises of filth beneath our feet.

She brought me to an alley brighter than the others, lit with enough torches for a small parade. Roistering, it was. On a Monday night. She pulled her hood lower and clutched the bag of food against her like a shield.

There was music now, in competition. A piano jangled against the weep of a fiddle across the way. Women painted and got up like a mockery of society ladies laughed at little Annie in her cloak, calling to me, "Ye'll have no fun with that one, bucko. She'll go weeping all the while."

A saddled mule stood tethered to a post.

"Here," Annie said, pulling me into a doorway.

A heathen hole it was. Although unexpected in its cleanliness, I will admit. I speak in local comparison, of course. And twas all lit proper inside, with no dark corners for skullduggery in the little room. There was a bar cobbled up, and tables made of planks and sawhorses. A trio in their cups sang to a squeezebox. Other patrons looked well past the singing. But there was a certain order to the wickedness, reminiscent of a garrison canteen. The sawdust on the floor was fresh.

The greatest surprise, though, was the busier of the two barkeeps. Molloy himself it was. With a clean shirt and garters on his sleeves, a new and sleek mustache all Irish red, and . . . an aspect of sobriety. But the fellow was born a dissembler, a master of falsehood and disguise.

"Jaysus, Mary and Joseph," he cried when he saw me. Fair shouting, he was. "By all the saints in Ireland and the sinners in London town! By the skirts of the blessed Magdalene! Tis little Sergeant Jones come up to see us!"

I would not have chosen to be the center of attention.

Molloy did all but leap upon the bar. "Hold your fire, boys," he called to the clientele, "for the man what lifts a finger at the good sergeant, and him a great major now, will have to fight his way through Jimmy Molloy."

He looked at the figure beside me and ran his hand over his hair. Hastening out from behind that counter of Satan, he grinned and said, "Sure, Annie, and we'll not tell Father Patrick that we've seen ye here tonight."

"Go on with you," the girl said. She still kept under the shelter of her hood. But her voice had a fresh warmth. Almost as if she were pleased at the attention from the low devil. "Here is a gift you don't deserve, and from a good lady."

Molloy seized the parcel and peered inside with the shamelessness of a savage. Then he remembered himself and set down the victuals.

"Will ye not go back into the lady's saloon?" Molloy asked my escort, with a glance around the room. "For tis safe and clean, ye know, and I'll keep out the ruinations till ye go again. But ye can't stay out here, Annie, for I cannot have such beauty distracting the boys."

Artfully, almost gracefully, he guided her into a back room. The Irish can charm, when they have a mind to. For a moment, I feared for the girl's welfare. But such thoughts were unfair. The Irish have their rules among themselves. And for all his wickedness, I never knew Molloy to harm woman or child. On the contrary, the fellow was afflicted with that profligate generosity you find only among the poor. The thief's hand is open when the banker's is closed. I offer this but as an observation, not in approval. Although I will admit thinking of Father McCorkle in that moment, suspecting that the fellow would have said that Jesus Himself got more respect from a thief than from a king. But look you. At times, the wisdom of the Gospels lies beyond us. Read without the filter of morality, we might mistake them for texts of revolution to make pale the doctrines of Mrs. Schutzengel or Dr. Tyrone. For it is a fact that society folk only made time for our Savior when they needed their water turned into wine in a hurry. Of course, the world has changed since then, and order is virtue, and too much thought breeds indolence and error. So let that bide.

Molloy come back out with respectable promptness, shutting the door behind him.

"She'll be in there telling her beads all the while, that one," he said. "Born for marriage, not sporting." Then he fair sang out. "Oh, Sergeant Jones, ye great major, ye. Just look at ye. Ye'll be a high general next. Like Wellington himself. 'Up Guards and at 'em!' I'd buy ye a drink and a dozen more, and kiss ye like me own mother or worse, but for I know ye'd call out an army o' constables after me."

He thrust out his hand and I took it.

"A round for all on the house," he cried.

That took care of the Irish.

WE SAT OVER A TRESTLE of planks by the rear wall. Pipe smoke mixed with the whiff of kerosene and the stink of sweat and liquors. I had expected to find Molloy as I had found him before, a beggar in rags. But here he was, shaven, employed and sober. Even if his employment was that of the devil, this was progress.

"I would not interrupt you at your work," I said, "but have only this night to speak to you. And speak to you I must. I hope it will not trouble the proprietor?"

He lowered a great slice of pie from his mouth and swallowed. Twas like watching a snake gulp down a rodent. Then he gave me the old Molloy smile that had got past many a sentry hours after the barracks was shut.

"Oh, the proprietor will give me the liberty, I'm sure of it." He waved a hand at the interior, as if surveying the lobby of a fine hotel. "For who do ye think his ownership is, if not James Molloy, Esquire, himself? Oh, Amerikee's a grand place for a fellow with ambitions."

"But . . . Molloy . . . when last we met, you were destitute."

He looked at me with that childish affection the Irish develop. "And who do I have to thank for me entry into the ranks o' the capitalists? If not himself, the good major? Though he was only got up to a captaincy then. And an't he looking grandiose under them shoulderboards? Ye'll recall the money ye give me that first night for old time's sake and for me services in the fray thereafter. Well, didn't I invest it? Oh, a terrible rooster he was, the gamecock of all Amerikee, with spurs like a *sirdar*'s saber. And didn't I win me a pile? And didn't old Dorsey go under, drinking both profits and debts? And then wasn't this fine place to be let? Why, the widow didn't wait til they'd waked him proper before she went hawking his substance. A sin and a shame, it was. But Jimmy Molloy was ever a friend to opportunity. Oh, tis a lovely thing to become a man o' substance, Sergeant Jones."

"Please, Molloy. It's 'Major' Jones. Sergeant Jones is dead and gone."

"And sorry I am for it. For wasn't he a lovely, tyrannical fellow? Why, I recall that day above Attock Fort, with the plague behind us and a thousand raging Pushtoons in front of us, and the poor captain dead as a rat got by a terrier, and the leftenant collapsed with the sun. And wasn't ye grand, the way ye took over the shreds o' the comp'ny, bayonet all bubbling with gore? I remember ye all a-thrusting, just sticking and clubbing away. Screaming the while, ye were. 'Who'll stand by me, boys? Who'll stand by me, men?' And the heathen buggers all around us, with their knives hungry for white meat. Who stood by ye then and brung ye back bloody when ye toppled down? Oh, didn't we have lovely murdering that day, Sergeant Jones? Weren't that a beautiful slaughter?"

"Twas long ago," I said. "And you were valiant, Molloy. I will credit that. Although you were undisciplined and a thief."

"'Let bygones be bygones,' says I. For I forgive ye the thousand cruelties I suffered under ye. I know ye meant 'em all for me own good. And sorry I am to this day about the regimental silver."

"Your own regiment, too," I said. "When the highlanders were but a low wall away."

"The shame o' the doings haunts me still," he said, smiling. "Oh, tis grand to remmynis, tis a loveliness worth the treasuring."

"Yes, Molloy. Under the proper circumstances, of course. And when events are recalled with proper decorum. But let us return to the present."

I regarded the man life had sculpted. He should have looked a ruin, but remained youthful in aspect. And handsome, in a low, unsavory way. Having devoured the pie, and the cake before that, he addressed himself to a shingle of beef. He did not seal his lips while chewing, but shared his pleasure with the wide world.

"I . . . offer my congratulations on your success," I continued. "Although I wish it were in another field of endeavor."

"Oh, Major Jones," he lisped through a great chew of carcass, "tis Amerikee, and a man o' business must give the public what it wants. Tis the way o' democracy and the path to profit."

I did not want to argue with the fellow. How can you convince the devil that hellfire is undesirable? Twas no time for lectures, in any case.

"Molloy, I . . . need your help."

He set down the beef. "Again? And didn't we just have wickedness enough with those Philadelphy fellows?"

"Yes. Again. For though you were a disgrace to your regiment, and your morals are weak, you have talents needed by your country."

"'Me country,' says he? Oh, mother, hide the jewels and hold your purse! For when they come down the lane crying about 'your country,' ye know they mean to pluck your feathers good."

"Look here, Molloy. You said yourself America's been good to you."

"And an't I good to Amerikee, then? Working like a beaten dog to set up me own business, struggling day and night, and giving out jobs right and left? An't I building the country up with me own two hands?"

"Please, Molloy. I need to talk to you. Seriously."

"An't me ears wide open to me old friend? An't I listening this very minute?"

"I need you to come to New York State with me."

"Are they fighting there, then?"

"Not yet. And I hope not ever. Look you. Ever a sly one, you were. With your mimicry and disguises and such like. This time you'd hardly need to pretend. For I'd only want you to be an Irishman, see."

"Sure, and you'll be explaining that, Major Jones?"

"In good time. You see, Molloy, our Union is threatened on many fronts. And there are rumors. Of risings and insurrections on the part of the Irish."

"Oh, and an't we great ones for the risings? There's none can rebel like the Irish. Though beat us down in the end the buggers do."

"I do not think it is a rising, see. There is something else. Trouble. And I cannot find the thread of it. So I need you to go among the Irish and find out what they are up to."

He looked at me darkly then. Serious at last. The mouth that was ever so quick turned still. When he spoke, twas in a voice reduced:

"An informer? You want me to go an informer?"

"I want you to serve as an agent of the government. You would not be betraying anyone you know or to whom you are bound in any way."

"Still, an informer . . ."

"An enrolled agent of the United States government."

"Oh, Major Jones," he shook his head, "and wouldn't I love to help ye? For hard, wicked devil that ever ye were, ye were square to me and sweet as me own mother with the honey o' understanding. If not for ye, the black English buggers would of give me twenty years in Delhi jail and not ten—although I was obliged to leave those premises early anyway, for the quality o' the accommodations was lowly and not to be endured, and thanks be to the black cholera for me blessed deliverance. Oh, don't I love ye for the justice that is in ye and the charity all reluctant? But I'm a great businessman now. Sure, and ye can see that for yourself. I can't go traipsing off to the wilderness and carrying on like a lad o' twenty. I'm a gentleman o' substance, with high responsibilities . . ."

He bent back to his eating.

"You won't do it then?"

"Oh, ye know I would if I could. But I can't, so I won't. And there it is. An informer . . ." He puffed his cheek and blew the idea to nothing, spitting shreds of beef upon the boards.

He had been my last hope. For the Irish were as shut to me as the thoughts of the Grand Chinee.

Molloy must have marked the disappointment on my face. As soon as he was finished with his meal, he wiped his snout and paws on the cloth that had wrapped it and said, "Oh, Major Jones, me lovely, darling man. Sure, and ye don't need the likes o' me, anyways. Nor are ye wanting such likes. For trouble I am, and always was. Me own mother, who was a great, pop'lar beauty back in Dublin, and every one o' me fathers in turn said I was trouble. And right they were. No, ye'll not be wanting the likes o' me for your delicate doings . . ."

I put my head down in my hand, searching my brain for ideas. "I wish Dr. Tyrone were here. Perhaps he could help."

Molloy perked up. "Help ye? With the Irish? That Orangeman? That black Protestant? Now, I'd not offend ye, Major Jones, and I've naught against the person o' the man, but ye'd be a fool to trust a low souper Protestant like that one."

"I'm Protestant myself, Molloy."

He waved that away. "Ye are but a Welshman, and not counted by the Holy Mother Church. For the Virgin knows that such are born benighted, and she'll intercede for ye and lessen your sufferings. But an Orangeman's damned to the blackest pit o' Hell."

"Dr. Tyrone is actually quite fond of you, you know."

"And don't I love the fellow meself? For he's sweet and full o' learning, and I'll not hear a word said against him. But he's damned for all that, and not to be trusted. Like every Orangeman ever born. Why, he'd not last an hour as an informer, that one. Sure, and the Whiteboys would set the pitch cap on him and hang him so high—"

I caught him by the wrist. "What did you say, Molloy? 'Whiteboys?' What are 'Whiteboys'?"

He did not lose his jocularity, but rolled on. "Sure, and nothing but thieves, the most o' them. For times are hard, and men are brought low. But long ago, in the days o' Black Oliver and down to the '98, they was the hardest o' patriot secret societies. 'All for Ireland!' 'Liberty or Death.' 'Erin go brach.' Oh, they weren't all high and fine like Tone and Tandy. But they made the Uniteds look like dolly-girls when deeds were to be done. Cutting the tendons on the landlord's cattle, they were. And sometimes on the landlord himself. Quick hands with a torch, that lot, though not so quick with their heads. It took the likes o' Father Murphy to manage 'em. And whenever they found an Irishman who grew too close to the English and betrayed his own, they'd set the pitch cap on him. Although I heard the cap was first thought up by a sergeant o' German George."

"The pitch cap," I said. "That would be pitch poured over the head? And gunpowder rubbed in it? Then set alight? And the poor man left to hang thereafter?"

He grinned in delighted agreement. "There ye have it! Just so. Ye've seen it yourself! Oh, sometimes they let the devil's hands free and he'll go tearing the flaming hair from his own skull and—"

Molloy stopped.

His face changed utterly. He looked at me with a greater sobriety than ever I had seen upon his features.

"Ye've seen it yourself," he repeated, in a flattened voice.

"I have."

"In these New York doings?"

"Yes."

He reached across the table to grasp hold of me, but thought better of it and only leaned in close. I saw the clots of wax on his mustache.

"I'm begging ye," he whispered. "If that's what ye found in New York, go elsewhere. For the likes o' them will kill ye horrible. They're worse than dacoits. Crueler than the Pushtoon."

"I will do my duty," I told the dark-eyed urgency the man had become. "At least I understand your reluctance to aid your new country now."

"Oh, bugger me country." His voice went up. "And every other country, too. For the truth is, they've done naught for the likes o' us. Your landlady's right about that, though smitten she is with Amerikee. And lucky we are, the two o' us, that we've still got our heads on our shoulders, and the use o' our arms and legs . . ."

He glanced down then. As if he could see through the planks of the table. To where my bad leg rested.

"Sure, and ye've done your share for two countries," he told me. "One after the other." Something like fondness colored his voice. "Leave Whiteboys and such be. For the sweet love o' Mary."

For the love of two Marys. The one he meant, and my Mary Myfanwy. How little such a fellow understood of duty and obligation. Molloy had been a brave soldier in his day, but courage is no more constant than the temperature, and physical valor is not tied to virtue. Perhaps he thought I relished the sordid business. Imagining that I had lost my senses since they made me an officer. The truth is that I only wanted to be home again, clerking in Mr. Evans's coal company office and lying in my nightshirt by my love, with my son in the next room. But we are not put upon this earth for our selfish pleasures alone.

"Thank you, Molloy," I said, rising. "Your information has been of value to me. Now I know what I am facing, see. I wish you luck in your endeavors." I looked down at that long-familiar face. "Abide by the law and avoid depravity."

The Irish are great ones for making every room into a theater. Such a despairing expression the fellow put on then!

"Oh, me darling man," he said, shaking his head as gently as a willow and smacking his greased lips, "your wife won't even see ye in your coffin. For they'll have to nail it shut to hide your ruin."

"AND WON'T HE BE HELPING YOU THEN, sir?" Annie Fitzgerald asked me, when we were almost free of the valley of the shadow that was Swampoodle.

"Helping me?"

The hood that covered her face turned toward me. "Sure, sir, and you weren't come all this way only to visit the likes of that one for your pleasures? But did he refuse you, sir?"

"Mr. Molloy . . . is engaged in other occupations."

She made a sound as if scorning all of England. "Always putting on airs, he is. And shows no respect to his betters."

"Now, now, Miss Fitzgerald. We'll have no talk of 'betters.' For this is America, see."

"And was it the Garden of Eden," she said, "there would still be better and worse." I had never known the girl to speak so freshly. "And what kind of husband would that one make, I ask you, sir, to some poor woman? When he won't do a bit for a friend? And one who was like a father to him?"

The girl was spanking angry. I would not have recognized the forlorn creature I had met three months before.

"I was no father to him, Miss Fitzgerald. For I was hard on him in ways a father is not. Besides, we were of an age, or near it."

"That one! He'll never be more than a boy. And a bad one, too."

We passed by a line of unfortunate women, each figure withered with the evening's failures. Annie Fitzgerald was so stoked up that I do not think she saw them. Or, perhaps, she had seen them too often.

"And I asked him to do more than 'a bit' for me," I continued. "His response was only reasonable."

"I'll give that one 'reasonable.' Letting down our kindly Major Jones. And won't he make a fine tale of your visit, though? Bragging how the world comes to his door!"

"Each man . . . must find his own way, Miss Fitzgerald."

She made a *hooomph* of a sound, fierce for the size of her lungs.

"That one couldn't find the pot beneath the bed."

We had come free of that vale of misery. A hack clattered by, and a constable leaned on a streetlamp.

Annie Fitzgerald stopped cold.

"Mother Mary!" she cried, laying her hand—delicately—upon my arm. "Oh, Major Jones! And didn't I forget the doings I promised Mother Flaherty? And me with only this single chance to go by? You know your way to the house from here, don't you, sir?"

"Miss Fitzgerald . . ."

"I won't be the hour," she said, already turning back toward Swampoodle. "Won't you make my excuses to Mrs. Schutzengel, sir? For she's good of heart and worries."

"I can't possibly allow you to go back into that . . . morass . . . alone."

She laughed gaily. "Oh, and you were always the gentleman, sir! A girl can tell you were raised by a steady hand. But you're not to worry. For we're not like your highborns, and the boys won't bother a girl who keeps herself proper."

She would not hear of my accompanying her. Then, slowly—for I am not quick in such matters—I saw that she was likely borrowing the opportunity to pass a moment with some fellow who had her affections. As Mr. Shakespeare put it, we must not "admit impediments" to such efforts, but wish young lovers well.

"Go you, then," I said, a touch embarrassed at my dullness. Yet, I felt some guardianship for the girl. She had been orphaned like myself. And life is hard even for those with two honest parents. So I called after her, "Beware false promises, now. And know your worth, Miss Fitzgerald."

She laughed like a plain little angel.

I WENT TO THE DEPOT EARLY, heavy in heart and soul. My bag was heavier, too, with the new uniform and all the aromatic provisions Mrs. Schutzengel had thrust upon me. With a tear in her generous eye. Those baked delights and ransoms of cold beef should have boosted my spirits. But I felt so alone I just stood under the roof of the platform, one step shy of the sleet coming down. I had not even had an opportunity to thank Annie Fitzgerald for her kindness, for she had not returned and must have stayed the night with Mother Flaherty.

An empty man, I was. Waiting for a train to failure.

I watched them loading cars of convalescents. The lines were quiet here, but sickness fired volleys in the camps. The shirkers transferring the weak from the ambulance wagons went roughly about their work, careless of the comfort of their charges, and heedless of the weather. For no one feels true gratitude to soldiers.

A pair of bearers dropped a boy in the slush and mud. The lad foundered, too weak to right himself, and the devils found it amusing.

I was just stepping off to interfere—and would have done so sooner any other day—when I heard my name shouted. By a long-familiar voice.

Twas Molloy. Dragging a bright carpet bag. The trouser legs below his soaking overcoat would have blinded a circus barker. On his head, one of those new Derby hats collected the sleet.

Glad to see him, I was. But I made him wait until I had given the ambulance crews a fine piece of Welsh temper and saw our boys properly berthed.

"I did not expect your coming this morning, Molloy." I kept my voice level, though it was a struggle. I made a great to-do of brushing the melt from my greatcoat.

He put on a face that rued his own folly, then shot me that smile I first saw in old Lahore. "Oh, and me conscience deviled me up and down so's I didn't know which end the porridge went in and which end it come out. Wicked, how the weight o' me obligations crushed down upon me. For conscience is cruder than famine." His grin stretched up to his ears. "And didn't I jump up then and say to meself, 'Our little Sergeant Jones—who's come up a major—is terrible in need. And how will Jimmy Molloy live with himself if the Whiteboys take him?' And here I am. Though how I'm delivered beside ye, I'm hardly awake to tell."

"I'm pleased, Molloy, that you have risen to your duty to our country." Twas all that I could say, see. Though I knew he come for me and not a flag. There are some things a man cannot bear in the morning. And I would not have such a fellow think me a servant of my emotions.

Now you will say: "We knew that he would come. For there are bonds that soldiers never lose." But I did not expect him, see. For hope does not make sound policy. And we must ever prepare for the worst in this lovely world.

We rode and talked and planned all the way to Philadelphia, sharing the food from my landlady's kitchen. He was a sharp one, I will give Molloy that. And he knew his people. His scheme to go inside them was ingenious. And brave. It even put me to worrying that I had, indeed, asked too much of him. For I would be just and not expect more of another than of myself. But by then Molloy was in fine fettle, enjoying himself like a child, and insisting that it was just like old times, only better.

As we drew into the Pennsylvania yards, he said but one thing that was out of place.

"Women," he muttered, "will get a man in trouble every time."

TEN

THERE WAS TROUBLE, BUT NO WOMAN IN IT. UNLESS you count the jailer's frightened wife. Men with guns and torches met my train. The police fellows had carbines, while most of the other men carried sporting pieces. A brace of hounds yearned after scent, tugging a plump man with a revolver along the platform. Outside the station door, a commercial traveler waited with his trunk and valise, doubtless recounting a lifetime's dishonesties as he watched the forces of law surround the train.

John Underwood stood beside a railroad man. The sheriff's hand lay on his holstered pistol.

As I stepped down, I caught the sense of things. The lawmen were not there to search the train, but to prevent a boarding. They surrounded the locomotive and the string of cars, while horsemen galloped ahead along the line. When the train began to move again, with the drummer safe in his coach and praying thanks, riders paralleled the wagons until the train surpassed their speed.

The sheriff come up to me right off, for I had telegraphed him from New York regarding my return.

"Don't you worry," he told me. "He won't get away."

"Who, then?" I hoped he would lead me inside the depot building to continue the discussion, for the wind was ripping.

"Nolan," he said. "That damned Nolan." He scratched a mighty ear. "Oh, for crying in a bucket. I knew they shouldn't have hired an Irishman onto the police."

"And what," I asked, for all was new to me, "did Mr. Nolan do?"

Underwood looked down at me, face boiling with chagrin.

"He killed the fellow who was set to answer all your questions."

THE SHERIFF DROVE ME TO LIBERTY STREET, to a Greek Revival house done up in stucco. Twas the jail. Passing by, you would have judged it a fine place for a family, for you could not see the harder portion from the front.

No sooner had we entered than the jailer's wife went wild. Wailing in a voice to chase cats. Mr. Meeks, the jailer and sheriff's deputy, sat in a corner chair, head down and hands clutched between his thighs. But his wife was up and going like a dervish.

"It wunt his fault," she cried. "He couldn't help it. Don't put us out in the street. It wunt his—"

"Nobody's putting anybody out in the street," Sheriff Underwood told her. But you know how it is when a woman has had too much time to think on a matter. Mrs. Meeks was set to speak, not listen.

"That dirty Irishman," she cried. "That Nolan. That's who it was. That Nolan." She looked at her broken husband. "I told him you can't trust no Irishman. I told him. But would he listen? Would he listen to me?"

"Theo?" Underwood said.

The jailer looked up. His face was gray.

"Theo, could you and the missus give us a little privacy for business?"

The man nodded. "Anything you say, sheriff." But he did not move.

The woman threw herself onto her knees. With a sideward glance at me. "I'm begging you. I'm *plead*ing, John Underwood.

My husband's an honest man, and he don't deserve to be put out into the street."

Small towns, see. They have their shames, but not the hardness of the city. Everyone knows everyone else, and must live with them. So John Underwood did not raise his voice, or scold, or threaten. No, he lowered his voice still further.

"Now, now, Sarah. Don't you worry. I know it wasn't Theo's fault. But I'd be grateful if you'd cook up some coffee. And you take Theo out and let him gather up his wits. It's been a hard day for everybody. You just cook us up some coffee, all right?"

Give a woman a task for her hands, see, and she will rest her mind.

Out she went, meek as a mouse and husband in tow, shutting the door behind her.

The sheriff shook his head. "Shock to 'em. Don't I know it? Never had such doings around here." He cocked an eye at me. As if a part of him still suspected that I myself had brought on all this trouble. "Found O'Connor with his throat cut. Right there in his cell. Back of his calves sliced through, for good measure. And what do you think of that? You kill a man, what's the sense of cutting his tendons? Sure isn't going to run off on you."

I said nothing.

"This morning, that's when it was. Sarah was off buying her groceries. And gossiping, no doubt. Well, some fellow Theo's never laid eyes on before comes running in yelling that I need him—that *I* need him—over at the number five lock. That we got another drowning. Irish fellow, the one who run in hollering. And who's here in the jail office just then? Just by sheer chance? Nolan. Our grand Irish policeman. And Theo leaves him here with the keys and everything else."

The sheriff sighed, investigating an ear with a sausage finger. "Damned lie, and nothing but. There wasn't any drowning. I was still up at the farm, just getting a late start, that's all. There's days like that." He looked at me, a truant child. "Wife's been ailing, you know." A flush of anger colored his brow. "They knew damned well where I was. Damned well." He grunted. "Then

Theo gets out to the lock. And there's no sign of a drowning. Not even a crow to pass the time of day with. Everything's just all froze up and waiting for the work gang to come around again. Well, he realizes something's fishy. So he rushes on back. And there sure isn't any Nolan, no sirree. Office here is empty as the tomb on the third day."

He looked around at the walls. With their legal notices and likenesses of criminals. "So now Theo's fretting. He goes and gets out his old dragoon pistol—Nolan didn't steal anything, at least—and he goes on back to check the cells. And what does he find but old Chauncey O'Connor lying there, every inch of him covered in blood. And the missus sitting by him and rocking and crying how I'm going to boot them out of the house for letting a thing like that happen. Well, first thing Theo thought was that the missus did it. She's got a temper, that Sarah. And Theo figures maybe O'Connor got smart-mouthed about the food. But soon as he came to his senses, he saw he'd been made a fool of. Letting Nolan alone in the jail like that." He sighed. "Theo did his duty, once he saw it. Say that for him. Ready to take his medicine like a man. Sent Jonah Clarke up after me. Met me coming down the Potter road. Told me about the killing and Nolan disappearing. First thing I did was to call everybody out—constables, police, for what they're worth, and all the fellows we keep on the rolls as reserve deputies. That's always been an honor kind of thing. Never had to call 'em up before. Well, I got 'em out on the roads fast as they could scoot. On *all* the roads. And you saw how we're handling the trains."

"This Nolan," I said. "Perhaps he's already gone. With a good horse. Surely, he wouldn't just wait to be taken."

Underwood twisted up his mouth until it seemed his lips would touch his ear. "There's the thing. Nolan's Irish. No horse of his own. And nobody's missing a horse. Morning train was long gone. Lake's froze, and the canal. So he must've gone off on foot. Or he's hiding."

I nodded, but meant nothing by it. "Tell me about Nolan, then. If you would, John."

He snorted. "Damned disappointment. Treachery, and nothing but. Must've been a spy for the Irish all along."

"What was he like? Young? Old? I would like to know, see."

"A murderer. That's what he's like. A damned murderer." He looked at me, baffled by his thoughts. Twas clear he was shaken, too. "Here I was figuring there was hope for the Irish. Seemed like young Nolan was the best fellow of all the local police—not that I have much use for any of 'em. But he kept himself sober. No funny business. Supporting his mother and sisters. And saving up to be married, so he always said. Seemed determined to be as respectable as normal people. Hardly seemed Irish—that's how they fool you." He shifted a clot of unpleasantness higher in his throat. "That Nolan fooled everybody. And more fool me."

Mrs. Meeks delivered coffee in tin cups. I suspect they were those used for the inmates, but no matter. The beverage smelled harsh and looked thin. She smiled and cooed, and you could feel her straining to hold her tongue.

"Thanks, Sarah," the sheriff said. "You go back out and sit with Theo now. He's had a hard day."

And out she went, trailing doubt and apron strings.

"Now, John," I said, "you made a certain claim at the station."

"Claim?"

"That . . . the murdered fellow, this O'Connor . . ."

"Chauncey O'Connor. Dead as a throat-cut hog."

"That he had been about to answer all my questions."

"That's right." Then he considered. "Or a lot of them, anyways."

"And who is—was—Mr. O'Connor?"

The sheriff shrugged. Whenever he did so, the lower half of his ears—those magnificent appendages—flared outward. "Irish. Old fellow. Well, maybe not so old. You know how they seem. Older for the drink. Although O'Connor wasn't the worst of 'em by a long stretch. Just liked his poteen. Every so often we'd bring him in to quiet him down and let him sleep it off.

Then he'd behave for a couple of months. No, he wasn't the worst of 'em."

"He came to you? As an informer?"

"Oh, no. No. We just brought him in drunk. He was down on Main Street, shouting his lungs out. How we were all going to see, how the Irish were going to show us, and how the Irish nation was going to rise up under the green flag of Erin. Any other time, I would've figured it was just more of their hooting and hollering. Nolan brought him in for disturbing the peace."

"Nolan?"

"Yep. Then he killed him. Because of what O'Connor said to Theo."

"And what was that?"

He smiled, the cat who ate the canary. "That 'President' Kildare was going to make the Irish a country of their own. And he didn't just say it to Theo Meeks. He was yelling it in the street when Nolan brought him in. With a pack of the saloon Irish trailing behind. Hollering that every Irishman was going to have his own home and land. That President Kildare was going to give it to them. That the mighty would be cast down."

He was pleased with his revelations. And clearly expected me to be pleased, too. When I did not reply, he continued:

"So, there you are, plain as day. Hate to say it, but I was wrong. Irish are up to their tricks, after all. It's a rebellion, all right. But now the cat's out of the bag." He gave a laugh that come close to a spit. "'President' Kildare. Fellow ever shows his face down this way again, I'll give him 'president.' We're going to nip this insurrection nonsense in the bud. You and me, Abel. Think we should send Bill Seward a telegram about all this?"

"There is no insurrection," I said.

He sat up. "What?"

"No insurrection. No rebellion." For I had thought hard during my journey, and found myself thinking even harder now.

"The hell you say. Why, the evidence is right in front of your face, man! *You're* the one who was making all the fuss about it!" He yanked a mustache end as though he would pull it off his face. "Now, with bloody murder right here in my own jail, and as good as an admission from one of the Irish, suddenly you don't . . . you don't . . ." His face went red as cured ham.

I put down my cup of coffee. Twas still near full, for the coffee was only fit for a jail, and then as a punishment.

"John . . . you've done good work. You've helped me. But I must ask you to trust me now. There is trouble, see. But no insurrection. For we have read the signs wrong, and must begin again. And do not annoy Kildare. Please. Let him go about his business. Until we see what that business is."

"If he even comes back. Once he hears about this."

"He will come back."

"Well, you sound pretty damned sure of yourself."

"He will come back. Because he is clever, see. If he would run, he would give himself away. And there is no good evidence against him. We do not even know what he's about. He will see as much."

"I bet he runs."

"We will see." The truth was that I was not completely certain. I could not think of Kildare without thinking of Nellie. And that clouded things. Perhaps it was only that I wanted them to return. Because I was not finished with either of them.

"Well, we damned well *will* know what he's up to," Underwood said. "Once we find that damned Nolan."

"You will find Nolan, that is sure."

"Don't I know it? And then we'll find out just what's going on. Rebellion and Kildare and the whole business."

"You will find Nolan," I said, but my voice was grim now. "But he will tell you nothing."

Piqued, the sheriff turned his head and gave me a side look. As if I were too full of myself. But I was only full of troubled thoughts. For the clearer one thing became, the foggier ten others appeared.

"Once I get my hands on Nolan," the sheriff said, "you can bet your bottom dollar he's going to talk. And that's a promise."

"John," I said, in a gentling voice, "you will not find him alive."

NOW YOU WILL SAY, "Well, where is that Molloy? He was not on the train with Abel Jones. And is he to be trusted, after all?" But you must wait for answers, for these things happen slowly.

Molloy and I parted in Philadelphia—for people always see what they shouldn't—and he went off to make his way alone. We had arranged the methods of our meetings. I tried to give him money from my funds, but he was wiser and saw that too much money always wants explanation. So off he went, with his Derby hat on his head.

I hoped that head would remain upon his shoulders. Without a pitch cap. For he would be on my conscience now. As for trusting him, look you. In some regards, he was more to be trusted than myself. For he had come to aid a friend in need, and there is goodness. While I was still not free of Nellie Kildare. And although I meant no baseness, Molloy was right. A woman will get you in trouble.

But let that bide.

Twas late when I left the jail, and whipping snow, but I went to see Father McCorkle. For I had thought on him, too, during my journey. And I had more cause to think on him now.

He made a fuss, all "Look what the wind blew in," and "How are ye, man, how are ye?" Yet he did not seem surprised to see me. With that knotting together of his black brows and his workman's shoulders.

His rooms smelled of a cabbage supper.

We sat by his fire again, but this time I declined his tea.

"Ah, Major Jones," he said, with the fire dancing on his face, "I see ye come back with heavy matters on your mind."

I inched closer to the hearth, for I had forgotten too quickly how cold it was in old New York.

"There is true," I said. "Heavy matters. And not unlike those weighing upon your own mind, sir."

He rocked back on his chair, a big man. "Is that so? And will we be welcoming ye into the Holy Mother Church? Or what do ye mean?"

"Nolan."

Oh, yes. I caught the fleeting darkness in his eyes. "I hear the boy's gone missing, Major Jones. And accused of a terrible thing, he is."

"A thing he did not do."

"And is that so? Sure, and I'm glad to hear it. For he was always regular to Mass, at least on Sundays. And cared for his mother, and kept his sisters decent. Won't they be pleased to know the boy's innocent?"

"They won't be pleased to know he's dead."

"Is he now?" He shook his head and sighed. "I had not heard that. Oh, the times are hard we're living in."

The fire snapped and flared, then calmed again. The brief rush of warmth was a lovely thing. I watched the flames and changed my line of talk.

"And how are the Latin lessons going?" I asked him.

"Oh, they get on well enough. But boys have little interest in such matters."

"I have heard, sir, that your Latin is excellent."

He allowed himself a little smile. "It was not bad in years gone by."

"I am told that boys who are not Catholics pay for lessons. To prepare them for their examinations, or even to go on to college."

"Tis a poor parish, and the little fees lessen the burden on my flock. Sure, and you don't begrudge me . . ."

"Not at all, sir. It is not the fees that interest me, see, but the skill."

"Tis not so fine. But have ye need of Latin, then?"

"Father McCorkle . . . do you know much about the Negro?"

"The sons of Ham," he said. "Are ye sure ye'll not take a drop o' tea, major? Twill clear your head of Latin and Negroes and what not."

I shook my head. "Thank you, sir. But it is the Negro I am interested in now."

He cocked a bushy brow. "Here, and I thought it was me lovely Irish ye come about. Will ye make an abolitionist of me, then?"

"I am told," I said, "that his sufferings have taught the Negro to dissemble. That, often, a Negro who can write a fine hand and read a sound book will nonetheless play the fool. For his safety, and to ease his way among those who prefer him unlettered and a fool."

He understood me.

"It occurred to me," I went on, for I would have things said aloud, "that a man who has better Latin than the schoolmasters at the Academy would not be limited to the speech of bog farmers and the vocabulary of the saloon."

He smiled. But it was different this time. "Ye'd have me spout like an English lord, Major? Taking on airs? When I'm only speaking to be understood by me own, who have not been to your fine academies?"

"A man may speak as he pleases. For this is America. But I think you are an intelligent man, see. A very intelligent man. Who plays the potato digger. To keep off trouble. But now I think trouble has come. And you know more about it than you will say. You put us off with homely speeches. And trap us in our prejudices."

"I've told ye, Jones, there is no rebellion."

"I said naught of rebellion."

"Oh, I've heard about O'Connor's carryings-on. The 'President Kildare' business. But the man was a famous drunkard. Addled. Pickled by drink. And as little as I like Kildare and his damnable doings, I'd not jump to the conclusion that the man's about to lead an insurrection."

"I said naught of insurrection."

"As for the Latin, every priest has the language. Some just remember it the better. It's no more than a trick of the mind, man. A few scraps of Latin do not bespeak a great intelligence."

He smiled wistfully, as if remembering. "I'm only a poor fool, like most men, and a priest with a poor parish. 'I am fortune's fool . . .'"

"And that is Mr. Shakespeare, not the Bible."

"What do you want, Jones?"

I took up the poker and teased the fire. To spare the man the rising. For he looked weary. I believe he went through every day a weary man. For much lay upon those shoulders. And muscles have no strength over matters of the soul.

"I believe I want the same thing as you, see. In the end. The welfare of your parish." I stirred the fire and glanced at him. But I did not stare. For there are times when a man must be left to himself. "I believe you know who killed O'Connor and Nolan. Oh, maybe not the individuals. But you know the cause. And the crowd behind the matter."

"I would never condone . . ." He near jumped from his chair.

I poked the stingy flames with the iron. "I did not say you liked the matters. Or had a hand in them. Only that you know. For I believe you are the one man who knows everything. Or nearly so. But you will not go to the law because you will not betray your own kind."

"A priest tainted with murder would be damned."

I nodded. "I cannot speak for your theology. Only for common sense. And common sense tells me that you know these things. Not every man can hold his tongue on his pillow or in his cups. And if the men do not come to you, the women do. They tell you things they do not rightly understand. But you understand them." I looked at him then. "What's Kildare about, sir? You can stop this business now."

He had put on a mask. A smiling mask. "Sure, and Major Jones, I've always heard tell that a Welshman's too clever by half and will tie himself up in knots. And I see that there's truth in the stories. For ye've gone off fantastical on me."

I would not smile with him. "You're making a mistake. Look you. You are not helping your people. You're hurting them. For they will only suffer in the end." I fear I waved the poker, as if it were the cane left by my chair. "Whatever the matter that's underway, it will not succeed. Whatever they have built up will crash down upon them. And then you will see hatred. And prejudice. And death."

He kept up that smile. But twas hollow. And brutal. "Are ye a prophet now, Jones? Or are ye only seeing things? Perhaps ye see Kildare's banshees and devils and haunts? Are they dancing around ye now? Have ye looked too long in the fire?"

"I've looked into hotter fires than this," I told him. For we are all vain and foolish. Then I edged toward him. "For God's sake, man! Protect your own people. Put a stop to all this killing, this . . . this madness. Don't let it go any further. For the love of God."

There was no living face before me.

"And what," he said, "would ye know about the love of God?"

THEY FOUND NOLAN IN THE MORNING, hanging from a tree where the road turned into the sheriff's farm. The pitch cap had been set upon him.

Underwood wanted to call up the militia. He raved about rebellion and elections and lack of respect. I think he was ready to hang the Irish by the dozen. And that would be just what the dark men wanted.

I talked sense into him at last. By warning of the impression of panic. Still, he raged back and forth in the parlor of his splendid home—twas no common farmhouse he lived in, and John Underwood was not a man who needed the job of sheriff to earn his daily bread.

"This is war," he insisted. "Nothing but a goddamned war."

I did not let him know. But he was right.

ELEVEN

WELL, THERE IS WAR AND WAR. AT THE END OF THE week, I had a letter from Mick Tyrone. Some of the pages were smudged a dark brown. Twas the look of blood. My friend had seen the kind of war I knew.

Headquarters, along the Tennessee
February 7, 1862

My Dear Friend,

I have seen the elephant. I had imagined that I knew something of war from street mêlées in Vienna and the skirmishes I attended in Hungary. Brutal as those affairs were, this was a different matter. I believe you understand me.

You have heard by now of our conquest of Fort Henry, but you will know to distrust the newspaper accounts. Certainly, it was a victory, welcome and worthy. But the ease of accomplishment reported by the journalists—few of whom were on the field—slighted the facts.

Perhaps you would excuse our initial confusion as attendant to the mounting of any grand campaign, but I must say that we boarded the steamboats with only the vaguest intuition of a plan. No doubt Grant, Foote and Rawlins knew our intent full well. We medicos, however, simply followed, like the rest of the army. I recall sudden orders, long waits, eternal lines, and blank faces.

I must say the spectacle was grand, though, when a fellow stood back. Dozens of steamboats and barges banked to the levee in the odd river light, as an endless flow of blue-clad regiments trudged up the planks to board. Odd, to see horses upon a deck. Toward the far shore, our gunboats gnashed at the water, snapping turtles of wood and iron, bristling with cannon and trailing smoke as they patrolled against enemy encroachments. I was startled at the number of women who attempted to board the transports, only to be turned back by the officers. Children and dogs ran about the embankments, while men with queasy stomachs broke from the ranks to perform the basest of duties squatting in full sight of a thousand of their fellows. As a medical man, I am accustomed to the body's mechanical functions, yet it was a sorry sight. The artist does not depict the full range of the hero's activities.

We made a grand procession sailing up the river. From each bend, a long succession of transports chugged along in the high, brown waters. It seemed to me an invincible display of might. May I say, at the risk of your mockery, that all felt a great exhilaration to be underway at last.

I did not see Grant until we disembarked. And that scene was but a greater chaos to me. It is the impedimenta of an army that the novice least expects. A mule becomes contrary in the mud, braking the progress of a hundred others. Soldiers made stevedores unload supplies without end, yet who can find that for which he seeks? Cooking fires appear, only to be scotched by officers wary of their smoke, and nervous boys finger muskets. Regiments form and sergeants bray, while quartermasters lay out bivouacs in conflict one with the other and disappointing to all. Grant stood watching from the deck of his vessel, unconcerned, a cigar in his mouth where his old pipe was wont to be. I thought that, should the Rebels strike our unloading, we would be beaten shamefully. But nothing transpired.

The plan, I now know, anticipated a coordination of forces, with our regiments of infantry advancing overland to take Fort Henry in the rear, while the gunboats steamed ahead and engaged in a duel with the fortification's cannon. I expected a grand panorama of battle and took the opportunity, while the orderlies established our field surgery, of joining a party of cavalry upon the west and unoccupied bank of the river. I went at the invitation of their adjutant, whom I had treated for a fistula. He should not have been astride a horse. But all wanted to partake of events.

We blundered through scrub trees and wallows for a time, until a scout led us to a promontory across the river from the fort. Dismounting, we took up positions amid abandoned gun emplacements. From our vantage point, no telescope was required to see the enemy's battle flag and the scurrying of cannoneers upon the ramparts. We also saw columns of men in gray, brown, blue—seemingly every color—departing the fort overland. We thought, then, that they would challenge our regiments in the field. In fact, they were fleeing. Only a brave rear guard remained to hold the fort.

Our gunboats closed toward the works and both sides opened with long-range guns. I will tell you that the Confederates, despite the wickedness of their cause, showed valor. They stood to their guns, despite the falling shot and spectacular losses. The gunboats paddled forward, engines groaning to drive those irresistible machines of war. The adjutant pointed out to me that the Rebel engineers had planned and built badly, and that the high water put our war machines level with the enemy's gunports. It seemed, indeed, as though our vessels might float right up to the walls and fire point-blank into la fortressa.

But where was the army? No sound of field engagements reached our ears, nor did we see the expected lines of blue break from the trees. The gunboats fired remorselessly. We watched their dark shells hurtle through the air, each impact followed by a great splash of debris from the earthworks. The slaughter was indescribable. Now that I have seen the human body disintegrated by shell, I better understand your loathing of war.

The defenders appeared as small as monkeys from our perch, yet we knew they were men. We held a firm allegiance to our own side, of course, yet one could not help admiring the bold rushing to and fro of men under fire, and the hasty serving of the guns by dwindling crews. Then a shell from one of our guns struck a magazine. The blast seemed to stun the very earth, and the smoke increased severalfold. When we could begin to see again, the interior of the fort had been cratered, the walls smashed, and guns lay bored into the earth, their carriages shattered. We knew then that we had won the day. Still, the Confederates would not yet yield. Toward the end, an officer discarded his sword and served one of the remaining guns himself. I know I shall never possess such valor.

For our part, the enemy's shot seemed to bounce from the armored sides of our vessels. The worst damage appeared to be to smoke stacks. I thought it a perfect example of the supremacy of the machine age.

Under a last, furious bombardment, the Rebel fire failed. Although I had imagined a relentless progress for our vessels, Captain Foote had kept them at a careful range, where few of the Rebel cannon could reach them. The Confederates could only suffer, with slight chance of retaliation. Loaned a spyglass, I viewed ruptured bodies everywhere along the Southron ramparts, and gutted mules behind the batteries, and blood so thick it discolored the mud.

The enemy raised the white banner, and the field fell silent. We still could not see our army.

I made my excuses to my mounted colleagues, for I felt I must return to the landing. Although it appeared that little harm had been done to our naval arm, a surgeon, too, has his duties. Incidental injuries could not be ruled out. Further, I expected we would extend treatment to the vanquished defenders who must face not only the pain of their wounds but the ignominy of capture.

After blundering about on my willful horse, I returned to the point of disembarkation and was ferried to the east bank. The first gunboats were just putting in. Grant, by the way, was in a lather, although those who have not observed him regularly failed to notice. The infantry, it seems, had become mired in the low country, all mud and creeks risen over their banks. The mass of the enemy, far from intending to engage, had fled toward Fort Donelson, twenty miles to the east and the principal Confederate fortification in the region. Overlooking the Cumberland River where it parallels the Tennessee, the citadel of Donelson intends to hold the forces of Justice at bay. But now that the Rebel designs have failed in part, I am confident they soon will fail entirely. As I write, Grant is preparing to move across the isthmus to lay siege to their works.

But now I must tell you what I truly learned of war. Fortuitous inspiration led me to make swift my return to the field surgery, for my untutored eyes had misjudged the loss to our own side. Even before the gunboats reached the bank, we heard the screaming above the shudder of their engines and splash of their wheels. Sailors and soldiers pressed into a waterborne role leaned out of hatches, or stood upon the walks, waving and shouting. All, even those miraculously unwounded, were splashed over with blood.

I leapt aboard the first vessel to approach the shore and entered hell. The armor had not repelled all of the Confederate shells, and others had entered through the opened ports. The darkened gundeck was a vision of slaughter. I could barely keep my balance for the slickness of the blood. I have heard that, in Nelson's day, the Royal Navy painted the decks and inner walls of its ships red to keep down the appearance of gore in battle. The practice wants revival.

I stood for a shameful moment, riveted. The lull of the great engines made the deck throb beneath my feet, and the screams seemed oddly far away. Boys flailed, untended, made freakish by the loss of limb and queer thrust of bone. All was shattered. Beams smoldered where fires had been imperfectly quenched. Wreckage, material and human, jumbled together. Some of their comrades tried to ease the suffering of the wounded, but most survivors had fled the cauldron of that ship. Speaking of cauldrons, a boiler exploded on another vessel, scalding men to death.

Somehow, I righted my will and went to work. Immediately, a fellow's artery exploded in my face—the poor man had turned to beg for help and a sharpness of bone cut him. I was nearly blinded and could only thrust my hand into the squash of his thigh until I found the source of the blood. Then I was helpless—I shall never go anywhere without my medical kit again—fixed to a man who would die should I release him. I called to a sailor to help me—the fellow was sitting there droll-eyed and useless—only to realize the man was dead and his stare vacant. Eventually, another sailor responded to my cries and I got him to hold his fellow's artery—a slippery business, that—while I tried to devise a tourniquet. But leather belts were too gross, nor would they hold in the slop, and rope was worse. The fellow convulsed and died as I struggled to help him.

Timidly, the boy who had crawled over to help asked me to look at his own impairment. In the gloom and slop and din, it was hard to make out exactly what had happened to him. Embarrassedly, and more dazed than pained, he let down the scraps of his trousers. There was a bedazzled expression on his face, I shall never forget it. The boy was nothing but shreds. I remember a ghostly voice, in that flat speech of the Westerner, asking me, "What kin ya see, doc? What kin ya see?" The truth was that I could see nothing but a hopeless stew of gore. And he was a fair young lad, though mere countenance should not move a man of science.

More help arrived, and we began clearing the men to the shore. One old fellow with a broken back babbled on as though he were being jollied home from a drunken evening. An army captain, seconded to the fleet, clutched the arm that had been torn from him, refusing to surrender it, cooing to it as though it were a baby. Those who had lost fingers or hands manning the guns were the lucky members of the crew, and half a dozen men had lost their sight.

When lanterns were brought aboard, I saw that I was in the cave of the man-eating Cyclops. Vital organs were strewn everywhere—one poor devil whose life should have fled instantly, lay stuffing intestines back into the cavity of his stomach. The queerest thing was that they were not his own guts, but those of a mate who had been blown in two beside him. Bones stuck out of the walls like arrows, and brains fell bit by bit from the wood above my head, like water dripping in a cavern. When I emerged to hasten to the surgery, those who saw me thought I was myself a casualty. I tasted other men's blood upon my lips.

We did our best, though paltry it was. The carnage I witnessed in Hungary, during the revolution there, had not moved the youth I then was to the degree this bloodletting moved the mature man. What was I thinking then, old friend, in life's April? How hard of heart is youth! I romped through suffering, regarding all as a clinical matter and a benefit to my studies. In truth, I had seen nothing to compare to this horrid day on the river, nothing of such bodily distortions, but never believe those who claim a man's hide thickens with the years. Wars are fought by young men because only they can bear it.

I am a man of science. But the heart will have its due. How hard it is to tell the orderlies, "Bring that one to the table," thus leaving the next fellow to die. One tries to choose wisely, to assist hope and avoid squandering effort on those who will not be rescued. But it is too much an imitation of the gods for me. I confess I prefer standing at my surgeon's table, allowing others to choose who will lie beneath my knife. I find I am a coward when I look into those faces blank with injuries yet unreal, or into eyes vast with the freshness of pain.

Last night, I longed for hospitals and order, for time above all. The skills I worked these long years to perfect declined to a fevered hacking and sawing, with a black-fingered assistant left to sew up what could be sewn and irons to cauterize the rest. At first, I tried to rinse my utensils in a bucket. But soon the bucket held nothing but crimson slime. I did my butchering through the night and into the dawn. They tell me I worked upon our enemies, as well, but I could not tell the difference.

What does it mean to the soul of which you speak, Abel, when a man finds himself in the midst of taking off a man's leg just because it is the easier course? What penalty that a boy will go legless because I was out of temper and grown impatient?

Not all the universities in the world prepare a man for this.

An old fellow who served in the war with Mexico tells me that this was nothing but a skirmish and the casualties light. It makes me wish I enjoyed your faith, for I do not know where I will find the strength for a real battle.

I will close soon, for I crave sleep. Tomorrow we will move with the army, and Brinton generously offered to have a letter of mine taken along with the military dispatches back to Washington, so I must seal this. I find, dear friend, that you are not only my most cherished correspondent, but forced to endure my confessions. How odd the needs of a man!

I fear I am jealous of your decency and disposition.

But I am selfish, and have not answered the queries from your welcome letter! Let me offer but a sketch, to be followed by an in-depth report when duty permits.

This "Doctor" Kildare sounds as though he is typical of the skilled mesmerist. Although I will not accord the art the merit of a science, there is something to it. The mind is unexplored, and surprises us. Most of the business is a nonsense, no more than a parlor trick. But I myself have been impressed by some demonstrations conducted under the strictest of conditions, first in Dublin, then in Vienna.

But I have seen the mesmerist's horrid failures, as well. My own "unexplored mind" read your missive and recalled a tragic circumstance I witnessed during my first years of study. It involved a fellow who sounds like a younger version of your Kildare—the name in the case was actually Kilraine, as I recall, and he was, indeed, a doctor. He had all the passion and conviction of youth, and declared that he could mesmerize a patient about to undergo surgery, eliminating all sensation. This was in poor, old Dublin, in '46, I believe. Chloroform and ether had not come into common use, and the restraint of a patient during surgery was a challenge. This Dr. Kilraine—a deep-eyed fellow, dark and handsome—finally gained the acquiescence of Dr. Joyce, the head of surgical instruction, to put under a trance a woman who would undergo the removal of a cancered bosom. We students watched avidly from the galleries, some skeptical, others hopeful of all that was newfangled. And Kilraine, who had only left his own student days a year or two behind him, enchanted us with the ease with which he robbed the patient of all sensation. She went into the deepest of sleeps. Here, it seemed, was a great possibility!

But tragedy followed. Thoughtlessly, the sleeper was not subjected to the usual restraint of straps and bindings. Midway through the operation, she awoke, screaming horribly, and sat up into the blade of the surgeon's knife. It pierced her heart. Dr. Joyce's reputation was, of course, secure. But Kilraine was forever discredited and dropped from sight. Of course, there is no relation to the fellow you encountered, I am but reminiscing. For you speak of a daughter of twenty, and Kilraine was yet unmarried not sixteen years ago. Thus it could not be the same man, even if the odds allowed.

I remember poor Kilraine, though. His humiliation, and subsequent degradation, was formidable. He was ruined. Yet, looking back, I believe he had the best of intentions.

As to the daughter of whom you write with such feeling, I am sorry. If your descriptions of her symptoms are correct, I see no hope. It is only a question of the speed of her decline. And do not waste your money upon shop remedies. They are useless. Tuberculosis is fatal. The only reported successes—and they are rare—come from the German-speaking lands, where the ailment is now treated by long residence in alpine retreats. Some claim the effect of the mountains is magic, but I don't suppose Miss Kildare is in a position to retire to Switzerland.

Lastly, I must confess that even science still has a few limits—I cannot explain the tricks performed by the girl. Yet, I have no doubt that explanations will be forthcoming with the years. We press ever forward!

With that as prelude, my views may surprise you, dear friend. I suspect there is more to such matters than we presently understand. I speak not of the supernatural, but of a few remaining natural phenomena that still resist our understand-

ing (though understanding will come, inevitably). Although most "mediums" and "spiritualists" have been exposed as frauds, a few resist all debunking. I do not think it a matter of spirits, although those afflicted with these "gifts" interpret it as such in their ignorance. Rather, I believe some individuals may possess still-unmeasured talents—not unlike an "ear" for music. Perhaps they "hear" more acutely than others.

I have been struck by the ability of a hound to read its master's mood—why should not some beings of higher evolution find themselves able to "read" the book of our faces, or to sense more about us than a clod may discover? Even a man of medicine must diagnose matters his eye cannot penetrate—and not all correct judgments are explained by reason. Let us but survive this war, dear friend, and science will unmask all riddles in the next decades. Your Miss Kildare may prove to be but a girl born with a form of "perfect pitch." Or she may prove devious, after all, and party to a foul hoax, deserving of our scorn. Or simply mad.

But I forget myself, and plead tiredness. For the poor young woman will not prove anything in years to come. She will be gone from us before that. Do I wound you? I would not. For your care comes through the pages of your letter and the fine voice of your lines. I wish I could offer hope for the girl, but you will never hear a lie from

Yr. Obt. Servt.
M. Tyrone
Surg. U.S.V.

AT TIMES I AM LIKE the Irish priest, confusing the words of our Lord with those of Mr. Shakespeare. I think of the Prince of Denmark in the graveyard, forlorn at the knowledge that his intelligence will never fathom the mysteries of the world. This life goes hard, and we are feeble creatures. I ponder mortality and injustice, when I should be thankful for the eternal promise. But let that bide.

TWELVE

THAT WINTER WAS THE HARDEST YOUNG MEN COULD remember, although old men insisted the winters of their youths had been colder still, and the snows deeper, and the cellars less abundantly provisioned. Whatever the truth of those memories, Penn Yan reached for an extra blanket, and woodcutters found generous reward for their labors. Signs that creaked in the wind froze to a stop, and the snow shoveled up higher than the shop windows.

You could walk across the lake, although none would do it by dark, for then you heard the groans of giants from the deep. When the women braved errands, they looked like Pushtoon brides, faces swathed and only eyes exposed. The wind cut. The toughest boys did not last half an hour at play, and when they buried Nolan, the policeman, the gravediggers had to light fires to soften the earth beneath.

A granite angel cracked in two as the navvies were shoveling the grave, and they ran. Old women said a darkness had come upon the land. They did not mean the war, but their own hills. Fort Donelson fell, but that was far away. Our celebrations were pale and brief, and Mick Tyrone had most of my concern, for war is hard on the good. The light lasted a bit longer each day, but the world felt heavy and old. The days grew too bitter for the horses to draw the sleigh over the hills, and I could only sit in my room and read, and think, or meet John Underwood at the jail to calm his fears.

And fears the good man had. He wished to please his people, and to keep them sure and safe. The death of a Federal man had been alarming, but finally the fellow was an outsider. The same went for poor Reilly, the informer, whose Irishness set him apart from the honorable citizenry. The last two had been Irish, as well. But their deaths were different, with one a policeman hung up by the gate of the sheriff's own property and the other murdered within the walls of the county jail.

Rumors flew of secret societies preparing to slaughter respectable folk in their beds, and the complaints began, and the letters to the newspapers, and the political scheming. When the Irish went door-to-door looking for work, they saw shadows moving behind the frosted glass, but got no answers to their knocks. Ladies glanced down nervously at their Galway seamstresses, and housemaids from Sligo found themselves locked in their rooms at night. Twas all I could do to keep Sheriff Underwood from arresting every Irishman who failed to tip his hat.

The priest, though, was the one who would not see the damage done and pending. I did not badger him, but saw him often in the streets, a black bulk bent against the wind as he rushed off to the shanty of a dying infant or descended upon a grocer to settle a fuss about a widow's debts. He pretended that nothing had changed. But there was a new hatred blowing down the valleys, and fear.

I heard of a rift between the priest and the Irish families that had got up to painted shutters and lace curtains, for such folk worried about the loss of the little respectability their efforts had earned them. What they asked of him I could not learn. But Father McCorkle scorched them. The priest lived to his reading of the Gospels, I will say that for him. For the poor were his, and I believe he would have carried them all in his arms like babes if he could have done so. On Main Street, his ravaged eyes looked past me without seeing. He was a true man of his faith, but should have spared his kind the coming ignominy.

Let that bide.

The winter slowed all things, excepting homeward footsteps. Jimmy Molloy did not contact me. We had agreed he would give his signal only when matters wanted reporting. But I followed him from a distance. The *Steuben Courier,* a paper from the county south of the lake, reported an epidemic of Irish misbehavior in the village of Bath. The outbreak centered on a transient fellow, one Seamus O'Bannon, whose excesses culminated in a saloon brawl that cracked the heads of two policemen and caused a constable to decline further employment. O'Bannon then enlivened the local jail with songs about Irish liberty, as well as with other tunes inappropriate for the ears of ladies and children, and the effect of his musical gifts upon his keepers was such that they arranged for an expeditious hearing. O'Bannon was offered the choice of enlisting in a Union regiment about to depart from Elmira or being remanded to state custody for grave crimes to be specified. The prisoner gave a brief patriotic declamation, swore he would put the military skills he learned under Her Majesty's yoke to work for Mr. Lincoln, then promptly slipped away from the two lawmen accompanying him to his muster. The authorities were seeking him in local Irishtowns and offered a small reward.

Jimmy Molloy had made his debut before his Irish brethren.

All I could do was to wait and hope. And I read, which is a lovely thing. I finished a most edifying history, *The Rise of the Dutch Republic,* in which the author proves that honesty and hard work decide the fate of nations. I also read those pamphlets given me by Kildare. The treatise on Swedenborg was a broth of sense and senselessness, the other sheets worthless. And I read the local weeklies, for I like a newspaper. Mr. Cleveland, the editor who had alarmed me in his quest for an interview, wrote a noble line and did not lack imagination—which, I suppose, is the essence of journalism. He published a piece speculating that America and Britain would go to war, that America would raze Liverpool and occupy London, and that our little Washington would become the greatest capital in the world. Imagine. I fear he does not grasp Britannia's might and majesty. Though it be rued, London's glory will last as long as Rome's.

And the Kildares, father and daughter, were ever on my mind. They were still off on their spiritualist tour, and the brown house in the hills slept dark and smokeless when I had John Brent steer our sleigh past it. Sheriff Underwood sent queries, of course, following the double murder. But Kildare was firmly fixed in Buffalo that day, displaying his daughter to rowdies at twenty-five cents a head.

I thought of her, and of how she had wounded me, only to see the good that she had done by it. For a lie had lain between my wife and me, an abyss of things untold, and long had I dreaded revelation. How great our secret fears become! Yet, my confession had only brought my wife and me closer, a thing I would not have believed possible, and the curve of my Mary Myfanwy's hand inked love into each word she wrote to me.

My days emptied. I had been everywhere, asking every blockhead the same dull questions, and I burdened Mr. Morris with my moping about the parsonage. I knew not what to do, while the fear of what might come swelled up in me. Twas fear of failure, too, for I would do my duty properly, like those good Dutchmen in the book.

Then one morning, reading the Gospels by a window, with sunlight pouring in to warm my shoulders and the first beads of melt from the roof making great plops on the front steps, I knew I had to stir. For I had let the winter mesmerize me as deeply as the Great Kildare himself might have done. Twas time to shake my bones and lift my feet.

A minute later I was in my bedroom, with a flyer in my hand. I had to think a moment to remember the date that morning, for the February days had grown identical.

If Kildare would not come to me, I would go to him. To the last grand performance of their tour, in the famed metropolis of Rochester. The show was still a night away, and the trains were steady.

I would observe Kildare from a safe distance and examine his tricks. This time, I would be the one in command, the scientist observer. I knew the course was right the instant I decided upon it. Suddenly, I was as confident as I had been despondent not a quarter hour before. Oh, a Welshman is a tenacious thing when you spin him up. I was ready to take on the world.

And I would see Nellie.

MAGNIFICENT ROCHESTER! What does it lack? Canals and railroads converge upon its fine harbor, while across the lake lies the Canadian shore of Britain's trading empire. Great mills adorn the falls of the Genesee, where a host of chimneys strive Heavenward. The city is even the center of telegraphic communication, with its Western Union company. Here the wealth of America's East embraces the harvests of its West in fruitful marriage. Arcades of multiple stories, shielded from nature's moods by vasty skylights, hold shops that would not disgrace old London town. There are more paved streets by thrice than in poor Washington, and the handsome boulevards and avenues are regularly cleansed of snow. A regiment of steeples and cupolas stands guard above the town's good Northern bricks, and Greek columns set a high tone, as though Ulysses had founded his final kingdom on the strand of Lake Ontario. Gaslamps brighten all.

I am told a man must see Venice before he dies—but I say let him see Rochester while he lives! With my first steps from the New York Central station, I felt invigorated—although one young rascal did try, unsuccessfully, to pick my pocket, for we are a race to despoil Eden.

I predict that Rochester will be among the greatest of America's cities in days to come, surpassing weary Philadelphia and even New York City in its glory. It is a very confluence of blessings.

Mr. Douglass lived at the edge of the city, where the farms retreated before the advance of progress. The native-born American is a curious fellow in his willingness to travel great distances to and from his work so that he may have his space and greenery about him in his hours of rest. It took me over an hour to make the walk.

The noble moor welcomed me, and I do believe his pleasure was heartfelt in that first instant. Yet, more than the usual sadness come up in his eyes then. Some uncertainty, some untold embarrassment marred the air. I could not figure the contradiction, for I saw no cause for shame. His house was decent, if not grand. Though not an abode of mirth, it was clean as a barracks just before the colonel's inspection, and who would not choose cleanliness and order over sloven levity? But as he introduced his wife to me, hesitation made him stumble. I did not understand that at all, for the woman appeared devoted and an enviable housekeep. I wondered if they had been fussing before my arrival.

Twas only over dinner that I grasped it.

His poor wife was, indeed, the cause of his dismay. She was a woman of sound domesticity, but not of intellect or cultivation. Her speech wanted correction, and even her gentleness could not disguise the coarseness of her manners. Her husband had risen beyond her. She could not keep the pace his life had set, and was no partner to the great man's soul.

And a great man Douglass was. Alarmed by my ignorance, my Mary Myfanwy had given me a fine scolding for my lack of respect in his presence, although I had done naught to give offense. I simply had not known of his achievements. Now that towering figure sat embarrassed by his mate's simplicity. For he was proud. And proud men see only what is lacking.

If it is better to marry than to burn, I am not convinced it is better to marry with too much youth. Look you. Who has not seen couples age out of symmetry, and passionate attachment wane to disappointment? I am blessed to have my wife a friend, and would wish such a blessing on all others. But there is no speaking to the young, for energy is their gift, not judgement. Too often, the beauty of form that sears the novice heart leaves naught but ashes in the aging breast.

I slept well, for mashed potatoes always make me settle. Following a morning tour of Mr. Douglass's printing office—a humble source of great affairs—I set myself to see Rochester properly. For we never know what knowledge may prove useful, and diligence is rewarded.

Of fine hotels there was a plenty, led by the Blossom and the Waverly. The latter establishment was grander than Willard's in Washington. I looked in to get the beauty of it, but took my midday meal at a farmer's hotel, where the portions were sound and the prices sensible. I would have liked to sit warm in the common room all afternoon, for it was cold outside, with a fierce wind off the lake, and my leg was a bother. But the fever, at least, was long behind me, and time must not be squandered. I roused myself and scouted all I could, from the great aqueduct to the last boatyard.

"There is prosperity," I thought. Even the Irish seemed busily employed, and sober at their ropes and saws and lifting.

I ended the afternoon at the farmhouse where Miss Anthony lived with her family. The land had been sold off as lots for new dwellings, but a residue of country charm remained. Apple trees held birds awaiting spring, and the air tasted lovely after the city's smoke. Too, my visitor's task was a happy one. My beloved wished Miss Anthony's signature to paste in our album. It seemed Miss Anthony was a figure of some fame, as well.

There is, I must say, a great deal of famousness in America. Mr. Douglass had presented me with a signed copy of his own life story—such printed confessions have become a national habit of late, arousing fear for our modesty. Why should we tell our secrets to the world? There is foolishness enough without addition. Of course, Mr. Douglass's reminiscences are meant to edify.

It makes a fellow think, though, to find a Negro has authored a book. How can we not regard such like as welcome among us? Reg'lar John Brent, master of horse and sleigh, might have said that the more books the African authored, the less of a welcome he would find. For he sees in us all a greater desire to look down than to look up. But I will believe better of my fellow man. We only need familiarity, see. Then brotherhood will come.

Miss Anthony was everybody's maiden aunt, stern of visage behind those tin spectacle frames, but soft in her doings. Her family kept a proper Christian household—Quakers, though we never talked devotions. Twas a home where there is enough for all, but never extra for any—though a portion will be found for one in need. That makes a goodly life. For Satan loves waste, while the Lord would have us value every morsel.

I set down my cup of coffee, into which I had introduced one sugar, though I wanted two.

"Miss Anthony," I said, "there is a thing I do not understand."

Her eyes rose behind the glass ovals.

"Mr. Douglass engaged in a seance with Kildare in Penn Yan," I continued, "but will not go to see his show in Rochester. I thought that he might join us. Embarrassment is it? At being associated with such matters in the public eye?"

She moved to pour more coffee, but I held up my hand to decline. For I had marked the thinning of the stream when last she poured, and would not shame her with an empty pot.

"Yes," she said, "Mr. Douglass is embarrassed. That he is. Although it has nothing to do with Spiritualism." She settled the pot on stained lace. "We have made progress, Major Jones. And we shall make far more. But progress is . . . uneven by its nature."

Her eyes glinted, but her voice avoided anger. She had the patience born of lengthy struggles.

"You see, Mr. Douglass is welcome upon the speaker's platform. But he's not . . . a colored man is not yet so welcome in the audience. Except at abolitionist meetings, of course. Certain rules still pertain in our dear Rochester. And they are ignorant, silly rules, when not repulsive. If he went with us tonight, he would be expected to sit at the back of the hall, where the benches are set high. 'Nigger heaven,' it's called. And even such seating becomes unavailable when sufficient white men purchase tickets." She sighed. "He takes such things to heart. If only he saw more clearly what women must endure."

I thought of proud Douglass, of his lovely cadences and lordly voice, of his newspaper and book. And of his needless shame over his wife. Reg'lar John Brent had called him "unhappy." Let us settle on that mild word. For we will never understand such wounds as his.

MISS ANTHONY DROVE US into town in a pony cart, which a boy minded for a nickel. A fog had risen from the lake, muting the gaslamps. You heard footsteps, but saw nothing. Until a human shape appeared a step away, only to vanish with another step. The wind was down and the night clung to the skin. A stranger never would have found his way. But Miss Anthony's course was sure.

From down the street, the Corinthian Hall was but a glow in the murk. We heard the hubbub of the crowd before we could reckon the edifice. Then, as we hurried across Exchange Place between the crush of carriages, the great building emerged. Tiers of windows shone golden through the fog and Roman symmetries made the hall appear grand as an opera house. Although I would not ascribe the wickedness of the French to the honest citizens of Rochester, this was how we might imagine Paris!

Now you will say, "Hypocrite yet again! This Jones would claim to be an honest Methodist, but here he goes frequenting a theater to gawk at a young woman." But I will tell you: Corinthian Hall was home to edifying programs and noble sentiments, and not the sad domain of scrambling players. And my concerns for Nellie were chaste. My visit to the hall was first a duty.

A rough crowd marred the entrance, composed of the penniless sort who hope for trouble.

Miss Anthony pulled her shawl tighter and leaned forward, a soldier on the march. I had to work my cane hard to keep pace with her.

As we approached the slot for paying customers, the hooting began. A fellow who had tied his cap to his head with a scarf hallooed, "There's the one wants to set women up on top of men. With the little soldier feller."

A second voice answered, "Well, *I* sure wouldn't get on top of *her.*"

They laughed. Calling Miss Anthony names as unjustified as they were miserable. For she was moral as a martyr, if extreme in her expectations.

"Just thinka them two going at it," a boy with half his teeth gone lisped. "Just thinka it."

Such was not to be tolerated. I turned on them, wielding my cane. But Miss Anthony seized my arm and drew me along.

"It's worse when we meet for women's rights," she said. "Or for the Negro."

"Bet that little feller fits right up under her skirts," a last voice yelled. "Pee*yoo!*"

Inside, the hall was brilliant as a summer noon. I paid for seats toward the front. Twas not an extravagance, for I felt I had to see what could be seen. And I will tell you, the audience was a revelation to me! If ruffians lurked without, the cream of Rochester's society had gathered within. I even saw a lady wearing diamonds! And plenty of parson's collars there were, with parson's necks behind them. On winter leave, officers glittered, their ladies graceful swans upon their arms. Bewhiskered husbands in their prime napped beside matrons whose hair had been gathered back tightly with ribbons and lace and splendid ornament. The younger members of the feminine division wore ringlets in rows or gleaming hair put up in the Roman fashion. Zouave jackets and garibaldis were the rage among the unmarried girls, and the new magenta satins shone between Genoa velvets of emerald green or havannah. My Mary Myfanwy, a born mistress of needle and cloth, could have sewn no finer garments. The dress put Washington society to shame, although I am not certain shame is felt in our poor capital.

Miss Anthony was welcomed by a few and known to many, but she made short work of social frivolities and remained a sturdy Quaker in her dress. As soon as we sat down, she nudged up her spectacles and readied pencil and paper.

The evening began with a lecture on Assyrian mysteries and the hierarchies of Babylon by a famous doctor of whom I had not heard. He claimed affiliation with a university in France, though his accent was flinty American. Now I take an interest in self-improvement and appreciate an elevated speech or sermon, but that fellow was dull enough to put a man into a snoring trance before the evening's mesmeric show began. Silly he was, too. But the crowd devoured every dusty word.

I snapped to life at the sight of Nellie. She did not come out with her father at first, but stood waiting back of the curtains. I could just see her.

Standing there, she looked pale unto death. Slender to disappearing. Yet she wore a greater beauty on her brow than all the splendid ladies in that hall. I thought that the man who married her might do naught but stare for a lifetime. Then I recalled she was not like to marry.

I do not understand why the Good Lord would create such beauty only to treat it so. But faith is our lot, not understanding.

Kildare himself seemed darker than ever, his midnight beard a veil to hide the man. He hypnotized a pair of fellows from the audience, chosen from the less expensive seats. He made them quack like ducks and waddle about the stage. Then the lankier lad stretched out between two chairs. Stiff as death, he was, with only his heels on one chair and the back of his head on the other. The stockier fellow sat upon his middle, feet in the air, without lessening the rigidity of the human plank. Next, Kildare convinced the bulkier subject that the other was his beloved. The poor oaf knelt and blubbered for the favors of his mustachioed companion.

Twas nothing to the least fakir of India. Naught but shabby circus doings. It played well with the rear rows, though. Kildare knew that he had to please them all.

He called for the dimming of the lamps. The flames flickered down in the chandeliers and sconces. Gloom settled in where the gas pipes ended and shadows quivered at the back of the hall. The stage alone remained a realm of gold.

Deepening his voice again, Kildare spoke of distant Arabia, of lost cities and secrets whose possession meant death to the uninitiated. His speech had a slow rhythm that put me in mind of tides. I don't know how he did it, but he kept deacon and dowager on the edge of their seats.

Soon the hall was his.

And then he brought out Nellie, leading her by a white hand held high. She was already in her other world. The bell of her sleeve hung down between her and her father.

She stood facing the audience, red hair free over satin. It was the very opposite of fashion to appear with hair undone, yet many a female heart must have filled with jealousy at the sight of her. In the odd light, I could not tell if her dress was gray or lavender, but no matter. She might have come in rags and looked a queen. A fairy queen, who needed no adornment. I read no hint of madness on her now. She cast a spell of peace and boundless distance.

Gently, as if he feared waking her, her father placed a chair behind her skirts then bid her sit.

The audience hushed. Breathless.

Kildare looked out upon them with those eyes.

"Who is in love?" he asked. "Who waits and longs? Who yearns?"

He paused, staring into the rear of the hall, as if he could not see the rising hands.

"Who would know the secrets of the future?" he called.

A hundred hands went high. Young men cried out, their voices half a plea and half demand. The fairer sex demurely volunteered.

Kildare stepped up to the lip of the stage, scanning the turbulent rows. Tormenting them with his hesitation. Letting them ache for attention, for a glimpse into eternity. He might have played the devil in a drawing room.

At last he called on two men of the cloth.

"Reverend gentlemen, I beg your assistance. To maintain the highest level of morality and decorum, as well as to confirm the veracity of the experiment, your humble servant requests that you select our volunteers. They must total ten, chosen alike from those formed after Eve and from the sons of Adam. If any be known to you and of good character, choose them first, so that the world may see there is no fraud."

Shameless, I call it still. Two white-haired vicars jumping at Kildare's bidding. Amid squeals of delight and groans of disappointment, they shepherded six young men and four young ladies to the stage.

A handy fellow produced a stool of the sort that does not interfere with a lady's crinolines, if I may be so blunt. Kildare adjusted it before Nellie, then turned to the audience again. Across the stage, three of the girls looked as though they already regretted their participation, while the fourth was flirting with the boys who had come up.

"Ladies and gentlemen," Kildare declaimed, "in the interests of delicacy, the conversations between my daughter and this young nobility of feminine beauty must remain private. But after each conference, I will ask the affected party to report to you the accuracy of our mystic intelligences." He folded his arms, flashing teeth amid his wilderness of beard. "The gentlemen . . . may expect no such mercies."

The audience laughed, but softly. With the grace of a Maharajee's servant, Kildare led a fretful missy to the stool. He whispered a last assurance to her and the young lady sat down facing Nellie, arranging her skirts about her. Back to us, the girl was a very hourglass, waist tiny and posture prim. Rows of brown ringlets flanked the pedestal of her neck.

Nellie leaned toward her. Curtains of red hair closed around the girl, until I could see but a sliver of her cheek. She began to fall, slowly, toward the prophetess, as if drawn by invisible ribbons. Then her chin rose and she paused in her swoon. She might have been offering her throat for a kiss.

Nellie's head began to sway, queerly, as I have seen the cobra do in rising from its basket. Slowing time to never-ending moments.

The girl jerked back. As if bitten. We all heard her gasp. Raising her hand to her mouth.

The audience jumped with the girl. We had become a single creature.

The lights lowered yet again, deepening the shadows. Nellie bid the girl come back to her. We could not hear, but understood the message on her lips. The girl leaned forward, sinking into the spell. Nellie brought her face, her lips, to the girl's ear. Auburn hair brushed the girl's cheek, cascading down her neck and breast like blood.

I had a sense that Nellie was draining the girl. Not of her blood, God forgive me, but of her soul.

Miss Anthony's pencil lay forgotten.

Nellie's lips brushed the girl's ear again, then glided down her neck and pulled away. She sat back like some legendary queen, her look triumphant.

No. Sated. She looked sated.

Kildare offered his arm to the girl and led her, shaking, toward the audience. Her face wore a lattice of tears. But she was smiling.

"Tell them," he commanded, extending a hand toward the audience.

"It's true," the girl burst out. "It's true. It's all *true.*" Then she broke down, sobbing and smiling as I have only known women to do in the deepest privacy. One of the reverend gentlemen helped her from the stage. He treated her like a sacred relic.

The second girl's interview ended wistfully, but with another confession that all had been accurately revealed. The third rose in a fit of joy, a child granted its wish. When her turn came, the flirt jumped up before her time was done, shouting, "I'll *never* have the beast, not in a hundred lifetimes!"

There was strange. We all knew she was wrong.

"Miss Kildare's a marvel," Miss Anthony whispered.

The first of the fellows sat down and leaned toward Nellie, anxious for those lips to find his ear. But Nellie kept her distance from the gentlemen, and spoke aloud. The great hall was so quiet her voice reached the rafters. Twas a deeper voice than the one I had heard on the hill. Fit to marshal the spirit world. The doubting girl was gone, at least this night.

Some of the maidens mentioned by name were in the audience, and swoons were not infrequent. The last boy fled the stage, fearing exposure.

But all this was prologue. When the game of hearts was done, Kildare led Nellie forward. She seemed to float toward us. Then he began that gliding passage of the hands over her, ending again by circling her eyes in a long, slow rhythm.

I felt my own eyes fighting a drowse.

When Kildare was done, Nellie stood with her eyes closed, hands extended from her billowing sleeves. Welcoming an invisible guest.

"In return for their gracious assistance . . . in maintaining the Christian virtue of this hall," Kildare announced, "our two reverend gentlemen may take the liberty of asking my daughter one question each. Any question, gentlemen . . ."

The first man, chiseled for a High Church parish, asked when the terrible war would end.

Her answer shocked, and might be marked the first failure of the evening. For it seemed unbelievable. With hardly a moment's hesitation, she said:

"Full three years more must pass. Three years of blood and sorrow. Then hate dies in the spring."

The hall broke into turmoil.

"But . . . but . . ." the minister stammered, " . . . the Union will win, of course . . . the . . ."

"Only one question, sir," Kildare said. "One question each. The strain is too great."

As the clamor subsided, the other preacher stepped forward. With a smug look. He was shorter than his colleague, and had the stoutness of the Lutheran.

"When," he asked in a mighty pulpit voice, "will our Savior return?"

The audience exclaimed at his boldness. But the man was undeterred. Even pleased at his effect, I thought.

"When will we again know the peaceable kingdom?" he continued. "When will the lion lie down with the lamb? When shall we look upon our Savior's face?"

I watched the rise and fall of Nellie's bosom. Expecting her to break down in a fit of coughing under the weight of such a test. But her disease seemed to have left her for the evening. In the course of the interviews, she had even gained a flush to vanquish her paleness.

"Never," she said.

You may imagine the shock in that hall. But she continued, voice rising to pierce us. "Never . . . until the day He is welcome again. He is not wanted now. Men's hearts are hard and cold . . . their hands hold fresh nails ready . . ."

"Blasphemy!" someone cried behind me. But the charge found little echo. Instead, the audience passed from its confusion into mourning. As if each man and woman knew the girl was right.

Kildare leapt to the rescue, face alarmed. He held up his hands for silence, calling out, "*Gen*tlemen . . . *la*dies . . . please . . ."

When he had them broken to a murmur, he turned to Nellie a last time and called, "Princess of the Ancient Mysteries . . . these good souls beg a response to the first reverend gentleman's unanswered question. What *is* to be the future of our beloved Union? Will it endure? What shall we see? What fate awaits this country?"

She lifted her face and said:

"Glory."

I OFFERED TO ACCOMPANY Miss Anthony home, but she would have none of it.

"Women must learn to fend for themselves," she said, get-upping her pony. The cart rolled into the fog.

Twas a relief, I will admit. For though I would behave as a gentleman ought, I hoped to intercept the Kildares as they departed. Dodging lamplit cabs, I hurried back toward the hall and met the last of the audience issuing from its doors. Slow they were, with somber faces. Clinging to the evening, or perhaps only to the false gaiety of the gaslamps. This was no night to pace through lonely rooms.

Hooks of conversation caught my ear.

"Nonsense, the war will be over by . . . Did you see the look on . . . They say she's . . . Oh, where the blazes did I . . . If you were Jesus, would you . . . felt it hovering, I *did* . . . My, what a lovely . . . haven't seen you in . . . I distinctly told . . . nothing but a diseased Irish slut . . ."

The last come from a woman's voice. For men will wound, but women speak to kill.

Just as I approached, Kildare swept out, leading Nellie along. She wore a velvet traveling cloak, with a hood that shadowed her face. The rowdies on the fringe of the crowd hollered about the "ghost girl," and damnation, but the respectable folk made way. You felt a mix of fear and yearning in them, an aching to reach out restrained by a peppery urge to run. A bit of it touched me. For we sensed we had approached a strange frontier, and the safety of what we knew checked the promise of that beyond. A coach waited. Kildare hustled the girl inside.

Neither gave a sign that they had seen me. There are blessings in a certain compactness of physique.

I thought that I had missed my chance—and had, regarding Nellie. But Kildare did not follow his daughter into the vehicle. He shut the door on her and tapped the driver's bench with his walking stick.

The coach pulled off.

A covey of ladies approached Kildare, holding out autograph books. He signed a pair of them, then announced, "I am called, I am called," in that actor-fellow's voice of his. And off he swept, cape trailing.

Now, you will forgive me if I admit I longed to speak to Nellie. I had thought much about her, about her words and doings, and had my bit to say and more to ask. But I count it a good thing that her father packed her off, for it left me no choice but to do my duty. And my duty was to follow Kildare.

I had not inquired for him at the hotels, nor at the police offices. For I did not want him to learn I had come to Rochester. Perhaps the girl knew. I know not what she sensed and what she missed, whether the future was clear as a painted picture to her, or but a boiling up of this and that. But I did not believe she would tell Kildare if she saw me in her visions. For there was more to that situation than the two let on. But let that bide. For now.

I hastened after Kildare, pursuing him into the fog. Away from the lighted front of the hall, the air was thick as guncotton, and the lamps but will-o'-the-wisps, teasing a fellow on. I dared not trail him too closely, and could not see much beyond the length of an arm. So I concentrated on his footsteps, the way we tracked the assassin to his lair in old Lahore. And I will tell you: Not a few British throats were cut in that distant darkness.

Kildare marched along with a purpose, fair slapping the pavement with his walking stick and careless of the ice. Twas hard to keep up with him. I could not use my cane, see. For it makes a wicked racket as I go, and sounds swell in the fog, and he would know it was more than the tapping of a gentleman's stick. So I scurried along, bad leg a bother. Yet, I would not make too much of the discomfort, for I was grateful to have the leg at all. Bull Run had almost won it of me.

We walked a quarter mile, I judge, down streets tucked up and others roiling sin. Where saloons sent out their lighted invitations, I had to slow and let him stretch his lead. Then the sad women called to me, for they imagined—hoped—I had slackened my pace for them.

Now, I would have none of them, as you would not, yet I will not judge the Magdalenes too harshly. For their Hell is here and now, and I had seen more than I wished of their lot in the Fowler case. Only think on it. To stand abroad on an icy night, counting on the Providence you have rejected to guide half a dollar to your bed, is to be damned before you shed your mortal husk. Tis fine to look out from your carriage, with your husband by your side and furs to warm you, madame. But it is a harder thing to look upon that carriage from without. And, if you will pardon me the honesty, not all husbands keep to their carriages when their wives are not by. The heart and flesh meander, and good fortune is not always born of justice.

The girls shivered in their cast-off gowns, while drunken hands played "Camptown Races" loud. Now I am a sufficient man, but know I am not grand or nobly handsome. So I must leave a bit of sympathy even with the wicked when a girl is disappointed by my passing.

I feared that I had lost Kildare's track. After the light of the bars and bawdiness, the fog seemed heavier still. More lost voices called their invitations. Perhaps they marked the queerness of my gait, and thought that I was drunk and fallen, too. Then, in the heavy dark, the voices changed to those of children.

There is sorrow.

I caught Kildare's footsteps again. Distinct and bold they were. Like the slap of his cane. He began to whistle. Shameless.

I shuddered at our surroundings. For I am an old bayonet and know full well the wantonness of men, but do not like to think upon such things as the purchase of a child. My heart hardens at those who would take such advantage. Christian charity deserts me.

"Lo, Kilraine!" a voice called. English as a fox chase.

And yes. He said, "Kilraine," and not "Kildare."

Kildare's footsteps ceased. As did the whistling.

"You're *late*," the Englishman accused. "And I'm *bored*. However *can* one amuse oneself in this . . . *vil*lage? It's duller than Scotland."

"I'm sorry, sir," Kildare said. Oh, twas his voice, and no mistaking. But stripped of pride and power of a sudden. "The performance . . . the first speaker rambled on . . ."

"All right, Kilraine. Done is done. Walk with me, old man. Tell me where we stand."

In that fog, all character was sound. Although I dared not follow closely enough to hear their speech—they lowered their voices as they got on to their business—the contrast of their footfalls and the tapping of their sticks told who was who. Kildare adjusted his pace to his companion, and his cane went out of rhythm. The other fellow strolled, easy as if promenading on Pall Mall, stick touching down lightly. The English gentleman has a way of capturing the world's attention by ignoring it.

I come along behind, trying to be quiet. With my rough stick unused, though it was wanted.

They walked and talked for a fair half hour, the Englishman's voice pitched high but imperious, while Kildare—Kilraine—remained subservient in tone, a debtor who has been told his loan cannot be extended. I ached to hear their words, but feared discovery.

Still, I had gained much. *Kilraine.* Oh, yes, I recalled the name from Mick Tyrone's letter. And isn't the world small for the wicked? But what on earth did the fellow have to do with a high English gentleman who fussed about in alleys where children were bartered? What should he have to do with an Englishman at all, him Irish and mixed up with rumors of Fenian risings, and murder, and mysteries?

One mystery more, that was.

We slipped back into a well-lit world. I recognized a street of better shops and fine hotels. Dull with the cold, a policeman shuffled between the gaslamps.

I yearned to rush forward and have a good look at the Englishman. But more light demanded more distance between us. Still, I saw his outline, slender even dressed for winter and as rigid in his posture as he was rumpled in his associations. I knew the type. They went to schools where there was time for sport, then made each other's sisters unhappy in marriage. The very best of Britannia's officers come of that stock, and the very worst.

They turned into the Waverly Hotel, Rochester's grandest. And that was a blessing, for I was able to watch them through a window as they talked amid plush and palms.

Graceful as a captain at a regimental ball, the Englishman turned toward me.

I *knew* that face. I could not put a name to it, and held it not in personal account. But I *knew* the man. Perhaps through the illustrated papers or the like.

He was pale, though not like Nellie. His complexion spoke of wealth and not of illness. A mustache grassed below a pointed nose. Slim and fair-haired, he was not handsome, but looked as though he expected the world to think him so. He slipped off his coat—twas fashioned with a quarter cape over the shoulders—and his finery set him off from every other fellow in that lobby. When a stout guest bumped him and erupted with apologies, the Englishman merely glanced down as he might at an errant dog.

Oh, the English. They disdain the world until it submits. It is their genius.

He gave Kildare a tap on the chest with the noggin of his stick, then smiled and turned away. As he strolled toward the staircase, the staff cleared a path for him, bobbing up and down like Chinamen.

Kildare stood in a slump. He wore the look of a man who had been taken where he did not want to go, then abandoned.

Snapping into motion, he fled. Trailing fear like a stink. He burst out of the doors before I could get well away, but still he failed to spot me. For all his yapping about visions, he seemed to see nothing at all now. He rushed into the fog and disappeared.

I let him go this time. For I had other matters to attend.

Inside the hotel I went, licensed by my uniform. I gave myself marching orders, since I had to overcome a certain reluctance to take the first step. I was entering upon a matter painful to me, see. Good money might be lost.

The Englishman was up the steps and gone. I picked out the steward who most resembled a quartermaster's sergeant.

"Look you," I said. "A fellow dressed up to the nines dropped this outside." I opened my palm to reveal a five-dollar gold piece. "An English fellow, see."

The steward reached for the money. "I'll give it to him."

I shut my palm. "I would know the man I'm doing proper. Does he have a name, then?"

The fellow looked me over. At first his face was pinched and cold, for he knew I was not a guest of the hotel. And his livery was finer than my uniform. Then he glanced about the lobby. Seeing the other guests were not attentive, he put on a street-corner face and said, "Whatever you're up to, it won't work, Jacko. That soldier get-up of yours won't fool nobody, let alone the likes of him. He's wise to all the tricks, the bastard. That's the Earl of Thretford, the richest man in England, and he don't need no five bucks." The steward held out his hand. "But I'll take it for not putting the coppers onto you."

He had the eye of one born to small triumphs.

I gave the fellow the gold piece without a fuss. For I was stunned like a recruit surrounded in his first engagement.

I shuttled off, leaning upon my cane again. The fog outside seemed welcoming, for my thoughts were dark and unclear.

The Earl of Thretford was not the richest man in England. He was, though, one of the richest, and among the most famous. At a time when the aristocracy despised industry and trade, his father had made investments scorned by his peers. The matter was a scandal in my youth. Now the son owned half of Manchester, a quarter of Sheffield, and at least an eighth of Glasgow. He even had holdings in sad Merthyr, where my father was broken and the Reverend Mr. Griffiths took me in. Arthur Langley, Earl of Thretford, was a great figure in politics, as well, an associate of Palmerston and Russell, and a favored shooting companion of Prince Albert, until that gentleman's tragic demise. To find such a fellow in Rochester, New York, consorting with the likes of Kildare or Kilraine or name him as you will . . .

I had so much to think on that I forgot to regret the gold piece.

THIRTEEN

"WELL, I HAVE BEEN A FOOL," I SAID TO SHERIFF UNDERwood. "And not for the first time, John."

His mighty ears sagged. "Guess that makes two of us, Abel." Consoling himself with a sip of jail-house coffee, he confided, "Never thought this darned job would be so much trouble. Of course, it's different for you, being a detective and all."

Detective?

I put down my tin cup. The jailer had not lost his job over the murder fuss and his scold of a wife retained charge of the cookery. Her coffee was a monstrous, cruel thing, and I pitied the prisoners. But the sheriff had shone a queer light on my doings, and my thoughts turned to myself:

Detective?

My mouth must have hung wide. For I had not considered matters in such a light. I was a military officer, doing my country's duty, and, temporarily, a confidential agent. Detectives were characters in the lowest of the weeklies, intemperate of garment, with little black cigars stuffed in their mouths. The wicked pursuing the wickeder. Had I not been a middle-aged man of thirty-three, I might have thrashed the fellow who called me such.

I let it go. For Underwood and I had other matters before us. And I think he meant it well.

"There is folly," I told him. "That I would fail to see the need of the thing. With even the least suspicion of Kildare, I should have tracked his journeyings. I should have got the authorities to report his meetings and the like. I let the man run wild."

Underwood nodded. "Funny, ain't it? How a thing seems so clear once you're behind it?"

I tapped the floor with my cane, a bad habit I was developing. "If he *is* involved in organizing the Irish for some scheme, then these Mesmerism tours give him the excuse to meet the local leaders." I gave the floorboards a sudden punch with my stick. "It's *worse* than a fool, I am. For even a fool would have seen it."

"What I don't get, though, is this Englishman." Underwood smoothed his mustache. "Rich fella like that. Now what's he up to? I thought the English didn't like the Irish?"

"They like them on their knees, well enough."

He sat back and crossed his arms. "Well . . . what do you make of it, Abel? What do you figure? About this duke fella, or whatever he is?"

The connection between Kildare and the Earl of Thretford made as little sense to me as to Underwood.

"What if he's just another of these spiritualist loonies?" the sheriff continued. "All crazy after seances and funny business like that?"

Now, sanity is not the first virtue of the English aristocracy, but I did not think the earl had come to Rochester in winter to embrace the occult. I shook my head, dismissing the notion.

The sheriff knocked his empty mug on the table. Between me going on with my cane, and him tapping like that, we made a fine racket. We might have been mistaken for seance rappers ourselves.

Underwood had the look of a puzzled child. On his great, red face. "Think he might be after the girl? Cougher or not, the look of her sticks to a fellow."

Given where Kildare—or Kilraine—had met the Earl of Thretford, I did not think the nobleman's interest lay in Nellie.

"It makes no sense to me," I said. "Yet, twas not their first meeting. No, John, they knew each other well, those two.

Master and man, they were. Kildare is on some business for the Englishman, that's sure. And I look for it to be a dark business. But what it is I cannot say."

He placed his paws on the swell of his thighs. "Oh, for crying in a bucket. Why did this Kildare have to pick Yates County? I ask you now. As if we don't have trouble enough with the war." He looked at me with a face that trusted, and I hoped I would not let him down. "Just this morning . . . old Howie Bates was running after me, hollering bloody murder. Wanted me to arrest his oldest boy so's he couldn't join up with the volunteers." Underwood glanced out through a window that wanted a cleaning. "This darned snow gets around to melting, the planting's going to go shy of hands. Houck boys just went off, too. And folks think I should stop 'em somehow."

"That would be wrong," I said. "And unpatriotic."

Underwood grunted. "Well, you try to tell folks that. Then stand for re-election." He looked at me. "War's a terrible thing, Abel. Don't I know it?"

The good man did not know it. For he had never served beneath the colors. Yet, he was right. For there is nothing good to say of war.

The sheriff looked out through the window again, chewing unspoken words.

"Blizzard weather," he said finally. "Look how close that sky is. Every day it holds off, worse it's going to be. Meanest winter I ever saw."

I rose to go. For I had a visit to make. Twas two days since the Rochester performance. I had come back a day late, by coach, so that Kildare would not encounter me on the train and no one might associate my journey with his affairs. The roads had been difficult, and the inns in decline where the railroad did not stop. The coaches were shabby. You felt loss, and change. From Canandaigua south, only sleighs could manage the roads. Where the rails crossed your course, you waited in the cold and watched a locomotive charge the future.

As I was doing up my greatcoat, I said, "Do not worry, John. We will get to the bottom of this." Poor Underwood looked as though the weight of the hills lay upon him. "For good men will put things right in the end." I looked about for my gauntlets, but could not find them. I fear I was distracted.

"Almost forgot to tell you," the sheriff said of a sudden. "Make of *this* what you can. Know who went running up after Kildare soon as he got back?"

"The priest," I said. "McCorkle."

Underwood stared at me, bewildered.

"The Great Kildare," I explained, "has great need of salvation."

Twas more than that, yet I withheld my suspicions from good John Underwood. For I would not accuse any man unjustly, and least of all a man of the cloth. Nor did I want the priest arrested too soon.

"AND MR. DOUGLASS SENDS HIS REGARDS," I said, standing well back.

Reg'lar John Brent nodded, readying a hideous beast for the harness. "Poor old Fred."

Yes. Poor old Fred.

"Well, then, Mr. Brent . . . what news in Penn Yan?" I was struggling to maintain my composure in that stable, for I found the place more loathsome than a snake pit. "Any fusses in my absence?"

He soothed the horse and buckled down the leathers. "I believe the citizens have had excitement enough, sir. The rumors are worrisome, though." He straightened his back for a moment and looked at me. "Major Jones, people are afraid. I'm glad I'm a Negro, and not Irish." He turned to the animal again, testing straps as a good sergeant will check a private's haversack before the march. "The talk of violence and insurrection is getting worse. It's supposed to transpire as soon as the weather breaks. The well-to-do are to be slaughtered in their beds."

"There will be no insurrection, Mr. Brent."

"Yes, sir. We agree on that. The Irish aren't as senseless as all that. But I'm beginning to wonder if there won't be a massacre."

I put my hand on the fellow's shoulder.

"A massacre?"

"Of the Irish," he said, looking at me now. "Fear leads to madness. And madness rides the stallion of violence." He patted the horse, which answered with a little neigh. "Some of the hotheads may get a mind to do unto the Irish before the Irish can do unto them."

I had not thought of things in that light. And felt the fool again.

Douglass had been right. John Brent was a clever man, and well-spoken, when we two were alone. He read relentlessly. That appetite for learning had cost him lashes before he ran north, and had cost him many a penny candle since.

"There will be no massacre of the Irish," I assured him. As if to reassure myself. "Sheriff Underwood will see to that. But . . . you agree with me, then? There's no Irish rebellion in the wind? It's all nonsense?"

You see, I had begun to doubt myself.

He lifted a second harness from the hooks on the wall, lugging it toward a great black snorter.

"Major Jones, have you ever visited our Southern states?"

I had seen the camps of northern Virginia, and served in one ill-starred battle on Dixie's soil. But that was not what the good fellow meant.

"No, sir, I have not."

He stroked and soothed the horse, then deftly slipped the straps and bridling over it. "Well, the citizens of our Southland live in constant fear of slave rebellions. It's a madness with them. A curse upon them, I would say." He bent to cinch the belly strap. "It doesn't matter that slave rebellions have been few, and small, and every one a failure. Or that the cost to the black man has ever been immeasurably greater than to his white master." I caught the corner of a smile on his turned-away face. Twas a bitter thing, although he was no bitter man. "Even old Nat Turner killed less of those folks than they kill of themselves every year, with their dueling and drinking and horse racing. And now this war. Yet, they live in constant fear of the man they hold in bondage."

The brittle smile changed. I could see but a fraction of his face, for he worked as he talked, yet his expression was as complex as any I have seen on a man. "You might even say there's a measure of justice in it," he continued. "In that fear of theirs. They've created their own nightmare. Surrounded themselves with it. Oh, they're fanatical about the notion of male bravery. The frightened are always obsessed with courage, Major Jones. But I suspect you know that, from your military endeavors." He wiped his brow with a coatsleeve, sweating in the cold. "I promise you, sir, this war will not be short. The Southron would rather die than admit his fears. Or face up to the error of his ways."

He turned his head and I could not see his face at all. He spoke to an invisible audience. "Whenever the fear becomes too great, these paragons of manhood take a stiff drink of whisky and hang a black man, or two—or ten—from a tree. Nor is hanging enough. Their victims are abused, sir. With abuses worse than those credited to our Irish." He managed a faint laugh. "They say it is done to teach my kind a lesson. But we know it is evidence of their fears. They live in terror of the world they've wrought."

I longed to leave that stew of horsestink and grunting and the banging of stalls behind me. But I wanted the wisdom of John Brent even more than I wanted to escape. Once upon the road, there were limits to the depths of a conversation. I stepped next to him, hungry to know more.

"But . . . you don't believe there will be a slave rising, Mr. Brent? Even now? With our forces marching to the succor of the black man?"

He looked at me. For an instant, derision commanded his features. It soon dissolved into sorrow.

"Major Jones," he said, "I believe you're an honest man and a good Christian. So I'll honor you with a frank answer. No. There will be no slave rebellion. Firstly, because the armies of our Union aren't marching much of anywhere, at the moment. Unless that squabbling out west amounts to something. Secondly, when they do march, they will march for their own advantage, not to free the black man. Our freedom, should it come, will be incidental. Until we, too, are allowed to serve in uniform, many will see such freedoms as may be granted us as unearned and undeserved."

His head fell as he turned to finish with the second horse. "The condition of the Negro resembles that of the Irishman, Major Jones. Although the latter is not held in chains. Neither will rebel, for each is too downtrodden. Consider our American Revolution. Was it made by the wretched? No, sir. It was made by gentlemen. Even Mr. Paine, whom I admire, did not write for the slave. He aimed his volleys upward, sir." He paused in his labors and looked at me. "Even the subsequent events in France, the Reign of Terror, must be blamed on the educated—sometimes I fear my own books. But then I turn again unto the Gospels." He shook his head in sorrow. "It's the well-fed who rise up. In hopes of being better-fed still."

He led the black, tugging on its bridle. I gave the creature plenty of space. "It's never the poor who make the revolutions," he said. "They swell the crowd, but do not rise until aroused by men who otherwise despise them, men who use them for their own ends. No, sir. The poor do not spend their time thinking about high ideals, but about bread and the avoidance of the lash . . . about gaining a bit of shelter for their families, if such they are allowed to have . . . and about living through each day. Easy, boy, easy now. That's just our friend, the major. No, the Irish will not rise. Not without a leader from another class. Even then, they'll need convincing. They know they have it better than they might. Why, I'd even wager that—"

Other footsteps trod upon the planks, and a sharp voice called for service. Twas a gentleman of the town, whom I had passed a time or two.

"Yassuh," John Brent answered, crimping down his shoulders and shuffling as he guided the horse toward the light. "Yassuh, Mistuh Farnum. Reg'lar John's a-coming. Ooooh, I be coming like I'se bee-stung. *Yas*suh."

I ASKED JOHN BRENT to take me to the highlands, to the heath that Nellie loved.

I knew she would be there.

The clouds hung plump and low, with a dirty look. As though the coming snow would fall unclean. The horizon closed, and the snow-clad earth showed lighter than the sky. I knew John Brent did not want to go up there, but go the good man did.

I had no fear of Nellie. But she was not alone in that half-forgotten world of moors and glens. I carried my Colt, belted beneath my greatcoat.

Twas cold. But now it was only discomfort and not misery that I felt, for I had my health again. At least, my health of body. My soul remained a vexed and troubled thing.

No singing now, not from John Brent nor me. No hymns or sprightly tunes to pass the miles. Those black-bellied clouds would not have it. And the road had thawed and frozen again. Reg'lar John had to pay attention, to keep the horses from breaking their legs. The sleigh skittered from side to side, threatening to plunge into a ditch.

We passed the taverns, Bull Run and Manassas, shut against the cold but plumed with smoke. The quiet was not of slumber, but of a world holding its breath.

No living creature showed itself. Even the birds were in hiding.

He knew his way, John Brent. He followed trails I had forgotten, where no sleigh or wagon had passed for weeks. Often, there was no track at all. He found his way by judging lines of trees and marking the shanties in the hollows.

Then we saw the hoofmarks. Plunging down the lane beyond our team.

Twas her. I knew it. Out riding. As if she could outrace death.

The heavens sat so low she seemed enfolded: A black wraith at the border of the world. There were no grand perspectives now, no endless ridges or burning twilights. Only the gunpowder gray of the sky, and the old-bandage color of the snow. As if a battle had been fought and lost. With only the girl left standing.

I got down from the sleigh. Recalling the wind from the time before, and my own desperation. Now the world held still. No flags of hair, no blowing capes. Only the smallness of her form across the heath.

"Careful, sir," John Brent said in a hushed voice. "Step clear of the places where the snow's sunken down. The ponds don't freeze properly up here."

I left him blanketing his horses.

She had been waiting for me. The Lord only knew how long she had been waiting. In that cold.

For me.

I trudged toward her, with the snow crusted hard. In the troughs between the drifts, my boots squeaked. I did not sink this time. I walked above the earth.

Like her.

Only I went like an old man, hands buried in my pockets. For I never had found my gauntlets.

She turned before I reached her. Perhaps at the sound of my boots. Or at the bidding of her spirits.

The snow had iced over where the earth fell away. I wondered how she kept her balance. So fearsomely close to the edge.

A new fur cap warmed her. Twas a dark, rich thing. Her hair fell from it.

"I thought you'd come to me in Rochester," she said. "After the performance."

"Miss Kildare—"

"Then I realized you had to follow my father. I understood."

"You saw me, then?"

"I knew you were there. I always know when you're there."

"But you didn't tell Kildare. Did you?"

She shook her head. "We cannot change the—"

"You didn't tell him," I said, "because you *want* me to kill him."

She gasped. Struck in the heart by a bullet of words.

"I . . . never . . . my father . . . I . . ."

"Stop it. He's not your father. He's no more your father than I am."

She bent over. I thought a fit had seized her, and feared she would tumble backward into the abyss. But twas only sorrow.

"I never wanted . . . I . . ."

I moved toward her. Carefully. And took her by the arm. Drawing her away from the ledge.

"I never wanted . . ."

"I know, girl, I know. I spoke too hard. We do not always see the thing we want." I smelled her sickness and her sweetness. The ends of her hair brushed the hand I had fixed upon her. Beneath the heavy sleeves I felt a wasting.

She wept.

"Does he . . . abuse you?" I asked her.

She shook her head. "It was worse in the madhouse. Please, don't let them take me back there."

Now you will say, "He must have been amazed at such an utterance." But I was not. For I had been thinking long on the matter. Look you. We label "madness" all that asks too much. For we want peace, and not cruel revelation. We have less patience with the seer than the sinner, and shun the least discomfort of the mind. When the parlor games are done, we'll have no spirits.

"Don't let them take me back there," she repeated. "Promise me."

"I promise," I said. And I meant it, Lord help me. "I will not let them take you to such a place again. For you don't belong there."

I was holding her like a child by then, though I know not how we come to it. She wept against the rough nap of my coat. Head upon my shoulder.

"I only want them to leave me alone," she whispered. "But they never will."

"It's all right," I said, though it was not.

"I can't explain it. Sure, and I'd tell it all to you, if I could."

"I know."

"She came to me again. By day. She told me all. She had a message for you."

I laid a finger across her lips. Her flesh was fever hot, her temples wet.

"I'll have no message, girl," I said gently. "For we must let the dead go. Twas me you heard, not her. I was the one who kept her from her rest."

I did not know if such a thing was true. I do not know if any of it was true, or if it was only Mesmerism and dreams. Let philosophers and men of science argue about such like. I only know the dying girl believed. And for that moment, I believed with her. Thereafter, I was free of it. But let that bide.

"It's all that I can give you," she said. "My visions."

"You have given me what I need, see. And there's an end to it."

"I've tried to find out for you. About his doings. With the Irish. But he tells me nothing. He locks me in my room. The way they did in the madhouse. Only now . . . he's the only one who comes to me. Who comes to me that way. It's better so. He's the only one. And he isn't cruel. He's not a cruel man. He doesn't hurt me. But he doesn't tell me the things you want to know. He says he'll put me back in the madhouse, if I don't do what he wants. I'd rather die than go back . . ."

"No one will—"

"*You can't know what it's like.* No one can know. The screaming. They never stop screaming. I'm not like them. I hurt no one, sir. Even when they let me be, I never can sleep for the screaming."

Twas then I understood her love of those highlands. And of their silence.

"Nellie, I must ask you—"

"I know," she said, shutting her eyes and squeezing more tears free.

"I *must* ask you about these matters. It is my duty, see. You say he tells you nothing. But when last we stood here . . . you insisted there'd be no insurrection, no rebellion. You seemed certain."

"I know there's none, sir."

"Do the spirits tell you that?" I was struggling to sort reality from madness. "Please, girl. Try to think clearly. How do you know such a thing?"

The clouds had lowered around us. We stood alone in the world.

"From the men he keeps about the yard. The O'Haras." I felt her body tense as if frighted. By one of her thousand ghosts. "They . . . came to me once. To my room. When he was away. They . . . only did it that once . . . they were drunk . . ."

I held her close and shut my own eyes, too. We might have been falling down over the edge of the heath, over the edge of the world.

" . . . they laughed afterwards . . . they . . . asked me if I'd be a princess . . . when Kildare was King of the French. You see? There's nothing like rebellion in the air. It's all a lark. For he'll never be king of the French. He's mad, too."

"You're not mad," I said. I knew not what she was, but would not shame her with a curse of "madness." Was she less sound than those who made this war? Or those who excused bondage from their pulpits?

I let her weep for a bit, then broke her hold. "You must come with me now. It's over, all this 'Great Kildare' business. We'll take good—"

She tore away from me. Face repelled, eyes gone to great horizons. She shook her head with the abandon of a child, whipping her hair from side to side.

"*No,*" she said. "They'll put me in the madhouse, sure. You don't understand."

"I won't let them. I promise you."

The shaking of her head slowed, and the sweep of her hair with it. "You won't be able to stop them. I know you want to help me. The spirits told me long ago. Your spirit's tall and strong. But you won't be able to stop them."

"You can't go on like this . . . Nellie . . . *please* . . . let me see you safe and cared for."

"I can't go with you," she said.

"Why?" Twas I who was the stubborn child now.

"Because you have your life. And I'm no part of it. Because you do not know the thing you want yourself. For men are blind, where women see."

"Why won't you come with me, girl? I'll see that you're looked after. There are good people in the world. They're not all like Kildare."

She laughed. "He's far from the worst."

"Come with me."

"No."

"Why, then?"

She mustered the saddest smile in the world. "Because I'm dying. Tis no secret, sir. And I won't die inside their walls." She looked around at the snow-clad world. "I'd rather freeze than die where they'd put me."

"My church could organize something for you. There are so many good people. Why, I could even take you to my own—"

She laid her fingers over my lips this time, for twas her turn to do the hushing. She wore no gloves herself, and her fingers were as cold as her lips had been fiery. "You can't ask as much of others as you do of yourself. Take your happiness. Have joy of it. Don't bring in temptation."

"Miss Kildare, I assure you—"

The smile turned wistful now. "We're twined, you and I. Two castaways. I've become her, don't you see? She's so warm. And

I've felt only cold for so long." She wiped a reddened hand across her eyes. "Now go. And leave me what I have."

"I can't just go."

She closed her eyes and breathed so deeply it lifted the bosom of her coat. "It's so wonderful up here. The smell. The clean smell. For years, I smelled only the madhouse." She breathed again, glutting herself on the frozen air.

"I can't just leave you," I said.

The deep breaths had calmed her. She laid her hand upon the sleeve of my coat.

"I'm not afraid of the dying," she told me. "I'm only afraid of dying their way."

"Please . . . you mustn't give up . . ."

She laughed. Lightly. Amused. But when she spoke, the laughter lay a thousand years behind her.

"I just want to die where it's clean."

And then the great gulps she had taken of the sky turned against her. She began to cough, naught but a sick girl now. Coughing and coughing. I moved to help her, but she thrust out a hand to keep me back. Staggering off into the field.

"Nellie!"

She bent as if retching. Gagging and gasping. Spitting upon the snow.

I went after her, but she had passed beyond me. She used the last of her will to straighten and warn me off.

"Leave me now."

"Come *with* me. For the love of God."

She shook her head and silenced me one last time. You could not paint such sorrow in a face.

"We'll never meet again," she said.

Twas final. I cannot tell you why, but I obeyed her. I watched until she was but a shadow in the gray. Then she was nothing at all. Hoofbeats galloped into eternity. They had naught to do with a living girl.

I looked down, and saw her blood upon the snow.

FOURTEEN

"A MYSTERY!" THE REVEREND MR. MORRIS CRIED. "A mystery, Major Jones! I found it there, just there." He pointed at the barren kitchen table. "A note, a note! For you!" He extended a filthy paper, folded up square.

to majur jones

"Spies and stratagems!" the good preacher continued. "Sneaking about, sneaking about! It was lying right there."

The fellow did not seem the least bit alarmed by the intrusion into his parsonage. Instead, he was excited. But think you of a country parson's life. He is a witness to sorrows repetitive, which he must share, but he is seldom called when joys are divvied out. And Morris had no wife. We spoke about the Bible in the evenings, and he wished to hear more about India than I could bear to tell him, and he brought me hard-wrought sermons to review. He wanted a friend, and I was all he got.

I unfolded the missive, with my greatcoat still upon me. And read:

atuk fart

Well, twas a wonder Molloy could write at all. If he could not spell "Attock Fort," he knew how to have a note delivered cleanly, and how to see a dirty day's work well done.

We had agreed he would contact me when he had news worth the telling. Our two-word code—wrought of our shared past—meant I would meet him in Hammondsport, at the other end of the lake, the day after I received his communication. I hoped eyes might be less watchful in another county.

"Is it a great secret?" Mr. Morris asked, with the eager face of a child. "Is it a secret?"

"Yes," I told him. "It is a very great secret, see. Now you are party to a high government matter, and lives depend upon your silence."

Oh, wasn't the poor fellow delighted. "I'll never tell," he said. "Not a word, sir, not one word. I'll go to the grave with the knowledge locked in my breast . . ."

I only meant to give him what he longed for, and no harm done. For who would not have a feeling of importance added to his life? Still, the fellow needed calming.

"There will be no great hurry," I told him, "about anybody going to the grave. We'll keep our secret quiet, you and I."

The fellow kept his silence. I wish I had been right about the grave.

IN THE MORNING, before I left for Hammondsport, I went to see Father McCorkle. To make a last plea.

"He's over ta church," the housekeep told me. "Praying for all ye sinners, and ta take off the snows."

Well, he was in the church, but not at prayer. I entered as quietly as I could, with no wish to disturb his talk with the Lord, but found him sitting below the altar, humming and polishing a communion cup. He did not raise his eyes, but went on with his doings, scrubbing the shining chalice with a fury.

I cleared my throat.

He remained bent over the cup. "Tis late enough ye come," he said. "The boards want a proper scrubbing today, not just a sweep o' the broom."

"Father McCorkle?"

He lifted those black brows. With a look first of surprise, then of wariness.

"Sorry to disturb, sir," I told him.

He set the chalice down, but held onto the cloth. "Ye've been a disturbance to me since the day ye arrived. Will there be no end to this nonsense, Major Jones?"

I stepped down the aisle. Into the cold depths of the place.

"There will be an end. And soon enough."

"Are ye leaving us then?"

He did not bid me sit, so I stood before him. "I will go. When my duty is done."

"And when might that be, pray tell?"

Now a man of the cloth must be an actor in our Lord's theater, if you will forgive such comparison, for his despair must not show, and he must impart hope where none belongs, and he must hear things decent ears would shun, and listen without meanness. McCorkle was a master of his roles. I sensed the return of the hostility he had shown me when they fished up the drowned girl. But it lay in the air, and not upon his features.

"I will go," I said, "when Kildare has been stopped. From whatever it is he is doing. I admit I know not what he's up to. But there is trouble. And I will stop it, see. And I will stop you, too." I did not falter under those fierce eyes. "I know you are a party to the business."

He put on his Irishness, and gave me the face they give the tax collector. "I don't know what you're talking about, Jones. And look at ye. All raging in here like a madman, and bursting with accusations. Have ye no sense o' decency, man?"

But I was not raging. My voice was calm. And I was decent and not mad.

"I suspect," I continued, "that it is some scheme to advance your Irish. And that there is great wrong in it. I do not know what has moved you to go along. Although I know you would favor the poor. But the business will end badly. And, if there is violence, it will end badly, indeed." I leaned forward, hands closed over the ball of my cane. As if I might weigh down upon the priest. "Consider the fears you're rousing. And all that might come of it. If the people of this county turn upon your flock. Then there will be blood. And an end to advancement. Is that what you want for your Irish?"

He looked at me like a cocky private, not a priest.

"Are ye threatening me then, Major?"

Twas the last thing I intended. "Look you, Father McCorkle. I'm doing my best to help. Lay aside these schemes, whatever they may be. They'll do no good, see. Turn from the business and help me."

He called up a smile. Twas meant to look jovial. But it was mean.

"Sure, and don't your people like to say that God helps those who help themselves? And don't they think it's fine to free the nigger, that pious lot o' yours? While letting the Irishman rot?" He sighed, with a sound more like a snore. "Here ye've gotten me talking all theoretical. And I'm patient with ye out o' pity. For it appears that poor Morris's silliness has gotten to ye. All his talking spirits and queer doings. Why, ye've been talking mad enough to want locking up."

"It is not Abel Jones who will see the other side of the lock."

His smile withered to a twisted thing. Still a smile. But merciless as famine.

"No," he said, "it may not be. But tell me, major. What do ye think o' the girl? Our Nellie?"

I did not see how she came into this.

"And what should I think of her?"

"Well . . . I'm hearing evidences that she's naught but a madwoman herself. I even hear she was locked away in the past, and for more than a fortnight. To keep her off o' decent folk, it was. And for her own protection. I wonder . . . if twould not be better to see her safely shut away again?"

There was wicked.

I smiled. Twas grim as any smile I ever wore. Over the nakedness of his doings. But I could not find one word to fit to this.

Of course, Kildare knew all, and would have shared the knowledge. My experiences during the seance come because the fellow had hypnotized me along with Nellie. Worried, I had asked poor Morris to recount all that had transpired that evening. The man knew nothing of a spirit from far India, though he had been sitting just across the table. The business had been all inside my head. Or twixt Nellie and me.

And now I saw the full extent of my blindness. Twas plain as day, and so obvious you have doubtless figured it before me. Kildare knew *all* that passed between me and the girl. And the poor child did not even know what she told him. For he had only to hypnotize her and have her recite, then order her to forget the recitation. She was his human tool. He knew my fears as well as he knew hers.

And he knew that I cared for her. Not in the way I cared for my wife, mind you. Or for my lost love of India. Nothing improper. But in a way for which we have no words. Kildare knew that I would not want her harmed. And he forewarned the priest.

I was not laboring against a world of gossamer spirits, but against the viciousness of men. Sharpened to a point.

"You'll leave the girl alone," I cried. But well I sensed my weakness.

No doubt, the priest did, too. Twas his vocation. He raised one eyebrow, and held up a weathered hand. "Oh, twould only be for the girl's own good, the confinement. For we cannot have her doing herself harm. Tis against the Church and true religion. To say nothing o' the meanness in neglecting the helpless likes o' herself. Letting her gallivant about in the cold, when everyone knows it only does her an injury."

Unbidden or not, I sat down. You see, I was unprepared for such cruelty, no matter all that I had seen in life.

Now you will say, "That priest was evil, and no true man of God." But I do not think it so. He did an evil thing that day. I will not excuse it. Yet, even then, I saw what it cost him. He hoped that he might do a greater good. McCorkle was, in truth, a saintly man, and such are ever prone to cruelty.

"I . . . will not permit it," I told him.

He raised both eyebrows now, and gave a laugh. "Oh, ye won't? And are ye her father then? Or family elsewise? What rights will ye call upon, and what laws?" His smile worsened. "For all the commotion, wicked minds might start to think ye'd taken advantage o' the poor child. Given such deep concerns, and ye no relation to her."

I ignored the worst of it, for twas meant to provoke. I only said, "Kildare is not her father."

"Oh, and is he not? Would legal papers lie? Why, ye'd have the devil's own time proving such a thing. I'd have to pity ye the shameless attempt."

"And his name's not Kildare. It's Kilraine."

Oh, yes. I saw a flicker in his eyes at that. But, fool me, I did not pursue it. For my mind was not a clear thing at the moment.

"It matters not a bit," the priest said, "whatever his name is."

"You'll kill her if you lock her up."

He shrugged. "An't the poor child dying already? Oh, tis a torment to see her." He held out a hand that was not meant to help. "Would it not be better . . . to see the poor thing warm and comforted as she goes?"

"I won't let you do it," I said again. "And I won't be alone. I'll have Mr. Morris on my side. And all the others who know her. Powerful people . . ."

This time he laughed out loud, bending down and shaking his head. "Oh, ye little Welsh fool," he said. With tears of laughter starting from his eyes. "Sure, and I can see ye've never been a priest or such like, for ye know not the first bit about your fellows. Do ye really think, then, that the good citizens will rally to the girl, when they learn they've all been made into laughingstocks? Taken in by a mad girl, fresh from the asylum? With her ramblings o' spirits and the like? And them all reverent and believing and open o' purse? How do ye really think such folk will be, when they learn they've been made into asses?"

I sat there in my greatcoat. Smaller than any man should be.

"What do you want?" I asked, after a long time had passed.

He became the practical man again. In outward form, at least.

"Oh, tis little enough, Major Jones. I'd only have ye cease your pestering. Let my flock go its way. And Kildare, too. For I promise ye, as I've done a dozen times, that there'll be no harm to your cherished Union, nor to the good people o' this town. Or to the bad ones, for that matter." His deep eyes stared into me. "Just mind your business. And we'll all leave Nellie to her foolishness."

I stood up.

"There's a good fellow now," McCorkle went on. "Don't go bothering where ye don't belong, and we'll none o' us see any harm. As you're a Christian man, will ye only agree to that?"

REG'LAR JOHN BRENT HAD KNOWN ME long enough to sense I was not in a sociable mood. He guided the horses and left me to my grump. Oh, I was in a stew. For you will think me a simpleton in the ways of the world, but I will not accept injustice. To think of what they would do to a dying girl to further their purposes covered the world in ugliness deeper than any snow.

And still I did not know the purposes they meant to further. I hoped Jimmy Molloy would have my answers, and not just blarney spent to warm the air.

We traveled down the west side of the lake, by a low, straight road that ran through tidy villages. Those whose work brought them out of doors took time to wave as we passed. It was a different world from those highlands east of the lake, where death and cruelty hid behind the beauty. The harness creaked and jingled as we slid along. The clouds drooped down, covering the hills and ridges, and the cold come off the lake to hurt your bones. Yet, this side of the lake felt all at peace, the houses built by men of sound decision.

With a snap of the whip, we passed a farmer's wagon.

"Major Jones?" John Brent leaned back toward me. "May I ask you, sir, if you plan a lengthy visit in Hammondsport?"

There was a note of concern in his voice. I wondered if there was danger for the fellow in the village, as well as in the high country.

"We will see, Mr. Brent. A problem is it?"

He nodded at the lowering sky. "I do believe we'll have a heavy snowfall. I was surprised it didn't begin yesterday. Feels like a big one coming."

"I will do my best to waste no time, then."

I hoped Molloy would be there. Waiting. Though he had been a thief and given to drink, I trusted his skills and his promise.

I pondered over Nellie as we drove. Trying to imagine the terrors and devils that beset her, and all of her own mind's making. No, that was not true. For her terror of the asylum was no fantasy, nor was the danger Kildare would betray her. I wished that I might see things through her eyes. But we are ever separate from each other, and she more so than most.

Sometimes, when my spirits weaken, I see our Savior's cross as naught but lonely.

I thought of her, so vivid in the snow, telling me we would not meet again.

Again, I wondered what she truly knew. Longing to rescue her from both her worlds. There was sadness. For I knew even then that I would fail her.

I pulled the travel rug tighter.

The south end of the lake drew in like a string bag. We saw the frozen boats and shoreline buildings. Hammondsport slept out the winter's day under a gray blanket. Ramshackle, the shops and low hotels looked too dull for serious vice. I knew there were pleasant houses higher up the hill, with a fine little army of Methodists to give the village mettle. I recalled that the townspeople—not the Methodists, mind you—had a scheme of growing rich by raising grapes for wine. I thought them just as likely to strike gold. For Temperance will put an end to drink in our lifetimes. Then where will such ambitions find themselves?

There was no masking my arrival, for small towns have eyes for things they should not see. I told John Brent to drive right up past the shops on the square, to lay aside suspicion. Then I had him stop before the Rhys home—abode of a fine Welsh family, whose welcome I had enjoyed on a previous visit.

Methodists, too. Twas a sober, pleasant house, set on the hillside, not far from where a high stone mill stood derelict.

The path was clear of ice and snow, for the Welsh are conscientious. I gave the door a rap.

Mrs. Rhys appeared in her apron, cleaning her hands from her kitchen business. She was surprised, of course.

"Why, Major Jones! A visit is it? There is good. Inside with you, then, for the heat will go out and the cold come in."

Now I am a proud American, and if you find a prouder let me know. But there is lovely to hear the lilt of the homeland in a voice.

And a fine visit it might have been, for the Welsh will cook you up proper, and not let you rise until your belly is so full of good things that you fear you cannot rise at all. But I had my duty.

"Mrs. Rhys . . . I was but passing, see. And wished to say hello. Is Mr. Rhys at home, then?"

"Missed him by a whisker, you did. He's back to the shop with his dinner in him."

"It's greetings I would leave him."

"But, surely, we'll have you for supper, Major Jones?"

"I cannot stay, mum. For there is duty to our government."

She shook her head in warm, Welsh sympathy—there is none finer or more sincere, I will tell you. For we are not like the English, who only have you in to get you gone. Twas cruel to come and not stay on to eat.

"Ah," she sighed, "isn't duty a terrible thing?"

"Mrs. Rhys . . . I have a thing to ask."

"Well, ask you, then."

"I would . . . like to visit your privy."

She shivered at the very thought. "You'll freeze to the marrow. And need there's none. For there's a pot in the cellar."

"I would . . . if you don't mind . . . rather use the outhouse."

She made a face. "Shy now, is he? And doesn't he know what it's like when you're ten to the house and no secrets?"

"I beg you, mum. Let me use your outhouse."

She rolled her eyes and slapped her hands on her apron. Miffed. "Won't stay to eat, he won't. But he'll go off traipsing through the snows on us. Is that the duty you're after doing? Well, go you, then. You know where the door lies."

I hurried through the house and out the back. Shutting myself in the frigid cabin, I peeked through the air hole until I saw that Mrs. Rhys was well away from her windows. And then I was out the door and into the trees.

I made my way through drifts and thickets, testing my way with my cane and thrashing down brush. Twas good it was not summer. For I was alone, unbothered by child or dog. Or prying eyes. I crossed a steep road cut into a hollow, then turned downward. The mill loomed, its knocked-out windows blackened eyes. You could see the man who built it had grand hopes, though they were dashed. Not old, the mill stood abandoned but for a part of the ground floor locked up for storage.

I did not see Molloy. I worked my way up to the wall facing the steep of the hillside and scanned about me. Cold stone, snow and trees. I did not want to walk around the building, for the opposite side faced a street, with houses on the other side. I hoped Molloy was not so foolish as to put himself on display for all to see.

Twas cold, and I fear I did a bit of Quaker dancing to keep me warm. The clouds crawled down the hills, and I well remembered John Brent's fear of snow. I could not afford to be trapped here while great events transpired without me.

Shivering, I leaned against a window sill. To ease the moment's pressure on my leg.

A hand grabbed me.

Molloy it was. Putting the fear of dacoits and assassins into me. He crawled out of the building. In which he had no right to be. For that was private property.

"I didn't know ye was a gandy dancer," he said, with that mile-wide grin on his mug. "Oh, me darling man, ye'll set me to admiring the Welsh yet."

I resumed my usual dignity. "Are you all right, then? No harm's come to you, Molloy?"

"Oh, a rare day that'll be, when the likes o' them troubles Jimmy Molloy. Major Jones, ye've no idea the great fools they are. They're touched in the head every one. Ye'd get to thinking there's something in the air up here."

Molloy was one of those odd fellows who appear dapper even in threadbare clothes. In a low manner, of course. He looked a sight, in his battered derby and overcoat.

And a welcome sight, if I am to be honest. For I felt more affection for the fellow than I like to say. I will not have you think me too soft-hearted, or the dupe of a confidence man. But he was brave, see. Irish though he was, he had his qualities.

"Tell me," I demanded. "Tell me what you've learned, man."

"Oh, an't it an embarrassment for the glorious Irish race? Tis the silliest thing I've heard tell in me life. Kildare leading 'em round by the snouts, and them following at his heels like the dumbest o' sepoys, all faith and nary a question. And the O'Hara boys, trading in government rifles and—"

"What's that? Government rifles?"

He looked at me. Amazed. "Well, blind me with a stick if I didn't think ye knew that much, at least? Ye didn't know about the guns they're after buying? And with gold, too? Direct from the arsenal, and sold by your fine Federal officers." He made a face of absolute disgust. "Oh, I've never trusted an officer in me life, and there ye see why." He glanced at me, then added, "Present company excepted, o' course. But then ye was a sergeant in your prime . . ."

"*Why* are they buying the guns, Molloy? How many? Where are they keeping them? What are—"

"Oh, Katie bar the door, for the man thinks he's a rushing racehorse. Would ye hold onto your drawers, Sergeant Jones?"

"'Major' Jones, thank you."

"Well, Major, sir, just let me get me answers out, so's we can look at 'em teeth to tail in the light o' day. Now first off, I can't say all what they've bought in the past, but I know they just bought fifty Enfield rifles. Fine and handy they are, too."

"How do you know that?"

"How do I know? Didn't I just unload 'em meself, and me with the pain in me back where that Seekh fellow put his boot till ye shot his face off. Why, do ye remember that day—"

"Where did you unload them?"

"Oh, up to the barn. On the farm where Kildare hangs his hat. With that quare, blazing daughter o' his, and an't that a shame the decay o' her?"

"Kildare has government rifles in his barn?"

"Well, government rifles they were. But now they're his."

"Is there anything else in the barn?"

He thought for a moment. "Only the uniforms. And a cow and a couple o' horses."

"Uniforms?"

"For the Fenian army. And handsome green, they are. Like the sacred flag o' Erin." He stopped and gave me another baffled look. "Ye didn't know that, either?"

"What's the army for? How big is it? What are they planning to do? And . . . how did you get them to trust you to such an extent?"

Molloy looked many things—he had a knack for disguises, that one—but I do not think he ever looked trustworthy. Of course, the Irish probably judge differently.

"Trust me? Sure, and don't they all love me? If it wan't all such a lunacy, I'd be tempted to join 'em meself. Treat me proper, they do. As befits a former sergeant o' Her Britannic Majesty, who can teach 'em how to stand-to proper, and to march and fix a bayonet."

"You were never a sergeant, Molloy. And your corporalcy didn't last six months."

Exasperation twisted that rubber face. "Sure, and didn't I have to tell 'em something? To convince 'em I'm worth the trusting?"

Yes. Of course. But I did not like his pretense to a sergeancy. For rank was hard-earned under the sun of India.

"I hope you're not teaching them too much," I said. "Or too well."

"And what would it matter, me darling man? For all their doings are no more than hoopla." He looked up the hillside as if looking into the future, and his face saddened. For he, too, was capable of sincere emotion. "Don't I hate the thought o' the boys dying by the dozen and marching off into captivity? For excepting Kildare and that Napper and Bull O'Hara, they're naught but poor bogtrotters all tricked into throwing their lives away. As if they'd ever teach the Queen a lesson. No matter how many hundred Kildare says he's raised in the cities. They won't make it through their first battle."

I grasped him by the arm. To force an answer. "For God's sake, man. What are you talking about? With your 'teaching the Queen a lesson,' and battles and hundreds of men?"

He shrugged. "The invasion o' Canada. What else?"

Well, that made me skip a breath. I watched a gray bird hop across the snow. And back again. Twas Molloy broke the silence, not me.

"Now an't that the craziest thing what ye've heard, Major Jones? An invasion o' the Queen's American dominions! And the Frenchies supposed to rise up in Kewbeck, as if a Frenchman could ever be trusted to raise a hand before the battle was won. And them going to set up an Irish kingdom, with the Frenchies in it, too, and all with a mob o' Mayo boys what an't got the alphabet between 'em."

"Canada," I said. To the frozen air.

"An't that the craziest thing ye've heard?" Molloy went on. "Twould never come off in a thousand years. So have no fears. There's no rebellion against the Union or such. Naught but a crazy scheme that will never work."

"It's not supposed to work," I said softly. For I saw it all now. Every bit.

Molloy looked at me oddly. I never knew him at a loss for words, but he took a moment to find his way back to speech this time. He reset the hat upon his head and his eyes hunted over me.

"Now . . . Major Jones. Would ye only be telling me the riddle o' that? Here's great preparations, and men all incited to die to avenge dear, old Ireland, with lovely, oiled guns, and all set to go as soon as the ice melts so's they can get across the river into Canada. And a priest to bless them on their bloody way. And . . . ye say it's not supposed to work? Now where would be the sense in that?"

"Molloy," I said, bucking up my spine, "if you were still in uniform, I'd see you decorated. You've done your country a noteworthy service. And now I need you to do another." I looked into that long-familiar face, into the eyes that were never serious even in a regimental lockup, at the mouth born to smile at life. The risk to him was greater than he realized. Or perhaps he did realize it. For Jimmy Molloy was never a coward, I must give him that.

"Ye'll be wanting me to keep watch over them still," he said.

"Yes. And you must let me know the instant they're about to move. The very instant, Molloy."

"But couldn't ye just go out and arrest 'em? With what I've told ye already?"

I shook my head. "It's best to take them in the deed. If only at the beginning. With weapons in hand, and all the men identified."

The skin tightened around his eyes. A troubled look, that. "Sure, Major Jones, sir. The boys don't know what they're about, and I'd hate to see 'em come to needless harm. Without Kildare they'd do nothing. For he's only talked 'em all into the doings, and they have no sense o' the foolishness."

"No man will come to harm unnecessarily. But we must make a thorough cleaning. Or the business will be tried again. And next time, your countrymen will bleed."

He tipped his hat forward and gave his hair a scratch. Lice, probably. "Well, I'll do it for ye. As ye know I will. And I'll move heaven and earth to let ye know the minute they're set to move. But I pity them, I do."

"There's a good soldier, Molloy."

He smiled wistfully. "I'm not a soldier anymore, Major Jones."

"No. Of course not. I forgot."

"Sure, and it's nothing. It's only old times ye were thinking on. But I would have one thing o' ye. For curious I ever was, and ye know it."

"What's that?"

"Just what I asked ye. What did ye mean that this invasion scheme's not intended to succeed? For what could be the sense in the likes o' that?"

"If I tell you, your life might be in even greater danger."

He shrugged. And smiled. "If they get wind o' me doings, my life won't be worth a turd. So I'd thank ye not to let me die in ignorance."

"I do not expect you to die, Molloy."

"And I'm not expecting it, neither. For twould spoil me plans. But what did ye mean that the Canada go is meant to fail?"

"Molloy . . . have you ever heard of the Earl of Thretford?"

"Can't say as I have. Though he sounds like a low, high-born Englishman."

"That he is. And a very rich Englishman. A man of power."

"Is he in Canada, then? Or what do ye mean?"

"He may be in Canada by now. When last I saw him, he was in Rochester. Talking with Kildare. Whose name, by the way, is Kilraine."

Twas his turn for bafflement. "Is an Englishman backing the Irish, then?"

"No. The Irish are backing the English. Had I not seen him, I never would have figured it out. And we would have been at war with England, and us wondering what happened."

"War with England?" To his credit, Molloy looked aghast. He knew what stood behind that thin red line.

"The Earl of Thretford . . . and his kind . . . represent industry . . . the mills of Manchester and such like. They want Southern cotton. And they'd gladly spend the lives it takes to get it. They want England to come in on the Confederate side. But they can't get the government to move. For Palmerston is cautious behind the bluster." I thought back on the land that had shaped my sorrows. "Kildare's the paid agent of Thretford and his party. He's to lead your invasion of Canada from American soil. With U.S. government rifles. And Lord Russell and Palmerston and the rest of them will have no choice but to respond as befits the dignity of Her Majesty. The rich will have their war. And we will see the Union broken. It's clear as day," I told Molloy, although this day was hardly clear.

"So . . ." Molloy said slowly, " . . . the Irish think they're striking a blow against the English. But they're really fighting *for* the English. So the English have an excuse to fight us."

"Exactly, Molloy."

He looked down, with a slow and solemn shake of the head. "Oh, Sergeant Jones, I tell ye. I don't know whether to pee or go blind."

Now that ungentlemanly comment reminded me that I had places to be, and a pretense to maintain. I hoped that Mrs. Rhys had not gone out to the privy to see if I was still alive.

"We'll stop them, Molloy. And we'll keep little fools from becoming great ones. You've done your new country proud."

But he was in no mood for praise that day. He stood there as sober as ever I had seen him.

"Bastards," he said. With unmistakable hatred in his voice. "The day will come when Ireland will be shut o' the dirty, pasty-faced English bastards."

"For now," I said, "let's just keep this country free of them."

I left him muttering. For my part, I went running. With the first snowflakes floating through the trees. Back of the Rhys's yard, I prowled about the outhouse for a moment. When I did not see Mrs. Rhys behind her windows, I made my way down to the back door.

When I come in, she had a washbasin waiting. And coffee and pie on the table. She shook her head maternally, as all good Welsh housewives do.

"You must be frozen to the heart of you," she said.

FIFTEEN

NOW THERE IS PIE, AND THERE IS PIE, AND I MUST pause to tell you. My mind was all on invasions of Canada and streaming snows when I come back into the house, but when Mrs. Rhys placed that bounteous slice in front of me, with its crust golden as the dreams of Midas and the filling red as rubies, I could do naught but sit me down and eat. For hungry I was, and there was courtesy to take into account, too. The good lady had baked it for their evening meal, twas clear, but cut it fresh for me. The oven's warmth was still in it, and cream spooned thick from the jug covered it over, and the flavor packed a wallop. Twas made of cherries she had put up, that pie, with black walnuts to take the sweet off, and oh, such a puckering beauty you will rarely hold in your mouth. That pie demanded more than I could give, for savoring was owed it, and second helpings, and a plush chair thereafter in which to glow and drowse. But time there was none.

The poor woman was baffled and amazed by my goings-on, but she bore it like a Christian and sent a lovely piece of pie along for John Brent as I dashed out into the snow again.

Now you will say, "Oh, this Jones is an eternal hypocrite. For he fair trumpets his respect for this Reg'lar John, along with his swelling regard for the Negro race, then leaves the poor fellow to freeze while he gluts himself sick in the warm with his own kind." But I will tell you: Firstly, Mrs. Rhys would have had him at her table and wondered only that he did not help himself to a bigger portion. And secondly, I would have had him inside, too. But he knew his world, John Brent. He never went needlessly into a white man's house, and never would he put himself alone with a white woman. For he grasped that innocence is ever weaker than suspicion, and tongues will tell more than they know. John Brent was regular, all right. And cautious, too. But let that bide.

He put up the horse blankets and off we went into the blow, with the flesh of cherries clinging to my gums. The storm had come out of the north, and the wind was up. The driving snow cut into the eyes of the horses, making them shy. Big flakes fell fast, and all of John Brent's skill was wanted to keep the sleigh on the road. Not halfway up the lake, we come upon a spilled-over log sled, and a mule down broken-legged and braying. Its jittered fellows fought the harness and worsened the beast's sufferings. A mile farther on, I had to get down and lead our team by the bridle, with the horse fear in me all the while and John Brent steadying their path. The snow grew so deep I could not lead the pair properly, and my friend had to turn to the whip—of which he was ever sparing—to carry us into the gale.

All the way I worried. For though we would do best to wait and catch Kildare deeper in his deeds and all uncovered, I had to get off a coded telegraphic to Washington warning Seward of what was afoot. Next, I must share my intelligences with Sheriff Underwood, then make a plan to bring up soldiers from Elmira to see the business of arresting these fellows done orderly. For where fifty rifles had gone, five hundred might have preceded them. We needed to find every store of arms, and break every conspiracy. It would not do to lock up Kildare—or Kilraine—only to learn that his plot would go on without him. A crushing was needed. Not cruel, but thorough. War with England would ruin us all.

We made it back into Penn Yan after dark, with the snow scraping the belly of the sleigh. John Brent dropped me before the parsonage, remarking, "I've got to get these horses into the barn. They're blown, sir." His strong features showed no self-concern, despite the cold, but only alarm for his animals. For he loved all that the Good Lord had created.

The truth is we were as blown as the beasts. There is a special weariness comes of the cold, and it slows a man's thoughts as surely as it does his limbs. Oh, I was born to be a fool that day.

I intended to thaw my fingers then set to work with my code book. After sending off the message to Seward, I would go by the jail to see if Sheriff Underwood was still there—although I suspected he would be gone home to his farm with such a storm upon us. For we would see no rebellion, nor invasion, nor common crime in such a snow as this.

Still, I was anxious to take matters in hand. For duty delayed is duty betrayed, and the man who begins by putting off a chore ends by putting off his salvation.

I did not even get inside Mr. Morris's front door before a boy ploughed up to me and gave my coat a tug. Snow cascaded from my shoulders.

"Major Jones!" he cried. "Major Jones!"

I had seen him somewhere before, but could not fix him. Then he wiped his nose with the back of his mitten and I remembered. He had begged a penny of me in the street a month before, and I had given him ten cents. He was the boy with the Irish face and American voice.

"What is it, lad?" He should not have been out on such a day, but inside, fed and warm. I pitied the lad and thought of my own son.

"Sheriff Underwood sent me to ya. He needs ya right now."

Oh, how I longed to go inside and thaw.

"Where is he, boy? The jail is it?"

The little fellow shook his head. "No, sir. He's gone home to his farm. Had to go real quick. Says to tell ya, 'Bloody murder,' and that yer to come to him quick, no matter what."

"More, then?"

He shook his head and shivered. "Kin I go now, sir? It's awful cold."

I gave him another ten-cent piece and sent him off.

There was hard. For I was cold and weary, and wanted my rest. I felt near sickness again and, despite the dark, my eyes were all bedazzled. But Underwood would not have sent for me on such a night had the matter not been urgent.

Murder was it? Again? And the constables and deputies no doubt out in the storm themselves, with a shivering boy sent to fetch me.

But what was I to do? John Brent could not take me, for his horses were spent. Besides, the sleigh would not cut through the depths of the snowfall any longer.

Now I am human like you, see. For a moment, I wondered if I could not plead the weather and stay in until the morning. And such I might have done, had a lesser man called for me.

I shook as much of the snow as I could from my coat and boots, and went inside.

Mr. Morris come running.

"I was afraid, afraid!" he cried, with his peaked hair aquiver. "A terrible storm! I prayed for you and our John Brent. I prayed! And now my prayers are answered! Isn't the storm terrible, terrible? A judgement, a judgement . . ."

"Mr. Morris . . . I must ask a favor, sir."

"A favor? A favor? Anything, anything!"

"I would like to borrow your horse."

"My horse?"

Yes, his horse. Twas a sad, decrepit animal, fit only for a preacher's gentle rounds. Yet, it was little less of a terror to me, for all that. I would as soon have mounted a dragon. But I saw no other way to reach Underwood's farm. For it was too far to walk, and my good leg was as frozen as the bad one, and the drifts were half as high as me and growing.

"The sheriff has called for me," I told him. "It is an urgent matter, see."

"Urgent? But the storm, the storm . . ."

"Your prayers will see us along, Mr. Morris."

The poor fellow looked at me in fear. He faced eternity boldly, but had his qualms about the day-to-day. And truth be told, the horse was precious to him. I have never understood the bond between the human and the equine.

"Prayer? Surely, surely. Yes, prayer. An urgent matter? You said it was urgent?"

"Murder," I said. Forgive me, but I knew the fellow liked a bit of excitement.

"Murder?"

"Murder."

He looked about himself, at tables and at chairs, as if a tool to prevent my foolishness might be found lying around like a book or a pair of misplaced spectacles.

"Then you must go," he said, despairingly. "Go, go. I'll saddle Priscilla. But you're all wet, all cold . . ."

"I will change my socks, and that will do." You will note that, selfishly, I did not try to dissuade him from saddling the mount himself. For I would endure horrors enough upon its back without attempting to girdle the creature with leathers.

"You know the way?" Morris pleaded. "You . . ."

I nodded firmly. For I had traveled the road past the sheriff's farm many a time, if in better weather, and I had visited him at his homestead twice.

"So cold," the preacher said, "awfully cold, the storm . . . the storm . . ." And off he went to help me all he could.

I changed my socks in haste and pulled on another length of unmentionables beneath my trousers. It made for a snug waist and seat. But the warmth was worth the squeeze. I repositioned the pistol for what little comfort I might have, then chose my greatcoat over my India rubber cape. For I wanted the warmth without the sweat of it. I should have taken the time to write a note, detailing all that I had learned. But my brain was as frozen as my fingers.

We think too little, and learn too late.

Morris led the horse around to the front, stepping high to make his way through the snow. I had a problem with the placement of my cane and fiddled about. Sitting a horse is an awkward business. And my shivering come not from the cold alone. For that sunk-backed beast seemed a viper to me. At last, I handed my cane down to the pastor.

"I will not need it to ride," I told him, "and Underwood will loan me a walking stick."

"Yes, ride, ride," poor Morris said. "Oh, what a dreadful night! It makes me fear the Apocalypse!"

I snapped the reins and rode off after murder.

I never lost my way. It was a trial, but I had not soldiered all those years for naught. If a man can find his way through the killing deserts of the Pushtoon and come out with all his parts still on him, he will not go astray in New York State.

Still, I often had to trust the horse and my instincts, for there was little enough to see. With the snow blowing against us and the dark down, my eyes found no more than a shroud of earth, and that close as the walls of a coffin. Only the trees by the roadside, white to windward and black on the lee, gave reassurance that we had not suffered a second Flood, and this time a frozen one.

Twas hard going for the horse. I hate the creatures, yet I will be fair. She did good service, though after some miles of plunging through the drifts she could do no more than plod. I sang hymns to help us both along, and the animal did perk up all startled at the handsome sound of my voice. Even a beast will take comfort in a nice hymn.

I sang out "Old One Hundred," for that one pleases me ever, with its feel of marching Heavenward. Then I gave the night "Rock of Ages," which, though newfangled, has meat on its bones. On I went through Watts and Wesley, with snowflakes darting into my mouth and the wind like the breath of the devil.

I prayed between melodies, asking for safe deliverance from the perils of the night. I know we are not meant to pray selfishly, asking the Lord for favors and comforts. But the horse was going feebly now, and the drifts looked as high as my shoulders, and I will tell you without shame that I was afraid. For men may be faced down, but nature is implacable.

Well, there are ever those worse off than us, and sometimes we are guided to their aid. Passing through a grove, under branches clacking in torment, I heard a human cry.

It made me jump, I will tell you. For the dark seemed full of devils, though I am not one for spooks.

I heard it plain.

A human voice, weakened and calling for help.

I saw the figure then. Plunged into the snow beside the road. Pleading with a desperate, upraised hand.

"Help me," a man's voice called, all broken. "Please . . . help me . . ."

I pulled up closer to the dark lump in the snow and, holding the reins tightly in my hand, let myself down from the saddle.

I dropped into snow up to my hips.

" . . . help . . . me . . ."

The poor fellow sounded Irish of a sudden. It occurred to me that he was likely drunk, and lost, and would have died had I not happened by. I felt a lilt of pride at the prospect of rescuing my fellow man.

I bent toward him, thinking of the Good Samaritan.

THE LIGHT SHOCKED ME. The world was naught but a blaze. Pain pushed outward from my head, greater than my skull, and the world wore a killing glare.

I shut my eyes again and went back under.

I do not recall any dreams, and my sleep had not been notched by day and night. I would tell you that I knew only a long darkness, but that is looking back. Then I did not know if my sleep was long or short, or if it was a sleep at all. Twas a nothingness. On dark days, when my devils come upon me, I fear eternity will be so. But then I turn again to my Redeemer.

I woke a second time. Moments later? Hours? Days? I was too wrecked to wonder. All was a jumble, and so that day remains. I have but scraps, stuffed in the pocket of memory.

A ceiling of unfinished boards, gray and uneven.

The smell of rough soap used in quantity. Prickly as briars in the nose.

Wind. Before I found the strength to turn my head and look around me, I heard the wind screaming to come inside. It strained the walls and smacked against the windows. A vandal of a wind, it was, with a sharp keen to it.

My face was cold. My body lay cocooned, but coldness pressed down on my eyes, my cheeks, my nose.

I did not try to move at first. I did not even think of it. Something in me knew I could not yet take on so great a task.

My eyes would not stay open. The light hurt too much. I hid behind my eyelids, letting myself sink again. Yet, something braked me before I lost consciousness, and I lay between the worlds. Perhaps I had a glimpse of Nellie's days. Thoughts rose vivid and out of rhyme, without the comfort of order. Images sought to lure me from all decency, and darkness seeped out of my corners.

I was visited by my Mary Myfanwy and our little John, by President Lincoln sitting in a coach, by flaunting girls that I had long forgotten and a drunken quartermaster recalled from India. The cholera dead rose, too, not least my mother. Countless phantoms robbed me of my peace, and those who should have comforted did not.

Do you believe we ever know ourselves? What hides within us, waiting to emerge?

Not sense, that's certain. If I speak of myself. I had forgotten the invasion of Canada and government arms and the Irish. I had no recall of my night ride through the snow. Twas as if my brain were going carefully with me, testing me with pictures from the past before bullying me back to present duty.

I remember turning my head as if called. The room was spare as a country chapel. There was a single window.

Beyond the glass, the sky was so blue that I want a better word to tell the color. I felt that I had never seen a sky so blue.

The wind howled and the panes shook.

Only then did I wonder where I was. For nothing was familiar. My sense of time and place had slipped askew. I did not know the room. Or the smells, at once familiar and foreign. I floated under my blankets, chill air on my cheeks.

Thinking was too hard and soon I slept.

I awoke to find a woman standing over me. She jumped when I opened my eyes.

"Du lieber Gott!" she said, laying her hand over her mouth in alarm. But then she lowered the hand. And smiled. *"Verzeih'mir. Hub's nit erwartet."*

She had a face just wearing beyond youth, with brown hair gathered back. All kindness she looked. Handsome, in a sound and solid manner.

Her eyes, though, were treasures. They poured over you like honey.

"You are . . . waking?" she asked, in my tongue. But I could not respond. I could only look up at her, an angel hovering over me. And then I could not do that much.

When next I woke it was dark. I felt a need to carry out a personal matter. Quickly.

Fortunately, my limbs had come back to me. With needles in them. Great complainers they had become, my arms and legs. And there was a business that wanted hasty attention.

I got up on an elbow.

Too fast.

The room swirled and hurt and pushed me back toward the pillow.

All I could think of was my need. I wanted to cry out. With no sense of past or future. I dreaded the embarrassment of soiling the bed. A strange bed, at that. A bed between worlds.

I bullied my way out from under the blankets, unsteady as if I were drunk. Which I was not, you understand.

My bare feet found the floor. The sharp cold of it. And I toppled over.

Then it was day and I was sitting up. The angel spooned broth into me. I could not remember waking, but suddenly the world seemed clear. Twas not, to tell the truth. But I thought it was. My head held a mighty hurt.

I had a sense of something gone wrong.

Of something gone terribly wrong.

" . . . day . . . is it?"

"Was?"

" . . . day . . ."

Her face was oval and full, with life's cares just beginning to mark it.

"Montag." She tipped the broth into my mouth. "Monday is today."

I tried to shake my head. I don't know if I managed it. "Date . . . *the date?*"

The question seemed to confuse her. "*Weiss nit. Muss mal gucken.*"

She took away the empty bowl. And left me with a child's sense of loss.

The sky was gray that day, but the wind was down. For the first time, I heard an infant's cries. It occurred to me that the poor woman had two infants to feed now.

Bits and pieces, pieces and bits. Molloy kept popping into my head, but I did not get the sense of it. Then I slept and dreamed I was confined in a madhouse—a place of horrors it was—and could not convince anyone that I did not belong there. I woke sweating, leaping up only to collapse back into dizziness, with the great ache ever in my head.

Isn't it queer how one little drop of thought can unleash a flood of memories? As when your life's love kisses you a certain way and erases the years? Well, I had no kiss, but, of all things, the pistol that the boys in my old company had given me come suddenly into my mind.

Where was it? For though I have no love of such instruments in general, that Colt was holstered in sentiment. I distinctly remembered having it with me that night.

The rest of the night returned in a blink.

And more come back to me, too.

My head throbbed. Too small a jug for so many thoughts. Fair clobbered I was by remembering.

I had to go. Had to warn Seward. Had to raise Underwood. Call up the regulars . . .

How many days had I lain there?

The room was ever cold, but now I fair froze at the thought that Kildare might already have launched his invasion, that our beloved country might be rushing toward an ocean-spanning war, and that it might be my fault.

The woman stepped in, just as I attempted to rise. I was got up in somebody else's unmentionables, far too large for me. Of course, I covered myself again. Unwilling to think of all that she had seen while I slept, or of the shames I doubtless had committed.

"Uniform?" I asked her. "Do you . . . have my uniform?"

She looked at me, unable to understand at first. But her confusion lasted only a moment, for the word is nearly the same in the German tongue, though they will speak it peculiar.

"*Ja*, we have."

"Please," I said. "Bring it to me. Please."

I know not what I intended, but she saw clearly that it was beyond my capabilities. "*Morgen*. Tomorrow, I bring."

I did not argue with her. For all my strength had gone into the request. I lay back.

"How . . . how did I come here?"

"To here?"

"Yes. What happened to me?"

She chewed her lip for a moment. Thinking. She had an openness that was her greatest charm, and gave all without calculation.

"*Weiss nit genau was passiert ist. Mein Mann* . . . my husband finds you. In much snow. You are dead, he thinks." A look of frustration come over her. "*Ach, wie sagt man? Sie waren grausam mit Blut geschmiert.* All blood is on you. He comes late from the wood-selling, *mein Mann. Dann hat er dieses komische Mägdlein gesehen. Schockiert, war der Gute. Es war nit richtig bekleidet, das Mägdlein.* The girl he sees. Her clothings are not enough. *Doch, es hat dich gerettet. Es hat ihn die Stelle gezeigt.* Alone, he is never finding you, she is showing him. *Dann ist es weg.* Without the girl to help, he never finds you. *Und* you die, I think." She sighed. "*Der Herrgott hat dich lieb.*"

Now I was not in my clarities, see. I let the remarks about the girl pass, thinking it a reference to a daughter I had not seen.

That evening, the woman brought me a dinner to fill a right belly. Twas no rich man's fare, but honest. She sat beside the candle, watching long enough to be sure I could eat by myself.

When she come back for the plate, her husband followed her in. Twas the first time I had seen him.

Tall, with shoulders broad as a yoke, he wore a full beard. But you only saw the true man when he stepped in close and the flame of the candle caught his eyes. Now husband and wife they were, and different in hue and stature. But didn't they have the same warm eyes? The two of them looked as if life were a constant gift they longed to share with the rest of the world. Overflowing, they seemed to me. *Overflowing.* Though not with worldly treasures. You would have known them for kindly sorts if you had met them in a prison or a battle.

"*Guten Abend,*" the fellow said.

Now I knew that much from dear Mrs. Schutzengel.

"*Goodenbend* to you, sir," I answered in my finest Dutch.

The woman took up the utensils. "My husband . . . helps you. If you want to sit by the fire and become warm. You are so strong?"

Of a sudden, the room's cold bit me. Few things in life have sounded as lovely to me as a place by a hearth did then.

Standing remained a trial, and walking was worse. Twas the dizziness that comes with a great crack over the head. I had a great scab on the back of my skull, where my assailants had, no doubt, expected my brains to spill out. But a Welshman is hard to knock down, and harder still to keep there.

The husband smelled of work and winter barns, of hay freshened with a pitchfork and sweat on leather. He helped me into a set of his own clothes, which were twice too big but served for modesty. Then he guided me out of that poor little room as though I were a child taking its first steps.

He placed me in a rocking chair, surprisingly gentle in his doings, then laid a quilt over me. Oh, that fire was a glory. The flames smiled, I tell you. I was close enough to feel the heat on my face. Only the dizziness would not settle at first.

When I come to myself proper, the couple were just done with their after-dinner chores. The woman lifted an infant from a low cradle and soothed it in her arms, sitting down in a chair across from me. Twas not so good a chair as mine, for they had given me the place of honor. The husband brought a kitchen chair and placed it close to the flames, then he fetched a big Bible—*Die Bibel,* they call it—with metal clasps. He sat down and opened the book.

He read to us by the firelight, tracing the lines with his finger.

"*Selig sind, die um Gerechtigkeit willen verfolgt werden; denn das Himmelreich ist ihr . . .*"

Even the infant seemed to listen. I knew not their tongue, but got the spirit. What better tonic for the wounded flesh than that tonic of the soul? The fellow could have read those words in Hindoo and would have reached me still.

When it come time to get down and pray, I struggled to join them on their knees. But I was too wobbly and only interrupted their devotions. Together, they tucked me back into the chair.

Then they spoke the Our Father, and no mistaking it. I did not know the words their way, but mumbled along. When they bowed their heads in silence—with the firelight coloring their faces—I said my own prayers, too.

They stayed a long time on their knees, with the woman clutching the infant. And what better attitude of prayer might there be, than a mother holding her child?

Even prayer was not enough to hold me. My mind drifted and I began to doze, only to wake again to a stabbing clarity. For the first time, I noticed the bed of bundled hay. Made up on the floor, behind the cradle. And I understood. The bed they had given me was their own. Twas all the bed they had, and they gave it to me to soil.

Would I have done a thing as fine as that?

Our selfishness resounds in our small lives.

I sat and watched them, husband, wife and child, praying on the splinters. Perhaps such folk will wait for us, on the day we are most in need, to help us limp across the River Jordan.

IN THE MORNING, the husband helped me down to breakfast at their table. The woman had my uniform—the one from Mr. Feinberg's shop—stitched up and cleaned. She handled it as if it were dangerous.

"How long was I . . . how long did I sleep? How many days?"

They looked at one another, then spoke in quick German. The woman began to count up on her fingers.

She stopped when she reached seven.

I sat up, spoon halfway to my mouth.

"I must go," I said.

The woman shook her head and looked at the man.

German again.

"*Es geht nur bis zur Scheune*," he said. "*So ein tiefer Schnee hab' ich nie gesehen.*"

"He says the snow is too deep. Only to go to the barn is possible. He has not seen such a snow."

"The road . . . how far is it to the road?"

She translated. She knew the distance well, but wanted counsel.

"*Die Strasse ist nit zu befabren,*" the man said. "*Geht nit. Keineswegs.*"

"My husband says it is not possible to go. The road is under the snow, too."

But which road? A main road? Were other roads open? If the snow was still so deep . . . then likely Kildare had not made his move. But I had to be sure. I could not loll about, shying from my duty. I had to be on my way.

I had the senselessness that follows a great, jellying whack on the noggin, see. They tried to reason with me, but I got on my greatcoat. A madman, I lurched into the yard.

Beyond the barn lay a white sea. We needed a Moses now, to part the snows.

I plunged ahead.

Stubbornness has its place in this life, and it has won not a few battles that rightfully should have been lost, but I fear I went to an extreme that morning. I charged the drifts where the house faced front and a road should have waited.

At first, I thought I would make a go of it, for the snow was crusted hard. I climbed up on the bank and limped along, careful of a slip. But not six paces out I broke through the surface. And found myself engulfed up to my chest.

The husband dug me out and carried me in. At the edge of a swoon, I asked him to put me on the bed of straw and to take his own bedroom to himself again, but he ignored me. Undressed, I slept the day out and the night.

Now the only thing duller than a convalescence is listening to a report of a convalescence. So I will spare you more of such matters for the moment, and let you take a breath.

Later, when I returned to the world of common days, I found a letter waiting from Mick Tyrone. Although I like things kept in proper order, I will share that letter with you now, to lift you from the boredom of my bed. And you will see my little woes were nothing.

SIXTEEN

Dover, Tennessee
February 26, 1862

My Dear Friend,

I hope my scrawl is legible. My hands shake. They have done too much these last weeks, and little well. I thought I was a man of Science. I'm nothing but a threepenny butcher. I wear more blood on my hands than old Macbeth and his wife together. Far more. My "medicine" is no more than a hacking at flesh and bone. What Rebel bullets left unfinished, my fingers completed. I have bathed in a river of gore and cannot sleep. Man is a beast, and I am but a jackal.

I will tell you of the struggle for Fort Donelson to purge myself of it. But first allow me to venture an answer to the query contained in your last communication. Given what I have seen of Mesmerism over the years, I believe you are correct in assuming that this Kildare may have lulled you and the others present into a trance while pretending to work his will solely upon his daughter. Once he had you in that waking sleep, it would have been an easy thing to suggest to you the presence of a soul dearly remembered and lost—you would have made your own choice of visions, requiring no previous knowledge on the mesmerist's part.

I do not credit your notions of a life beyond the grave—we are naught but food for worms—but, in the caverns of the mind, we do keep others "alive" in some sense. Kildare asked you to "see" a thing you longed to see, to believe what you wished to believe. It is how the confidence man succeeds, whether he is a mesmerist or not.

As for the girl, I advise you to break all bonds with her. You cannot save her. Nor is she yours to save. Your kindness and attachment leave you vulnerable. Turn away. Such people drain our strength. No doubt, her sort gave rise to the legend of the vampire. It is only a question of whether her sickness or her madness will first overtake her. Turn away!

Doubtless, my counsel seems cruel to you. But a doctor learns some things. Even on the battlefield, we must turn from the cries of the wounded who cannot be rescued in order to save those who retain a chance at survival. You, too, must concentrate upon those who have a chance, and leave the doomed behind. It is life's stern rule.

Far from heartless, my friend, I find I bear too much emotion to do my job as well as it might be done.

Molloy's remarks opened an old wound, although your innocent discussion with him had no such intent. It saddens me to read of the old, hard words spoken in a new and hopeful country. Yes, I am an Irish Protestant by birth, though I have left both the religion and the land behind. What of my birth? Why should it mean I cannot like Molloy, nor he old Mick Tyrone? These swift, unreasoned hatreds will forever be the downfall of the Irishman.

Molloy would have me and my forebears no more than tools of the English. Yet, my grandfather died fighting against the English at Ballynahinch, in the rising of 1798. He fought for Ireland's freedom. His thanks were death and the confiscation of our lands by the Crown. The English hanged his brother, too, although the man was innocent of any involvement with the rebels. The family tie was enough.

My own father, born to wealth, matured in penury. He made himself a doctor through sacrifice and will, determined that our family would rise again. He died in the early years of the Famine, of typhus, while treating the starving and diseased of his county. Yes, he was an "Orangeman." Indeed—a Protestant who went into dens of affliction a priest would not enter. He died serving those who despised him, and brought home the typhus that killed my sister.

Do you understand now why I will have nothing of their nationalism? Why I believe that universal brotherhood is the only sensible path for mankind? These hatreds must be laid aside forever!

Hatred! It seems I cannot escape it. We exult in slaughter, Abel. Even Darwin cannot explain the extent of our thirst for blood.

I must tell you of the battle.

After the swiftness of Fort Henry's fall, the soldiers thought they were off on a lark. Even the weather smiled upon our ranks, warming until you would have mistaken February for May. Marching across the neck of land from Henry to Donelson, the troops cast off their blankets and overcoats, as well as not a few haversacks and other impedimenta. When I made the journey myself after concluding my duty at the old field hospital, the countryside looked like a battlefield without bodies. All the litter of war lay beside the roads and trails.

Yet, fate plays hardest with those who take her for granted! No sooner had we invested the lines about Fort Donelson than winter returned with icy ferocity. The Confederates, though besieged, slept snug in their cabins and tents, while our men lay upon the ground, squirming together like worms in a jar as they attempted to gain some warmth from one another. It is a wonder the entire army did not freeze. The human body is, truly, a wonderful mechanism, and full of contradiction. A mass of men will survive freezing nights, and a boy will pull through the amputation of his every limb, yet a light tap on the head will kill the giant. This war makes me feel as though I am constantly learning, yet I can never quite say what it is that I have learned.

We expected a siege and, eventually, a surrender. Our gunboats made a run at Fort Donelson, too, but had not recovered sufficiently from the duel for Fort Henry. Our boats were run off, at a high cost. Yet, Grant appeared untroubled. When I visited our headquarters, which had been established in a country cabin, he seemed the calmest of men, confident that his course was right. All believed we had the Confederates trapped.

Of course, I am learning that warfare is largely the art of dealing with the unexpected. With the snow thick over the earth and the roads coated with ice, the Rebels broke from their entrenchments and attacked. I recall the moment I heard the cannon's roar and the first snap of the rifles. I was seeing to a boy paved over with boils. He could not sit or lie or even bear the weight of his woolens upon him. The eruptions needed lancing, and such would be painful. He stood there with fear and sadness in his eyes, a child got up as a soldier, and I was just about to call to an orderly to assist me when the ground shook and the lantern swayed from the pole of my tent.

It might have been our own forces attacking, yet, inexplicably, I knew it was the reverse. The sounds arose well forward and to the south, carrying easily through the cold air. After a moment, it became clear that this was more than another skirmish. I shouted to the men to prepare for casualties and to have the ambulance mules put in harness. The fellows went ploddingly about their business, especially the hostlers. Our ambulances had not yet been needed, the few casualties we had suffered being easily managed by those vehicles assigned within the brigades of foot. But the human mind fascinates me endlessly—I do believe I will make the brain the object of my study when this war is over. Somehow, I knew that we had a hard day's work before us. I tore into all of them, shocking man and beast. They had believed me a cool, methodical fellow, chary of speech. But I was in a fury that day.

With sufficient activity underway beneath our tentage, I decided to lead the ambulance train forward myself. The truth is that I wanted to see the battle (Will men never learn?), although I sincerely believed I might be of best initial service at the medical posts closer to the lines. Nor did I trust our team-

sters to make their way with much speed unless attended, for we are sent the dregs of the service and the worst of the civilians hired on. Few teamsters wish to serve the medical arm, for there is less profitability than lies in ferrying general supplies.

Our first battle was with the roads. The ice cost us more mules than did hostile fire that day, and I took my poor horse along through the woods beside the track, since he found the going easier there, despite the snow's depth. We had to change teams and leave a pair of ambulances behind. I did have the presence of mind to order the derelict vehicles pushed off the road so they would not impede military movements.

My impression of battle is that it is, above all, confusing. We passed between regiments at rest, dawdling as if nothing unusual was afoot. Meanwhile, the blasts and crackle of battle had spread until the sound encompassed the entire world before us, although now and again we heard an individual shout distinct against the din. The first stragglers appeared, and the ambulatory wounded. No matter how light their injuries, each of the latter had one or two unscathed companions anxious to help them rearward. A number of them expected me to put them aboard a hospital wagon and turn the vehicle immediately. But I feared we would need those vehicles for men of lesser fortune and I scorched the selfish with language of which you would not have approved. Words were all I had, I fear, for in my anxiety to see that other men did their work properly, I had forgotten myself and rode off without buckling on sword or pistol.

I feared defeat. Healthy men came toward us at a run, their weapons cast away. The eyes of terrified boys swelled horse-like, while grown men wailed that all was lost and that the Rebels were on their heels. We worked our way through a good mile of deserters and debris, and gave way twice to line ambulances heading rearward packed with men who would never again be whole. Closer to the front, mounted troopers chased cowards with the flat of their swords and, sometimes, with the edge. We seemed in the midst of disaster.

Yet, the gunfire did not slacken or rush toward us. Some in Union blue were standing to put up a fight.

I hurried the ambulances along. Thinking on a thousand things, I looked casually to the side and saw blue ranks on a slope below me, visible only from the waists down, upper bodies blurred with smoke. One after another of them splayed backward. But the line held. I still saw no Confederates.

We had to pause while a regiment came on at the double, tripping in the slush the road had become. Then a battery nearly ran us into a ravine, racing forward like madmen. An officer screamed at me:

"Get those goddamned meat wagons off the goddamned road."

I pressed forward. In the background, I heard a wild keening, a high banshee scream, that chilled me. It was odd, you see. I do not recall a fear of the bullets spitting past—but that queer shouting made me want to flee.

Men surged back and forth across the road, sometimes moving by company but often in smaller groups. Lost officers shouted regimental numbers, while sergeants cursed their charges into line. I noticed how many soldiers lacked gloves, and remember thinking that their hands must be awfully cold on the steel and wood of their muskets.

A quartet of our soldiers came marching along, escorting three forlorn prisoners. You will not credit this, but only one of the captured fellows had proper shoes, while the worst off had only rags upon his feet. They looked crushed. And, yet, there was a residue of anger in them, but whether at themselves, their own superiors or at us I cannot say. They looked like they had been ill fed all their lives. I could not imagine that such ravaged creatures might make worthy soldiers.

The guns boomed all around us. Black smoke floated over white snow. We had taken on enough badly wounded men to turn three of my ambulances around, while, another had lost a wheel to a ditch. Two went astray, and I had only a pair of vehicles left with me.

Down in the trees, men shouted for ammunition. I saw the orange belch of cannon, but could not see the guns themselves. It was midday, but the sky had burned twilight pink above the smoke.

A boy clawed at my bridle, asking me if he would be all right. I nearly slapped him off before I saw that his skull had been sliced away.

I would not have thought such a one could live. But he was standing upright, tugging at my horse and speaking clearly, if hastily. "Will I be all right, sir? Am I gonna be all right?" With half his brain exposed to the air and blood down the side of his head. He should have been dead, or at least unconscious.

I called for an orderly to help him into an ambulance.

The boy's face calmed and he smiled. He let go of my bridle. "Thank you, sir," he said. "Thank you a hundred times." With that, he pitched backward into the muck, eyes wide, brains squeezing out of him. He was dead, as he should have been well before. I was glad I offered him that last, false comfort.

I still could not find a proper line of battle. The fighting seemed all a-tilt. I thought I saw General McClernand in the distance, but may have been mistaken. We passed one of our batteries, where man and horse lay dead, the guns silenced. I wondered if the battle had somehow passed us by, if I had led us astray.

I had a sketch of the roads—no proper map—and I pulled off my gauntlets to draw it from my pocket. Then it happened. A gray-brown line swept over us, shrieking. That banshee howl came from the Rebels, you see. It is some sort of battle cry. You might have thought a tribe of primitives was attacking.

How do men manage battle? Everything happens so fast. One instant, I was unfolding my sketch of the tracks and lanes, the next the enemy flowed around us. Most of them rushed by, driven on by officers in proper uniforms. But a pack of ragged men surrounded me.

"Git off thet harse," a fellow in a farmer's hat called through broken teeth. Their speech is so curious I had difficulty under-

standing the man. Another of them, a boy in scavenged breeches, grasped my reins. I recall the redness—the awful redness—of his ankles in that cold, and the unmatched brogans on his feet. His rifle was as tall as he was.

"Git down, you sumbitch," the farmer fellow said.

I felt I needed my horse. To attend to my duties.

"Look here," I said. "I'm a doctor. I'm here to care for the wounded."

Farmer rammed his muzzle into my ribs. It hurt not a little.

"Git down, or yer gonna be a daid doctor. Git off thet harse."

It was no good arguing with them. I dismounted. I have no idea what they thought they had accomplished, for none of them climbed up in the saddle. They simply trailed after their comrades, leading their booty behind them.

I clambered up beside the teamster on the lead ambulance. His face was white. I had to manage the horses until he came around again.

"Damnation," the driver said, over and over.

In a swale of scrub timber, we found a devil's harvest. They must have stumbled upon one another. For every man shot, another lay in the snow with his head smashed or his face crushed inward. Now you have spoken to me of the bayonet, but few men use them here. They employ their discharged muskets as clubs, or use their fists, or rocks, or even their teeth. I did not see a bayonet unsheathed all day.

It is as well, for such wounds do not heal.

We loaded the ambulances without preference to the allegiance of the wounded. Some of my men complained, but I cut them short. A wounded man is a soldier no more. We left those whom I judged as doomed behind, for two ambulances were nothing to the numbers of the fallen. I will never forget that: Men with their guts strewn around them, pleading for succor, or lying broken-backed, or hemorrhaging beyond my capacity to aid them. A man may be fully sentient on his way to death, and damning eyes followed my progress. Those men will carry their hatred of me with them to whatever lies beyond the grave. For I was the one who walked among them, saying, "Take him, but not that one."

They cried for mothers and sweethearts, or wished me to Hell, as our wagons creaked away.

And then I found the horse. Not my own, but another. He was standing by the side of the lane, with his head down, as if sniffing for grass under the snow. I do not believe I have ever seen a more beautiful stallion outside of a racing paddock. That horse was bred for running, not for battle. What sort of man had brought him to the field? The saddle was no military issue, but sleek and oiled soft, and the thick cloth beneath it was gray with a yellow border. One of those high Southern gentlemen must have ridden him into battle. I knew not the rider's fate, but from that moment the horse belonged to me. I called him "Reb," which the fellows thought a great joke.

Mounted again, I guided the ambulances back along our route—or believed I did. I could not always recall which fork to take, and clouds of smoke had settled in the hollows, thick as a London fog. The battle continued at a furious heat, but we seemed well away from it again. I shall never understand war's turnings.

I led the wagons across a frozen stream bed, careful of the wheels and wounded—for the latter's cries and pleas wrenched the heart. At once, my spirits soared! I saw a ridge ahead of us and our flag waving handsomely between the bare trees. My horse, too, longed to run toward those dark blue ranks, as if he had changed allegiance with his change of rider. But I dared not hurry the second ambulance, which was having difficulty with the streambed.

A horseman broke from the ridge and rode for us at a gallop, slashing his horse with a crop. He applied great energy to his task and reached me just as the second ambulance pulled free.

"Sir," he cried, pulling up breathless, "General Grant sends his compliments and asks"—here a brief pause and pant—"if you could hurry these ambulances along"—pant—"so our guns may fire upon the enemy." He gestured to whence we had come.

A gray line of a thousand men stretched across the fields.

I moved the ambulances as briskly as I could, keeping the suffering of the wounded in mind. The moment we reached the shadow of the slope, our cannon opened fire over our heads.

Grant waited atop the ridge. His staff officers, most of whom I knew, wore pale and serious faces, but the general smiled and motioned me over.

"My apologies, sir," I said, saluting. "I did not comprehend the situation." I think he heard me, despite the discharge of a nearby battery.

His smile broadened.

He reined his horse closer to mine. Grant is, by the way, a superb horseman. He leaves his staff behind on their jaunts.

"Doctor," he said, "you are one brave fool."

Another section of guns released its salvo. My horse, to its credit, did not shy, and I leaned toward the general. I felt I must say something in response, for though clearly a fool, I had not the least bravery to my credit.

Grant spoke again before I could find appropriate words.

"Looks like you've picked up quite a mount there," he said. "But I can't have my officers making off with contraband. It's illegal, Doctor."

"Sir . . ." I stammered, ". . . General . . . the Confederates seized my own horse . . . they . . . I . . ."

He winked at me and called out above the shouts and volleys, "Well, I'm going to look the other way, Doctor Tyrone. This once. But the next time you come upon a horse of that quality, I want him turned in to my headquarters so I can induct him into Union service myself."

Just then, General Wallace trotted up, with a worried look. I believe I have mentioned him in a previous missive. He has a special fondness for the classics.

"General," I heard him say to Grant, "my apologies for the violation of your orders . . ."

Grant shook his head. "No apologies, Lew. You did just right. My thanks."

The battery fired canister down the road. The louder report made every horse prance or rear—except my mount and Grant's. General Wallace's bay took an effort to control.

Grant . . . seemed unshakable.

"What do you think, Lew?" he asked.

Wallace's horse had a last dance, then submitted. The general stared off toward the enemy, although there was little to see for all the smoke. "I believe we will hold, sir."

Grant nodded. "That we will. Got 'em now. Damned fool Pillow. Had his chance and lost it. Now he'll take his whipping." Then he remembered me. Looking up from a dispatch he had begun to scribble in the saddle, Grant told me, "You are dismissed, Doctor. With my compliments for your valor."

Now any man likes such words applied to him. But what shall we do, my friend, when we know our actions did not merit such a response? I rode off feeling a fraud.

You may hear complaints that Grant was not at his post when the attack began that day, for he was in conference with our Naval arm upon the Cumberland, some miles below the fort. But he "rode to the sound of the guns," as you old soldiers say. Lew Wallace was the hero of the hour, for he moved his regiments where they were needed without awaiting permission. He shored up McClernand's broken line. To those upon the field, it seemed a desperate day. But Grant was unperturbed from start to finish. A man of astonishing calm, he appears to see through the mystifications and confusions of battle with uncanny clarity. Medical Science would, I think, find him an interesting subject.

I rode back to my butcher shop. For such it was. The contest went on without me, but I saw its hideous residue. I like to think the note Grant was writing as he sent me off was the order to General Smith to counterattack the Confederate works. For hollow though we know such matters to be, we all would feel ourselves a part of history. And I had little else of glory.

With the Rebels contained and their defenses compromised by their own inadequacies, their surrender was only a matter of time. The night before they struck their colors, a cavalryman named Forrest slipped his command through our lines to escape, refusing ever to surrender to Yankees. But the remainder of them surrendered well enough. Their officers were full of bluster and nonsense, but the men wept in their shame. We captured nearly as many of them as we had soldiers of our own.

The following days were a blood-soaked blur to me. With human wreckage enough of our own, we had to take responsibility for the captured Confederate wounded, as well. The houses of the little town of Dover were full of bleeding men. We did our best for them, but there were not enough skilled hands or supplies. Despite Dr. Brinton's remarkable efforts, we are not yet a service fit for war. In the end, we will lose as many to gangrene and neglect as fell upon the field.

I cannot write of all the horrors that lay on my surgeon's table, for no language in my command contains words of sufficient description. I would need to make the noises of a brute. I began by trying to save limbs and ended by sawing away lives. I know, I know. You will insist that I must have done some good. But not enough, my friend. The carnage was too vast. For every two I cut, one died. And for every one I cut, another perished waiting for my knife. We buried the bodies or torsos in temporary graves, but the ground was frozen hard and willing hands were few, so we burned the mounds of limbs that fell from our surgery tables. That will always be my image of our great victory at Fort Donelson: a heap of limbs soaked down with kerosene and set ablaze, blackened fingers curling against the sky.

Grant wants to move south, but there are reports of jealousy over his victories. We are stopped, and know not when we will proceed. Perhaps it is as well. The next slaughter can wait.

Before I close, I must tell you of an incident that occurred this afternoon. The affair began a week ago, shortly after the surrender, when I rode into Dover to ascertain the needs of the Confederate wounded. I made my rounds, spending hours in makeshift hospitals that were little more than charnel houses.

Not all of the attending physicians appeared to be men of advanced skill. Twice, I took over at tables where a country doctor was destroying the remnants of a life. I fear I was sometimes rude.

As I prepared to leave the village, a delegation of Confederate officers on local parole approached me, asking if I were not a surgeon. I told them that I was, indeed, although not as much of one as I had long imagined myself to be.

"Doctor," the ranking man began afresh, with the deceptive softness of the Southron gentleman, "I must swallow my pride and ask a service of you. As a gentleman and man of medicine, I hope you will not refuse me, sir." He was a small, upright fellow, bald-headed, with his hat held at his waist in supplication. His uniform, once fine, was tattered.

"What's the trouble?" I asked. Or snapped, perhaps. For I was weary. And his sort were the ones who made this war.

"Doctor, there is a young man who I fear will die if not attended. A young gentleman, sir. He requires a surgeon."

"Can't your surgeons do it, man?"

He lowered his eyes. In shame at the need to beg me. "Doctor—Major, sir—this here young man is the son of a senator from Miss'sippi. His father is a powerful man. Our doctors . . . are afraid to operate on Captain Barclay. They insist he cannot be saved, sir, and will not touch him. I fear they do not want the blame for his death under their knives, sir." He brushed a finger across his eyes, then cocked his head back proudly. "It is a disgrace, sir, and I am mortified to discover such cowardice among my own people."

I went to look at the officer. Now I always insist that patients be treated equally, whether rich or poor, as beautiful as Helen or ugly as mud. But our hearts are moved against our will. The young man, a captain while yet a boy, was blond and handsome to break the heart of every girl in his state. But his days of romance were over. He stank of urine, as he will for the rest of his life. Both his legs were shattered at the hip, and he had suffered dreadful local mutilations. His legs were rotting on him, and I have never seen a surer candidate for gas gangrene. He should have undergone amputation days before.

I made no secret of his advanced condition, yet I gave him a choice. I had no chloroform with me, and the Confederate supplies were long since depleted. I could either operate immediately with nothing to allay the pain, or return in the morning with an adequate supply.

The young man looked up at me with steady eyes of blue. "Doctor Tyrone"—he had instantly digested my name, as these "gentlemen" will—"I would not be so discourteous as to expect such a journey of you." He gathered himself for a moment. "But I would be grateful for your present services in relieving me of these legs. I have grown tired of them, sir."

We lugged him to a knacking yard. I made the bastards wash their knives and saws, which had not seen water in days. Then I set to work. His friends held him down, although one of them soon found he was unequal to the task and left the table weeping. The young captain suffered dreadfully, I assure you, although I am a quick saw. He did not so much as groan. Nor would he even bite down on a rag. He closed his eyes and fought himself, ashamed at his body's quivering rebellion as I took his legs off. I have never seen his like.

Well, this afternoon, with time to spare at last, I looked the fellow up. I found him alive, bedded in a chapel that had been turned into a hospital. The other Confederate patients ignored me, turning their backs on my blue coat. Not one asked me to so much as examine a wound (their bandages, I must tell you, were filthy, and I will see to the matter). But the young captain recognized me at once, greeting me with a display of gentility. I fear I was a bit gruff, for I am no friend to aristocratic airs, but he pretended not to notice. He might have been holding court on a grand estate.

In fact, he lay on the floor, on rancid bedding stuffed with hay. But he smiled so easily you would have thought him on holiday. He barely winced when I examined my gory work. I think, by the way, that he will heal.

Suddenly, I sensed a change in the air. A cold curtain of hostility descended. I heard whispers, and noted that the men's eyes were fixed upon me.

An armless man with a massive beard knelt by the captain's head, bending—no, tottering—down to whisper in his ear. With sidelong glances at me.

The captain looked at me harshly, almost hatefully, for a moment. Then his face smoothed over again.

"Doctor Tyrone? The men say you are riding my Buster."

I failed to understand him. Theirs is a very foreign form of English.

"Buster," he whispered. "My horse. The boys say you are riding my horse."

I understood it then. I hastened to form excuses and explanations, but the captain reached out and closed a hand over my wrist before I could speak. He had lost his legs and more, but still had the grip of a man happiest out of doors.

I began to blather about finding the animal, but the young man did not let me finish a sentence.

"Buster loves his carrots, Doctor Tyrone." Tears glazed his blue eyes and he let his head sink back on the ticking. He released my arm. "You feed that horse plenty of carrots, hear?"

The captain called out then, not loudly, but in a voice accustomed to command since childhood:

"Boys, I have asked the doctor to look after Buster. He has kindly obliged me." But he sensed the men were still unhappy with the situation, so he continued, "We must be generous with our enemies. Doctor Tyrone here is going to need him a real, fine horse when we send him and all the rest of the Yankees skedaddlin' back where they came from."

The room was fiercely silent for a moment, then another voice said, "Damn right. Damn sure, you're right, Cap'n."

They all began to hoot, to shout and yelp. Next came that wild banshee call of theirs.

As I left that room of limbless men, they were singing a buoyant song about their flag. I fear this war will not end as soon as we might wish it done.

I am enclosing a list of books and a few banknotes. My dear friend, when next you pass through New York or Philadelphia, please inquire as to the availability of the titles. That is, of course, if you should find the time. Give preference to the medical works, especially those on vascular matters. Although I yearn to read of higher things, I am determined to make the most of my grisly profession. I will not accept that all this butchery should pass without an advance in knowledge.

Please think fondly of
Yr. Obt. Servt.
M. Tyrone
Surg. U.S.V.

SEVENTEEN

IT WAS A LOVELY COW.

That is what my host said. I am sure of it. Standing there, brushing the animal's brown back, he looked my way and said, *"So 'ne schöne Kuh, nit?"*

I do not speak the German's weighty tongue, but my acquaintance with Mrs. Schutzengel, followed by my convalescence in this country household, had quickened my ears sufficiently to follow a bit of talk here and a scrap of chatter there. Ah, the mysteries of language! How little truth there is in any tongue, despite our ceaseless appetite for speech! All words are shadows. Only faith brings light. The Welsh know words are weak, and thus we sing.

Anyway, twas clear the fellow was fond of his animals. His kind would rather talk of cows than kings. And bless such men, says Abel Jones, if the wish be not presumption.

I was walking again. If slowly. Head a bit dazed and unwilling. But we cannot give in to our weaknesses, and I was supported in the flesh as well as in the spirit. *Herr* Kempf, my host, had whittled a cane to help me on my way.

If only the snow would have left us! We were prisoners. Deep into March, the south wind held its breath. You know how April's scouts ride out ahead, sneaking past the winter's sentinels to wake the earth into bright rebellion. The first scents rise, of earth and wet and life. All is reborn beneath a strengthening sun, and hearts swell in a hymn of wordless praise. This year, the earth slept on and whiteness reigned. March would not move, as if the very calendar had frozen. The snow still blocked the course to the main road. I ached to leave, to go back to my duty and stop Kildare before the deed was done. But the drifts had set in hard and kept us pinned.

Work done, *Herr* Kempf turned from the cow and sighed. His smile faded and earnestness overtook him. He gestured that I should follow him. Toward the gloom at the back of the barn.

Now, that was a well-kept barn, I will tell you. Neat as the family household. The animals were groomed, their stalls showed cleaner than the inns the county round, and the harness racked on the walls gleamed with oiling. The plow sat polished and ready, and fresh grease squeezed from the hub of the wagon wheels. Your German will not starve from neglect of his business.

Twas cold in the barn, yet I was delighted to be up and about. The smell of hay and even of horse sweat reeked life, and the wind crying through the boards sang of my good fortune. I was alive, though other men had not intended that I remain so. It was lovely just to be.

Still, my joy was tempered by dread. The world beyond spared no time for idylls. I feared what might have happened in my absence. I thought of Nellie, too. And between, behind and above all other thoughts, reveries of my Mary Myfanwy and young John haunted me as no ghost ever could. If ghosts there be, which I will not believe.

What if my sweet beloved thought me dead? What had my wife been told? How had she felt on the day no letter from me arrived, with none to come thereafter? I wished I had bought her that damnable—pardon me—sewing machine.

Herr Kempf beckoned me along, for I was not yet quick. I scuttled down between the hay bales, learning the length of my new cane. Though it was morning, musty twilight reigned. Fairy dust drifted between the eaves.

"Ist 'ne gute Scheune, nit?" he asked.

I understood only that something or other was good.

A stack of crates and chests rose against the back wall of the barn. He began lifting them down. I moved to help him—for I felt my strength returning—but *Herr* Kempf waved me off.

"Sollst ruhen," he said. *"War fast 'nen Totschlag, dass Du bekommen hast."*

He seemed almost bad-tempered now, which was not the fellow's nature. Twas as if he had been set to a task he longed to avoid.

I sat me down on a bench of hay, with the dust sweet in my nose.

At last, he reached the chest at the bottom of the stack. Before he opened it, the good man straightened himself and took a deep breath. Then he bent to lift the lid.

The container might have been full of serpents, the way he reached inside.

He lifted out my pistol, the Colt the boys from my old company had given me, with its fine engraving and embarrassing inscription. Now I do not love firearms, and might wish them gone from the world, but my heart swelled at the sight of that particular instrument. For we may think high thoughts all we want, but our sentiments will have their say.

He held the pistol out by the barrel. But he was not offering it to me. Only displaying it.

"Kommt nit ins Haus, die Waffe," he said. *"Verstehst?"* He tried, for the first time, to speak in English to me: "No in *unser* house." Shaking his head to make certain I understood.

I nodded. For I understood him better than he knew.

He stuffed the pistol back in its hiding place. If I had nursed any doubts, which I had not, they would have been vanquished by the sight of the weapon. The men who had attacked me had not bothered to search under my greatcoat, or even to pat along my sides. Thieves would have taken the pistol sure. My assailants had wanted to kill me only, and believed they had. But for the storm, they might have strung me up and given me the pitch cap.

Herr Kempf gestured toward the barn door. *"Gehen wir, ja?"*

I followed him back out. Into the sunshine. Twas bright enough to blind, and I stepped carefully. For even the best-tended barnyard remains a barnyard.

I was a steadier man than I had been the day before. And better I would be the next day, too. When a Welshman sets his mind on his improvement, stay out of his way.

That morning seemed to grace the world with confidence. The sky was a handsome blue. For the first time since my beating, the sun fell warm upon my shoulders. I stopped and raised my face in exultation.

An icy drop from the barn roof struck my cheek.

The snow was melting.

Herr Kempf looked at me.

"Morgen gehen wir zur Hauptstrasse. Ich helfe dir."

I did not understand a word he said. But his good wife come out just then, to take up the fresh-laid eggs.

She went by us at a perk, explaining:

"Tomorrow he helps you to the road."

THE LADY OF THE HOUSE made a chicken dinner that last night. This was on a weeknight, mind, when so rare a bird was forbidden the family pot. The hen died in my honor. The Kempfs were good souls, teachers of kindness.

What was I to them? Despite my uniform, I might have been a criminal, or otherwise deserving of my fate. Yet, I woke up in their own bed. The money had not been taken from my pocket by my attackers, so I offered to pay for my board. Neither man nor wife would hear of it, for they lived in mercy's dominion.

There is true religion, see. I speak not of Christian, Jew or Musselman, of Hindoo or the countless kinds of heathen. For did not Jesus look beyond the name? Tis kindness, not severity, that lets us gain a little peek at Heaven. Now you will say, "This Jones speaks like an infidel. Saved is saved, and damned is damned, and done." But I will tell you: Those who would put harshness in religion are no Christians worthy of the name. Look at that young family, with poverty their neighbor and lifelong work their fate. Were they not better Christians than a prince? I say we must keep true religion from the grip of the old and bitter, and place it in the hands of those who love.

Father McCorkle did not err in all his judgments, I will give him that. He understood why Jesus loved the poor. Had he understood this world half so well as he understood our Lord, we would have all been spared a share of misery. But let that bide.

We sat and ate by the firelight, and snow broke from the roof. Thump after whumping thump of it come down, with drips and drops and drips between the avalanches. The night felt even warmer than the day. I imagined the ice breaking on the canal, and windblown waves on the lake, and boats and armed men sailing to do wrong.

We ate the bird stewed up with homemade noodles, graced with carrots and onions from the cellar. A bit of salt, and the *Hausfrau* had a dish that would have tempted Adam out of the Garden. Lovely puffs of biscuit sopped the leavings.

"There is good," I told them between bites.

Afterward, we prayed on our knees by the fire. The little one lay solemn in the cradle and there was a heaviness upon my hosts. You might have thought they saw what lay before me. Yet, all I had told them was that I must reach the town as soon as possible.

We sat by the hearth thereafter, drinking hot water and honey pricked up with nutmeg and clove. The Germans have a way with winter things.

"I must thank you again," I said, to liven the drowse into which we had sunk.

"Nein!" the woman said quickly. "The *Herrgott* you must thank. And the girl. Who is so strange. Without her, there is no finding of you."

Of a sudden, I remembered that earlier conversation, that other mention of a girl. My head had been spinning and my thoughts disordered with the seriousness of the injury upon me. But now the words rushed back. I recalled assuming a daughter was involved. Yet, daughter there was none grown in the house.

I felt uneasy.

"What girl?" I asked. "How was she strange?"

The woman glanced at her husband, but did not ask him again. She had heard the story often enough.

She shrugged. "The girl . . . maybe she is a woman. *Doch jung*. Young. By the road, she is standing. *Sehr komisch, hat sie ausgesehen.* She is looking not all right. Not with the right clothings for the coldness."

"Did he see her hair? Did the girl have red hair? Was she slender? A slender girl with red hair, was it?"

The woman asked her husband. He shook his head no.

That baffled me.

Herr Kempf read the befuddlement on my face and spoke to his wife. She weighed his comments for a moment, then said, "My husband does not understand these things still. He is only coming home. *Im tiefen Schnee.* All is snow. Then the woman is calling to him. With the hand only, not the talking. She is in the trouble, maybe, because so little clothings she has. He stops the wagon *und* is following after her. Then you are there. In the snow. With so much blood. *Mein Mann* looks up to ask the questions and—" the woman popped out a breath—"like this she is gone. In the snow *und die Nacht.* She must freeze, I am thinking. With her little clothings."

A chill gripped my heart.

"But what did she look like?" I demanded. "How did she *look?*"

The woman asked her husband another question. As he replied, he bobbed his hands, palms up, in a gesture of incomprehension.

"He says," *Frau* Kempf told me, "that he is not believing if he is not seeing. The girl has clothings like the *Prinzessin* of the Sultan, in the stories for the childrens. She is very beautiful, with the brown skin and her not many clothings." The good wife looked at me. "Is this not strange?"

WE LEFT IN THE MORNING, with my pistol returned to me. You guess my thoughts, so I will not report them. I was a man with one eye on the future, the other focused on a quitless past.

The going was hard. Later, they told me I had brought the winter of the decade with me to Yates County. Brown with mud, the high fields wanted plows, but the swales hid deep in snow. Now, humility is a virtue ever in short supply, so I will tell you frankly of my shame. I am not tall—though height is not everything in a man—and still lacked something of my normal strength. I could not have made my way without my guide. He helped me through the drifts where I stuck fast.

Once, he carried me like a child.

I wonder sometimes what it must be like to be tall and comely. I would not be envious, but look you. It must be an easier thing to be born long of leg and conquering handsome—though life is hard enough for all, I know. But think how it must be to go through life admired at first glance, body formed to overcome all challenges.

Well, we must be content with what we are given. We know what we are made of, you and I. Isn't it a miracle when someone loves us?

The day was not all trials. Birds sang. The melting went the faster for their songs.

The farm lay at the edge of the world, and it took us half the day to reach the main road. *Herr* Kempf stayed by me until a wagon come along headed south toward Penn Yan. A farmer fellow let me share his seat behind the horses. After helping me up and deflecting a last barrage of my thanks, my host strode off across the sodden fields.

The driver did not say much for a mile. Dour, he chewed tobacco, spitting off the side into the slush. When he did speak, it was to the horses, not to me:

"Damned foreigners are ruining this country."

THE DAY WAS DYING when we reached Penn Yan—a town I was not meant to see alive. The sky had clouded over and the farmer grumbled. He said a storm was coming, but I did not mind at all. I welcomed the prospect of more snow now. For snow would block Kildare. Until I could determine where we stood, and send my telegrams, and arrange for the militia.

My hopes were dashed. The storm arrived, but snow did not come with it. Just as I climbed down by the parsonage, I felt a drop of rain. I did not reach the porch before the Lord's artillery began to sound and bayonets of lightning cut the sky. The rain attacked as I slipped through the door.

It might have been the summer rains of India, the way the pellets come punching at the earth.

I heard sounds from the kitchen and rushed toward them. All were surprised. Myself at finding Mr. Douglass visiting, and the Noble Moor by my appearance alive. But Morris was the one who took the cake. The old expression never was more apt—the preacher looked as if he had seen a ghost. I fair thought he would take off at a run.

He began to stammer. "You . . . but . . . dead, you're dead . . . we thought . . . my horse . . . no body . . . my horse, Priscilla came back and—"

I had a hundred questions I longed to ask. But one question had place before all others.

"Have there been any messages for me?" I fear I was shouting. For the slowness of the journey had set me to brooding. "Any messages, man?"

"Messages? Messages?" The poor fellow acted as if I had spoken in an exotic tongue.

"Yes. Messages. For me. It may be urgent."

He rose from his meager plate. "Yesterday . . . just yesterday . . . yes, yes . . . a message, a message!"

I nearly leapt upon him. "Where is it, man?"

"Where? Where?"

"Where's the message?"

He shook his head. Leaden raindrops struck the roof and walls. "Don't know . . . must think . . . you were dead . . . dead, you see . . . gone over Jordan . . . never thought . . ."

"On your desk, perhaps?" Mr. Douglass interposed. A boom of thunder followed on his words.

Mr. Morris looked as if he had been assaulted with yet another foreign term. "My desk? Desk? No, no. In the dustbin. Thrown away." His alarm grew even more intense. "I do hope Mrs. James hasn't emptied—"

"Where?" I shouted. "Which dustbin?"

Morris launched himself toward the next room. I followed, with Mr. Douglass trailing, caught up in the excitement.

" . . . Dead . . ." Morris mumbled, " . . . gone over Jordan . . . everybody thought . . . over Jordan, passed over Jordan . . ."

He reached for a paper-stuffed cylinder beside his desk.

I took it away from him, dumping its contents on the old Turkey carpet. As I rummaged through the scraps, I had to slap poor Morris's fingers away. He only sought to help, but was a trouble.

The rain pounded at the windows. It come colder now. Sticking to the glass then sliding downward. Its sound was that of shots heard on a flank.

There it was! A sheet of schoolboy's paper, folded up and sealed. Inscribed, "to majur jones."

I tore it open.

if not ded hury Kildare leevs
on canal barj tomorow after dark
guns and men and gold he wil
atak canady I am with him hury

EIGHTEEN

"YOU WILL DO IT, SIR, IF YOU WISH TO SAVE OUR Union!"

Mr. Douglass did not move. Behind his mighty shoulder, Mr. Morris leapt about in a dance of enthusiasm for the task I had assigned him, but the great Douglass only stared down at me. His hands tested the air at his sides, clenching and falling slack again, and his face had taken on the maroon hue of fine leather.

I know fear. I am not the blustering sort who will pretend he has never been afraid. Oft was the time when only the dread of failing in my duty saved me from abasement. I have seen fear gnaw at men, on the eve of battle or faced with disease. Some are afraid of serpents. Worst are those who see into themselves.

"I . . . my weapon is the pen . . . not the sword . . ."

I was abrupt with the poor fellow. For time was our enemy.

"Well, throw your inkpots at them, man. We need you with us."

"Need, need! We need you, Fred," Mr. Morris sang. "Union, save the Union . . ."

Now I do not suggest that Frederick Douglass was a coward, for he was not. Fear shadows us all like a padded-foot assassin and leaps out when our guard is down. For all his daring speech, Douglass long had led an ordered life, with the turmoil of bondage decades behind him. Twas the unexpectedness, see, of being asked to take a gun in hand that threw him. His was a world of boundaries, and well he knew the fate of the black man who lifts his hand against his white brother, no matter how just the cause. And I had made it clear we would be outnumbered.

Outside, the Lord's cannon boomed and lightning smote the earth. Sleet slapped the windows, clinging to the glass, and the wind wailed. When the world goes thus awry, old voices bid us keep to our firesides.

"I . . ." Douglass, never at a loss for words, could hardly begin. "I . . . dare not . . ."

I turned away. Brusquely, I'm afraid, for I have a heathen temper when there is a fight before me. It comes from my sergeanting days in India, when the lads needed to fear me more than the enemy. I waved to Morris to start him along on his errand. For the good preacher was to find John Underwood and bring him to meet me, along with any arms and men the sheriff had at hand. Just at the door, I turned again to Douglass.

"You will go," I told him, "to the livery stables. Tell John Brent to bring his horses, properly saddled and without delay, to the door of St. Michael's. Do that much at least, Mr. Douglass."

I did not know if we would be out-rifled ten to one or worse. I wanted every hand, and had drawn Morris and the Moor a sketch of the conspiracy in order to enlist their help. Morris had risen to the call with such alacrity that I feared for his welfare, should he be entrusted with a gun, but Douglass withered. When I needed him to swell.

Looking into the eyes of the bold orator one last time, I understood why slaves do not rise up. We men burn such deep fears into our fellows that they cannot overcome them in a lifetime. I have seen it in myself, when thrust among the rich. The onetime servant fears the master always.

If he would not raise his hand, I hoped Douglass would at least raise our horses. For we would have to ride hard to overtake the barge before it issued from the outlet canal. I dreaded that prospect more than I did the looming confrontation, for I am not happy on a horse in sunlight, let alone upon a night like this.

I pulled on my India-rubber cape, set my hat upon my head, and followed Mr. Morris out the door.

Heaven blasted us. Just as it did the old king on the heath. Colt hard against my hip, I told the preacher:

"Pray as you go, Mr. Morris. And have the sheriff show you how to load."

I HAD MY OWN TASK BEFORE ME, though twas one of little hope. I bent into the sleet, holding my hat to my head with a naked hand. My gauntlets had long been missing and my fingers stiffened as I marched through the town.

I was off to see the priest, you will have guessed. For only he could halt this wickedness now, by calling on his Irish to desist. I did not think he would help me, for he was in it deep. But we must do all we can to hinder bloodshed. And I will tell you: I felt my share of fear, just like Fred Douglass. I wanted to see my wife and child again, and to live long. I would have liked to call up the militia and let a thousand others share the burden. But look you: There was no time for dallying. A man must stand to his allotted duty, just as our gentle Savior stood to His.

McCorkle was the key.

I found him by his fire reading Scripture. I rushed inside without the slightest knock and stood there sodden, dripping like a fish.

Had the Angel of the Apocalypse come in with fiery sword, I do not think the priest would have been amazed one bit the more. He sat up as if pricked immodestly and his eyes went huge in the firelight.

"But . . . you're . . ."

I shook my head and spoke though numbed lips. "*Alive,* Father McCorkle. For the O'Hara boys are faulty executioners. And now you are wanted, see. To put an end to this wickedness. For you have had the measure of these matters from the beginning, but do not know what lies behind the doings."

"Sure, and I haven't the one notion o' what you're raving about. Have ye been conked on the pate, then, and all disordered?"

"You do not know who stands behind Kildare. But I will tell you. For the sake of your Irish and the Union both. Kildare is paid with English gold. Your parish folk will cross the river, and the Royal Artillery will be waiting on the shore. To welcome them with canister. Those who do not fall under the volleys will throw down the rifles they know not how to use." Oh, how clearly I could see it! "And they will be Her Majesty's prisoners. But they will have done what is wanted of them by Kildare and those behind him. They will have served their purpose. The moneybags of Manchester and Birmingham will have their war and their cotton. And the Irish will be their fools again."

The priest's expression did not change. But his eyes narrowed. I would tell you they clenched, as if eyes were fists, to give you the sense of them.

"I don't know what all your blathering's about, Jones. But I'm beginning to think there's a touch o' the Irish in the vexed blood o' the Welsh, for it's a terrible gift for imagining ye have. And a great love o' the talk. Will it be banshees next? Or the Devil's Coach Devour at the door?"

Outside, the wind wailed. The little house fair shook under the storm's assault. Drops of wet fell down the chimney, hissing into the fire.

The priest glared into the burning. "You're a fool, Jones. A daft man. And no good to anyone."

But his voice was different. He spoke like a poor actor, mouthing lines in which he has no confidence.

"I am a fool," I said. "I give you that. But fools may be forgiven." I took a step toward the crumpled blackness of him. "And you, Father McCorkle? Will you be forgiven? For sending your boys to death or captivity? On a hopeless mission? Arranged by English gold?"

"Ye Welsh," he said. "Forever calculating, ye are. With your little paymaster souls. Our Lord's mission was hopeless, too."

"I will stop Kildare. With you or without you." Certainly, my voice sounded more confident than I felt. "I'm telling you it's all an English plot, man. To use the Irish to provoke a war. For the love of—do you really think they have a chance to conquer Canada? There'll be no rising of the Frenchies. Naught but a slaughter there'll be. And widows and orphans for nothing."

He turned on me. Face scorched by the fire. "Damn ye, Jones. *Damn* ye for a lackey and a dupe. It's nothing but their dancing dog, ye are. And not even fit for a jig, with the crook o' the leg on ye. They've crippled ye, and still ye beg their bones." His fist pounded the table and it shivered like an invalid. "The Irish will be free."

"Not in Canada, they won't."

"We'll rise. We'll rise and show the world."

"You'll rise to nothing. You've been betrayed."

"*Liar!* Tis nothing but a damnable liar I see before me. A Judas. Coming to bait me with your nonsense about English gold. A lying little Welshman, and a Judas."

I smiled a little, as we do when we are struck hard, and clutched the grip of the cane *Herr* Kempf had whittled. "Haven't you wondered where Kildare—Kilraine, I should say—where he gets his money? Do you think his bit of magic with the girl brings so much in, then? Do you know the price of an Enfield rifle in the middle of a war, man? Or of uniforms, or boats, or provisions? Do you know where the money comes from? From an English lord, I tell you. From a wicked dozen of them, most like. But twas only the one I saw in the streets of Rochester, giving Kildare his instructions. There is your Judas. Your informer. It's Kildare."

"You're a filthy Protestant liar."

I closed toward him. But not in anger. For my desperation was beyond the reach of insult. The commotion of horses out in the street told me it was time to go.

McCorkle began to rise. I think he would have liked to strike me a blow.

I slapped my hand down upon his Bible. Flat upon the Scriptures, may the Lord forgive me. Our faces come spitting close.

"Damn me for eternity, if I have spoken one false word, Father McCorkle. We *need* you to come along with us. To stop this. Before it ends in blood." I was pleading with every mote of my being. "I cannot say who will live and die. Only that your people will lose, one way or the other. And the price they pay will be a high one. There will be no freedom or glory in it, only shame and betrayal." How can you reach such a fellow? "I *beg* you, man. Come with me and talk to them. Tell them what I've told you. Stop this . . . this madness . . ."

He was a statue, not a man. A statue of a hard and vengeful prophet.

"I will not go with ye," he said. "And damn ye."

Twas time to do my duty, so I told him, "Damn me, you may. But stop me, you won't. And the blood will be on your hands."

The fiercest smile I ever saw deformed his lips.

"May it be your blood then," he said.

HUNCHED AGAINST THE STORM, four horsemen waited in the street. Their flesh and weapons shone beneath the lightning. I wished they were more, for there would be a plentitude of Irish.

Two empty mounts waited, heads lowered, on the flank of the little party. One was for me, the other for McCorkle. I cannot tell you in Christian words how I felt toward the priest at that moment.

John Underwood was there, massive, with a carbine slung barrel-down. Douglass had come, after all. A hunting piece lay across his saddle and, despite the weather, he looked like a prince at his sport. Morris carried a shotgun nearly the size of himself. I have never seen a man so ill matched to arms. A good gust might have blown him away. Last of the four was John Brent, whom I had not expected.

"The priest will not go with us," I told them all, casting my voice above the slap and spatter of the sleet.

"Oh, for crying in a bucket," the sheriff said. "I could've told you that."

"Well, we will leave the horse," I called. "The Lord may move him still."

Underwood shook his massive head in doubt. Water flew from the brim of his hat.

"And which shall be mine?" I asked John Brent, steeling myself to mount. I wondered at Brent's presence. I had not told Morris to ask for his participation, only for his horses. I worried for John Brent, see. For he must live on in the town as a black-skinned man, while Douglass could leave with the morning train. Even if we won the day, the Irish would never forgive him.

Brent tugged a canvas from the saddle of the horse that was to bear me. "Quickly," he told me. "Get up before it gets wet."

I rose at his command, with only a bit of trouble from my bad leg. I tucked my cane beneath my cape then spread the sour rubber around me. My stick would fair impale me, if I fell. But I had ridden off without my cane once and would not do so again.

The saddle was dry and snug. Brent was ever a thoughtful man. I wanted to say something to my benefactor, to give him a last chance to change his mind about coming along. Yet . . . was he not a subject of our Union? And was this not an hour of need?

Twas as if he read my mind. Leaning over, he spoke into my ear.

"I've driven for you all winter, Major Jones. You get to know a fellow along the road. If I didn't stand by you now, I'd never call myself a man again." Then he laughed. "Besides, ole Reg'lar John has to keep an eye on his horses."

I held onto the reins a bit too tightly and the horse shied.

"Her name's Betty," Brent told me. "Give her a little slack now."

I was about to call out to John Underwood, to ask him to lead our pursuit, when another horseman come slopping fast up the street. We sensed him, then heard him, but hardly saw him until he pulled up and the sky bleached white again.

Meeks, it was. The deputy. Spattered in mud, with melt soaking him and his horse.

So we were six in all.

"Eli Denton," Meeks shouted, breathless, "says they passed his way . . . maybe two hours ago."

Underwood straightened. Putting me in mind of a dog that has caught a scent.

"Two hours! Only two hours!" Morris crowed. For he knew more of canals and the speed of their traverse than did I.

"Who is Eli Denton, then?" I asked, with the icy rain striking my face. I had taken off my hat so I would not lose it at a gallop. For a proper hat costs money, and the braid and brass cost more, besides. The hat was stuffed beneath my rubber cape. For a head can dry more cheaply than a new hat can be purchased.

"Denton's got the keeping of the first lock," Underwood answered me. Then he turned his horse into the street and let a whoop. "Come on, boys. We've got 'em now."

I was glad that one of us was confident.

THE SHERIFF WAS A LION. How sadly we misjudge our fellow men. I well recalled my alarm during our first interview, when he sat across the table from me, with his bulk and those ears and his doubts. I suspected then that he was composed of appetites only, a creature without a core, and not worthy of his occupation. He had proved me wrong that very day, and now, in the face of greater odds, he charged forward like a young hussar—though I had learned that he was over fifty, and not the man of forty that he seemed.

He had to wait for stragglers several times, for we were horsemen of different pedigree, and only John Brent rode with a skill equal to the sheriff's. Once, I will admit, Underwood had to come back after me, for my horse had strayed in the darkness and the storm. I was embarrassed to be the cause of the least delay. I bounced along behind him, with ice crusting my eyebrows and shame in my heart.

We rode across the heights, lashed by the heavens. Twas hard to see, and cold, and as desolate within a man as without. But I am an old bayonet and know that the weather is as hard on the enemy as it is on ourselves, and he who takes a grip has the advantage. They would not see or hear us, or expect us, and we might gain surprise to raise our chances.

The going was hard, for the roads were muddy ice and the fields icy mud. I mustered the courage to kick my mount in the flanks to spur her on, for riding behind the others left me a target for the clots their mounts kicked up. I must have looked a sad, ramshackle thing.

Sheriff Underwood stopped us in the center of a field. A wild place, it was. Lightning stabbed the earth and lit our faces. Horse eyes bulged.

"Stay here," Underwood told us. "Abel, you tell 'em about handling their guns, in case they don't know. Give 'em a dose of your soldiering business. I'm going to have a look along the gorge."

He would have done well on the Northwest Frontier, that John Underwood. He knew the scout goes best who goes alone.

"Look you," I said, as my horse strayed sideward, "the first thing is to clear the mud from the barrels."

Obediently, they swung their weapons into their arms.

"*Don't point them at each other,*" I said quickly. "They are wet now, and likely will not fire. But one will take a friend's life out of spite. Point the barrels downward, gentlemen."

"Won't fire? Won't fire?" Morris exclaimed. He cradled the shotgun in his arms, as if it were a slighted child.

"Yours may do a damage, Mr. Morris. For it is a fine piece and has a hooded mechanism. But I cannot speak for those with caps exposed." I looked around me. The storm seemed to have weakened just a little. Or perhaps I was becoming conditioned to it, for a man can become accustomed to anything. "Remember, gentlemen: if your guns do not fire, theirs will not, either. And they do not know that yours are wet for certain.

They will have their doubts, and doubts are fatal. Which of you have pistols in your belts?"

Meeks murmured, and John Brent raised his hand. No doubt Brent kept one loaded in his barn for the day the hateful came hunting. Underwood would have a revolver, as well. With my Colt, that made four.

"Do not take them out, but keep them dry. I will tell you when to draw them. For they will be our weapons in the fight, if fight we must."

"I have no pistol, sir," Douglass said, with just the least crack in his voice. "I would fulfill my role, Major Jones, and not stand idly by."

"Pick up the first that falls," I told him.

UNDERWOOD RETURNED IN A COAT OF MUD. He must have gone crawling. When he spoke, he aimed his words at me.

"They're down there, all right. Don't I know it? Lanterns front and back of the barge, lit up like a society ball. Good thing, too. Still have to get snot-close to see anything. There's two mules drawing along the towpath on the near bank, with Napper O'Hara—the young one—on 'em with a switch. Mules are strung one behind the other, so they'll block a shot from up near the front. Half a dozen Irish out on the deck with staves, breaking up the last of the ice as they go."

"Armed?" I asked.

The sheriff shook his head. "Couldn't tell for certain. I'd bet that Napper's got a pistol tucked away. He's the wilder of the two, though Bull's the meaner. If the boys on deck have rifles, I didn't see 'em. But seeing's the problem down there."

"And Kildare?" I asked.

"Lamp's lit in the cabin, so I figure he's in there keeping dry. Probably with Bull O'Hara. Bull's the one I'd watch. He'll shoot straight."

"You know the ground, John," I said. "Where's the place to take them?"

"Next lock down," he said without hesitating. For he knew his business. "Deep one, sharp fall. Steepest part of the gorge, just about. Let 'em get into the lock, but we won't let 'em get out. Hard for 'em to get away on foot, with the banks so sheer."

If it would be hard for them to escape, that meant it would be equally difficult for us, should things go poorly. But I said nothing. For his spirit was up. And spirit has carried many a battle that should have been lost.

The sheriff was a sort I knew quite well, the man who moves briskly to keep a step ahead of his concerns. Such a man will carry the breastworks. Or fall before them.

"That's good, John," I said. "You have done us a fine reconaissance." But I was thinking: one O'Hara by the mules with a pistol. And Kildare was no trained fighter, so he would be over-armed. With two pistols, at least. And a gambler's gun concealed. If he was in the barge's cabin, his powder and caps would be dry. The same went for the other O'Hara brother, the one who worried the sheriff. And if the half-dozen Irishmen with the staves were armed, as well? What about those shut below the deck? Were the Enfields still in their packing cases? Or was each man primed to kill his way to Canada?

And where in God's name was Molloy? He had the sense to place himself discreetly, yet worried I was. For danger might come at him from either side if a battle erupted. Now a trouble he was, that one, with a past stained black as the devil's behind, begging your pardon. But he had done me fair and done me proud. I did not want to see a brave man fall.

And . . . and he was my *friend,* see. For friendship is a strange thing on this earth.

My companions sat on their horses, with the sleet down their necks and up their cuffs. Of a sudden, I realized they were waiting for me. Even Underwood looked for orders now. They saw me as the man who knew his killing.

It is a shameful distinction.

"Let's go, then," I said. "You will lead us to the spot, John. And I will set each soldier, begging your pardon, gentlemen, each *man*—"

"Can't hear ya," Deputy Meeks shouted.

I nodded. Twas just as well. "Let's go," I repeated with greater vigor. "We need time to put each man in his place."

The fields were muck and mire. Approaching the lip of the canal gorge, we dismounted. And I was glad of it, though walking had a queer feel after the ride. The mud wanted our boots. John Brent tied our horses. I asked him what might be done to keep them quiet, but he had thought that far without my bothering him. He paired each with a favored stablemate.

"I can't do anything about the thunder and lightning," he said. "But horses feel best in their preferred society. Just like people."

A single whinny might collapse our hopes. For a moment, I considered leaving Brent up with the horses, to soothe them. But we needed every man. Twas not so much a matter of *being* strong as of convincing Kildare and his boys that we were a mighty band.

"Careful now," Underwood said. He sent Meeks down the slope first, to test the way. Then Morris disappeared after the deputy. "Get your hand away from that trigger, Reverend," the sheriff called. "It's slippery going down."

He stepped up to John Brent, Douglass and me. "Be a miracle if Morris doesn't blow a hole in the boat then kill half a dozen of us for good measure."

"John?" I said to the sheriff. "It's a bit hard to tell, see. But I have a sense that I know this place."

"You go on down now, Brent," Underwood said. "You next, Mr. Douglass." He wiped a big hand across his face and a flash outlined those massive ears. "You know it, all right. Remember that poor little mick who drowned herself back in January? Down there in that lock, that's just where it happened." He sputtered a laugh and shook his head, as a man will when the world is unbearably hard. "Wasn't McCorkle a coot that day?"

I recalled the girl. The dark roses of blood where the grapples stabbed her. And the sheath of gold that wrapped her as a shroud. She had been thin, with the hair of a mermaid.

The thunder rolled down from the hills and across the heath. It seemed so odd to me, that winter thunder. For thunder is ever a summer affair in my memory, whether storms over the Black Mountains or the monsoon trumpets of India.

A horse moaned and shuffled.

I followed John Underwood down, and slid, and lost my cane in the brambles.

Well, I could stand without it. And shoot straight, if need be.

WE WERE NAUGHT BUT PIGS in a wallow after tumbling down the slope.

"His name is Jimmy Molloy," I told them, "and he must not come to harm. For he is a brave one, and has done good work."

"But how will we know him?" Morris asked. "How will we—"

"There is trouble," I said. "For he is a great one for disguises. Got up fancy, he is a fine-looking man, in a low and devious way. The last time I saw him he wore a Derby hat, but likely he'll be wrapped up for the storm. His hair is red, but you will not see that for the weather."

The sheriff grumbled. "Now I've got secret fellows running over my county. Oh, for—"

"He is a good man, John. And clever. He will find a way to let us know him."

I hoped that I was right.

I reconnoitered the site, while Underwood and Meeks checked the lockkeeper's shanty. Twas empty, but the upper gates of the lock were open wide. Ready to receive the barge. Perhaps Kildare had sent men ahead to open the locks. We never saw them, if he did. They may have taken shelter with a bottle, with the hard weather upon them. And good riddance. As for our position, it was poor. In the narrow defile, our ambush could easily be turned upon us, with a treacherous climb at our backs. We would take our stand at the foot of the embankment, in the underbrush, on ground slightly lower than the towpath. With naught but a ditch and the path between us and the conspirators.

Had they been soldiers and experienced, I would have spaced my comrades well apart, to make it seem the barge was all but surrounded. But these were simple men caught up in trouble.

I put each man in place, none more than a half-dozen paces from his neighbor, so each would have the comfort of sensing his fellow by him. I lined them up in a rank, to lessen the chance of them shooting each other. Although we did not separate, I divided us into wings of three men each, one centered on me and the other on the sheriff. I told them it was tactics. The truth is that I wanted those of less experience on either side of Underwood or me. The sheriff had Meeks to his left and Morris to his right, while I stood between Brent and Douglass. It would be our duty to bolster them.

We were crouched in the thicket, centered on the lock. The heavy gates made a fine prison for a boat. They would be trapped until the lower sluice was opened, and for a time thereafter.

Underwood called to me, in a reduced voice. "That light up there. That's them."

Twas no distance at all.

Hurriedly, I gave out final instructions. "Those of you with pistols, draw and prime. But keep them under your capes until they're needed. Do not touch the triggers until I challenge the barge. And do not point the barrels along your legs or at your feet in the meantime."

I scurried along our thin little line, twisting on my bad leg.

"Mr. Morris," I continued. "You will point your shotgun at any armed men who bunch together. Aim it at their bellies, and shoot if you feel menaced. But none of you must draw until I call the challenge, understand?" I lowered my voice. "Keep to your places. And keep you still. Do not stand to reveal yourselves. Let them wonder how many we are, and where."

I watched the lantern sway along the gorge, then made out its twin a bit behind. The lights seemed to grow in size with every second.

"No one is to fire unless Kildare's lot begins shooting," I said in a hushed voice. Only the slap of the sleet let me risk continued speech. Foul weather is the hard friend of the infantry. "Or if you hear my command, or that of the sheriff. Understand?"

The men made little noises of agreement, and I could sense their fear. Twas no longer a lark, or a fine gesture, or even a duty. Now it was living and dying. Twas easier for me, of course, as it always is for those in charge. We hear of the weight upon the colonel's shoulders, but the weak link in the battle is the private alone with his fears.

"Stay down now," I whispered, taking up my own position. "And be quiet. And don't forget Jimmy Molloy." Then I prayed.

A plan is nothing against fate. Our lives might end in a single volley.

A new sound come toward us. Almost a crying it was. Between the claps of thunder, we heard groans. As of a giant undergoing torment.

I wanted to ask what it was, but could not break our discipline. Later, I learned it was the noise of the barge grinding the last of the ice against the sides of the canal.

The lantern at the front of the barge disappeared, although its aura remained in the air. The lead mule had come between us. They were that close. The first lantern reappeared, then faded behind the trailing mule, only to shine out again. Despite the blow and sleet, I could see figures straining on the deck, working with long poles. I saw no rifles. But all was still obscure.

I felt the wet come up through my boots. Cold as a widower's handshake. The wind screamed down the gorge.

Their voices come over, all Irish. *Would ye put yer back into it, ye wort'less bugger? It's frayzin' I am, Napper. Tell Boylan he's wanted. I'm frayzin', I'm frayzin' up dead. Swate Jaysus, would ye stop yer flailin'? Swate Jaysus . . .*

What were they but fools? McCorkle had been wrong. I was not the dupe, though fool enough. These were the dupes of empire and of wealth, of all the great lords and the cruel Kildares. Twas hatred blinded the priest, as hatred blinds all those who embrace it.

Damn it, me fingers! Push, would ye push? I'm frayzin' . . .

I did not want to fire on such fellows. But I would do what needed to be done.

And then a wicked voice broke out in song:

The swate-heart o' Dublin,
'Er name was Light Sally,
She'd do it for sixpence,
Just back o' the alley . . .

That Molloy. His lascivious tenor invited his fellow countrymen to join him. And the poor, benighted Irish did.

Singing, they come toward us.

I had a fix on Molloy now. But my companions would have no sense of him.

Napper O'Hara trailed the second mule. Just as the sheriff had said. I saw the lamplit cabin on the deck, imagining silhouettes on the oiled cloth behind its windows.

O'Hara stopped the mules, letting the boat drift into the lock.

A little time now, I thought. Easy, fellows, easy. I sensed the breathing of my comrades, for I could not hear it in the squall or over the wawling of the Irish. The sleet stiffened. It struck the wood of the boat and the trees like arrows, and left a cutting feel upon the face.

Twas shivering cold. My fingers would need prying from my pistol.

The lead mule started forward on its own, drawing the second animal behind it. The younger O'Hara, Napper, ran up and gave the first one the switch across its eyes. Angry, no doubt, that his brother was warm in the cabin and him king of the mules. Lucky I was that those boys had not killed me, for they were the sort that have joy of their meanness.

The boat moaned, timber against ice, against stone. The Irish with the staves were not in uniforms, but in rags, shabby even in the faint light of the lanterns. The uniforms were for Canada and death, not for the likes of us.

Twas miserable work they were doing, but that is the lot of the Irish in the best of times. They had to hook one great chunk of ice out of the water, with six of them pulling, to let the boat snug to the lock. Their song broke down under the effort.

The barge was level with us now.

The poor navvies looked as if they were dancing as they worked. Though their feet were planted firmly on the deck of the barge. Twas the swaying of the boat that gave them their rhythm.

The wet upon me now was not the sleet, but sweat.

Jaysus, Mary and Joseph, would ye heave?

Perhaps Kildare had powers beyond the trick of Mesmerism. Perhaps a bit of the girl's gift had rubbed off. He stepped out of the cabin, pulling on his slouch hat. As if he sensed us. Or perhaps it was only to oversee the business with the lock.

Bull O'Hara followed him. Elder and thicker than his brother, with a beard to rival his master's.

Kildare peered into the darkness. Twas uncanny. He was looking almost exactly at the spot where I had crouched down.

Well, let him see. If the light was enough.

I rose and summoned up my old sergeant's voice.

"In the name of the United States Government, you are all under arrest. Surrender your weapons."

My boys ignored my earlier instructions and leapt to their feet beside me. Twas not proper doings.

Kildare and the Irish did not obey me, either.

Bull went for a pistol, and Kildare drew out two of his own.

"Drop 'em, Kildare," John Underwood shouted. "Or you're first."

Napper slipped behind the trail mule's haunches, fingering the trigger of his revolver.

I feared a slaughter.

"Don't shoot," I commanded. Or begged. "Hold your fire. Everyone."

Guns were up all round.

"Kildare, you'll not go farther. The militia are closing on the outlet," I told him, though it was a lie. "Surrender, and save yourself. Save the men who trusted you."

Twas as if two firing squads opposed each other. Kildare and the O'Haras against the rest of us. With the Irish dumb in wonder.

We faced off almost close enough for fists, weapons extended and gathering sleet.

Out of the corner of my eye, I saw Molloy ease toward the rear of the pack on the deck.

Thank the Lord, I thought, the rest of the Irish were not armed. They just stood gripping their staves. Waiting for a sign or an order.

The boat's rocking settled a little, though the storm churned on.

"You lied to them, Kildare," I tried. "Tell them how you lied."

I was just about to tell them myself, when the rest of the Irish emerged. Climbing up from the bowels of the barge. First two, and then a dozen. Then more.

They were armed with the Enfields.

Gunmen lined the barge, from the cabin back to the stern. I could no longer see Molloy.

"It would appear," Kildare said, "that my militia has arrived a bit earlier than yours, Jones. Now shut your mouth. And all of you put down your weapons, or we'll fire. Take aim, lads. Napper, collect their guns."

A line of rifle bores steadied their aim on us. Still dry enough to fire, most likely. The Irish did not look properly trained. Still, a volley from so many barrels would be deadly.

Napper eased out from behind the mule, pistol up and ready.

"Stay right there, O'Hara," the sheriff said. His voice was unshaken. And angry. "Or I'll shoot you dead as a lamb chop."

"Men," I tried again, "this is treason. You could be hanged. You've no hope at all . . ."

Just as Kildare mouthed the word to fire, I felt a new presence beside me. Now I am a veteran soldier, and should have heard him coming. I can only plead the darkness and the weather. And my fear.

"No hope at all!" McCorkle bellowed, shoving past me. He stretched out his arms, as if to gather in his flock. "Ye've been betrayed, me darlings, and by that one." He pointed to Kildare. "For he's in the pay of Englishmen and it's not but a trap ye will—"

Kildare shot him.

The priest fell. Beside a mule.

The animal kicked and brayed, driving Napper into the ditch.

"*Lies,*" Kildare screamed. "*He lied.*"

The world exploded.

I do not know who fired when, only that guns went barking. I shot Kildare, God help me. And put a bullet in his breast.

The mules were mad. High above the gorge, our horses shrieked.

Both O'Haras were blazing, and I heard the wrong voice cry. Then the O'Haras fell. One just after the other. Napper in the ditch and Bull on the deck.

And what of the Irish with their Enfields?

No rifle fired a shot. For none was loaded. Molloy had seen to that. Most of the Irish dropped their guns and jumped for the far bank. But half a dozen stayed to go after Kildare. Weapons raised as clubs.

His people knew McCorkle's worth.

The Great Kildare had climbed back to his feet. Pulsing blood in the lantern's light. Warning off the Irish with his remaining pistol. His eyes shone huge, despite the whip of the sleet.

"Don't kill him!" I shouted. "I need him alive!"

But the Irish have their own rules among themselves, and they were deaf to me. They closed toward their countryman.

"I'm shot," a voice cried. "Lord, I'm shot."

The rear mule slumped, belatedly feeling a wound and braying piteously. The harness dragged the lead mule down.

Kildare staggered backward to the bow of the barge. Lashed by the wind. Swaying. Struggling to keep his feet on the uncertain deck. He held his pistol out at arm's length. Pointing it first at one of the Irish, then another. Still, they edged closer.

Instead of firing at them, he turned to face the darkness.

"I'll kill you, Jones," he called, with the sleet punishing his eyes. His voice had weakened, but I heard him clear. " . . . kill you . . ."

He fired his pistol toward the bank, seeking me with bullets.

Mr. Morris stepped onto the towpath and triggered his shotgun.

Kildare flew backward over the lip of the boat. Plunging into the icy water, between the prow of the barge and the wall of the lock. Likely to be crushed, if not yet dead.

Swift as a cat, a figure shot across the foredeck, leaping into the water after Kildare.

Twas Jimmy Molloy.

The last of the Irish gave us a look-over, dropped their rifles, and fled after their fellows.

"I know you!" Sheriff Underwood cried. "I know every damned one of you."

"John," I shouted. "That's Molloy in the water. My man. Help him. *Please.*"

For Underwood was stronger, and strength was needed now. Along with a good reach.

"Meeks is shot," the sheriff called to me as he dashed for the edge of the canal. "But he'll keep."

Douglass ran to aid the sheriff, peeling off his cloak. Poor Morris stood stiff in amazement, shotgun still in his hands, while John Brent calmed the mules.

I limped over to the priest.

He lay behind the crumpled mule, as still as the beast was a-quiver. I bent to move him to a more fitting spot. Thinking he was dead.

But he was not.

He opened up his eyes—just long enough to read my face—then they fell shut again.

"I damn you still," he said, and died.

The devil's own streak of lightning found the lock's machinery. Twas a great bolt and blast, blinding and deafening. I knew not what it was at first, for it turned me around and sat me on my hindquarters in the mud.

By the light of it, I glimpsed a figure up on the rim of the gorge. Standing where our horses had been tethered.

I did not imagine her, I tell you. I saw her plain, even to the red hair darkened by the wet of the storm. She had gathered her shawl about her, drenched skirt pressed by the wind. I saw her white face and white hands.

I *saw* her.

And then twas dark again.

I scrambled up the bank. Clumsy without my cane. Grasping limbs, brush, the mud itself.

"Nellie," I cried.

She had been right. I had killed Kildare. One way or the other.

"Nellie!"

When I reached the high fields, they were empty. And Nellie Kildare had vanished from the world.

MEEKS WAS SHOT IN THE LEG. I could not tell the quality of the wound for the filth of us, but the bone seemed unbroken. The deputy would likely live and prosper. One of the O'Haras would live, as well. Napper, the young one. But prosper he would not. His brother lay among discarded rifles, mouth open to the sleet as if it were whisky.

We did not find Kildare that night, but Molloy bobbed up spitting and the sheriff fished him out.

We crowded around my old acquaintance, who was wet through to freezing. His brogans had come off in his struggle with the waters of the lock, and his rag of a coat was gone with his Derby hat. Douglass offered his cloak, which Molloy, shamelessly, accepted.

"Begging your pardons, gents," he said, "I'll just be going into the fine, warm cabin o' the barge for to be rid o' me rags. Oh, I'm cold as a beggar and worse."

I followed him. Queer, the things that strike you after a fight. The cabin smelled of kidneys fried in butter, Kildare's last meal. Perhaps it was the Lord's way of reminding me that, justice done or no, I had shot a man. It made me treasure Molloy's gesture all the more.

I diverted my eyes from his increasing nakedness and spoke my piece:

"Molloy . . . I must say . . . I . . . Jimmy, that was one of the bravest things I've ever seen. When you are properly dressed again, I would like to shake your hand."

Something made me look up. Perhaps I was too weary for propriety. And I saw the look of wonder on Molloy's face.

"Sergeant Jones—I mean, *May*-jor Jones, begging your pardon—what the devil are ye on about now? And what brave deed are ye praising me for? For I'm mystified by yer ramblings and tabulations."

"Why, your selflessness, Molloy. The raw courage of it. The Christian way you threw yourself into the water, risking certain death to save Kildare."

He shook his head slowly. In astonishment.

"Are ye mad, then, Major Jones?" he asked me. "I wouldn't have risked a splinter for Kildare. But didn't the man have his pockets loaded down with gold, and lovely English gold at that, and don't I hate the wasting o' good money?" Bare as the first of our kind, he slumped down in a chair cut from a barrel. "Oh, it broke me heart to see the man go over."

NELLIE DISAPPEARED INTO A CONTINENT AT WAR. I hope she found a little peace before the end, and that she was not harmed further by the hand of man. I never will forget her.

Nor did others discard her memory. There is strange, the way we are remembered. Twas long years later, in a time of peace, when I come up to visit the Falls of the Niagara with my Mary Myfanwy. We detoured to Penn Yan to visit my old friend John Underwood. He always kept a good table, and his wife was jolly. But that is not the matter of it.

Summer it was, and we had taken the buggy down to the lakeside to promenade with our ladies. Oh, slower we were, but fine men still, and of good heart. Well, there we were, strolling and watching the boats out on the water, when a grand fellow sauntered up, tipping his hat to the ladies. Underwood introduced him as the new sheriff. I looked hard at the fellow, for he seemed familiar to me, as if I might have known him as a boy. The face was Irish as cabbage at the end of the month, with a turned-up nose, but his speech was plain American.

Anyway, he invited us into a big, striped tent where a celebration was in progress. Underwood seemed to think the young sheriff a fine fellow, so we accepted. It was an Irish revel, got up by some charitable association. Times had changed, you understand, and the Irish were not entirely disreputable. Why, they even had tablecloths down. Nor was there the least scent of alcohol.

I remember that it was lovely and cool there in the shade, with the sides of the tent rolled up, and we indulged in a round of root beer, though it sometimes gives me wind. A handsome young fellow sang to a piano brought down from the town, fair weeping through their ballads full of loneliness, then turning the mood gay, but never saucy.

He closed with a mournful tune of local provenance—for the Irish make a song of all they touch—and the lyrics made me sit up proper. I still recall the refrain:

Soft as the lilacs,
With long, fiery hair,
Sweet, magical beauty,
Sad Nellie Kildare . . .

My Mary Myfanwy, who looked so lovely in her white summer dress, asked me why I was crying. I took her hand and told her I was a silly old man.

But I must tell you of my departure from Penn Yan. Not in those later years when life was golden, but in the midst of war.

Twas the lambkin end of March, when the brown earth ripens and a sniff of the air lifts your heart. The sun was out and shining. John Underwood come down to the station to see me off. Mr. Douglass had already departed, gone to New York City to pay a call upon Mrs. Stanton and to visit a German acquaintance. I had said my farewells to Mr. Morris, as well, who was off to the war. The regiment he had signed on to chaplain was leaving Elmira that very day. The good shepherd was proud as a field marshal in his regimentals, and I feared for the Rebels if they ever got within range of his sermonizing.

The sheriff stood there, grand and hale. We had worked well together, John and I, and we had saved most of the Irish from the gallows, though Napper O'Hara would hang and three more would see a prison. The traitors' ring was broken, for the present, and the English would not have their excuse for a war on our account. Much haunted me—not least Nellie and the priest—but still I felt a sense of satisfaction. Perhaps I had not done badly by our fine country. For if I could not lead again in battle, I wished to do my little bit behind.

All with the Lord's help, see.

I grazed my hand over the lovely walking stick John Underwood had given me as a parting gift. It was too fine to use, but his sort cannot be told such things. So I made a show of wielding it, although the rude cane carved by good *Herr* Kempf was more fitting to the likes of me.

"There is lovely," I said to him, admiring the stick in the sunlight. "I would call you 'friend,' John, if I may?"

"Oh, for crying in a bucket. If we're not friends after all we've been through, I—"

We heard the whistle of the train approaching.

I thrust out my hand. "You are a good man, John Underwood. May God bless you."

We shook, and if the big fellow did not go soft around the eyes! He dropped my hand and gave his ear a tug. "John Brent would've come down to see you off. But folks have their ways about them around here . . ."

"He is a good man, too."

Underwood nodded. "Don't I know it?"

The train chugged down upon us.

"And Meeks is convalescing properly?" I asked.

With a squeal of wheels on rails, the locomotive slid past us. Halting on cushions of steam. The coal smoke made me think again of home.

"His Sarah's driving him crazy. And then some. He'll get up as soon as he can, trust me. Here, let me give you a hand with that crate."

I let him help me, for the sewing machine was heavy. I had managed to persuade the shopkeeper to sell it even below the price he had posted as the "lowest ever," and the "bargain of the century." Leaving just enough of my husbanded pay for modest sustenance on the journey to my beloved—although she would need to spare me a dollar from the cup in the kitchen to get me back to Washington from Pottsville.

I had put on my good uniform for the occasion, and the conductor was respectful and did not hurry me. Still, I did not wish to keep others waiting, for that is inconsiderate. Underwood helped me up with my baggage.

We shook hands a last time, and he jumped—heavily—from the train step. Down on the platform, the conductor raised his wand to unleash the power of the locomotive. And then I heard a shout.

"Major Jones! Major Abel Jones! For the love of Pete, somebody find Major Abel Jones! Don't let that there train go!"

"A moment, please, and my apologies, sir," I said to the conductor as I stepped past him again. Underwood gave me a curious look. For a sheriff wants to know all that goes on.

It was a telegram from the President's office. I gave the breathless messenger a nickel, though it spoiled my economic calculations. What was to be done? Virtue is temperate, not miserly.

I opened the message and read:

AJ. Report immediately to Major General Grant, Army of the Tennessee. Present location southwest of Nashville. Authority to commandeer railroad stock, vessels, or other transport. Waste not a moment. Great danger. Trust no one. Go armed. JN.

HISTORY AND THANKS

THIS BOOK OWES MUCH TO THE GENEROSITY OF others. Don and Donna McIntire of Hammondsport, New York, were my guides and flawless hosts as I learned to love the land surrounding Keuka Lake. No country could ask for better citizens, and no guest for greater hospitality. Frances Dumas, the Yates County historian, gave time and expertise, answering questions I did not yet know I had. She is a credit to her office, deeply knowledgeable, ever helpful, and determined that the past shall not wither. At the Yates County Genealogical and Historical Society, Kevin Bates kindly made period newspapers and other references available to me, offering more than was asked. Matt Syrett, of the Hammondsport Public Library, surfaced volumes I would not have had the wit to seek. Marion Springer, assistant historian at the Steuben County Historical Society, responded generously when a blustering November wind carried me into her office. Each of these citizens clearly love their land, its people and their past. Where I have erred or "amended" history, the fault is mine, not theirs.

This novel is as accurate as I could make it, from patent medicines to battlefield details, but I have taken some liberties with history and believe the reader has a right to know. While figures such as Sheriff Underwood and Stafford Cleveland are loosely drawn from historical persons, the Reverend Mr. Morris and Father McCorkle are fictitious. I do not mind hanging great ears upon a sheriff, but will not hang imaginary sins upon men of the cloth. While the schism in the local Methodist Church indeed took place, and Penn Yan hosted two Spiritualist conventions in the late 1850s, Mr. Morris's peculiarities are devised, not documented. As for the Catholic congregation of St. Michael's, they enjoyed the services of an Italian priest through much of the period. Civil War–era Fenian invasions of Canada are the stuff of historical fact and tragic failure, but Kildare's effort is early and invented.

Elsewhere, fact trumps fiction. The taverns of Bull Run and Manassas *did* stand at a crossroads on those high moors, and Yates County was divided into its own North and South, with violent confrontations. The Irish were troubled and troubling, for prejudices unthinkable to us were universal then. In the middle of the nineteenth century, Spiritualist beliefs and seances penetrated sober religious households by the tens of thousands, attracting many clerics with their promises. Those admirable souls struggling for women's rights often found inspiration in the spirit world, as well. And there *is* something inexplicable in those hills above that crooked lake. Yates and Steuben Counties even today attract religious dissenters, with an Amish migration from Pennsylvania to the less spoiled glens of western New York. Stafford Cleveland, a splendid newspaperman, wrongly predicted war with England, but rightly foresaw the rise of the United States as a world power . . . there is much more, and I encourage the reader to discover it for herself or himself on a visit to the Finger Lakes, with their evocative beauty, history, hospitality and ever-better wines (Abel Jones was wrong about the victory of Temperance, although the movement left us more temperate as a nation, and should be thanked, not mocked).

A last debt that must be acknowledged is to Rudyard Kipling. Those who have read that decent man's works will recognize the "quotations" from his masterful short story, "Without Benefit of Clergy," in the past of Abel Jones. I cherish Kipling. Attacked as a creature of imperialism by those who know him only through a hand-me-down reputation, he wants a fair reconsideration. Kipling transcended the petty hatreds of his times, and loved the world through which he passed with a naivety and joy worthy of Abel Jones. In his stories, novels and poems, love and friendship broke forbidden barriers—his best work was defiant of the givens of the Victorian and Edwardian ages in which he wrote. Even today, not one of the remarkable writers produced by India or Pakistan since independence has matched Kipling's portraits of old India, whether of the Grand Trunk Road in *Kim*, the commonplace dangers of a Northwest Frontier still wild today, or the unexpected love that crosses lines of color, religion and position. Nor has anyone written better of the common soldier. He was humane, true of heart, and less fallible than most. I wish only that those who dismiss him would read him first.

I hope this book will please the citizens of Yates and Steuben Counties. It is honorably meant. If I did not describe an Eden, I came as close as I could. For the highlands by their lake move me as they moved Abel Jones, and I found the people as worthy as he found them. God bless.

AUTHOR'S NOTE, 2012

I'M EXCITED ABOUT THE RE-PUBLICATION OF THE "BY Owen Parry" series of Civil War mysteries and am grateful to Stackpole Books for undertaking it. The novels featuring Abel Jones have attracted a cult of followers, and the most frequently asked questions I field as I travel and talk on other subjects are versions of "When's the little Welshman coming back?" While I hope to add new books to the series in the future—after fulfilling other writing commitments—I'm glad Abel's able to huff and puff and pontificate through these first six novels again. His character was always a joy to write.

Of the six books in the series (thus far), *Shadows of Glory* holds a special place in my heart. It's the quietest of the novels, with the hush of a winter landscape and high notes best conveyed by the image of long red hair blowing madly in a snowstorm. *Shadows* has some of the richest—and darkest—vignettes in the series: Mysticism intertwines with sorrow. I believe the opening churchyard scene may be the best thing I have written, and no character ever enchanted me as did poor Nellie Kildare. Many a reader has chosen a different novel as his or her favorite tale of Abel Jones, but this ghostly book haunts me still.

Of course, authors are notoriously poor judges of their own work.

But let that bide.

—Ralph Peters, aka Owen Parry, March 2, 2012